Other books

Amanda Cadabra and T...
(The Amanda Cadabra Cozy Pa... ..ok 1)

Amanda Cadabra and Th.. Cellar of Secrets
(The Amanda Cadabra Cozy Paranormal Mysteries Book 2)

Amanda Cadabra and The Flawless Plan
(The Amanda Cadabra Cozy Paranormal Mysteries Book 3)

Amanda Cadabra and The Rise of Sunken Madley
(The Amanda Cadabra Cozy Paranormal Mysteries Book 4)

Amanda Cadabra and The Hidden Depths
(The Amanda Cadabra Cozy Paranormal Mysteries Book 5)

Amanda Cadabra and The Strange Case of Lucy Penlowr
(The Amanda Cadabra Cozy Paranormal Mysteries Book 6)

Amanda Cadabra and The Hanging Tree
(The Amanda Cadabra Cozy Paranormal Mysteries Book 7)

Other books published by Heypressto

50 Feel-better Films

50 Feel-better Songs: from Film and TV

25 Feel-better Free Downloads

Want to read more about Tempest the Cat? Get the FREE short story prequel to Amanda Cadabra and The Hidey-Hole Truth at https://amandacadabra.com/free-story-tempest/

Copyright © Holly Bell (2022). All rights reserved.

www.amandacadabra.com

This book is a work of fiction. Any references to real events, people or places are used fictitiously. Other names, characters, places and incidents are products of the author's imagination. Any resemblance to actual events, places or people, living or dead, is entirely coincidental.

www.heypressto.com

Cover art by Daniel Becerril Ureña

Chartreuse@heypressto.com
HollyBell@amandacadabra.com

Twitter: @holly_b_author

Sign up and stay in touch

Follow Holly on Bookbub

Amanda Cadabra
AND THE NIGHTSTAIRS

HOLLY BELL

To Steve and Lianne

CONTENTS

Introduction 15

Chapter 1. 16
A Grand Opening

Chapter 2. 21
Amanda Rises To The Occasion

Chapter 3. 25
The Corner Shop

Chapter 4. 30
Janet Oglethorpe

Chapter 5. 35
Amanda's First Day, and Edward Nightingale

Chapter 6. 42
Finley

Chapter 7. 49
Tempest's Plan, and Fire Alert

Chapter 8. 54
A Smoking Stall

Chapter 9. 61
Thomas Does His Thing

Chapter 10. 69
Harsh, Lunch with Mother, and No Picnic for Amanda

Chapter 11. 78
Sharon and Gary

Chapter 12. 82
Ellie Gives The Inside Track

Chapter 13. 87
Intelligence HQ

Chapter 14. 92
The Walker

Chapter 15. 97
A Warm Reception

Chapter 16. 102
The Sleeper

Chapter 17. 106
The Reader

Chapter 18. 110
A Division of Labour

Chapter 19. 116
Dumb Blondes, Mrs Vine, and Erik

Chapter 20. 121
Desecration

Chapter 21................126
Janet Just Wants

Chapter 22................130
The Big Tease, Beards, and Temptation

Chapter 23................136
The Curate

Chapter 24................141
Ordinary People

Chapter 25................145
Amber

Chapter 26................151
At The Naughty Prawn, and Humpy

Chapter 27................156
The Wisdom of Claire

Chapter 28................162
Nick

Chapter 29................166
The Chancer

Chapter 30................169
Ask Me Anything

Chapter 31................172
Recap, Recall, and The Sword of Damocles

Chapter 32................176
Matty

Chapter 33................180
Memories, and Thomas's Perturbation

Chapter 34................185
Another Body

Chapter 35................189
A Tentative Suggestion

Chapter 36................196
Linnie

Chapter 37................200
History Lesson

Chapter 38................205
A Dangerous Habit

Chapter 39................209
Hillers and Humpy, and Lost and Found

Chapter 40................215
Woodie's Pedigree, The Museum, and Pressure Point

Chapter 41................219
The Glass

Chapter 42................224
The Wisdom of Aunt Amelia

Chapter 43 . . . . *229*
Covert Preparations

Chapter 44 . . . . *235*
The Prop

Chapter 45 . . . . *239*
Beyond The Gate

Chapter 46 . . . . *244*
The Cloister

Chapter 47 . . . . *249*
The Refectory

Chapter 48 . . . . *256*
The Study

Chapter 49 . . . . *260*
The Guest Chamber

Chapter 50 . . . . *267*
The Night

Chapter 51 . . . . *272*
Retreat

Chapter 52 . . . . *275*
A Change of Habit

Chapter 53 . . . . *280*
Jane is Alarmed

Chapter 54 . . . . *284*
Pressure Points

Chapter 55 . . . . *291*
Wait Until Dawn

Chapter 56 . . . . *295*
Confession

Chapter 57 . . . . *300*
Defiler

Chapter 58 . . . . *304*
The Letter

Chapter 59 . . . . *308*
The Nightstairs

Chapter 60 . . . . *313*
The Cloister and The Hearth

Chapter 61 . . . . *317*
The Bait

Chapter 62 . . . . *321*
The Pieces

Chapter 63 . . . . *326*
Armed

Chapter 64 . . . . *331*
The Road to Ruin

Chapter 65 . . . . *337*
Baker Steps In, and Amanda Owns up

Chapter 66 . . . . *341*
The Burning Question

Chapter 67. . . . .*345*
Family Time

Chapter 68. . . . .*351*
Potential, and Aunt Amelia's Warning

Chapter 69. . . . .*354*
The Party

Chapter 70. . . . .*361*
The Brains Behind the Operation

Chapter 71. . . . .*365*
Who Told The Bishop?

Chapter 72. . . . .*368*
Treasure

Chapter 73. . . . .*373*
The Judgement of Wallace

Chapter 74. . . . .*376*
The Wisdom of Humpy, and a Present for Amanda

Chapter 75. . . . .*380*
Amanda's List, and Tempest Solves Two Mysteries

Chapter 76. . . . .*385*
Amanda's Theory, and Questions Old and New

Author's Note *391*

About the Author *393*

Acknowledgements *394*

About the Language Used in the Story. *396*

The Cornish Language *397*

Questions for Reading Clubs *398*

Glossary. *400*

A Note About Accents and Wicc'yeth *407*

The Last Word … For Now. *408*

The Village of Sunken Madley

Key

1. Amanda's House
2. Sunken Madley Manor
3. The Sinner's Rue Pub
4. The Library
5. St Ursula-without-Barnet
6. Medical Cent
7. Priory Ruins
8. Playing Fields
9. The Snout and Trough Pub
10. Post Office/Corner Shop

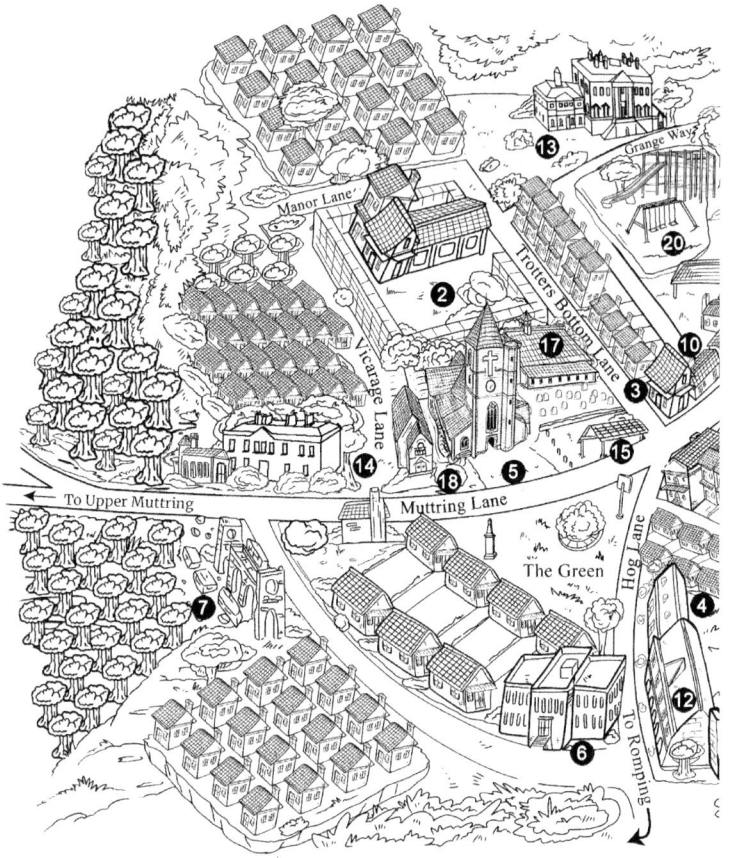

11. The Orchard
12. School
13. The Grange
14. The Elms
15. The Market
16. Vintage Vehicles
17. Church Hall
18. Rectory
19. The Big Tease
20. Playground

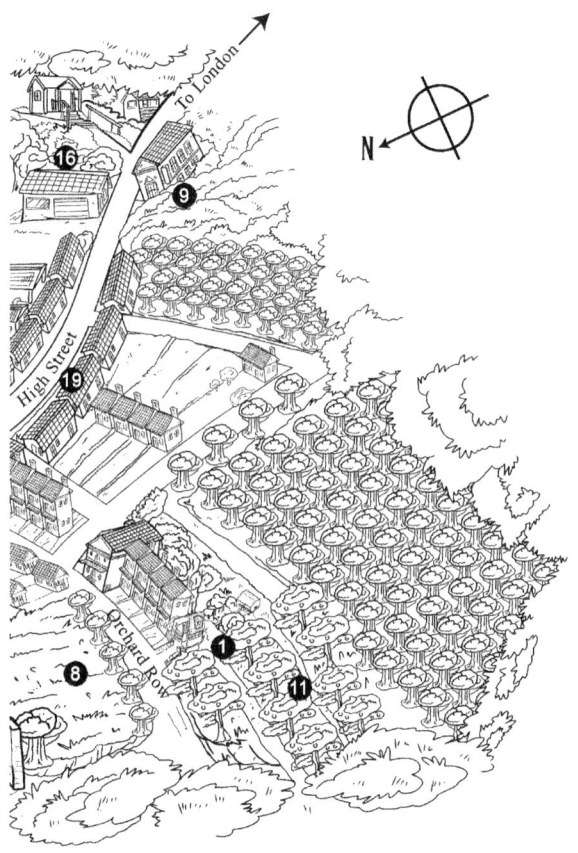

Plan of Sunken Madley Priory

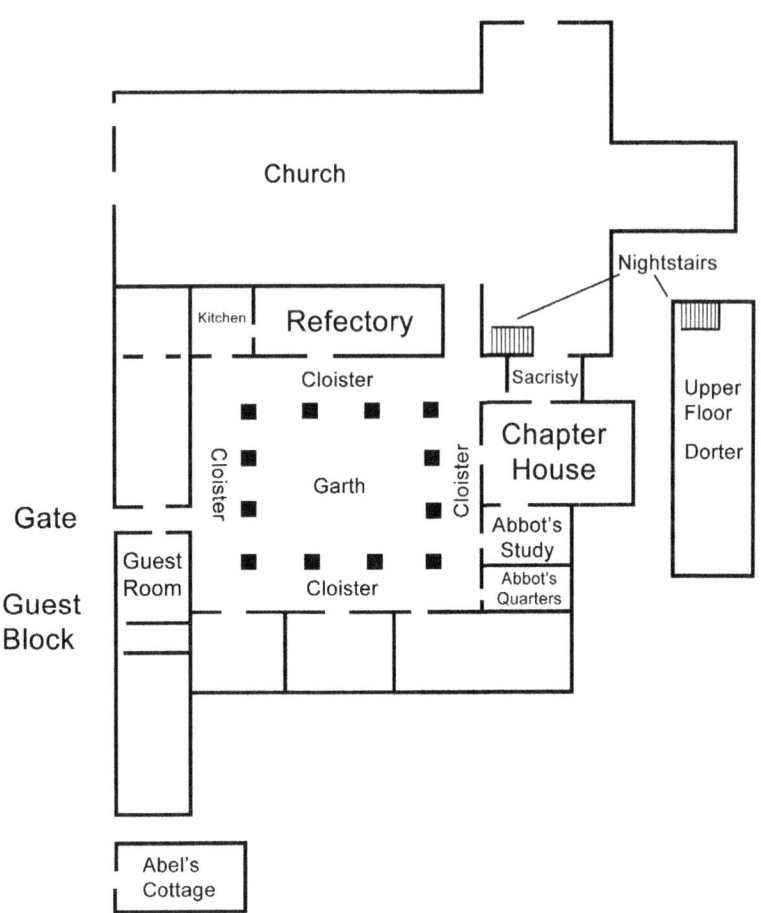

Seating Plan in the Refectory

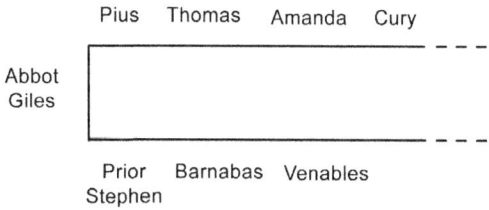

Map of Cornwall and the South of England

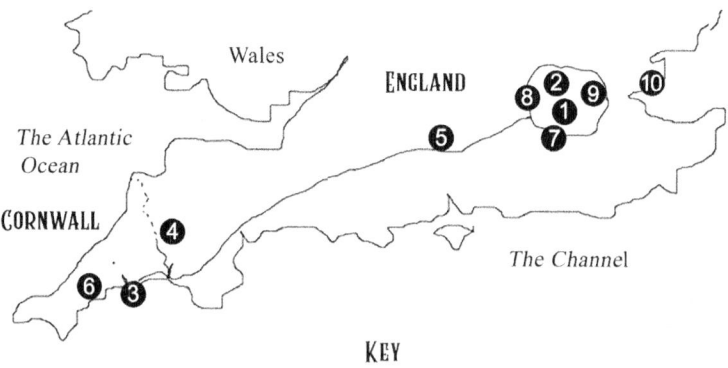

Key

1. London
2. Sunken Madley
3. Parhayle
4. The River Tamar & the border
5. M3 Motorway
6. Bodmin Moor
7. M25 Orbital Road
8. Heathrow Airport
9. Stratford
10. Southend-on-Sea

Magic

is always pushing and drawing

and making things out of nothing.

Everything is made out of magic …

So it must be all around us.

– Frances Hodgson Burnett

Introduction

Please note that to enhance the reader's experience of Amanda's world, this British-set story, by a British author, uses British English spelling, vocabulary, grammar and usage, and includes local and foreign accents, dialects and a magical language that vary from different versions of English as it is written and spoken in other parts of our wonderful, diverse world.

For your reading pleasure, there is a glossary of British English usage and vocabulary at the end of the book, followed by a note about accents and the magical language, Wicc'yeth.

Chapter 1

∽

A GRAND OPENING

It was a blissfully sunny August Sunday, and, as the villagers expected, Amanda Cadabra and her irascible feline companion were making their way towards their favourite picnic spot. Jonathan, the dazzlingly handsome but incurably shy assistant librarian, had raised a hand in greeting as they'd passed.

Witch and familiar took the slope up towards their goal at a gentle pace; Amanda because exertion was no friend to her asthma; Tempest because he believed that 'rush' was a speed reserved for extreme emergencies, but otherwise for peasants. He sniffed delicately in the direction of the picnic basket.

Amanda chuckled.

'Can you really smell ham through the container? It has a tight lid. Not that lids or locks have ever held you back, Mr Fuffy-wuffy. Well, you won't have to wait much longer for lunch.'

Their goal was in sight. The one-thousand-year-old priory, long since an unremarkable ruin, lay on the northern edge of the peaceful English village of Sunken Madley. It was situated just before the last of the habitations gave way to the trees of old Madley Wood. Years ago, Amanda had illicitly, but very discreetly, used some magic to erect a platform on what remained of a portion of the upper floor. They would visit on fine Sundays, Amanda to think and Tempest to survey his kingdom and … eat.

But today, today was going to be different. Amanda felt it before she saw it, saw it in the shadows.

She stopped a few yards away, staring towards the ground.

'Oh, Tempest. Oh no …. Not here … please, let it not be … *here*.'

* * *

Several days earlier, Detective Inspector Thomas Trelawney of the Devon and Cornwall Police, and now also of the London Metropolitan Police, was standing in his new office. It was strongly redolent of fresh paint and new carpet.

The office, together with his flat, occupied part of the ground floor of The Elms, one of the largest and oldest establishments of Sunken Madley. The village, still rural in spirit, was pleasantly situated just three miles south of the Hertfordshire border and 13 miles north of the Houses of Parliament. It was rather different from his Cornish coastal home town of Parhayle, but all in all, Trelawney was happy to be here.

Having looked around the room, he turned his hazel eyes toward Bryan Branscombe, the village builder, and smiled.

'You've done wonders, Mr Branscombe.'

'Thank you, Inspector. Very nice of you to say so.' Bryan pushed his hands more deeply into the pockets of his light grey overalls and gazed at the carpet to hide a blush.

He was still getting used to accepting compliments. Bryan looked up again, at a slight angle, being somewhat shorter than Trelawney's six feet. 'Sorry about the delays,' he said for the umpteenth time. 'But the gas explosion at the Puttenhams left them without a kitchen, so I couldn't leave them, and then I had to sort out the plumbing at Pipkin Acres. It's a residential home, after all.'

'That's quite all right. I've been busy with various things back in Cornwall myself, and I believe Miss Cadabra has had a few rush jobs on. But here we are now, and I can see it's been well worth the wait.'

'Thank you, Inspector. Here, would you like to check the facilities?'

Thomas had already been shown the milestones in the refurbishments of his new flat and office as they'd been reached. However, this had something of the air of a grand opening, albeit with just the two of them.

Bryan had cleverly made the small loo appear to be part of the stretch of cupboards that ran from the right-hand edge of that essential room to the end of the wall opposite where the desk would be. That centrepiece of furniture was to be set in front of the attractive bay window, with the door to the hallway of The Elms on the left and the entrance to Thomas's new flat to the right. The woodwork was painted matt white; the walls were mushroom, and the carpet a warm beige. Pleasant, welcoming and serviceable.

'The desk will be over this afternoon,' Bryan told him, 'as soon as Miss Cadabra has finished with it. I'll bring it over.'

'Thank you, Bryan. I don't know how you managed to get it to her workshop.' A generous present at the end of the last case and something of an heirloom, it was a gift from Miss Armstrong-Witworth of The Grange. A handsome Victorian partner desk, it was furniture crafted to last and, thought Thomas, must weigh a considerable amount.

'Oh, that's all right, Inspector. All part of the service. Moffat helped me get it onto the van to take to Miss Cadabra. You wouldn't think a man his age could be that strong. Must be one of them bodybuilders in his spare time! Iskender –'

'– who owns the kebab shop?' checked Trelawney, who was still getting to know the village.

'That's right. Gave me a hand the other end, and then Marcus, your neighbour, will help me get it back here.'

'But I can –'

'No, no, Marcus says he wants to do it. What with you sorting out that business and clearing his name as a suspect and all.'

'Most kind. You must let me give –'

'No, Inspector, that's quite all right. Mrs James takes care of all that. But I wouldn't say no to a jar down the Sinner's when we're both free.'

'You're on.'

'Did I hear my name spoken?' asked Irene, knocking on the office door that gave onto the hall.

'But not in vain, I assure you. Do come in, Mrs James,' called Trelawney.

'Thank you, Inspector.' His new landlady trod lithely into the room and turned her head, adorned with short blonde hair, towards her builder, 'All done then, Bryan?'

'All done, Mrs James. Just the desk arriving soon, and I expect Miss Cadabra told you, Inspector, she's waiting on the staining of your coffee table for the sitting room until you've seen the colour of the leather on the desk. So the two echo, as they say, in different parts of the flat.'

'Of course, Amanda told the inspector,' said Irene, smiling at Thomas and briefly laying a maternal hand on his grey-suit-jacketed arm. 'It's all absolutely splendid, Bryan. What about the flat?'

'Perfect,' said Trelawney.

'Good, good. Well, Bryan, I think you deserve a bonus.'

'Very kind of you, Mrs James.' Then, nodding brightly at Trelawney, 'You and Miss Cadabra can start work then.'

'Not yet,' stated Irene firmly. 'The paintwork and carpet need airing for at least three days, I'd say. They'll be no friend to her asthma else. Is the paint on the window frames dry, Bryan?'

'Yes, completely.'

'Well then, with your permission, Inspector, if you're going to be here for a while …?'

Irene began to open all of the windows, top and bottom. 'Ah, yes, good idea,' Thomas approved. He went into his flat through the door at the right-hand end of the office and opened the entrance to the side passage that ran between the house and the annexe, which he knew all too well. He opened the kitchen windows and the French windows giving on to the extensive garden, with its distinctive avenue of elms that gave the house its name and had featured so significantly in the last case. The memory flickered through Thomas's mind before being recalled to the present by the voice of approval from Irene:

'That'll get a good through draft.'

'Three days?' Trelawney checked. 'For all of the chemical odours to dissipate?'

'Yes. Then,' advised Irene, 'ask Amanda to come and try it.'

Chapter 2

Amanda Rises to the Occasion

Amanda, meanwhile, in the furniture restoration workshop bequeathed to her by Perran, her grandfather and mentor, was trying something rather more challenging.

'Well done, *bian*,' said Perran, addressing Amanda by his pet name for her since birth, the Cornish word for baby. He, her grandfather, was, strictly speaking and in vulgar parlance, dead, like his wife, Senara. Amanda, however, knew better than to use such a word, but instead described them, as she had been taught, as 'transitioned': to another plane of existence, that was. It was one, as far as Amanda could judge, that seemed to be a whirl of cocktail parties, excursions to exotic locations, and luncheons with disconcertingly legendary figures from history.

Right now, however, they were engaged in assisting their granddaughter with her magical skills. The scene was being regarded with a mixture of *ennui* and amusement by Tempest, a permanently grumpy feline in a furry collection of storm greys, out of which glowed two yellow eyes.

He might have been regarded as Amanda's familiar. Tempest would have corrected this misapprehension as Amanda was, in his view, his pet and cumbersome charge for whom he would have only grudgingly admitted a certain affection. To Trelawney, he was a malevolent creature of, no doubt, disreputable provenance. By contrast, to his adoring witch, Tempest was Mr Fluffykins and other names that denoted to their object how utterly he had her wound around his little finger.

Tempest occasionally paused in his observance of Amanda's endeavours to exchange glances of cordial dislike with Granny. Both Senara and Perran had been responsible for casting the complicated and dangerous enchantment, late one night in the workshop, that had reincarnated him. But it was Granny on whom he pinned the unforgivable charge. Neither the years nor her transition had dimmed their mutual disregard for one another. Granny, naturally, knew precisely who and what he was, as did Perran and Mrs Sharma. However, in spite of Amanda's careful enquiries, no one was telling.

'I can see your progress,' commended Grandpa, his accent flavoured by his Cornish origins. 'You're holding the handles more loosely now.'

'Yes,' replied Amanda, who, dressed in her green boiler suit, was kneeling on an old door on the floor. 'I think,' she added hesitantly, pinning back up the untidy plait of mouse-brown hair that had flopped down onto her shoulders, 'I might try letting go. But you'll steady it if I …?'

'Of course, pet.'

Amanda had screwed in four handles, one along each edge of the door. Facing a short edge, she gripped the ones on either side of her, took a deep breath and focused. She said softly:

'Aereval'

The door lifted slightly from the floor with only the tiniest of wobbles. Amanda took it up six inches then, relaxing her hold on the handles, slowly and carefully released them. She gradually lifted her arms, feeling the thrill of being airborne.

'Look, Grandpa! Look, no hands! – Oh!'

It must have been the loss of focus that allowed the door to tip and slide her forward. Her eyes flew open. Her hands reached back frantically for the handles as Perran lifted a finger and steadied, then lowered, the makeshift vehicle.

'Phew! Thank you, Grandpa.'

'You're all right, *bian*,' he soothed.

'Splendid effort, Amanda dear,' Granny encouraged her. 'I suspect you are somewhat distracted.'

'I am?'

'You are expecting a telephone communication, are you not?'

'Oh,' Amanda returned airily, 'yes, the inspector did say that the office might be ready today for us to begin work officially. The furniture restoration has to come first, though, except in … well, pressing circumstances.'

'But both your new position as consultant to the inspector and your day job are dependent on your developing your abilities as village witch, however secret that office must remain.'

'Yes, Granny.'

'And you're coming along nicely, *bian*,' assured Grandpa, from whom she had inherited her particular magical gift: levitation.

It was the hallmark of the Cadabras, a farming clan on Bodmin Moor, from whom Perran had apparently become estranged on the day he had eloped with Senara of the witch-clan Cardiubarn. Amanda found the story adorably romantic. Granny had bequeathed her another skill set, which had been extraordinarily useful. But it had equally got Amanda into a great deal of trouble and nearly brought destruction upon the village. For the Cardiubarns were spell-weavers.

If her grandparents' lessons since she was six hadn't sunk in, Amanda certainly knew it now: magic was a serious business. It was to be used sparingly, absolutely not in the sight of Normals – non-witches – and never, ever upon humans themselves.

There was a whole list of dos and don'ts that Amanda had learned over the years. Amanda liked rules. You knew where you were with a good rule. But then … there were times when ….

Chapter 3

❦

The Corner Shop

Magic practice over with, Tempest had made it patently obvious that the fridge was lacking in Devon double cream, his latest whim.

'It's on the list.' Amanda waved towards the notice board near the kitchen door that led to the hallway.

The relevance of this statement was lost on Tempest. His voice sounded, as usual, clearly in her head:

The word is on the list; the cream is elsewhere.

'Fine,' she sighed. A visit to the hub of the village was clearly called for before Amanda could start on the inspector's coffee table, which was to be stripped and sanded prior to applying the new stain.

Five minutes later, Tempest was leading the way to The Corner Shop from the racing-green Vauxhall Astra. This had been bequeathed to Amanda by Perran, together with the business, and bore the legend in gold down each side:

Cadabra Furniture Restoration and Repairs

Amanda heard Joan the postlady say, as she pushed open the shop door with its characteristic:

Ding!

'Well, I don't know. Seemed nice enough from her letter. Hello, dear!' she interrupted herself, leading the chorus of greetings from the assembled company.

'We was just talkin' about a visitor, dearie,' explained Sylvia, the eighty-something lollipop lady. Her staff of office, a round 'Stop' sign on a pole used for arresting traffic and allowing the school children to traverse the road safely, gave her job its name. Currently, it was leaning in a nook behind the shop door. 'Joan's long lost somethin'-or-another 'as turned up.'

'Oh, that's nice,' Amanda replied politely, who had difficulty with the idea of family ties. 'Erm ... is it?'

'That's what we're wondering,' put in Dennis Hanley-Page – dashing septuagenarian and owner of Vintage Vehicles – whose zest for life was undimmed by the mere passing of years. 'Some sort of second cousin?'

'Yes,' answered the curvaceous Joan, pushing a stray blonde curl off her face. 'Said she was investigating her family tree, and I turned up. Said since losing her parents, it's suddenly become important to her, and so she "reached out". Offered to stay at one of the pubs but, well, I don't know, somehow the way she put it ... I feel I must put her up, really.'

'She might be very nice, and you two could hit it off,' came the voice of Nalini, her willowy form approaching from the mysterious back of the shop. She reached below the counter, extracted a gourmet treat from a packet, laid it on a paper napkin, and ceremoniously handed it over to Amanda. She, in turn, placed it on the floor in front of Tempest, waiting at her feet for his tribute. He and Mrs Sharma exchanged glances that only they understood, and Tempest sampled the delicacy. Their unfathomable relationship had been the same from Day One and had always mystified Amanda. Tempest's list of humans for which he had a measure of respect was a singularly short one.

'Well, I must just wait and see, I suppose,' responded Joan philosophically.

'Your grandmother's cousin's daughter's niece, did you say?' enquired Dennis.

'So she says, or something like that, but my grandfather's cousin passed, so I can't ask him.'

'Might be that 'e didn't know about the daughter if you know what I mean,' Sylvia hazarded, with a gentle suggestive nudge of her friend's arm.

'That did cross my mind,' agreed Joan cheerfully.

Ding!

The door opened to admit Mrs Yarkly, who nodded a greeting to the occupants of the shop. They duly responded. Mrs Yarkly was known throughout the village as a woman whose delicacy regarding certain matters was of heroic proportions. She was, however, an individual whom Amanda rarely encountered and, therefore, whose face had long since been forgotten.

'Just crackers, thank you, Mrs Sharma. I've been having an unfortunate,' she lowered her voice so that her final words were barely audible, 'Bathroom Experience.'

'Oh dear,' sympathised Amanda. 'Tiles falling off the walls? That can happen, especially with poor-quality adhesive or grout. Of course, that can also simply lose its integrity with age. Or, you could be right: it could be too wet if they're new, but I don't think ground-up crackers will be the best ....'

Mrs Yarkly was frowning. That was one of the few expressions Amanda recognised, and she paused to ask, 'Are you all right, Mrs Yarkly?'

'No. Not *that* sort of bathroom experience, girl.' Holding her right hand at shoulder-level, with a flick of her index finger, she pointed discreetly and briefly towards her lower abdomen.

'Ah, a ... a digestive issue,' Amanda correctly inferred.

'*Pre*cisely.'

'Oh dearie,' intervened Sylvia, 'you want to pop along to Mr Sharma, the chemist, then. 'E'll give you just the thing: clear up a loose stool in minutes.'

Mrs Yarkly was affronted.

'There is nothing amiss with my furniture. I'm sure it isn't the way I've been sitting. Besides, isn't that more your department?' she asked, turning to Amanda, now struggling to maintain her countenance with a suitably grave expression. She was rescued by Nalini, who intervened smoothly with,

'Here are your crackers, Mrs Yarkly. We wish you a speedy recovery from your indisposition. And I'm sure my husband would be more than happy to assist you.'

'Thank you. And, Miss Cadabra, I saw that my sister's extremely valuable antique cabinet isn't repaired yet.'

'It's on my list.'

'You do know our aunt works for Trading Standards?'

'I'll get there as soon as I can,' Amanda promised meekly.

As Mrs Yarkly departed, another was arriving who would easily have been a match for the truculent lady. Through the open door could be heard the peremptory call of:

'Churchill! Heel.' This heralded the entrance of Miss Cynthia de Havillande of The Grange, a tall and impressive figure and the oldest and most venerable resident of Sunken Madley. The aged terrier, named after the late prime minister, looked around cautiously for Tempest, saw he was distracted by a delicacy and settled happily behind his mistress's ankles.

'Good day to you all,' Miss de Havillande wished the assembled company warmly, to which they responded with equal geniality. 'I can't stay. A pint of milk, if you would, Nalini; I promised Moffat I would bring one. He is making scones. Regarding the next ball, to wait until the autumn Feast of St Ursula of the Apples seems to me to be too long a delay. However, we shall be thin of company, so I propose a party on the last Saturday in August, to mark the end of astronomical summer. Or is it meteorological?'

'Meteorological, Cynthia,' supplied Nalini with a smile.

'Thank you, my dear. Yes, to mark the end of meteorological summer.'

A chorus of approval greeted this offering.

'Splendid. Amanda, no preparation need be made on the ballroom; it shall be held in the large salon. Although it is not a formal ball, gentlemen shall be expected to attend in jacket and tie and ladies in some sort of evening-appropriate-wear. Perhaps you would be good enough to spread the word.'

'Lovely,' approved Sylvia.

'No problem there,' responded Dennis.

'Yes, I'll let people know on my rounds,' promised Joan.

'And Dennis,' Miss de Havillande addressed him peremptorily, 'if you must drive one of your deathtraps to the party, perhaps you could approach at a reasonable speed and not send the gravel on the drive flying into orbit when you skid to an uncontrolled halt.'

Mr Hanley-Page grinned.

'Don't worry, Cynthia, I know that pre-historic Range Rover of yours can't manage any but the smoothest surface.'

'Hmph!' There was an ongoing vehicular feud of long-standing between the neighbours. It was no more than skin deep, and this was Cynthia's way of acknowledging a hit.

Having paid for her milk and bade the throng farewell, Miss de Havillande exited with the inevitable call of:

'Churchill! Heel!'

Chapter 4

JANET OGLETHORPE

Janet Oglethorpe, some two hundred miles to the north of The Corner Shop, neatly folded her dressing gown onto the ordered pile of clothes and toiletries and pulled down the lid of her wheelie suitcase. She called, in a Yorkshire accent, to her husband, for the third time,

'You sure you'll be all right without me? Don't answer. You'll exert y'self.' She closed the bag, put the padlock in place, and hauled it out of the bedroom of number 18 Bardsey Lane, Wigworth End, and down the stairs.

'Aye, love, I'll be reet as rain,' came the patient response.

'You won't 'ave me t' do fer yer. Since y' heart, I've 'ad to do all around 'ere. It all falls on me. Me that 'as all the responsibility I 'ave.'

'Aye, love.'

Janet came into the sitting room, where Keith Oglethorpe was comfortably disposed on the sofa, with his hands clasped behind his head. It still bore its enduring thatch of strawberry blond hair that she'd noticed at their first meeting.

'Feet off table. How many times 'ave I got to tell yer?'

'It's not like we eat off it, lass,' he responded good-naturedly with his automatic reply.

'And put that thing away, poisoning y'self, and what with yer 'eart.'

'It's just a tad of flavoured air.' Keith hid the vape pipe his daughter had bought him for Christmas. He'd given up smoking as per doctor's orders, and Linnie had given him a rather grand Meerschaum-looking device and some nicotine-flavoured e-juice to go with it. 'I've told yer, love, it's perfectly safe. The juice is food standards; yer could put it in a cake and eat t' ingredients. Probably do yer less 'arm than all that sugar yer put in yer tea and all them biscuits.'

'I need me energy. With all I 'ave to do. It all falls on me now.'

'I'm well on t' mend,' Keith soothed. He looked at her, wondering, as he so often did, what had become of the soft, round, pretty girl he'd married. Over the years, she'd become harder and thinner and, well … harder. They had met at a dance. He'd seen her at once, all off-the-shoulder ruffles and big hair. Now her brown coiffure was close-cropped: 'sensible'.

Janet Oglethorpe, she was then, and they found they were distantly related. They had lived near his family home until it had passed into Keith's hands. It had been with the Oglethorpes for hundreds of years, starting off as a decent-sized dwelling for the time but growing to accommodate the needs of the occupants. And then, of course, they'd done the side extension where Freddie and his mate had a room and ensuite shared throughout university. Bit older than Freddie. A late bloomer. He was a nice chap. Bit of a chip on his shoulder, but then who hadn't? Had Freddie kept in touch with him still? All the way down there in London.

They'd added a conservatory so Linnie could do her horticulture. She'd done well making such a go of that. Had her own place and market garden now, and she and her husband seemed happy. Would be nice to have some grandchildren up here, but Freddie had taken care of that. Freddie kept saying, wistfully, he wished mam and dad would move down there, but Keith loved this old house too much. At least … it was family… Of course … they could always … but Janet … her job.

He'd been proud of Janet. She'd risen through the management structure of the department store in York to become the Woman In Charge. She ruled with unsmiling and absolute efficiency. Keith had readily offered to move his small office into the home to look after the children and the cats. The children had grown up and left, and the cats, after making more cats, had made their transition to another plane of existence and, likewise, their offspring.

But Keith had never given up hoping that, someday, the girl he'd married would re-emerge. Even though Linnie had told him her aunt had said Janet had been like that forever but knew a good man when she saw him, and had shown him the side of herself that he wanted to see. Even so, Keith had never given up.

Keith had liked having the house as his domain. Until what Janet always called his 'heart'. It was only a mild attack but meant that his life had moved to the ground floor, and Janet had taken some half days off to 'see to things.'

She had attacked the 'project' with her customary zeal and set about 'sortin' out the 'ouse'. She'd cleaned from the attic to the cellar and back again, imposed a strict regime for the restoration of her husband's health, and, unexpectedly, turned her attention to 'family.' In the process of which, she'd discovered some sort of half-cousin down south.

'Oh, aye? You're goin' to visit 'er?' asked Keith, trying to keep the hopefulness out of his voice. It would be nice to have the place to himself for a bit. And Janet was clearly embarked on a new project.

'It's me duty,' replied his wife shortly. 'It's family. I've arranged f' services to visit twice a day and give yer y'dinner and y'tea.'

'Ta, ar lass.'

Yes, over the years, she'd become a lot smaller on fun and a lot bigger on duty. Although he secretly wondered if it was just an excuse to do the things she really wanted to do.

'Only be about a week, p'raps a bit more. I'm due four weeks of 'oliday, and I'll be in reg'lar contact with t' office.' And now here she was about to be off down the A1 towards somewhere between Hertfordshire and London. 'Details is on t' desk, but I'll call.' She came over and gave him a dry peck on the cheek. 'Be'ave while I'm gone.'

'Course love. Where is it you're goin', again?'

'Chuffin' ekk, I told yer: Sunken Madley.'

* * *

Amanda, with Tempest's desires satisfied, however temporarily, was comfortably ensconced in her favourite retreat: the workshop. She was testing various yellow-green wood stains on pieces of wood of the same kind as the inspector's coffee table, which was housed temporarily towards the back of Amanda's restoration space.

She wore a dust mask, even though the sanding of this piece of furniture was being conducted several feet away.

'*Sessiblin,*' she called. A block wound with abrasive paper ceased its systematic sweep of the table's surface. The hose-like arm of the Hoover that had been following the sanding block lowered itself to the floor. Tempest emerged from his burrow, deep within into a pile of clean furniture covers, and telegraphed his displeasure at the appalling racket that had been disrupting a nap.

The legs of the inspector's furniture had already been done, and Amanda was satisfied with the result. She put the lid on the second sample tin of stain and checked that the wax on the desk had gone off and was ready for buffing.

'*Mecsge,*' Amanda called over to the pot on the electric hob on the opposite side of the room. The brush began stirring.

'*Cumdez obma,*' she summoned a roll of chartreuse green leather down from the rack above and carefully cut it to size.

In an effort to distract her familiar from his displeasure at the recent noise from the vacuum cleaner, she offered, 'This time tomorrow, my first official day in the official office. Imagine, Tempest!'

Must I? he thought.

It had already been agreed that Amanda would bring a large, paw-selected cushion to be placed on one of the extra chairs in the office for the comfort of Tempest. Much as Trelawney had rather the cat – or whatever it really was – were elsewhere, the inspector thought was best to placate him.

Amanda applied glue, then fitted the leather into the surface of Trelawney's desk and wiped off any excess adhesive. She stood back to assess the effect. One final touch: she buffed the wax to a soft glow.

'Yes, Tempest, I think he's going to be pleased.'

Chapter 5

୬

Amanda's First Day, and Edward Nightingale

The office smelled only very slightly of fresh paint and the new leather inlay. They sat for the first time on either side of the partner desk that had, in Miss Armstrong-Witworth's words, come home. The executive chairs were in light tan leather and accommodated Trelawney, with his back to the window, and Amanda, facing him, ready to begin.

He was used to doing this sort of thing on his computer. However, Thomas knew that Amanda thought better with more tangible objects and, besides, it might help them both. Accordingly, he put the A3 printout of a map of Sunken Madley between them.

'First of all, Miss Cadabra,' he opened, addressing her as they had agreed: formally for work situations, reserving first names for off-duty, 'thank you for sharing what actually transpired at The Manor back then. Not dealt with precisely by the book but ….'

'Yes,' agreed Amanda. 'I thought you'd say that, which is why I didn't tell you,' she added frankly. He shifted uncomfortably in his chair. It was at once awkward and disarming.

'Well, as I say, thank you. I do appreciate it.'
'And it's off the record?' she checked.
'Yes.'
'And I know,' Amanda admitted, a shade contritely, 'that I did use magic in a way that I really wouldn't do so now, after … everything.'
'Quite,' agreed Thomas, 'Erm, … To move on ….."
'Aren't you going to put a red cross on The Manor?' asked Amanda, pointing to the place on the map.
'Ah, yes.' Trelawney, as he made the mark, heard his colleague sigh,
'I wish we had a corkboard and red string,' she said wistfully.
He grinned. 'I'll get you one for Christmas.'
Amanda looked disappointed.
'That's ages away,' she pointed out.
She sounded so much like his young niece and nephew that he could not help laughing.
'Well, sooner perhaps, but let's not waste the morning with a shopping trip to the stationers, shall we?'
'Yes, you're quite right, Inspector.'
'Very well, Miss Cadabra. So we've put a cross on Sunken Madley Manor. Next.'
'Next: Lost Madley. Well, Little Madley, I suppose it is again now.' She went quiet. He noticed. There was something she hadn't told him, and still … the memory rose unbidden of her walking out of the night into the lamplight when he'd driven up to the Asthma Centre in that strange annexe to the village, and he'd suddenly thought, 'Lili Marlene'.
Suddenly, Amanda surprised him by saying,
'I suppose … I should tell you what happened there.'
'Well ….' Thomas was taken aback.
'After all, now there's no reason not to,' Amanda considered.
'Erm, … thank you. Yes … please.'
'Maybe we should make some tea first.'

'Indeed,' he concurred with feeling. 'Let's christen the new kettle.'

A few minutes later, mugs of tea, shortbread and gingernuts on the desk beside them, Amanda clasped her hands and, looking directly into Trelawney's eyes, began:

'You see, Inspector, it was like this ….'

* * *

Edward Nightingale's cologne was subtle. His dark hair was carefully tinted to disguise the very first threads of grey, and his nails were manicured. His doctor had said it was important to like what he saw in the mirror. And it pleased his mother to help, and he liked to make her happy. She always said that as she owned a salon, the least she could do was make sure her son was always well turned out. Besides, it was good for business for the ladies to see him in there, and had he thought about that phone number she'd given him from Cassandra Thornton?

There was no shortage of phone numbers. But he was looking for more than … he didn't know what … someone off the bottle, that was for sure … but more than that …. Anyway, right now, he needed to keep his mind on his future. And it could be a very bright future. If he played his cards right. His brown eyes checked himself in the mirror, and he patted his stomach. A couple of extra pounds there, but bumping up his gym regime would soon sort that out. I'm a new man, he reminded himself. He put on his blazer and adjusted his tie. This is a fresh start. The past is behind me.

It had been an odd path. After his law degree and a short stint in a contract law firm, he'd got diverted into the theatre, via media paralegal, and into a small private performance company. It had been surprisingly lucrative, and he'd had hopes of being able to impress …. until …. He hadn't quite staked his shirt on it. And a good thing too. It hadn't gone totally according to plan. And then *she* …. After the emotional … collapse ... and a spell in a discreet private hospital, when he'd been urged by his doctors to consider a change of career, now he was back … back to the law and …. maybe more. Put things right. For himself … for the family. A phoenix. That was right. A phoenix rising from the ashes.

It was perfect. A sort of work experience assistant to a solicitor. In a quiet village.

* * *

'So we put a cross there,' said Trelawney, adding a red mark to Lost Madley.

'But I don't see any connection,' observed Amanda, rising slightly from her chair to arrange the skirt of her orange dress more comfortably underneath her.

'Patience, my dear consultant. Early days. Let's move on.'

'The church hall. Well, of course, you know all about that.'

Suddenly the vision flashed into Amanda's mind of that brief glimpse of the inspector ripping off his t-shirt just as she passed out. She banished it at once. It had no bearing on …. on anything.

Trelawney looked up at the slight pause to see Amanda giving her head a little shake. 'All right?'

'Oh yes, yes, absolutely,' she responded hastily.

'So, next: The Grange,' he prompted.

'Again, no connection. Accidents do happen,' Amanda replied glibly.

Oh, there were entire volumes she wasn't disclosing here, thought Trelawney. He knew it with absolute certainty.

He looked at Amanda. 'Are we sure that we have absolutely *all* of the information pertaining to that case?' he asked carefully.

Amanda was very sure that *she* did, but knew he was fishing.
'Yes, as sure as we can be,' she replied easily.

He didn't want to push it, not this early on in their official working relationship; the paint barely dry on the walls. He'd interviewed – no, actually won commendations for his interview technique. He'd been across the table from the most devious of criminals in the course of his career. Yet, for some peculiar reason, it infuriated him that Amanda was even more skilled at evasion, misdirection, distraction, and downright obfuscation. And yet … the one thing she had never done – and he was certain would never do – was lie to him. Given his disastrous and heartbreaking domestic history, this meant more to him than she could ever possibly know. He instantly calmed down and asked gently,

'You're certain you've told me everything about that case?'

Amanda treated him to a wide-eyed kitten stare. It was hypnotic. He found himself wanting to believe whatever words she was about to treat him to.

'You've got all the notes from at the time. What else can I tell you?'

It was hopeless. Long ago, when he was a child, his grandmother had asked him to choose an eel for a pie from a basket of them. The species could have taken classes in Slippery from Amanda. He gave up.

'Right …. A cross on The Grange then. Moving on ….'

'The library. Again,' commented Amanda, relieved that there was nothing to hide about this one, 'you know all about *that*.'

'Indeed I do. You're quite sure about the translation of what that … oracle woman said?'

'Yes, it was definitely something like you must find or solve "the secret of Sunken Madley".'

'And that was all she said?' Trelawney checked

'On that matter, certainly,' answered Amanda regretfully.

'All right, well, it's a journey. And we've only just started. So … the library.' He put a cross over it. The next one's off the map.'

He drew an arrow pointing west and wrote 'Cornwall' next to it. 'But that doesn't mean it isn't connected.'

'Agreed,' said Amanda 'Finally: The Elms.'

He added the 'X. 'And that brings us up to date.'

They looked at what they had.

'If we had a corkboard, we could use push pins and tie them all together with *red string,*' Amanda pointed out yearningly.

Trelawney suppressed a grin. 'True, but for now, let's make do with our marker pen.' He drew lines between the crosses, and they stared at the map between them. Silence ensued until Amanda sighed.

'Well, I'm not getting any inspiration.'

Thomas ran a hand through his short, light-brown hair, an unconscious gesture, absorbed from his mother, that somehow helped him to think. 'Well, let's try excluding things. It's not to do with the people involved. Would that be fair to say?' Trelawney suggested.

'Yes.'

'Nor, at first glance, the locations.'

'Oh,' interjected Amanda, a thought occurring to her.

'Yes?'

'Well … maybe we're not thinking in the right dimension.'

Trelawney frowned in momentary confusion, but then his brow cleared.

'You mean … time?'

'Maybe … not just time but … well … the dimension where Granny and Grandpa are, except, of course, there might be ….'

'… more than one of them?' Somehow the word 'dimension' made Thomas more comfortable with the notion. It sounded scientific, at least. 'Might there be something more they could tell us about that in relation to our puzzle?'

'I don't know.' Amanda was doubtful. 'They're extremely vague on the subject.'

Yes, thought Thomas, it's always been clear where she gets that from. He asked aloud,

'But I take it you've never asked them about it in this context?'

'True,' she admitted. 'No, I haven't.'

'Might that be a line of enquiry we might, tentatively, pursue?'

Amanda nodded decisively.

'It's worth a try.'

Chapter 6

Finley

Round eyes and ears gave him something of the look of an amiable monkey. Which is precisely how his loving sister would have described him. On the whole, women found his appearance pleasing, but it was his apparent good humour that won him female companionship.

Finley – Finny to his family and Fin to his chums – tended to be known as a bit of a chancer. Even his sister would have said that. And right now he saw no reason to pass up an opportunity that might pay off. Probably nothing in it, but why not? He could come up with a story as well as the next person, actually a lot better, really. But that wasn't the only reason he was heading north.

There'd been this girl … woman … it had only been that one date, and then he'd lost her number. But he'd never forgotten her, and he'd never been able to find her again. He'd only had her name, which was so common it was probably just a profile nickname, and the vaguest idea of where she lived … in some village up towards the Hertfordshire border. She'd been different. At first, he'd given her the usual act: good listener, liberal, accepting, fascinated, ready to commit … and then, as the evening progressed, it had begun to turn into the real thing … things. And afterwards, the more he'd remembered and thought about her and their time together, the more ….

She hadn't called him. Her profile had disappeared from the dating site where he'd seen her. And Stew, that idiot, had played that dumb trick with the card she'd written her number on. With the wind that day, he'd never have had a hope of catching it. But still. Just a mate mucking about. There were plenty more fish, after all. However, the prize had yet to come his way. And now …

Finley wandered into his sister's spare bedroom, where she was now packing his bag. He put a gentle arm around her shoulders and kissed her cheek.

'You don't have to do that.'

'I know. But I've only got one brother, and he doesn't come to stay every day.'

'Often enough, though.'

'Course, I love having you around. Now, are you going to tell me any more about what this … venture is about?'

'I can't say any more, Angie.' He sat on the bed, bouncing a little with excitement. 'Just that it could be the big one.'

She shook her head. 'The big one, the big one. The big one has got you into more trouble than I –'

'No, but it could,' her brother insisted. 'Set us all up for life: you, me, Mark, the kids.'

'I'm fine,' said Angie, taking a last look around the room for any items that might have got missed. 'I've got a job I like, it pays the bills, and we're all happy.'

'Yeah, but I could give you more if I could just ….'

She went to him and put a hand on his cheek. 'I worry about you, Finny. You're a good person, but sometimes you walk too close to the cliff edge. Sometimes I think you want to jump.'

'I … I know I can be a bit of a lad.'

'Don't you think you're getting a bit old for that? Shame you never found that girl.'

'Well … maybe, I just might …. Anyway, Nick and Stew are going with me.'

'Oh no,' said his sister with foreboding.

'Oh, they're all right,' protested Finley in a persuasive tone.

'You think everyone's all right. And every*thing*. Half your trouble.'

'Well, with them along, at least it'll be a laugh, and it's Nick's birthday, and he likes the country. Well, it's country-ish anyway.'

'And you're not telling me where you're going?'

'I'll be in touch,' Finley promised.

Angie saw him to the door, where they said their goodbyes.

He put his case in the boot of his blue MG, got into the driver's seat, slid his phone into the slot and tapped at the screen. Google maps enunciated:

'Directions to The Snout and Trough, Sunken Madley.'

* * *

With a trial schedule of one day at the office and the next in the workshop, Amanda was now back in her green boiler suit and, regarding the set of loose-limbed chairs, arrayed ready for her attention. Normally, she always experienced the slight thrill of the 'before', knowing the delight of the owner that would inevitably follow the transformation she was about to effect.

Today, however, she approached it with a somewhat desultory air. Giving herself a little shake, Amanda declared decisively:

'Music, Tempest, that's what we need.'

He put in head down under his paws. His human's ideas of what constituted music usually differed widely from his own.

Amanda switched on the vintage Roberts radio, which had come with the bequest to her by Grandpa, to listen to her favourite channel. A new song was just being played. The writer, however, having discovered with evident pleasure a new rhyming couplet, had alas, thereafter, been deserted by the muse and was supplementing the lapse by repeating it over and over again.

She switched to her second favourite music channel, where a young lady was insisting, in a rapid succession of words, that she was no longer thinking of her ex. The illogic of this repeatedly affirmed statement was too much for the listener, who essayed the classical channel. A plainsong chant issued forth dolefully and, from what she could catch of the Latin, was dwelling on the twin subjects of sin and death. Amanda sighed and abandoned her search. She crossed the room to a drawer stuffed with CDs, hunting for one that might inspire.

'This isn't like me,' she observed Tempest, who had now raised his head, safe from the unsatisfactory airwaves. 'Whatever is the matter with me? Am I ... a little ... bored?'

In my presence? Tempest marvelled to himself.

'Oh, dear. Can it be that I've become addicted to ... excitement? Oh no ... have I become addicted to ... murder?'

* * *

Amanda and Trelawney had made no further progress with linking the Sunken Madley incidents. They were, nevertheless, taking a gentle walk to The Snout and Trough to celebrate Amanda's first week officially consulting in the new office. It was a warm, idyllic day, hedges billowing over old walls, lobelia cascading in purple waterfalls.

Having reached their destination, Sunken Madley's 'The Other Pub', while Trelawney inspected the possibility of indoor seating, Amanda went to the garden to check if it would be pleasant to eat outside.

It was quiet. A couple from Pipkin Acres, a woman at her laptop with a glass of white wine, and a convivial party of three men. The one sitting opposite Amanda suddenly rose. He was a little over medium height with reddish brown hair and wore a white shirt with a narrow, muted purple stripe. He came towards her with a smile.

'Amanda!'

To her bemusement, he advanced and kissed her on the cheek.

'Ah … er … hello?' she managed to respond. Facial recognition was not one of her strengths.

'Amazing. I had no idea you lived round here.'

'Erm.'

'It's me! Fin, Finley.'

'Ah,' she replied, still none the wiser, but he ploughed on enthusiastically,

'That was a great night, Amanda.'

Night? Thought Trelawney, walking up to join her.

'I have to admit I was really disappointed when you sent me that text saying you'd had a great time but didn't want to meet up again. But, of course, I respected your decision. I still do.'

'That's very … understanding of you.'

The man became aware of Trelawney and, a little nervously, acknowledged him with a smile and friendly nod.

'Oh, hello. Well, I don't want to keep you two.'

'Yes, well, I hope you and your friends enjoy your stay in Sunken Madley,' replied Amanda with a polite smile. 'We'll just, erm,' she looked at Trelawney with a gesture towards the dining room, 'lunch?'

Trelawney returned the man's amiable nod and accompanied Amanda inside the pub.

They chose a table on the opposite side from the garden, sat down and looked at their menus. The Snout and Trough was currently being enhanced by the presence of an Ethiopian chef who had transformed fine dining into gourmet, so there were plenty of new delights to choose from. After a couple of minutes, Thomas remarked casually, without looking up from the entrées,

'You don't remember the ....'

'No, I'm afraid not,' replied Amanda easily.

After a short pause,

'He seemed to remember you particularly well,' Thomas observed.

'Yes, he did, didn't he,' Amanda said vaguely. 'The mafé chicken looks delicious.'

'Hm, yes, I'd like to try that. ... He seemed ... like you had a date.'

'It's altogether possible.'

'Drinks?'

'Hm, perhaps a mango juice,' responded Amanda thoughtfully.

'I meant, perhaps you had a drink together.'

'Oh yes, we might have,' she said cheerfully, studying the puddings.

'Dinner even?'

'Well, er … could have been.'

'And …?'

'No idea.' She looked up contritely. 'Oh, I'm sorry, Inspector, I'm not much help. Is it important?'

'Well, he is a stranger to the village,' Thomas replied tactically.

'Ah, true.' She nodded enthusiastically. 'In the interests of keeping a watchful eye on the village, yes, I suppose it might be useful to know more about him. You never know, do you? I tell you what,' Amanda added brightly, 'let's ask Claire. We usually went on double dates, you see, but sometimes, of course, we went our separate ways and then met up later.'

'Really? I mean, erm, of course, there's no reason for suspicion about simple visitors to the village.'

'Indeed, they'll probably be gone by Monday morning at the latest. But as I say, we can always ask Claire.'

'Ah… I expect there's no need. Just … tourists.'

Thomas was disarmed by her complete lack of either embarrassment or interest in the scene that had just taken place in the garden.

He had to admit that he was strongly tempted to drop in on Claire but told himself that that would be wrong. It would look like he was ... which, of course, he wasn't. Or checking up on ... his colleague, which would definitely be beyond the pale. No. The past was the past. And this wasn't even *his* past. And it had no bearing on anything, and the best thing he could do was to just forget all about it and have a pleasant lunch together.

'So ... any ideas for pudding?' he asked cheerfully.

'We won't get any work done this afternoon if we have some,' she pointed out ruefully.

'I think we've made as good a start as we can and deserve a half day off.'

Amanda leaned forward, round-eyed with awe

'Are we really allowed to do that?'

'Considering the all-nighters we've done and shall almost certainly be doing in the future, I'm sure we've clocked up sufficient hours to enjoy whatever downtime comes our way. As an autonomous unit.'

'We're off-duty?'

'We're off duty, Amanda.'

'Then, Thomas!' she responded, her face wreathed in smiles, 'I'd like to have the Berbere-spiced Pudding.'

'Dark chocolate and avocado?'

'Yes,' Amanda confirmed with glee.

'And I'll have the Injera Bread Pudding,' Thomas decided.

She leaned forward once more and asked confidentially, 'We walked here, didn't we?'

'We did, if memory serves the last twenty minutes,' he agreed.

'Then we could have wine.'

Thomas laughed. 'Yes, let us sink ourselves utterly in debauchery.'

Chapter 7

TEMPEST'S PLAN, AND FIRE ALERT

Saturday passed without incident until later in the day. But it began in the workshop. Once again, Amanda, green-boiler-suit-adorned, knelt on the old wooden door with the handles, which she now held lightly.

'Now, *bian*,' Grandpa encouraged her. 'Nice and relaxed …. Breathe …. That's right ….'

Amanda closed her eyes and murmured:

'*Aereval*.' The door rose gently a few inches off the floor …. a few more …. Amanda released her hands and raised her arms a little.

'Good, good,' came the voice of Perran.

Suddenly the door tipped forward, and Amanda grabbed for the handles, eyes flicking open to see Perran steady and lower her with a soft gesture and a smile.

'Well done, *bian*, your highest yet.'

'What went wrong, Ammee dear?' enquired Granny.

'All at once, I thought of surfing!'

'And the door tipped back like a surfboard riding down a wave.' Senara diagnosed correctly.

'I just feel, even when I am level, that the balance of the door is all wrong. And that's why it tips forwards even if I try sitting back a bit.'

'Balance?'

Tempest, observing from the comfort of a pile of old curtains that had yet to be cut up into rags, yawned in a marked manner. Granny glanced at him with suspicion.

Oh dear, he thought, the answer is so blantantly obvious it might as well be inscribed on the wall in letters three feet high. How humans had managed to invent the wheel was beyond him. Of course, they only *thought* they had invented it. His money had been on another life form entirely, and how right he had been. He could give his human, or Perran, but not, of course, That Woman, a hint. If he wasn't so exhausted. And so, instead, he put his head on his paws and went to sleep.

* * *

Joan said Janet had settled in and was no trouble. Always washed up her cup. Helped out wherever she could and told Joan all sorts of things about the family that she hadn't known. Perhaps not the most cheerful of souls; in fact, she seemed to have a bit of a chip on her shoulder, but … it was nice the way she was taking such an interest in Joan and Jim's lives and the village.

Meanwhile, Tempest, fresh from his nap and emerging from the workshop, had delicately sniffed the air …. There it was … yes … the unmistakable aroma of … new … cat.

Oh, not the emergence of one of his ill-gotten offspring into the world. That was so familiar it barely made its mark on his olfactory radar. No, this was definitely mature or, at least, maturing. And not the tang of a male either … but the perfume … hmmm. At once, an idea came to Tempest ….

Every lady cat in the village, and several beyond its borders, had become intimately acquainted with Tempest. They naturally regarded this as a notch on the side of the basket, and something of a conquest, especially the ones with distinctive-looking progeny. But, as Tempest considered it, all had succumbed to his charm. Except One.

She with the cream coat of silk, the sapphire eyes of fire and the heart of ice. Natasha, the Nevskaya Maskaradnaya, who surveyed her kingdom from a favourite window of The Grange.

Tempest had run through most of his armoury: charm, gifts, and indifference. He had been keeping his distance since the last seasonal ball at The Grange and had been pondering the strategic moment to re-enter the lists for her affection. And now …

Marcus and Roberta had moved from the main house at The Elms into the annexe, and their romance, it appeared, was continuing to blossom. The couple had asked Mrs James if they might have a pet. Irene had readily agreed. It looked like they were going to be permanent tenants, and she had asked Bryan to install a cat flap for them. Irene also said that she would be happy to have the kitty's company during the day while she was at her jewellery-making. This, over the years, had grown into a profitable concern.

The pair had duly made a visit to the cat rescue centre. They had, that very Saturday, returned with their new family member. Bella, in the first flush of maturity, was young and beautiful, in a tortoiseshell array of gingers and chocolate browns, with a white bib and paws. Roberta had taken the Friday off work and Marcus the Monday, to have four days between them to get her settled.

As Tempest savoured the fragrance, an idea came to him. It was popularly referred to as "green-eyed' and monstrous. This was not a tactic that had ever occurred to him before. He had, of course, observed humans employ it in relationships, with inevitably and entertainingly disastrous consequences, and in courtship, with varying and unpredictable results. He himself had never had what he would regard as a rival, but … it was about time that She started to appreciate his efforts, which had been prolonged and, in his book, arduous.

Once Bella's pets were out of the way, perhaps he might take this new lady for a stroll.

Natasha had to admit she was growing a little bored. Her life had undoubtedly been enlivened by the sporadic appearances of Tempest. Not that she had any intention of accepting his advances. He was admittedly the most dashing male she had ever encountered, and the notion of kittens was by no means repugnant. Still, she abhorred grey and intended the next generation to be adorned with blue, not those yellow eyes that glittered in that uncannily seductive manner. Hmmm, yes … they definitely …. but no. She would remain firm, at least in her own mind, but that didn't mean she wouldn't allow him to … entertain her ….

* * *

It was as they were emerging from the village dance class that the call came. Sunken Madley was not the sort of place where the residents did anything together except gossip. However, they had united behind the Rector's efforts to raise money for the church hall by holding a weekly Latin-ballroom class. Sandra, the proprietor of the Snout and Trough, provided a function room, and her sister Vanessa, who had taken rather a shine to Trelawney, provided the office of teacher between her appointments as a physical trainer.

Most of the costs of rebuilding the hall were now covered, but there were still bits and pieces to be paid for, and by now, everyone had grown to enjoy the classes. Especially as seasonal balls were now held at The Grange, hosted by Miss de Havillande, her boon companion and co-owner of the house, Miss Armstrong-

Witworth, and Moffat, the self-styled butler, who was, in truth, the house and estate manager.

It had been a special night, with the dance lesson held later in the day than usual and followed by a social dance. Bidding farewell to their classmates, Amanda and Thomas strolled companionably down the path to the car park.

'I know it's late, but we haven't eaten, and I'm hungry. Shall we get a takeaway?' she suggested.

'Yes, after our exertions, I'm sure we deserve ….'

His phone rang. He answered it.

'Nancarrow? …. Aha. Any casualties? … Well …. Good. … Hm, yes, I know …. Hm … yes, yes, I do think it warrants my return. I'll be there as soon as I can. Thank you.' He hung up with a sigh. 'I'm sorry, we'll have to postpone.'

'You're recalled to Cornwall. I understand. It's quite all right. Is everything …?'

'A fire. A stall was set ablaze. Appears to be arson.'

'Then you must go at once.'

Amanda dropped him off at The Elms.

'I'll keep you posted,' Trelawney promised as he undid his seatbelt.

'All the best with the investigation.'

'Thank you.'

'Goodbye, Thomas.'

'See you soon, Amanda.'

Chapter 8

A Smoking Stall

It was still dark when Trelawney arrived. Forensics had found no accelerants, but it was an old wooden structure that had had its home next to the fish market for many years and must have gone up like tinder with little encouragement.

Detective Sergeant Harris pulled himself up to his full average height, waved a hand above his dark hair on seeing his boss approach, and went to meet him.

'Hello, sergeant, what's the deal?' asked Trelawney as they walked over to the embers.

'Hello, sir. It's the Losow's stall. Fruit and veg.'

'Anything more on what started it?'

'No one had poured petrol over it or anything like that, sir,' Harris told him as they stood at a safe distance from the smouldering ruin. 'Could it have just been teenagers having a smoke and being careless with the cigarette butts?'

'Possibly.'

'They're not likely to own up to it,' remarked Harris.

'Hm.' Trelawney looked around. 'Are the Losows here?'

'Their daughter took them home, sir. But they said they were tucked up in bed, and no one suspicious was hanging around the stall anytime.'

'All right. But let's see if anyone was seen by anyone else around the stall, shall we? Tomorrow.'

'Yes, sir. I don't think we can get any further tonight. The show's over, and everyone's gone home.'

'First thing, we'll make a start.'

'I'll do the house-to-house, shall I, sir?' suggested Harris as Detective Constable Nancarrow joined them.

'Hello, sir,' she greeted Trelawney. 'Thank you for getting here so quickly.'

'Hello, Constable. Not at all. Right, tomorrow, yes, please, Harris, see to the house-to-house and Nancarrow, do the hotels and bed and breakfasts.' Parhayle, in the summer, thronged with tourists. 'See if any of the visitors saw anything.'

'Yes, romantic summer nights and all that. Walks on the beach under the stars,' added Nancarrow with the slightest trace of wistfulness in her voice as she glanced up at her boss.

'Quite. Well, get a good night's sleep, both of you.'

'Yes, sir,' said Harris.

'You too, sir,' Nancarrow answered with a warm smile.

Sunday morning found Trelawney taking a stroll around the area where the conflagration had taken place. Tourists passed, looking curiously at the tent covering the remains of the stall and the crime scene tape. Some even took photos on their phones.

Ah, thought Trelawney with a smile, here comes Morwenna from the Estate agents in Lowarn Street.

'Morning, Inspector, caught the pyrotechnic offender yet?'

'We're working on it.'

'Wish I could help, but I was in St Austell last night. How's, erm … the Chief Inspector? All right, is he?' It was she who, according to his Gran Flossie Trelawney, described his best friend, mentor and boss as 'the thinkin' woman's crumpet'. She gave a wink. 'Give him my best.'

And here was Mrs Chelsea James — no relative as far as he knew of Irene, his landlady — and her daughter Izzy, of number 8, Wiley Street. It was one of the rare occasions on which the 8-year-old appeared clean and almost tidy, even her unruly blonde hair that normally looked dirty, in spite of her parents' best efforts. He'd encountered her Sunken Madley counterpart, weeks earlier on The Elms case, in the person of Frankie.

'Morning, Inspector,' replied Chelsea in answer to his greeting. 'Say good morning, Izzy.'

'Mornin',' muttered her daughter, clutching her deep lavender teddy closer and regarding Trelawney with a suspicious eye.

'Good morning, ladies. I expect you've heard about the fire.'

'Yes,' agreed Chelsea, 'and I wish we could help, but we were all home all evening and then in bed. Sorry.'

'Did you hear anything unusual?' asked Trelawney.

There was a pause while Chelsea thought back.

'No ... no, nothing until the sirens. You know, the fire brigade and so on. Sorry, Inspector.'

'That's all right. If you do remember anyth—'

'We will. I hope you'll forgive me, but I must get to the shop. In-laws are coming over. Lovely couple, I'm very lucky, but my brother-in-law is coming too; I just got a text. He's back from college and has decided he's vegan, so I need to get a nut loaf or something. I'm doing a proper roast Sunday lunch, so the joint won't do.'

'Of course,' replied Trelawney understandingly. That reminded him. Gran Flossie would be expecting *him* for Sunday lunch, case or no case. And he did have to eat at some point.

'But I'll ask them all and my hubby if they saw or heard anything.'

'Thank you.'

'Well, goodbye, Inspector,' said Chelsea. 'Izzy?'

'Bye.'

'Goodbye, ladies.'

There was no one around for a moment. Thomas looked up at the sky. Blue, limitless. A wind coming off the sea. The scent of seaweed and the tang of salt in the air. People milling happily through the streets of his home town. He put his hands into his trouser pockets, closed his eyes and smiled into the sun.

Hearts at peace under a Cornish heaven, he thought, adapting from the Rupert Brook poem. The faint sound of groaning came to his ears, and he opened his eyes to see a group of teenage girls walking towards him. Trelawney knew them all by sight though not by name. They invariably moved as a cluster and seemed to adopt a generic make-up strategy. He'd learned to differentiate them by small variations in appearance.

'Ladies, is something amiss?' he asked, fairly certain he knew the answer.

'Hangover,' said Erin, the tallest one. 'We were partying last night. Jas's birthday.'

'S'right,' agreed the darkest-haired one. 'My birthday.'

'Her 'ouse, so we wasn't doin' no underage drinkin' in the pub or nothin',' put in Maddie, the fairest one.

'Yeah, I stopped over,' added Stacy, with the longest hair.

'And the rest of you walked home?' enquired Trelawney.

'Yeah, we were safe enough. We didn't get given no rosehipnol or nothin',' assured Erin on a jovial note.

'Good. Did you see anyone near the fruit and veg stall? Or anything unusual?'

'I don't remember,' they sighed in unison.

'Sorry, Inspector,' apologised Courtney, the curly-haired one, 'I'm a complete blank.'

Trelawney felt that, although she was not the sharpest knife in the drawer, this was an overstatement.

'What time did you go home?' he asked, doubtful of an accurate response to this one.

It was met with a mixture of shrugs, 'dunnos' and 'sorrys.'

He shifted tack.

'Did any of you see any of the others to their door?'
'You wha'?'
'Course not.'
'Was it still dark?' Trelawney suggested.
'Might'a bin', 'Erm …', and 'Well …', were the various replies.
'So,' he summarised, 'none of you can vouch for the whereabouts of any of the others after what time?'
'Dunno.'
'We did start on the shots pretty early,' admitted Jasmine.
'All right,' he concluded.
'Sorry, Inspector.'
'Yeah, sorry.'
''Ere, Inspector,' said Erin with a grin, 'don't tell my mum I'm a suspect!'

Trelawney noticed Maddie was looking uncomfortable. But even before that, his instinct was alerting him that there was more she could tell.

'Well done, ladies, for managing to get up before midday. Where are you all off to?'

Erin pointed towards Kastel Street.

'Daisy Chain. Their coffee's our hangover cure.'

'It is splendid. Well, enjoy your day,' he bade them, 'and if you do remember anything that might be useful, please call the station.'

'Sure.'
'We will'
'Seeya.'

They ambled a few yards before Trelawney called Maddie back.

'I have the feeling there is something you'd like to tell me, Maddie. You won't get into trouble.'

'Well … Gabby went off with 'er boyfriend earlier.'

Trelawney looked around.

'No, she's … she couldn't get up this morning. We'll take 'er a cup round later.'

'And Gabby's boyfriend is …?'

'I don't want them to get into trouble or nothin'.'

'I'd just like to talk to anyone who was out last night in case they saw something that can help us track down the arsonist,' he assured her.

Maddie's face assumed an expression of horror. 'Oh, my days! Yes, before he murders someone!' she uttered dramatically.

'So if you could, please, ask him to get in touch with me,' requested Trelawney.

'I promise. But Ty's all right. He is *really*, you know, deep down.'

Good grief thought Trelawney, grateful that he had no daughters.

'When my 'ead clears, Inspector, I'll try really hard and see if I can remember anythin', and I'll get the others to do that too.'

'Thank you, Maddie.'

Was that all she was hiding? Was she ally or perpetrator? Hard to see what motive she could have or the young lad in question.

Back at the station, Trelawney and his team looked at what they had so far. There was no CCTV camera covering the area of the stall. At least, photos and footage on social media gave some idea as to who turned up when the blaze was spotted or was already there.

Trelawney caught sight of a face in one snap that he knew: Bradley Rowe. He'd been in trouble before. But that was Halloween when he'd stolen a load of fireworks for a stupid dare and set them off on the beach. Hopefully, the arrest and court appearance had subdued his eagerness to impress his clueless comrades.

Thomas was a little preoccupied at the Sunday lunch table, and Gran Flossie and Granddad Trelawney, used to that, happily supplemented the conversation themselves together with Polly and Wella, his young niece and nephew. However, the pair of them groaned with exaggerated disappointment when their uncle said he wouldn't be able to watch *Wreck-It Ralph* with them because he had to find out what happened to the Losow's stall.

Refreshed by the excellent roast beef, Yorkshire pudding, gravy, roast potatoes, parsnips, carrots, peas and cabbage, followed by figgy 'obbin for pudding, Trelawney, if somewhat full, returned to the station.

The inspector searched his memory banks. Of course, then there was, hm, Hardy Hughes. He was the perpetrator in the last arson case Trelawney had dealt with. Could have turned nasty, that one. But surely, Hughes was still serving time at Her Majesty's pleasure in Exeter Prison. He asked Nancarrow to check.

'Yes, sir …. He's … out on probation.'

'Check with his PO regarding his movements, please, Constable.'

'Yes, sir.' She extracted the number from the records and dialled. Presently she reported. 'His parole officer says he's been a model parolee since he got out. She has no reason to suspect he was involved. She will ask him, though, if he saw or heard anything that might be useful.'

'Thank you, Nancarrow.'

The station was being bombarded by calls from other stall holders and shop owners. Were they safe? What were the police doing about catching the criminal? Whose stall would be next?

The following days turned up no leads that did not end in a cul-de-sac. Someone donated a trestle table and a couple of fold-up garden chairs, and Michelle Losow's mother said they could borrow her old gazebo from out the loft. That way, they could open as usual, though, of course, it wouldn't shutter and lock up like their old stall. But it could do until the insurance company assessed the value of what had been lost.

Chapter 9

❦

THOMAS DOES HIS THING

'Good timing, lad,' Mike, salt-and-pepper hair hair taking a slight buffeting from the wind coming through the front door he'd just opened, welcomed his younger friend in with a clap on the shoulder.

Hogarth's wife was away from their home overlooking the sea in nearby Mornan Bay, off in Spain for a few days, and so he had excused himself from cooking. Instead, Mike had retrenched to their menu from his still relatively recent bachelor days. 'Food's just arrived.'

'Hello, Mike,' Thomas greeted him with pleasure. 'Yes, I thought I saw the delivery bike from the Chennai riding back past me.'

Having unpacked their aromatic provision onto trays – Chicken Tikka Masala for Thomas and Rogan Josh for Mike, with servings of rice and naan – they helped themselves to lime pickle and mango chutney from jars in the kitchen. Relaxing his tall fit frame in a favourite armchair opposite Thomas, Mike invited an update on the day. They discussed the case, but no inspiration occurred. They finished their meal and had twenty minutes until the jam roly-poly would be done in the oven.

Cups of tea steamed on the table in front of them.

'Well, I hope something comes to light soon,' remarked Thomas. 'Plenty of calls from the shops and stall-holders. And as I say, just that unlikely handful of suspects, and not a whiff of a motive among them.'

'Hm, and on a Saturday night, too,' agreed Mike. 'People merry, pubs chatty, music playing or those at home up watching television. All distracting.'

'Not like a weeknight where everyone is trying to get their eight hours in before the working day when an unusual sound might stand out.'

'Hm. I know that it's very early days yet, but if you need a shortcut, you could always ….'

Thomas looked ill at ease.

'Oh, I don't know. Mike.'

'You've used it in Sunken Madley, haven't you?'

'Yes, but … here … here in Cornwall where … isn't that a bit … risky?'

'Ah, you're thinking if there are any surviving Flamgoynes or Cardiubarns lurking?'

The remnants of the now dispersed, and mainly deceased, rival witch-clans was a matter that never entirely left Hogarth's mind. "Amanda Cardiubarn" she had been born, the sole survivor, it was hoped, of that clan. Her nefarious family of spell-weavers had met their, some might say, timely end in a minibus that plummeted over a Cornish cliff. It was the old cold case that had brought Trelawney to the doorstep of 26 Orchard Way that day.

It was during the course of the investigation that Thomas discovered the truth about his own strange connection to the Flamgoynes, known for their powers of divination, through his paternal grandmother. A truth with which he was still struggling to come to terms. And the ability that he had taken for granted as ordinary had turned out to be a genetic legacy from the worst sort of people.

It was to be hoped that none remained active of either clan. But no one could be sure.

'If there are any left,' hypothesised Thomas, 'who are in their right mind, or what passes for it, and I use ....'

'Magic?'

'Yes, that. Well, won't they detect it?'

'That's possible. But they're not looking for you, lad. They're looking for Amanda. On the alert, either to stay away from or for revenge. No, I think you can, without undue risk, do your thing, Thomas.'

'I have so little to work with ....'

'Just have a look.'

'All right.'

The room was quiet, just a sleepy bird or two outside the window, the wind from the sea below wafting the curtain slightly.

Thomas closed his eyes and waited. In the darkness, he saw it: the lines of light, like a long exposure photograph of car lights on a road. The first, gold, racing, racing and now others of orange, green, blue on its left, and another out further to the right, glowing deep lavender. Racing, racing, coming into parallel, then closer and crossing with an explosion of light, and now something else. This was new. A bright star ... no ... the sun, rising before him and racing up to the zenith, then gone. Blackness.

He opened his eyes, yet looked unseeing into the middle distance.

'I know something,' said Thomas.

'What do you know, lad?' Mike asked gently

'Just one person. Not collusion, I mean, no accomplice ... and this morning. It was someone .... someone I ... I saw or ... thought of ... this morning. Before noon, before the sun was overhead.'

'Good. Good. Well done, Thomas. So who's the list?'

'The girls – you know the ones – and the boyfriend of one … Ty, and the fireworks enthusiast.'

'And the offender out on licence?'

Thomas shook his head. 'No … I thought of him later, after lunch, in the afternoon.'

'At least you have a list. A row of shells, and you just have to work out which one the pea is under.'

'Exactly.'

'Let your subconscious slow cook that for a bit,' Mike encouraged him. 'Meanwhile, what's new in Sunken Madley?'

'Oh well, we had our first week, or rather half week in the new office.'

'Excellent,' commented Hogarth.

'Made a start on the whole "riddle of Sunken Madley" thing,' Thomas continued.

'Splendid.'

'And, er, some new visitors to the village.' The studied casual note caught Hogarth's attention, of which he gave not a whit away.

'Oh yes?' he enquired idly. 'Anyone interesting?'

'Not really, erm, a relative of Joan the postlady, and, erm, a … just a tourist, I think, making a prolonged stay.' In spite of his best efforts, the slightest inflexion of tension, and minuscule dialling up of the casual tone on the mention of the latter, encouraged Hogarth to pursue but softly.

'Prolonged stay? In Sunken Madley? That's a bit unusual, isn't it? Don't they normally just drop in for a meal or the weekend, at most?'

'Yes, yes, they do. I did think it a trifle unusual,' Thomas agreed nonchalantly.

'Still … wasn't someone you recognised from police files or anything?'

'No. No, but, erm, actually, Amanda … that is, he, err, knows … well, had met Amanda before. Or so he claimed.'

'Really? A furniture restoration customer?' Mike asked blithely.

'Er, no ... they had a ... a date. It didn't come to anything,' Thomas hastened to add. 'Just an evening: dinner, and that's all.'

Hogarth regarded his younger friend with kindly amusement.

'Dear me, Thomas, you're not ... can it be .... that you're je–?'

'Certainly not!' he protested at once. 'That would be absurd. It would be ridiculous to be jealous of someone's history.'

'Wouldn't it just?' Mike replied impishly. 'Especially when Amanda's had her nose rubbed in your romantic past, old chap, in the very recent past.'

'Oh yes ... that,' Thomas agreed, uncomfortable at the memory.

'And was Amanda disturbed by that?' asked Mike, making the most of this opening. did think it trifle

'Well, no ... just ... withdrawn, I'd say. But then I explained straight away, and it was all fine.'

'And Amanda didn't explain about her romantic encounter?'

'Well, yes, she did, that is ... Amanda didn't remember him. You know how she is with people and faces,' Thomas added, 'but she said, with not a care in the world, that Claire would, and I should ask her.'

'And ...?'

'Of course, I didn't. Although, Claire would be enlightening, no doubt.'

'Yes...?'

'Well, I gather that they've done quite a bit of double dating in the past, so there must have been a few of them. Dates, that it. And, well ... It's just that ... well, I only had one or two ... involvements to explain *about*,' Thomas concluded, followed by a breath out.

'Ah .... and you've just discovered that Amanda has an entire back catalogue. How many husbands?' Mike asked.

'Well, ... none, but ....'

'Partners?'

'None.'

'Memorables?'

'Well, … just one, I think,' Thomas owned, loosening up and beginning to see the humorous side of his emotional predicament.

'But nevertheless,' remarked Mike, 'Amanda has not been spending the last 15 years locked in a tower, asleep in a glass case in Madley Wood or in the cellar of a palace singing *One Day My Prince Will Come.* How shocking. No wonder you're perturbed. Your expectation was entirely reasonable.'

Thomas blushed and grinned.

'Oh, dear. I do see what you mean. I suppose, subconsciously, I was …. Not very 21st century of me, was it? I suppose I hadn't actually been *thinking*: just … responding … when the truth is … it's rather a compliment, in its way.'

'Just so. If Amanda has searched for the right match and come up empty heretofore,' Mike pointed out jovially, 'but appears to enjoy your company….'

'Yes, I do think she does. Although, at times, I think she's just patient with me … yes, I think Amanda does enjoy the times we're together … professionally … and socially. Yes … yes, she does …. And, at times … just now and then … more … but even so ….'

'Yes, yes, and you're right to bide your time,' approved Mike, getting up to check the progress of their pudding in the oven. 'Get used to your working partnership before you try for any other.'

'And I have to be sure… that the two – work and personal – could … mesh,' said Thomas, coming to his feet to help with the custard.

'Yes, you do,' Mike replied firmly. 'Or you'll have the villagers of Sunken Madley to deal with!'

* * *

The following day, between them, at various times, Trelawney, Harris and Nancarrow interviewed the girls and Ty. Ty's father said his son had slept over at Gabbie's, as was agreed on Saturday nights. He was a good boy and not one to get into trouble.

Gabbie's mother said, yes, they'd heard them come in, and she'd gone down to make sure they'd locked the front door properly, and they had. They were good kids.

'Could either or both have left at any time during the night?' Trelawney enquired.

'Not without setting the dog off, Inspector. The bolt's always been noisy.'

'Yes, love!' called her husband. 'I'll put a drop of oil on that this week.'

'More chance of aliens landing in the back garden. No, but I've oiled it myself for all the good it does. Oh! But here's someone who would tell you if she could.' A golden retriever had trotted up and was sampling the new array of aromas that Trelawney had brought in with him. 'Melyn, here,' she said, leaning down to pat the dog. 'You love Ty, don't you? Course you do.' She looked back at the inspector. 'Believe me, if either of them had tried to go out, she'd have been off our bed like a shot, woken up both of us.'

According to Harris and Nancarrow, the other girls' parents said that their offspring were in no condition to go anywhere last night. Erin's mother, Laurie, said she'd heard her daughter come in and make for the bathroom. She'd tied Erin's hair up in a scrunchie for practical reasons and left her to it. The other parents had similar tales.

The former fireworks enthusiast had been up in Newquay for the weekend, surfing on Fistral Beach.

Trelawney shook his head in confusion. But his 'thing' had shown him clearly; it was someone he'd met or thought of on Sunday morning. There must be an alibi to be broken. But whose?

By the following Saturday, it was clear that the police had got as far as they could for the time being, and Amanda received a text.

On my way back. Won't be there in time for the class, alas, and lunch with mother tomorrow. See you Monday morning. T.

Safe journey. See you 9-ish Monday :)

Chapter 10

❧

Harsh, Lunch with Mother, and No Picnic for Amanda

Harsh Biggerstaff thrust the nose of his new pet into the face of his younger sister.

'Ruff!' he shouted. She yelled and ran to her mother.

'Now Harold,' remonstrated Mrs Biggerstaff.

'It's Harsh; how many times do I have to tell you, Mum?'

'Yes, well, Harsh. We said you could choose a dog as a reward for doing so well in your exams, but if you start bullying Ellie again, it's going straight back, do you understand?'

'Whatever.' He pulled his hoodie off the hook in the hallway.

'Where are you going?'

'Out.'

'Harol– Harsh!'

'I'm going to walk it, okayyy?'

'Well, keep him on the lead. He doesn't know us or the area yet.'

'Whatever.'

'How come you did so well in your exams anyway?' asked his sister, regaining her composure.

'Coz I'm a genius, thick'ead,' Harold replied meanly.

'Or you copied, moron,' replied Ellie smartly.

'Watchit,' he warned her.

Harold clipped the new lead onto the dog's collar.

'Can he be my dog too?' Ellie asked wistfully

'No,' came the flat answer.

'Can I come and walk him?'

'No.'

'Mum, can I have my own dog?' Ellie called.

'We'll talk it over with your dad.'

'Or a cat,' Ellie added thoughtfully. 'Cats are way better … and more intelligent.'

'Won't suit you, then, will it?' Harsh taunted her.

'We'll see, Ellie. Harold, got your phone?' Mrs Biggerstaff checked.

''Course.'

'Well, be home for lunch.'

'Whatever.' The door slammed. Outside, Harsh looked around, trying to decide on the direction to take, but then the dog chose for him.

* * *

Thomas turned his key in the door of Penelope Trelawney's Crouch End house, his school holidays home from the time his parents divorced when he was 10. He heard voices in the sitting room. One was his mother's, but …

'Darling!' she exclaimed with delight, emerging into the hall. 'Come in; Smoky's here!'

He hugged his mother, then followed her, asking, 'Smo–?'

'Allegra, but Smoky to the old cohort,' explained a smiling woman with long wild dark hair dressed in deeply distressed jeans and a black biker jacket. It was open to reveal a t-shirt bearing the legend: Sorry for nothing. 'Thomas. Glad you arrived in time. Lovely to meet you. I'm just off. Popped in while I was around to catch up with your mother.' She turned to Penelope. 'Oh, he's gorgeous, Penny,' then back to Trelawney with enthusiastic curiosity, 'Are you *really* a policeman?'

He laughed. 'Yes.'

'He's a detective inspector,' said Penelope with pride.

Smoky shook her head in wonderment. 'Well, colour me psychedelic. Whoever thought, when Penny threw that brick through the police station window, that one day she'd produce one herself!'

This was new to Thomas. He looked in consternation at his mother, who had suddenly discovered that the sofa cushions needed plumping up.

'Really?' he enquired casually of Smoky.

'Oh yes, but we're all reformed characters now, aren't we, Penny darling? Although I always say you can take the punk rocker out of the rebellion, but you can't take the rebel out of the rocker. Anyway, must dash. See you Tuesday night, darling. Pleasure meeting you, Thomas. Bye now.'

Penelope returned from waving her friend off at the front door to find a frowning son standing on the hearth rug in true Edwardian disapproval.

'*Mother!*'

'Yes, dear?'

'You threw a brick through a station window?'

'Yes, but it was all a mistake,' Penelope explained calmly. 'My aim was off.'

'What were you aiming *for*?' her son enquired suspiciously.

She looked around the room with an air of innocence,

'Oh, erm, a hat.'

'Hat?' he pursued.

'All right. Helmet then,' confessed Penelope.

'What!? A policeman's helmet? You've never told me any of this!'

'No, dear, because I knew you'd fly into a pucker and see how right I was? Besides, it's all ancient history, and I was never caught. Lot less CCTV in those days, thank goodness. Now, let's go and finish making the lunch,' she added without skipping a beat. 'You can lay the table.'

Thomas, however, did not consider the conversation finished. 'But –'

'And make sure you use the napkins in the *left*-hand drawer, not the right.'

'And *why* is your friend's nickname Smoky, may I ask?'

'You don't want to know, dear,' replied his mother wisely. 'Left-hand drawer, and be a lamb and grab some more rosemary from the pot outside the back door.'

'I –' Thomas attempted once more.

'And, darling, you can open the wine now.'

Reaching the conclusion that there was no doing anything with his mother, Thomas sighed resignedly and went in search of the corkscrew.

* * *

The ruins of the thousand-year-old priory on the north side of the village were not listed or even, apparently, "of interest". It had somehow slipped through the net of heritage legislation. But then, Sunken Madley was not the sort of place people came to, or if they did come, they remembered it only vaguely: except for the pub or the stained-glass windows in the church, or the excellent food served just inside the gates, at the Snout and Trough.

The priory was, however, a notable destination for Amanda and Tempest on fine Sundays, and the place where she thought most clearly or where she could simply revel in the beauty of her surroundings.

But today, today was going to be different. Amanda felt it before she saw it, saw it in the shadows.

She stopped a few yards away, starting towards the ground.

'Oh, Tempest. Oh no …. not here … please, let it not be … *here.*'

He lay face down, Amanda checked for a pulse, but the injury to the back of his head and the red stain on the bare earth was testimony enough. She made the call.

Trelawney had agreed to his mother's table rule of putting his phone on silent while they ate when there was no case going on. Consequently, Amanda's effort to communicate went to voicemail.

No problem. She dialled his deputy.

'Ah, if it isn't our Miss Cadabra,' said Detective Sergeant Baker with his customary dry humour, which always somehow steadied her. 'Where is the body this time?'

'At the priory. A teenager.'

'Seen anyone around?'

'No, sergeant.'

'The inspector not picking up?' asked Baker.

'Not yet. He's at his mother's and might have his phone on silent.'

'All right, miss. I've got his mother's number. We'll all be right there. Just you sit tight unless you see anyone suspicious, in which case you leg it, understand?'

'Yes, sergeant.'

'You all right, miss?' Baker checked kindly.

'Yes, sergeant. Thank you.'

'Good. Be right with you,' he promised.

While Amanda waited with Tempest, she could not help looking, not at the body but towards the place, the place where she had thought she had seen him. At least, she'd *thought* it was a him. Just a couple of Sundays ago, wasn't it? … Yes … wasn't this the place? …

That day, as they had approached for their picnic, Amanda had had a … a sense, was it? Of… a weird but, on the whole, she thought, kindly presence, yet anxious, fearful even. There'd been a quick movement of a hooded head, a face looking out for a moment, then shifting quickly back behind a pillar, like a squirrel might do. Amanda had gone closer, right to the pillar. But there had been no one there. Just a … an aroma, perhaps … yes … sage. Yet none was growing nearby. It passed. It had been a peculiar experience. Amanda had wondered if she'd imagined it but … now ….

What if whoever had been there had witnessed what had happened to the poor boy? It was possible. Yes, the hooded figure was almost definitely what some might call a ghost, someone from another time that shared our present space. It was probably prudent not to mention it to the inspector. It would undoubtedly discomfort him, and he needed to pursue his normal methods. Yes, best not to say anything. At least … not yet.

* * *

The body of the young man had been dragged into the shadow of the ruins, judging by the tracks. Any footprints beside it had been hastily scuffed over; the only ones were from Amanda's shoes and the inevitable cat paws.

'There are some over here, sir,' called Baker. The grass was patchy, and in the bare earth on the verge by the road, prints were clear to see.

'Dog tracks? Or fox?' asked Trelawney.

'Dog, sir,' said Baker. 'But none to be found. Coming from the direction of where the chap was dragged from. 'We'll have to check if they belong to any of the dogs who walked here this morning. But if we're in luck …' Baker crouched down and moved crabwise by the walls and pillar of the ruins wherever there was grassless ground. 'Here. Nose print. As individual as a fingerprint. I'll get flash 'n' dabs on it.'

'Good work, sergeant.'

Trelawney went back over and squatted beside the body. Vinyl-gloved, he carefully searched the boy's jeans pockets. These, however, contained just a housekey and a smaller key on a Thor's hammer keyring, a phone, passcode protected, a fiver and some coins.

It seemed pretty clear how he had met his end, but, as always, he deferred to Dr Carter, the medical examiner, who had arrived promptly and was now approaching.

'Definitely deceased?' she asked severely.

'That is, as ever, your judgement call, but all signs of life are gone.'

'Good,' the doctor replied shortly.

Trelawney knew she did not mean that unkindly.

'Yes, I know how you feel about being called to an extant subject, who is the province of the medics.'

'Indeed.'

He wisely gave her space and retreated to join Baker and Amanda. Nikolaides was seeing to securing the crime scene.

'Are you all right, Miss Cadabra?' asked Trelawney.

'Yes, thank you, Inspector. A little shaken. These things don't ever seem to get easier.'

'Quite understandable, miss,' responded Baker comfortingly.

Presently, the medical examiner rose from beside the body, and Trelawney went straight over to her.

'Dead at least three hours. Rigor mortis has set in. I'd put time of death somewhere between 8.15 and 9 a.m., but don't hold me to that until you get my report.'

'Of course, Doctor,' said Trelawney.

'Death was caused by a blow to the back of the head.' She knelt and pointed. 'See these stone flecks? Age-old method of dispatch, probably as old as hominids. Two million years of evolution, and we're still hitting each other with rocks,' she observed dourly.

'Indeed,' he agreed.

'I might have more for you later,' Carter told Trelawney. Then, 'I'll have to get you back to the table, won't I?' She had a disconcerting habit of addressing the deceased under her inspection. 'And then you can tell me all about it.'

The ambulance crew came over, took up their burden and ferried it to their transport. The medical examiner stripped off her gloves in an onsite-business-concluded manner. She took a couple of steps away, looked over her shoulder and, in a moment of compassion that always took Trelawney by surprise, added,

'Tell his family he wouldn't have suffered. The boy would have been knocked unconscious for the few seconds before death.'

'Thank you, Doctor. I'll tell them.'

The murder weapon was not far to seek. It had been cast away into the grass. There was nothing distinctive about it: hand size, wieldable. A stone from the ruin. There was sufficient patchy grass around the priory remains to muffle the killer's footfall. No prints.

The local police were stretched thin, especially with the double murder on the extremely dodgy Hydout Estate in the west of the borough. Baker and Nikolaides asked around the village, and Trelawney and Amanda checked with everyone who was home at The Elms. All were asleep, had alibis or were away. Irene said that she had spent the night elsewhere in the village but had neither seen nor heard anything at that hour. Amanda had a shrewd notion of precisely where Irene had been and skilfully diverted the inspector from pressing her on that point.

They moved on to The Manor. Hugh and Sita were having a lie-in after having had the grandchildren over on Saturday. At The Grange, the ladies had been up betimes, had had breakfast with Moffat, and discussed the end of summer party for the village. Hillers – Hillary – Miss de Havillande's niece, and Humpy – Humphrey – her spouse, were staying, and the former had been present at the breakfast table during the window in which the death had occurred. Humpy, however, had been out walking. Where was he now?

'Gone to visit Barnet Hill Museum,' supplied Hillers, a stout woman of middle years, somewhat above medium height, with a fresh complexion, and eternally dressed in tweeds. 'A favourite haunt. Or should I say 'fave spot'?' she asked with her characteristically cheerful if bracing, demeanour. 'Isn't that what the young people would term it? Or am I already out of date?'

'I'd have to consult my niece on that one,' said Trelawney with a smile. 'Could I call your husband?'

'Oh yes, but the chances of him picking up are somewhat remote, dear Inspector. Humpy exists in his own little world when he's revelling in history; bless him,' replied his wife.

And so it proved. Humpy did, however, eventually answer the call but said he'd seen nothing out of the ordinary that came to mind. He'd walked all around the village and visited the orchards but couldn't say at what time he'd been anywhere, not off the top of his head. However, he promised to think about it.

Nikolaides had gone around with a photograph of the young man, starting with the estate adjacent to the priory. A resident had identified the victim as one Harold Biggerstaff of 31 Hedgerow Way.

Chapter 11

SHARON AND GARY

Trelawney broke the news as gently and kindly as possible. They mutely nodded acquiescence to the presence of forensics and photography to go over their son's room in the hopes of finding clues to the identity of his assailant.

Consequently, the inspector went outside and called in what Baker referred to as 'flash 'n' dabs'. Next, he and Amanda made their way upstairs, following Mrs Biggerstaff's directions to Harold's bedroom. They were greeted by an unmade bed and an open drawer, out of which Harold had, presumably, pulled a t-shirt. This much could be seen in the gloom of the closed curtains.

Once these were drawn, they could see the foundations of a pleasant room furnished courtesy of the ingenuity of Ikea. The window shed light on a poster of an animé character pulling a sword from a stone. There was another of a multicoloured trainer shoe exploding, and a third announcing: Computer Games Don't Make Us Violent: Lag Does.

Sure enough, there was the desktop, the games console and various controllers. The computer was password protected.

Hopefully, there would be a login written down somewhere; otherwise, it would take a couple of days for the IT wizards to crack it. But the desk itself revealed nothing beyond schoolwork. Neither the wardrobe nor the drawers were much help, but under the bed was an old-fashioned brown leather suitcase. Trelawney didn't want to pull it out before the team had done their work but reached in a gloved hand and tried the latches.

'It's locked,' he said, getting up and straightening his jacket. 'Could you get this, please?' Forensics went down and dusted for prints; the photographer took her place on the floor and captured an image of the case.

Sharon appeared anxiously at the door.

'Let's make some tea,' urged Amanda, and the lady of the house took her back downstairs and into the kitchen. But the distraught woman's hands were shaking too much to fill the kettle, and all she could do, at first, was vaguely point to the tea caddy and biscuit barrel. 'Please go and sit down with your husband, Mrs Biggerstaff. I'll bring this in.'

'Thank you, dear. I think I will before my legs go from under me.'

It went to Amanda's heart to see the woman's distress. She had to remind herself that Harold was likely in the, respectively, reassuring and bracing company of Grandpa and Granny.

Minutes later, Sharon and Gary Biggerstaff sat, nervous and shocked, side-by-side on one stretch of the L-shaped sofa, with Amanda and Trelawney on the other. The couple sometimes stared at the blank plasma screen on the wall opposite as though for comfort or inspiration about what might have happened to their son.

'Yes, Inspector,' said Sharon, putting a hand on the top of her short, dark-blonde hair as though to help her remember, 'that's all he said, that he was going out with the dog.'

'Could he have been meeting someone?'

'He didn't say, and I didn't like to ask. He got a bit worked up if he thought I was trying to pry.'

'Harry did need careful handling,' agreed her husband. 'You found his phone, didn't you? And there were no texts or calls, right?'

'It's passcode protected. Would either of you know …?'

The parents both gave a definite shake of the head to this.

'Oh no, Inspector,' Gary answered firmly. 'Especially not since he turned eighteen. Even before that, we believed we should respect the children's privacy. I know they're only kids at the end of the day, but … you gotta have some trust, you know?'

'I understand. How about your landline?'

'Harry hardly used it. To be honest, *we* don't use it much, but I never heard it ring or heard Harold talking on it. Did you, Sharon?'

'No, not at all.'

'Harold kept a case like a suitcase under his bed,' Trelawney asked on a different tack.

'Yes,' confirmed Sharon, 'he called it his "safe". We thought it was right, especially at his age, he should have some private … well, you know. I clean his room sometimes – well, just go round with the Hoover when I'm doing the rest of the upstairs – and, naturally, he wanted to have some things out of sight of his mum. But he kept it locked. At least, he said he did. I never tried to open it.'

'Could the key on his keyring with the housekey be the one for that?' enquired Amanda.

'Yes, dear. I mean, Miss Cadabra, I expect so. It belonged to his granddad. In those days, a teen would have kept girly mags in there, but these days it's all online, isn't it? I can't think what he kept in there, but yes, he was 18, and it was his own business. Seemed only right.'

'Understandably,' Trelawney responded. He looked around. 'Is there a dog?'

'There *was,*' answered Gary. 'Just got him this morning.'

'Harold took Woodie with him when he went out,' added Sharon. 'Seems he ran off because no one's seen him, and he hasn't come back here. Hope he's all right.'

'Yes, indeed,' Trelawney agreed. 'I expect so. Hopefully, someone will find him and report it. I have to ask this, Mr and Mrs Biggerstaff. Can you think of anyone who might have had a grudge against Harold or might have wanted to him harm for any reason?'

'Well ….' Gary tried to begin, then ran out of steam.

In the awkward pause, Trelawney's eyes took in the wedding photo on a shelf. It showed the couple in rather slimmer days, with a less pepper-and-salt Gary with more hair at the temples. But looking at the way they sat close together on the sofa, with his hand over her clutched ones, it seemed to Thomas that theirs was a love that had grown, rather than diminished, over the past 20 years. There was also a happy family snap of the two of them with their children: a son and a daughter.

'It's been … difficult,' said his wife hesitantly.

'They don't want to say,' called a youthful voice from the staircase in the hall.

Chapter 12

ELLIE GIVES THE INSIDE TRACK

A girl, whom Trelawney judged to be around 10 years of age, in dungarees over a blue and white striped top, came into the room. She flopped herself down on the sole armchair opposite Trelawney and Amanda's wing of the L-shaped sofa.

'Oh, this is Ellie, our daughter. Ellie! Say "hello" properly,' Sharon bade her.

Pushing her large-framed glasses further up the bridge of her nose, with a sigh, Ellie got up, went over and shook hands gravely as introductions were made. Trelawney could not help but observe the disordered state of her fringe and long hair that rivalled Amanda's wilful coiffure. Miss Biggerstaff returned to the sofa and looked at them assessingly.

Trelawney put a general question: 'Ellie, is there something you can tell us that might help to find your brother's killer?'

She transferred her gaze to her parents, who nodded with an air of resignation.

'Answer the inspector's questions, love,' urged her father.

Ellie needed little encouragement to speak candidly:

'They don't want to say that Harold was horrible. He was a nightmare. And I know we're supposed to be all sad and everything, but I'm not going to pretend because he was ghastly to me, and I'm glad someone else thought so, and I won't have to live with him for one more day, and you can lock me up for saying so, but it's a *fact*.'

'But Inspector,' intervened Sharon, 'he wasn't always like that. He used to be such a sweet boy, and the children got on so well.'

'He was going through a period of adjustment, you see, Inspector,' urged Gary.

'He used to be nice,' said Ellie drawing up her legs and crossing them as she settled into her narrative. 'That was back when he was ordinary. Like me.'

'Ordinary?' asked Amanda.

'Well, I'm not exactly catalogue-model attractive, and I don't have a problem with that. And it used to be that Harry wasn't either, but then he started growing up and getting tall and fit, and girls started noticing him, and he started getting popular, and then it was like I was something nasty on his shoe. Like none of us was good enough for him.'

'It was such a change, you see, Inspector,' explained Sharon, 'and like Gary says, he was trying to find his feet, and we ….'

'We thought we should be understanding, and he'd get past it,' added Gary.

'Bet he wouldn't have,' returned Ellie with frank pessimism. 'And this morning, he was vile to me. I don't know why *he* got a present, and I didn't.'

'He did do better than we expected on his exams,' mitigated Gary.

'And we thought a dog might help him with … whatever he was going through,' Sharon explained. 'You know? Responsibility and a connection with someone or something outs– to bring him out of himself.'

'You just got the dog this morning?' asked Trelawney.

'That's right. From the Maysea Dog Trust. Lovely shelter and rehoming place. Seemed like a nice little thing. Of course, pets do mean extra work, but we just thought if it helps … *helped* Harold …', she trailed off.

'Mum means, get him to give two thoughts to someone outside his narcistic self.'

'You saw him as a narcissist, Ellie?' Amanda probed gently.

'Yes, we did Greek myths with Miss Chandra, and we did about Narcissus, and she told us about narci– that personality, and I looked it up, and it was my brother *all* over!'

'I see.'

'So, was there anyone who was offended by his behaviour?' Trelawney pursued.

Ellie replied readily:

'Yes: me.'

'Ellie!' chided her mother. 'What will the inspector think?'

'Apart from you?' intervened Amanda, 'Someone who took offence at what he said or did and could have harmed him?'

'Oh, I see. Yeah, I couldn't stand him, but I wouldn't have killed him. I was just waiting for the day he left home and I could have his room. And now his dog, too, of course.'

'So … someone else …?'

'I dunno. I think he upset a lot of people at school. Started wanting to be called "Harsh". I don't think even his friends liked him all that much, and I know for a *fact* that Amber dumped him, and who can blame her?'

'Ah. Amber?' asked Amanda.

'Amber Tang. My friend, Sahana: her brother is in her class,' answered Ellie, as though this was self-explanatory.

'Anyone else specific that Harold could have really upset?' pursued Amanda.

'Well … no, but I don't know his friends. Not now. I used to. But not since he got all I'm-so-above-you.'

'Thank you, Ellie,' responded Trelawney. 'Mr and Mrs Biggerstaff, are you acquainted with any of Harold's friends?'

'I'm sorry, Inspector,' apologised Sharon. 'He ... he stopped bringing friends round. I think they used to get beers, go off to the playing fields or the woods and hang out there. You'd have to ask at the school, Inspector. I expect they'd be able to tell you something there. But ... he's left, I mean, he *had* left school this summer, and he didn't seem to be in touch with them any more.'

'Thank you. If you can think of anything that might be helpful or just anything you recall, please let me know.' He passed over a card to Sharon and another to Gary.

'What about me?' asked Ellie.

Trelawney duly handed her one.

'Thank you, Inspector.'

'Thank you, Miss Biggerstaff, for your help.'

'Well, I hope you catch whoever dunnit. I'm glad he's gone, but killing people is out of order,' Ellie pronounced fairly.

'I'm glad we agree on that,' replied Trelawney with suitable gravity.

'Inspector,' said Sharon, 'You will find whoever ….'

'We'll do our very best, Mrs Biggerstaff. That I can promise you. Just give us some time,' Trelawney requested kindly. 'It's a process.'

'Of course,' replied Gary, getting up and shaking hands.

As they walked away from the front door, Amanda stated, 'I like her.'

'Her?' enquired Trelawney.

'Ellie.'

'Yes, I could see you two could hit it off,' he remarked wryly.

'Where do we go from here? The school?'

'Well, Baker is there, and I don't want to cramp his style. Nikolaides is asking the neighbours if they saw anything, so – Ah, that reminds me; I need to make a call.'

'Sure.'

He dialled. 'Hello, Constable. Could you call the evidence locker to see if they have Harold's keys and, if so, get them back to us? ... Thank you. How's it going with the neighbours? ...

Of course … Yes. And could you track down a school leaver from Sunken Madley School called Amber Tang …. Thank you, Nikolaides.'

'So, how about … we find out who's new to the neighbourhood?' Amanda suggested once he had hung up.

'Apart from, er, Finley, was it? Yes, Good idea. In that case ….'

They spoke in unison:

'The Corner Shop.'

'We can't be sure everyone will be there on a Sunday.' Amanda looked at her watch. 'Hm … the cricket should be over. I suppose it's possible.'

'The match will have gone ahead, I suppose?'

'Yes. People will have heard the sirens and the flashing lights. One or two might have stopped to ask what was happening.'

'They'd have just been told there'd been an incident. Ah yes, that wouldn't have warranted abandoning the cricket.'

Chapter 13

INTELLIGENCE HQ

Ding!

'Good morning!' Amanda and Trelawney greeted the assembled company, for they were in luck.

'Hello, Amanda, Inspector,' came the replies from Joan the postlady, Sylvia the lollipop lady, Dennis of Vintage Vehicles, and Jim, Joan's husband. They had all dropped in on their way from the cricket. Sylvia's husband had gone ahead to the Sinner's Rue to 'get the drinks in.'

Dennis was in conversation with a lady from the village whom, predictably but erroneously, Amanda was pretty sure she'd never encountered before.

'Yes, Mrs Mungle, an interesting chap, George Clooney. Drives a 1958 Chevrolet Corvette, the same model as I'm tinkering with at the moment.'

Mrs Mungle frowned and asked with elevated volume: 'Courgette?'

'Vette,' Dennis enunciated carefully.

'He's a vet, is he? I thought he was an actor.'

'His car, Mrs Mungle, It's a Corvette.'

Her face lit up with comprehension. 'A Corvette?'

'It's an American car,' Dennis explained.

Mrs Mungle nodded enthusiastically,

'Oh, very nice. I always liked rock-n-roll when I was a girl.'

They chorused a farewell as she departed. No sooner had the shop door closed than Sylvia turned to Trelawney.

'Well, Inspector, 'ow's your incident going?'

'I think,' put in Jim, 'Sylvia means "how is the investigation proceeding?" Inspector.' After being made redundant, Jim had turned a hobby into a growing business as a village support baker for the teashop and pubs, as well as a private caterer. He'd even just got an engagement for one of Irma Uberhausfest's famous, and occasionally scandalous, parties for the over-70s.

'That's right,' Sylvia confirmed. 'The investigation. Terrible thing. Used to be such a nice lad too. Many's the time 'e used to thank me for seein' 'im safe across the roads.'

They already know the identity of the victim? wondered Trelawney. Then thought, of course, they do. This is The Corner Shop.

'I can remember,' sighed Joan, 'when he was a litte'un running down the path to get the post.'

'Then 'e shot up and started thinkin' 'e was the great I Am,' added Sylvia.

'Still,' put in Dennis, 'that's not a crime punishable by death.'

'Indeed not,' concurred Trelawney.

'Well, we're sure you and Amanda will get to the bottom of it.'

'Good morning Inspector, Amanda, what can I do for you?' asked Mrs Sharma, emerging from the back of the shop.

'Good morning, Mrs Sharma,' Trelawney replied.

'Hello, Aunty,' responded Amanda sunnily. The Cadabras and Sharmas had long been close. Mrs Sharma senior had often babysat the little 'Ammee', enthralling her with tales of India.

Neeta Sharma reached her willowy form down below the counter for a napkin and bag of extraordinarily expensive cat treats. Thomas observed the ritual with fascination as she handed the napkin to Amanda, who placed it before her familiar. He duly accepted the tribute, and a glance of mutual respect passed between Nalini and Tempest.

'Actually, we are here for some information,' responded Trelawney, dragging his attention back to the investigation, 'although I do rather like the look of that Walnut Whip,' he had to add.

'Of course,' replied Mrs Sharma, selecting the most pristine for him.

'I know,' said Joan. 'You're here to find out "what's hot and what's not" in the village, right?'

Trelawney looked doubtful.

'*New*comers,' Sylvia elucidated helpfully.

'Exactly,' agreed Amanda.

'Well,' declared Joan with excitement, 'I have my very own Exhibit A, if you please.'

'A previously unencountered fruit from the family tree,' explained Dennis.

'My grandmother's brother's … oh, something or other. It's not like we 'ave a family Bible passed down from 1583 or whatever. Just stories I remember from when I was a girl, more like. Anyway, there she is on pedigree.com or whatever the website is.'

'I think you mean "ancestry", dearie,' nodded Sylvia. 'Pedigree is for dogs.'

Joan laughed.

'Well, let's hope she don't turn out to be a right bi–'

'Thank you, Joan,' intervened Trelawney, 'and Sylvia. So this relative arrived recently?'

'Yes. Janet Oglethorpe is her name, and she arrived, well, yesterday morning, Must have set off at the crack o' dawn.'

'And is she at your home now?'

'Yes,' said Jim, 'keeping an eye on the pie.'

'The pie?' asked Amanda with interest.

'Jim's got one in the oven, love, to take over to the Biggerstaffs,' responded Joan.

'Well, they won't feel like cooking with all the shock and everything,' explained Jim, 'and it's no trouble for me. Just mince meat, onion, carrot, peas and gravy.'

Joan took his arm affectionately.

'Heart o' gold, my Jim.'

'So he has,' agreed Amanda readily. 'Just like his wife.'

Joan blushed. 'Aww, go on with you, dear.'

'Well,' said Jim philosophically, 'you do what you can, but, like they say, life goes on, and us all going around with long faces is not going to bring him back.'

'Indeed. So,' enquired Trelawney, touched by this exchange but steering attention back to the matter in hand, 'where was your visitor this morning between 8.15 and nine o'clock?'

'Oh, she was in bed. We all were,' responded Jim. 'The one day my Joanie gets a lie in, see? No post on a Sunday.'

'Of course. Up with the lark, both of us, every other day,' concurred Joan. 'Janet too, by all she says.'

'Did you get up earlier at all to get something from the kitchen or use the bathroom?' Amanda suggested.

'Not the kitchen … well, we was fast asleep and when we wasn't … well we 'ave an ensuite so ….'

'Would it have been possible for Mrs Oglethorpe to have left your house without your knowledge?' hazarded Trelawney.

'Well ….' Joan looked at Jim. 'I suppose …'

'I think we'd have to say yes, Inspector,' agreed Jim. 'Like I say, Janet's there now if you want to ask her yourself.'

'Thank you, Jim.'

'As for other new faces,' Dennis took up the thread of the enquiry, 'now, of course, we don't count our lovely new teacher. I think she and John are in London for the weekend, anyway, but there's a couple of chaps up at the Snout and Trough, although visitors there aren't unusual.'

'And the new boy at Erik's,' added Sylvia.

'Well, "man",' amended Joan. 'Some sort of assistant or trainee solicitor or suchlike. Very nice looking and lovely manners about 'im.'

'Better keep an eye on 'im, then,' teased Jim.

Joan grinned back at her husband. 'Seems a proper gent. I'm sure he's not the sort to press 'is advantage.'

'And just to save you askin',' put in Sylvia, 'I was at 'ome in bed with my other 'alf.'

'And I was tinkering in the workshop until 9 when I took the BMW 750iL out for a spin,' Dennis contributed.

'One of them Bond cars,' explained Sylvia.

'Thank you,' responded Trelawney politely.

'Did you pass the priory ruins, Mr Hanley-Page?' asked Amanda hopefully.

'No, my dear. Took the high road the other way. Wish I could be more helpful.'

'And that's the lot,' summarised Joan. 'Unless you count the Curate.'

'The Curate?' Amanda queried.

'New, self-funded. Kay. Lovely lady. Arrived coupla weeks ago, I think. Helping out our rector. Lots to do with sorting out the plans for the new church hall.'

'Ah, I see.'

Tempest completed his treat, Thomas paid for his Walnut Whip, and, with thanks and farewells, they departed.

As there was uncertainty as to the assistant legal eagle's whereabouts, Amanda called Erik. Another legacy from her grandparents, he'd been their family's solicitor since he'd taken over when Mr Prewdent had retired to take up a second career as a trombonist with the noted Wild Fling Jazz Orchestra.

Erik answered and said he hadn't seen Edward today as it was Sunday, but he was lodging at the Sinner's Rue for now.

Chapter 14

❧

THE WALKER

They found a quiet table in the Sinner's Rue near the fireplace. This had been filled with greenery: pots of plants placed artistically at varying heights. It was not cosily blazing logs, but still provided a pleasant focal point for the room.

Trelawney showed his warrant card as ID.

'I am Detective Inspector Trelawney, and this is my consultant, Miss Cadabra. Thank you for agreeing to talk to us, Mr Nightingale.'

'Oh, not at all, Inspector. Amanda Canasta?' enquired Edward.

'Cadabra,' she corrected him politely.

'Cadabra ... Cadabra .... Aha, you must know Dunstan Froggit!'

'Erm ... must I?'

'Yes! I remember... I never forget these things. Few years ago. Said he dated a girl with an odd name, and she lived in the upper reaches of the outskirts of the metropolis.'

Amanda searched her memory banks, but they were drawing a blank on any further data. It was not the sort that they maintained.

'Ah,' she responded noncommittally.

'Said he thought it went well, but you declined a second round ... er, meet.'

Out of the corner of her eye, she could see Trelawney regarding her with some amusement.

'Hm,' she replied vaguely, 'well, you know how these things are.'

'Oh, absolutely. I expect it was the job. Not suitable for everyone to partner up with.'

Amanda had no idea what that was, although the 'not suitable' might offer a clue.

'Still following the same career path, is he?' she fished.

'Absolutely. Finished third in the regionals.'

'Oh good.'

'But it is a risky sport, no arguments with that, and the strain on the spouse .... I do understand. Last year, a friend had a date with an awfully nice young woman. Thought it went swimmingly, but the morning after, she confided that she was a secret agent. Licenced to kill and everything. Well, I don't know if you'd know him. I worked there for a short time: Bond and Breege. I have worked in legal in finance since I left uni – head hunted. Splendid chaps and chapesses but rather stuffy, and I couldn't see them being happy with one of their senior staff being married to someone in that sort of line, you see.'

Amanda, for a moment, folded her lips resolutely to suppress a smile and nodded in a manner that she hoped came across as sympathetic. She did her best not to catch Trelawney's eye.

'Well, I'm sure you were right, and it was a good judgement call.'

'But you really don't recall Froggit?' he asked her earnestly.

'I'm afraid n–'

'Ah!' Edward suddenly cried. 'Cadassey! That was it: Arabella Caddassey.'

Trelawney intervened smoothly.

'I'm so glad we got that cleared up, Mr Nightingale. But the reason why we're here is because we're canvassing the neighbourhood –'

'Oh, you have my support. I have always supported our fine boys and girls in blue.'

'Because there has been a murder.'

'A ... a what?' Edward looked from one to the other in consternation. 'But ... in this village?'

'Yes, Mr Nightingale. We are hoping that someone may have been out and about and seen something that might be helpful.'

'Oh ...well ... let me see. Yes, I did go out. I headed up to where I thought the footpath might be that goes through one of the woods and up towards Hertfordshire.'

'So you went ....?'

'Let me see.... Get my directions right .... Erm, east, yes, let me see ... up ... delightfully odd name ... Trotters Bottom.'

'Behind the pub,' supplied Amanda helpfully.

'That's it.'

'Did you speak to anyone along the way?' Trelawney asked.

'Well, just the staff at the Sinner's Rue. I thanked them for breakfast, and they asked about my plans, and I told them where I was off to.'

'About what time was this?'

'Oh .... about 8, I suppose.'

'And during your walk. Did you see anyone then?'

'Well, few people are up at that time. I expect someone must have seen me. I think I passed a dog walker, at least. Oh, I think Mr Frank, is it? He was outside cleaning one of the pub windows when I left.'

'That's very helpful, Mr Nightingale.'

'May I ask what brings you to our fair village,' asked Amanda in a friendly tone.

'Of course, Miss Cadabra. I had some traumatic events in my life, and they affected my health. I was advised to consider a more settled way of life than the theatre.'

'The theatre?' she asked with surprise.

'Oh, I see. No, not as a performer, no. More of a legal consultant, producer, that sort of thing. Yes, so a small firm more or less in the country, but still within reach of dear old London, seemed the perfect fit for a new start.'

'Your first time here, is it?' Amanda pursued, with apparently amiable interest.

'Yes, I haven't previously had the pleasure.'

'I hope you have some friends here to help you settle in.'

'No, but Erik is most kind.'

'Indeed he is,' she agreed warmly. 'Well, we wish you all the best, don't we, Inspector?'

'Of course,' answered Trelawney, 'and since you were one of the few people abroad this morning, I do hope you won't mind if we're to come back to see you again?'

'Oh, not at all, not all, my dear Inspector. It's a serious matter. Anything I can do to help. Ah yes, your card, thank you. If I recall anything I might have seen then, of course ….'

'Thank you, sir.'

'Best wishes for your new start,' Amanda bade him kindly.

'Thank you.'

They walked out of the pub and into the car park.

Trelawney looked at his partner.

'What do you think?'

'Well …. Look. No, let's get in the car,' Amanda replied with suppressed excitement.

Once settled, she opened Google maps on her phone and showed him the screen.

'Sunken Madley. Now … see ….' she zoomed in. 'If he set out at 8 o'clock and walked east, then through this path, he'd hit the trees of Madley Wood. He could have doubled back in an arc, going from east to north through the trees, crossed the High Road when it was quiet, come at the priory from the north at the edge of the Wood, and arrived before the window when the murder could have taken place closed.'

'And … that footpath crosses the road Mr Hanley-Page would have taken.'

'Yes, so he might have been seen by Mr Hanley-Page or another driver. The time he was seen could give him an alibi or not.

'We'll check that then. In case he had opportunity.'

'And,' added Amanda, 'I'm sure for all his health issues, he's capable of raising a rock. Even if he does seem to be a bit of a nitwit.'

Trelawney nodded.

'Means and opportunity, then. But, Miss Cadabra, not ….'

'I know.' Amanda signed. 'Not motive.'

Chapter 15

༄

A Warm Reception

'So you were on front of house last night?' Trelawney asked Vanessa, who was on reception. She was dressed in a black skirt and a neat white shirt with a name tag on the left shoulder. It was a contrast to the sportier dance-class-teacher attire, in which the village beheld her on most Saturday afternoons.

'That's right, Inspector.'

'Do you remember Mr Flemming and his friends coming back?'

'Yes, they rolled in after midnight, but well before 1, when we turf all the visitors to the bar out and lock the front door for the night. All the guests have to be back by then unless by special arrangement.'

'What happens if they come back after?' asked Amanda curiously.

'If they wake us up to go down to the door, then they can expect an extra charge. The kitchen closes at 11, last orders at the bar then, and we shut up shop at midnight unless by special arrangement. The rooms do have snacks supplied and minibars. Naturally, we always do our best to accommodate the guests.'

'Makes me almost want to stay here myself,' remarked Trelawney.

He received a glowing smile for this.

'You would be very welcome,' Vanessa told him warmly.

'I'm sure. Do you recall anything about them: Mr Flemming and his friends? What were they like when they … rolled in?'

Vanessa looked at him ruefully. 'Oh, merry … you know. Been celebrating some game or other they'd been watching at the Sinner's. One of them had a hand on his forehead as though he already had the hangover that was almost certainly awaiting him this morning. It was actually a slight injury. Just a graze, and I cleaned it up with some cotton wool and disinfectant and put a plaster on it for him.'

'That was kind of you,' Amanda said.

'It wasn't really any trouble. We keep a small first aid box under the counter for any cuts and bruises.'

'Do you still have the cotton wool?' Trelawney asked.

'Erm … I … I actually wrapped it up in a tissue thinking I should bag it as sort of clinical waste, and meant to get a bag from the kitchen, but then another guest came in and needed something.' Vanessa looked under the counter. 'Oh dear, it looks like the cleaning lady found it. But she bags up all the rubbish and puts it out in the hopper for collection. The binbag will still be there. Don't worry, Inspector, I'll find it. I'll know it when I see it, you see. Just leave it with me.'

'Thank you, Vanessa. That's most kind of you: not a pleasant job. Which of the men was it that had the injury?'

'Oh … Mr Flemming, yes.'

'What impression did you get of the three of them?'

'Nice enough. A bit of the city boy about each of them. Bit millennial yuppie, if you know what I mean. Or that was how they wanted to be seen, I'd say. Ageing lad really, but harmless enough … I would have said. I didn't really have much to do with them. I didn't check them in when they arrived; Sandra did that,

I expect. I just handed over their keys last night, tidied up Mr Flemming, and wished them a good night.'

'You've been very helpful.'

'If I can remember anything else, shall I call you?'

'Please.'

Sandra came out of the restaurant with a welcoming smile.

'Hello, Amanda, Inspector. How is it going?'

'Hello, Sandra,' Amanda replied genially, 'Early hours. Vanessa says you checked in your guests?'

'Yes, our only ones this weekend, but three out of four rooms is a good booking. And yes, I did.'

'What would you say they were like?'

'Well … lads … well-spoken, sort of a mixture of posh and East London, I suppose. Bit flirtatious, but that goes with the territory. All wanting to feel like "he da man" and all of that nonsense. You know what boys are when they're together, falling over themselves to impress one another, but I did think they were a bit old for all of that. But still,' Sarah chuckled kindly, 'I suppose people want to prove themselves in some way or another, whatever their age. I suppose I'm still trying to prove to my mother that I can succeed as a businesswoman rather than as a wife. Hm … really must book an appointment with the therapist!'

Trelawney smiled. 'Did you have any contact with them apart from reception?'

'I did help out in the restaurant on Saturday. Busy night, and I served their table. They seemed like a cheerful party.'

'Do you remember what they were talking about?'

'Hm … yes, let's see … yes, because they asked me – well, when I took their order, I just asked them if they were comfortable and enjoying their stay, and they all said yes, it was great, all good, and that was all. Then when I brought the drinks, they had started that game: what would you buy with ten million pounds or something. They were still playing when I brought the starters and then the main course when they asked me what I would buy.'

'What did you say?' asked Amanda, her face lit with curiosity.

'Well,' Sandra replied both dreamily and frankly, 'the first thing I'd do is pay off the mortgage on this place. I'd hire more staff. Maybe someone to run this place while I took trips all over the world to see how the best hotels are run.'

'Then what did *they* say?'

'They were surprised and said most people would just give up work and have fun if they hit the jackpot. But I said this *is* fun, this pub is my dream, and I love it. And they all laughed and said something like, that was cool.'

'Which one of them said they would just give up work and have fun if they hit the jackpot?' enquired Trelawney.

'Well … hm … yes, Mr Gosney, I think his name was. And then Mr Flemming said, "Yes, no more daily grind for me." And the other one Mr … they called him Stew, said, erm, … "I'll drink to that," and they all raised their pints, and I said, "Enjoy your meal, gentlemen," and went to greet a new party of diners.'

'Thank you, Sandra. And this morning?'

'I was a bit distracted. One of the diners from the previous night had come in very worried because she thought she'd dropped her wallet, and we were all trying to help find it.'

'So you weren't at the reception desk all morning?'

'No, I was helping her to look in all of the places she might have lost it.'

He turned to Vanessa, hopefully. She shook her head.

'I wasn't here. I had my personal trainer hat on: clients all day except for when I taught the dance class.'

'So there were times when no one was on the desk, and any of the guests could have gone in or out?' Trelawney asked them.

'Yes, Inspector,' agreed Sandra. 'I'm afraid so.'

'And the wallet?' asked Amanda.

'The cleaner had found it behind one of the loos. It must have dropped out of her pocket when she ….'

'I see. You have an honest cleaner.'

'Of course. The lady offered a reward, you know, but Shelley wouldn't take it. I trust Shelley and all of my staff implicitly, Inspector.'

'Good. I'm sure it's reciprocal,' Trelawney responded warmly.

'I hope so. I wish we could be more help. I honestly do. This is a dreadful matter.'

'True,' replied Amanda. 'But I trust it won't affect business here at the Snout.'

'I doubt it. You know what people are like. A murder adds a certain macabre fascination, even glamour, to a location. You know about the pub in Muswell Hill and the very dark story about long ago everyone being poisoned or whatever. It's all claim to fame. Lovely pub, by the way.'

'Like a haunted part of the pub?' Amanda suggested.

'Oh, if only we had a ghost! But the agency is completely out of them,' Sandra jested with a theatrical sigh.

'Alas,' said Trelawney drily.

Chapter 16

∽

THE SLEEPER

'Well, Mr Flemming is waiting for you if you'd like to speak to him now,' Sandra offered. 'I'll show you the way.'

'Thank you,' Trelawney replied.

'Could we have a pot of tea, please, Sandra?' requested Amanda.

'Of course, and I'll add some biscuits.'

Sandra had given them a corner table and put reserved signs on the ones surrounding it. Finley stood up warily, but Trelawney extended a hand in a friendly manner, saying,

'Mr Finley Flemming?' Amanda noted the piece of sticking plaster high on his forehead, partly hidden by his hair.

'That's right,' he replied eagerly, clearly relieved at being able, at least, to answer the first question easily.

'We meet again. Thank you for seeing us. I'm Detective Inspector Trelawney,' he introduced himself, showing his warrant card, 'and this is my assistant and consultant, Miss Cadabra, whom I believe you already know.'

'Yes,' he responded, visibly relaxing at Trelawney's pleasant tone and calm manner.

'Hello,' Amanda greeted him amiably, 'I ordered some tea on the way in. Is that alright?'

'Erm, yes, yes, great.'

They sat down, and Trelawney opened with, 'So, Mr Flemming, as you may know –'

'Yes, I – I heard. There's been a … a fatality. Must be terrible. For everyone. I mean …'

'That's right. It is, and we want to get to the bottom of it as soon as possible, as I'm sure you can understand.'

'Oh, I can, I can,' agreed Finley emphatically.

'So we're hoping that you may be one of the people who may have been out this morning and maybe seen something that could lead to finding the person who did this.'

'This morning?'

Sandra arrived, bringing the tea personally, and set it out with a smile.

'Here's a little jug of oat milk for you, Amanda.'

She withdrew as they thanked her.

'Sorry, Inspector,' Finley continued, 'I was asleep up in my room. We all were. We'd had a bit of a night of it. Got a bit carried away, to be honest, watching the game in the Sinner's Rue. My mate Stewart jumped on my back, and I fell and hit my head on the hearth. Stupid, really. Oh, he didn't mean any harm. It's me. Accident prone. In and out of A and E so much, the staff know my name,' he joked. 'But I really needed to sleep it off. That and the beers and the … shots and things.'

'I see,' the inspector replied neutrally. 'So, what time did you leave your rooms?'

'Erm, sort of about 11-ish, I think. The kitchen was really nice and made us a late breakfast. That did help.'

'Usually does, doesn't it?' remarked Trelawney sympathetically. 'What time then did you see your friends for the first time in the morning?'

'Well, then, at breakfast. We texted, and then Nick said he'd call down to reception and ask about food.'

'Did you see anyone, staff, for example, before you left your room at around 11 to come down to breakfast?'

'No ... no, not unless, you know, staff have a key, and they looked in to see if they could clean the room or something.'

'And,' asked Amanda, pouring the tea, 'did you hear anything unusual?'

'I didn't wake up until half ten – thanks, no sugar – and then I texted and had a shower to try and wake myself up.'

'How is your head this morning?' she enquired solicitously, adding milk and sugar to her cup.

'It's ok, thank you. Bit sore if I press it,' Finley said, putting a hand to his thick brown hair, 'but it's fine.'

'And your friends are now …?'

'They checked out after breakfast and went … home, I suppose.'

Trelawney put in, 'It would be very helpful if we could talk to them.'

'Oh, sure. I can give you their contacts.'

The inspector slid his card with a phone number on it across the table. Finley, thumbs twitching across the keyboard on his phone, soon transferred the information while Amanda and Trelawney enjoyed their tea and shortcake and gingernuts, respectively.

'Excellent, Mr Flemming,' Trelawney thanked him. 'Would you be able to tell me where they work, in case it's easier to find them there?'

'Yes, er, Nick, er, Nicholas Gosney, works at West's Bank. He's part of a management consultant team at Canary Wharf, and Stewart Croft is assistant manager at Third Equinox, a private gym there. That's how we all met. I worked at Barfax, you see.'

'The bank?'

'Yes. Equity analysis. I can send you the details if you like?'

'Please.' And presently, 'Thank you, Mr Flemming. Now perhaps you can tell me what brought you to Sunken Madley.'

'Oh, just a jolly. Celebrating Nick's birthday. A break from the daily grind, you know how it is.'

"And what is the nature of your particular daily grindstone, Mr Flemming.'

'I work in an estate agents.'

'I see. Thank you.'

Trelawney then excused himself on the pretext of going to sort out the tea bill in case there was anything Flemming might confide in Miss Cadabra.

Left alone together, Amanda said kindly, 'I do hope this unfortunate incident hasn't put too much of a damper on your holiday, Finley.'

'Oh well, you know …. Of course, it's terrible, but … these things do make for a good after-dinner story,' he admitted.

'True.'

'Of course … if you felt like cheering me up ….'

'Well,' responded Amanda readily,' if you're still here on Saturday, we have a Latin-Ballroom class in the afternoon with Vanessa, who looked after the cut on your head last night.'

'Really?' he replied politely but unenthusiastically.

'Vanessa is a personal trainer, you know.'

'Right. Well, I think I'll go for a walk in the woods.'

'Oh do, our Madley Wood is beautiful. And you should see our orchards too. We are very proud of them.'

'Ok, will do.' A silence fell, and Amanda spotted Trelawney near the dining-room door and rose.

'Well, thank you for your help, Finley.'

'Sure, Amanda.'

She joined Trelawney, who asked, 'Get anything more?'

'No. Just that he's not interested in dancing but is going to take a walk in Madley Wood.'

On the way out, Trelawney asked Sandra if she could check with the cleaning staff to see if any had looked in on Nick.

Chapter 17

∽

THE READER

'Tarts,' said Jim, putting down a plate on the kitchen table in front of the three guests. 'Damson. Gluten and dairy-free batch for the Big Tease, fresh from out the oven. Might still be a bit hot so take care with the jam.'

'That's lovely, Jim. Thank you so much.' Amanda eagerly moved one onto her cake plate.

'Here's your teas,' said Joan putting them down on the table with the sugar bowl.

The couple sat down with Amanda, Trelawney and Janet around the table, which was topped with a vinyl red gingham cloth that Jim used when he was baking. He'd wiped the table hastily when they'd arrived, and it was still a little floury, as Thomas had just discovered and was brushing his arm to remove the off-white powder from it.

'Sorry, Inspector.'

'No, no, this is your workplace, Jim,' Thomas replied good-naturedly, 'and there was only a very little of it.'

'So,' opened Joan. 'What a thing to happen! This morning was it?'

'That's right. Between 8.15 and 9 o'clock. So we're trying to find anyone who might have been out and about then and saw or heard something that could help.'

'Sorry, Inspector, like I told you, we have a lie-in on Sundays. We came round about … Oh, not till what would you say, love? … After 9… 9.30 p'raps? I did wake up about 6-ish, then went to the bathroom, but straight back to sleep, me.'

'Yes, that's right,' agreed Jim. 'We always know when the other one gets up, though it doesn't wake us properly out of sleep, if you know what I mean. I did the same, but about 4-ish, and straight back into the Land of Nod, Inspector.'

'And you, Mrs Oglethorpe?'

'I woke up at 6, at my usual time for work, but then, yes, I was able to drop off again after a bit of a read.'

'Oh yes, I find reading helps,' put in Amanda, in an understanding tone. 'Was it a novel?'

'*The Business Manager's Strategy Guide* – Melina Kit-Werque,' Janet replied repressively.

'Ah. Yes, I expect that would put me to sleep,' Amanda replied candidly.

Trelawney took up the questioning again. 'And you slept through until …?'

'9.30, when I went down to make a cuppa. I 'ope it wasn't me as woke you up, Joan.'

'Oh, might have been, but that's all right, love; I usually come round about that time on a Sunday. Don't I, Jim?'

'Pretty much,' agreed her husband. 'We do sometimes go back to sleep again… later. But seeing as we had a guest, we got ourselves together about 10.30.'

'When Mrs Oglethorpe was ….' Trelawney enquired, turning towards the lady.

'In the kitchen, weren't you, Janet?' suggested Joan.

'That's right,' she stated.

'And very kindly offered to cook breakfast for us all,' added Jim.

'But,' put in Joan, 'we said, "let's go down the Big Tease for a treat and have pancakes." And so we did. Lovely they were too!'

'Well, I hope that apart from this morning's unfortunate incident, you enjoy the rest of your stay as much as your visit to the Big Tease,' Trelawney bade Janet politely.

'That's very kind of you, Inspector.'

'I understand you are a member of Joan's family.' Amanda put the question in an interested tone.

'That's right. I was looking into the family tree. Well, you get to a Certain Age, and so many of the people who remember you from your younger days have passed, and you start to become more conscious of the transient nature of this life,' Janet went on dourly, 'and, naturally, look to your roots.'

'You do?' enquired Amanda curiously. She knew that both Mrs Uberhausfest, who was in her nineties, and Sylvia, in her eighties, had said, one day, that they had no interest in 'digging up family'.

'That's right. You're too young to understand, I expect,' responded Janet, somewhat depressingly.

'Probably,' Amanda agreed diplomatically.

'So many people emigrate or move to places that are difficult to travel to, so when I found out that second cousin Joan was only down the motorway here, well, I felt Moved. You see, I believe in Family,' Mrs Oglethorpe declared, as though it were an article of faith someone was challenging.

'You have family back in …?'

'Wigworth. Yes, I have my husband. Our two children have flown the nest. Our son is in London, and I shall, of course, be visiting him and our grandchild this week.'

'I see,' said the inspector smoothly. 'Well, thank you all for your time.'

'Wish we coulda been more help,' sighed Joan.

'Not at all.'

'Delicious tarts, Jim!' Amanda complimented him enthusiastically.

'Here. Take a couple for your tea break, you two, and make sure you eat them. Keep up your strength to find the killer,' he recommended heartily.

They made their farewells and returned to the Ford.

'Joan and Jim can alibi each other,' pointed out Amanda. 'But no alibi for Mrs O, then.'

'Quite,' agreed Trelawney.

'I have to say, she's a bit of a chilly soul. I can't help rather hoping she dunnit.'

Thomas smiled at this. 'One rarely gets that sort of wish fulfilled, I'm afraid,' he said understandingly.

Amanda remained optimistic. '"Rarely" doesn't mean "never".'

Chapter 18

A Division of Labour

Back at the office, Amanda and Trelawney summarised what they had so far, not that there was much of it.

'Newcomers with no alibis,' summarised Amanda, standing by her beloved whiteboard. She began writing with a black marker pen. 'Finley Flemming and his two friends, er …?'

'Nick and Stewart,' Trelawney supplied.

'Thank you. Janet Oglethorpe … Edward Nightingale.'

'And the Curate.'

'Six then. And not a breath of a motive between them,' she sighed. 'Of course, the only person with any sort of motive is Amber, Harold's ex-girlfriend. But why kill someone if you can just … terminate the relationship? It's a lot tidier.'

'Not to mention a lot more legal,' Thomas added.

'Well, of course, there's that,' Amanda conceded. 'But you know, what if it's not just about the person but the place? It's very old. What if there is a connection to the past that might bear exploration,' she ventured.

Trelawney could see where this might be going. He was keen to avoid the use of magic, with which he was still uncomfortable, to delve into the mists of time on an errand that would, at its best, be inordinately high-risk. Thomas deftly headed it off at the pass.

'That is always a possibility. However, let us exhaust the current line of enquiry, shall we?'

'Yes, Inspector,' Amanda replied meekly.

He eyed her somewhat suspiciously. Thomas knew that tone. It meant that whatever notion she had in mind was not likely to be dismissed. Not unless he could get this case solved using good, solid proper police methods.

'All right, the Curate won't have time to chat to us on a Sunday,' he assessed, 'so I suggest we call it a day and take it up tomorrow. Let's get some background on our list of remotely possibles. See if we can find any connection to Harold whatsoever. We could start with Erik if he isn't busy.'

Trelawney's phone sounded. 'Nikolaides? … Good … ah, and inside? … Aha, that'll make the techies happy. … Yes, please. … Excellent. Thank you, Constable.' He hung up and looked at Amanda with a smile. 'The smaller key on Harold's keyring fits the suitcase under his bed. Nothing unusual in there – personal items – except a password book.'

'Oo, including the ones for the computer and phone.'

'Yes. Nikolaides has volunteered to stay late and see if it yields anything helpful to our investigation.'

'Wonderful. About Erik ….' Amanda had an idea. 'Why don't you go and have a chat with him while I do the job hanging over my head at Mrs Vine's?'

'Hanging over you?'

'Her rather dotty and forbidding sister was chiding me for not having done the job yet. But the two of them are like chalk and cheese. Mrs Vine is in the know about what goes on around here and is very ready to share. I could pick up something useful while I'm there, as well as getting Mrs Yarkly off my back. She was hinting darkly that she'd have trading standards on to me if I was dilatory. Oh, I don't think that that was a threat with any teeth, but it would kill two birds with one stone.'

'Good idea. Is it an all-day job?'

'I don't think so. Anyway, I think Erik might be a bit more forthcoming with just you.'

'Really? All right, then, we'll reconvene at ….'

'The Big Tease?' Amanda suggested at once. 'Alexander and Julian might have heard something.'

'Good idea. 12.30?'

'Yes.'

'You're sure you wouldn't like to be there for the interview with your solicitor?' Trelawney checked.

'Well, I think Erik might … welcome another … just you …. Well, you'll see.'

'All right. I trust your judgement.'

'You do?' Amanda beamed.

'Of course; you are, after all, the expert consultant on all things Sunken Madley.'

'So I am!'

* * *

The next morning found Amanda getting back on the door in the workshop, asking,

'So you can't give me any information on yours or any other dimension or clue or hint at all to help me solve this riddle of Sunken Madley?'

'Like we say, *bian,* the path will open up, all in good time,' Perran answered patiently.

'Quite,' agreed Granny. 'Now, to more important things: levitation practice.'

'I do have a murder to help solve,' Amanda pointed out.

'Yes, you're very busy and important at the moment,' Granny acknowledged, 'But so is this. Remember that this sort of expertise can mean the difference between life and death.' Senara gave her granddaughter a knowing look. Amanda had to acknowledge the truth of this statement.

'Yes, Granny.'

'And ... relax,' began Grandpa.

Amanda closed her eyes, breathed and pronounced,

'*Aereval.*' The door rose. She dropped the handles, it rose further. Suddenly it tipped forward. She opened her eyes and tried to steady it herself. Perran had to intervene and bring her back down to earth.

'I don't know what's going wrong,' she said, frustrated.

Tempest rolled his eyes and burrowed into the pile of curtains. One always hoped against hope that they would get there by themselves in the end.

* * *

Erik, a fit man of medium height, blue eyes and brown hair showing only a hint of grey, gestured Trelawney towards the comfortable client's chair. He offered tea, which was accepted with thanks. Thomas liked the man but had also only recently observed to Amanda that Erik was a man of guile, subtlety and intelligence. Trelawney needed him at ease in spite of his lack of an alibi.

'How's the case going?' Erik was asking as he busied himself with the kettle and tea caddy.

'Still in the trees.'

'Can't see the wood for them?'

'Exactly,' agreed Trelawney. 'But I'm hoping you might be able to help with that.'

'Of course, Inspector. Any way that I can,' Erik assured him, pouring the boiled water into the pot.

'Thank you. I see you make your tea old-school.'

'Oh, when I'm by myself, it's bag and mug, of course. But the clients always seem to like it, and nothing but the best for the inspector, or The Corner Shop Four would have my head on a plate.'

Trelawney could not help smiling at that.

'I have to say I like that: The Corner Shop Four.'

'Perfect for a bank heist,' commented Erik.

'I do hope not,' replied Trelawney sincerely. 'If I ever had to pit my wits against that little group, I'm not sure who'd come off the worse for it!'

'Too true,' Erik agreed heartily. He put the tea tray on the desk between them with milk, sugar lumps and a plate of chocolate digestive biscuits. 'Shall we let it brew a bit?'

'Please.'

Erik sat down at the desk. 'Now, I'd begin by asking how I can help, but I'm well aware that I have no alibi for the time when the unfortunate incident occurred.'

'Well, let's put that to one side for the moment, shall we? After all, you have no traceable special connection to the victim, even if you may have had opportunity and means.'

'Thank you for that. But I do understand. You've got to do your job.'

'Off the record,' Trelawney offered, 'I can say this much. I don't know you well, Erik, but from what I do know of you, I don't think you committed the murder.'

'I appreciate your saying that.'

'Your assistant, however, he's new to the village?' asked Trelawney.

'That's right.'

'Is it your practice to take on assistants from time to time?'

Erik shook his head. 'No, not really, but … well, Edward was a special case, and I felt a certain affinity with his … situation, and even a sort of responsibility.'

Trelawney was surprised, 'His situation? You were responsible for it?'

'Perhaps I should explain.' Erik checked the pot. 'I think this is brewed enough.'

'Please.'

'A few years,' opened Erik, pouring the tea into the white china cups, 'well, *several* years back, I had a bit of a wobble, shall we say. It was a bad time for me. My business partnership came to an end, and my marriage ended somewhat abruptly – well, of course, all the signs were there but … well, perhaps I should go back further. Dear me.' He smiled slightly and added milk to his tea. 'I sound as muddled as my clients. I'm usually so good at presenting things.'

'Believe me, I do understand.' Trelawney followed suit with the milk.

'Well. Thanks, old chap. I mean, Inspector.'

'It's fine,' Trelawney assured him, tonging a sugar lump into his cup. 'Go on … in your own time. However, it comes.'

Chapter 19

༶

DUMB BLONDES, MRS VINE, AND ERIK

Amanda, meanwhile, was standing in a large room. The sideboard was at the right-hand end. At the other, was a baby grand piano upon which the householder seemed to have absentmindedly deposited three large, white, faux-fur off-cuts. Amanda eyed them curiously.

'They're gorgeous, aren't they?' Mrs Vine, sister to the bathroom-experienced Mrs Yarkly, observed the gaze of Amanda, who continued to regard the objects with bemusement while enquiring,

'Is it an art installation?'

Mirabella Vine gave a peal of laughter.

'Each is a work of art, isn't she? My exquisite girls, three generations of pure white Persian kitties. Priscilla, Evadne, and Charybdis.' At the sound of their names, the trio revealed their heads rising from the midst of the mounds. Amanda observed the deep blue of three pairs of eyes, behind which there appeared to be somewhere between very little and nothing at all.

They were undeniably extremely striking: thick, long luxurious coats of snow and orbs of indigo. Dumb blondes, Amanda couldn't help thinking.

'Not only are they my darlings,' went on Mrs Vine, 'but also Prissy and her daughter Evadne have produced some absolutely gorgeous litters of kittens. And without wishing to appear vulgar, I hope I can tell you, my dear, just between us girls, that people are willing to part with considerable sums to own one or more. Charybdis is still too young for such things if you know what I mean.'

Amanda gulped. A response had clearly been invited, but only three words kept repeating themselves in her head: Oh. My. G¬—

And here He was. She had hoped against hope that Tempest had wandered off to explore the garden and, preferably, the other end of the village. A hope that was in vain from its very inception. For he was inevitably drawn to the lodestone rock.

'Erm,' she began.

'Oh, don't worry about dear sweet Tempest; the ladies are not in heat. I can safely promise that they won't be in the least bit interested.'

Prior to Tempest's entrance, the three heads had lowered themselves back into the mounds, and the eyes had shut.

Now, granddaughter Charie not only raised her head but also craned it forwards as though she had just been presented with an entire fillet of prime Alaskan salmon. Daughter Evadne opened her eyes. The matriarch was naturally too sophisticated for such common behaviour, but her tail distinctly tapped twice.

'They are indeed very fine,' Amanda managed to utter.

'Oh, thank you, my dear. Will you be all right with your asthma? If they stay down this end of the room.'

'Oh yes, thank you, Mrs Vine, I'll be fine. I have a mask anyway.'

'I'll leave you to it then. Prissy, Evie, Charie, be good girls now.'

Amanda strongly doubted this adjuration would be complied with. She looked at her familiar, still lounging nonchalantly in the doorway.

'Tempest!' she whispered admonishingly.

He turned his handsome head in her direction. If he'd worn glasses, he would have looked over them at that moment. Amanda shook her own head helplessly. There was nothing to be done but to trust that the ladies would remain virtuously up on the piano and just enjoy the eye-candy on the threshold.

The last thing she wanted was to be presented with a basket of misbegotten grey kittens from yet another irate owner of a pedigree queen.

Amanda set to work. While moving the Vines in, the width of a doorway had been misjudged by an inexperienced employee of the removal company. One of the drawer handles had been torn off, damaging the wood where it was attached. The whole sideboard also needed a good clean and polish.

During the course of the next two hours, Charybdis descended to the Aubusson under the piano. She crossed the gleaming parquet, followed Tempest out of the door on the far right opposite the piano, and returned sometime later.

Next Evadne.

Last, Prissy, who first outstared Tempest before jumping down and leading him out of the door on the left.

Finally, the job and the felines were finished. The three white furry mops were back on the table. Purring. Amanda had been unable to stop herself from observing the rake's progress. It had had all the appalling fascination of a traffic accident.

'Oh, look! He's cheered them all up!' cried Mrs Vine with delight as she sailed back into the room. 'I'm so glad you brought your dear little pussy along. I was sure that seeing another kitty so handsome would perk up their spirits. I heard he goes everywhere with you. So, so sweet!'

'Well … erm, and you're sure that none of them is ….'

'Oh quite, quite, my dear. That is … I *think* so.' She hurried into the kitchen. 'Let me just get the kettle going. I have the tea things all ready.' She soon re-emerged and came to the end of the room. 'Well, that's a beautiful job you've done on Uncle Waldo's sideboard. He would be so pleased. Such a dear man. And very fond of our feline friends, you know. And here. I had it all ready for you,' went on Mrs Vine, handing Amanda an envelope.' She lowered her voice confidentially. 'Cash. My second husband was in the building trade. Such a nice man. Had his ways, of course, as we all do. People really should take more care on ladders.'

'Oh dear, Mrs Vine, I had no idea your husband was killed falling off a ladder.'

'Oh no, he was killed when someone *else* fell off the ladder. They were carrying a hod of bricks, you know. The doctor said it was very quick. That's how I met my third, you know.'

'The brickie?'

'No, the doctor, dear. We've been married for five years this autumn,' she told Amanda happily. 'He transferred to Barnet Hill, you know, and so we decided to up stumps and move to your delightful Sunken Madley. I'm sure you'll meet him some time.'

'Yes, I expect so.'

'Not, of course, that the brickie wasn't a nice man and his father, oh, was just lovely. Nothing he didn't know about buildings. Loved the old ones, and he'd be very upset to think of anyone committing murder and desecrating our dear old priory.'

'Do you think so?'

'Of course, strictly speaking,' added Mrs Vine, 'I suppose the village has been doing that for years.'

* * *

Erik's story didn't make for easy listening. It was all too parallel with Thomas's own experience. He more than understood when Erik concluded with,

'Yes, so when I heard from a friend in the trade about Edward Nightingale and how things had gone pear-shaped for him, I wanted to … pay it forward, as they say. I felt a wish and a responsibility to help someone as so many had helped me.'

'Of course. Pear-shaped, how exactly?'

'Well, although he has no children, it was a similar situation: he discovered his domestic partner and his business partner had become involved, and he had a significant setback financially when a venture failed. It's really not surprising that his health has suffered as it has. He has his quirks, as we all do, but I admire the man for rebuilding his life the way that he is doing. I hope Sunken Madley will do the trick for him.'

'Thank you. I appreciate your sharing all of that with me. Please, I do have one more question.'

'Fire away,' Erik encouraged, getting up and going to the sideboard to switch on the kettle for a refill.

'I know you've already spoken to Detective Sergeant Baker. But can you tell me anything about Harold Biggerstaff?'

'I wish I could,' replied Erik, putting teabags into the pot. 'He's never come much in my way. A troubled youth, I gather, though. He'd got a bit of a rep as a bully. I tell you what, best person to talk to is Kieran. Kieran and Ruth. They could tell you what the word on the school street is about him. He'd left, but it was the same school, although they'd have had nothing to do with him, but, they'd likely either be in the know or know someone who knows someone who is.'

'They're at the hub?'

'Good grief, no. Too wrapped up in their books and each other, and Kieran with his cricket. But it's often the way, that the people the least interested in gossip hear the most.'

Thomas thought affectionately of Amanda, who didn't seem to be able to avoid it in spite of her strenuous efforts.

'Thank you for not minding my approaching your son.'

'Not at all. He'll want to help, and so will Ruth. And interview them yourself, together. I think Kieran rather looks up to you, and Ruth thinks you're not an idiot, which is high praise indeed.'

Trelawney laughed. 'Said that, did she?'

'Oh yes. I can testify to that under oath, m'lud!'

Chapter 20

༄

DESECRATION

'Have we – has it, the village, been actually *desecrating* the priory?' Amanda asked Mrs Vine anxiously.

'Well, yes, but … no, not really. It's never had any protected status, you see, dear, and we've always just … helped ourselves, if you know what I mean?'

'Not exactly,' responded Amanda, a little at sea.

'Well, I doubt you'll find a home in the village that hasn't got a bit of wall or garden feature or carved this-and-that that didn't come from the priory.' She pointed out of the kitchen window. 'My rockery.'

Amanda looked out. 'Very pretty, Mrs Vine.'

'Thank you, dear. All of that's from the priory. And my neighbour's done her lovely little stepping stone path with rocks from there. It goes right across her pond. Ever so pretty.'

'So the priory doesn't belong to anyone?'

'Well, of course, it belongs to *someone*, but they've been going round in circles for years trying to find out who. It must be one of the big houses, but no bits of paper have turned up yet, and meanwhile, well, it's the village's, like it's been for this many hundred years. Used to be a bit of a spot for romantic occasions, if you get my drift, but then people just went off it. Oh, it might have been some silly thing about seeing the ghost of a monk or whatever. Anyway, the Wood is more popular now. I remember, my husband and I –'

'Well, thank you for sharing your story with me, Mrs Vine, about how you two met.'

'Oh, they always say Miss Cadabra is so easy to talk to.'

'Do they?' Amanda returned, managing admirably to keep the weary note out of her voice.

'I'm making us a nice pot of tea. And I've got some smoked salmon here in the fridge for the dear little kitty.'

'Thank you, Mrs Vine, but –.' Amanda encountered the glare from 'the dear little kitty', who was feeling peckish.

'Oh, come along; it's the least I can do. I have some very fine teas. Used to be my twin passions: teas and dogs,' she said, gesturing Amanda towards a seat at the kitchen table, 'and it's already brewing.'

Amanda looked around for any signs of canine presence.

'Oh, not now,' Mrs Vine explained, going over to a corner of the counter to fetch a deep powder blue Huntley & Palmers Dundee Cake tin.

She took off the lid. 'Fairy cakes! Yes?'

'Lovely!'

'Yes,' continued Mrs Vine, who rarely lost the thread of her discourse regardless of the number of detours. 'Lovely as the puppers are, they're too much trouble, I'm afraid, with all of the walks and so on, they do need a lot of attention. I have to say,' she added, with a nod in the direction of the piles of white fluff purring on the piano, 'my girls' wants are few in comparison.' Mrs Vine took some smoked salmon from the fridge and served Tempest. 'But I still love the woof-woofs. Yes, I used to help out at Crufts, you know. Oh, I heard there was a dog at the scene of the crime! Do you know what sort?'

'No .., it, er, he or she is missing.' Amanda bit into the perfect sponge and icing confection: a simple cupcake with the top sheered off, then cut into two and set like wings in the topping. 'Hmmm.'

'Julian's best,' commented Mrs Vine. 'Too bad you don't know the make and model, so to speak. Some dogs are better at finding things than others, but he might have been able to lead to something, if you'll excuse the pun.' She took the lid off the teapot and peered inside. 'We'll let it brew just a bit longer. Of course, oh!' Mrs Vine abruptly interrupted herself.

Amanda regarded her with some concern, but the lady then resumed her discourse with a glow:

'Verena Greenfoot dropped some precious jewellery the other day. Perhaps that was it. People only think of magpies and monkeys, but some dogs are absolutely *mesmerised* by shiny things. Oh, it's true. So … you must forgive me, dear. I've always been an avid reader of Agatha Christie and so on, but could the killer have dropped a valuable ring or … or locket – it's so often a ring or a locket, isn't it? With poison in or a telltale photo or microfilm or something, isn't it? – and Harold's dog found it, and Harold refused to give it back, so the killer "took him out"?'

'Well …'

'And then covered their tracks? From all accounts, not that one wants to speak ill of the dead, of course, but in life, it does seem Harold wasn't a terribly nice boy. I'd bet he'd say "finders keepers".'

'I'm sure the police are following up all leads,' Amanda responded diplomatically.

Mrs Vine smiled and nodded, then looked at the teapot. 'I think that's enough, or do you like it stewed?'

'Now is fine, thank you.'

'Here's milk – oat, as I know dairy isn't helpful for your asthma – and sugar. Help yourself. And some cold water. It's a crime, some say, but I'm no snob, and I expect you have to be getting on. And have another cake,' she added, seeing that

Amanda had finished her first. 'Anyway, you'll mention what I've said to the inspector, won't you, dear?'

'Of course, Mrs Vine. Thank you for your thoughtful suggestion,' Amanda smiled, composing her cup of tea, accepting another cake, and adding, 'You never know where an idea might lead.'

'I expect you've been helping the inspector to round up the usual suspects.'

'Erm, who might they be exactly, Mrs Vine?'

'New people. *Strangers*, as dear Mr French is always saying. It took *us* a while to earn the rank of "village" after we moved in, I can tell you, but apparently, we got it quickly, would you believe? But the new people all seem so nice, though … I do think, well … I don't want to say, as I like Joan so much.'

'I shouldn't think you'd be saying anything Joan hasn't,' Amanda replied frankly.

'Well, I met her relative – Janet, isn't it? – in the High Street. Joan introduced us. Seemed polite and friendly enough, but I wasn't sure just how genuine she was, you know?'

'Really?' prompted Amanda.

'Though you can't really tell on first meeting, can you? Now that gorgeous solicitor assistant, well, if *he* settles in the village, I can see him attracting quite a bit of attention from a number of ladies. Lovely manners. Oh yes, held the door of the chemist's open for me when I went in.'

'That's nice. Do you recall what he bought?'

'I think he just asked for a tonic … a pick me up, you know? One of those vitamin things, probably. Why? You don't think,' Mrs Vine asked excitedly, 'he was after some *poison* or other do you?'

Amanda smiled. 'I doubt it. It's not an over-the-counter sort of thing.'

'No, no, of course, it isn't,' Mrs Vine laughed. 'I am getting carried away, aren't I? Anyway, as I say, lovely man, and if I didn't have my Anil, I think I'd be in the queue! Oh, and the Curate's lovely. Just had a *little* chat, but I do hope that she stays.'

'Have you come across the visitor staying at the Snout?'

'Someone's staying there, are they? Well, that's nice for Sandra. But no. Well, you tend not to, don't you? Visitors are usually here today and gone tomorrow. Oh, you've finished your tea? Like another cup?'

Tempest was looking restless, and Amanda had the impression that the well was now dry, and so replied politely,

'It was very nice, but I think I'll be getting home.'

'Well, here,' urged Mrs Vine, putting two fairy cakes in a napkin, 'take one each for you and the inspector for later.'

'Thank you, you're very kind,' Amanda accepted warmly.

They walked out to the front door, with Mrs Vine calling on the way to the cats on the piano.

'Well, I think we've all enjoyed your visit, you and your little friend there,' she nodded toward Tempest, 'haven't we, girls? Well … bye for now, Amanda. I'm sure I'll have some more jobs for you.'

'Goodbye, Mrs Vine, and thank you!'

The door having closed behind them, Amanda turned to her errant feline, sashaying along beside her.

'"All enjoyed your visit"? *You!* All three! You have no morals whatsoever!'

Finally, thought Tempest, she understands me.

'And if I'm presented with three baskets of grey kittens and a huge bill, it's coming out of *your* caviar fund!'

Tempest smirked up at her. She had clearly made no impression upon him whatsoever. Amanda ventured into territory where angels fear to tread.

'You know, you'll never get anywhere with Natasha if you keep going around the village like some floozy who's anyone's for a sandwich.'

For a moment, Tempest's gait stiffened, and his eyes narrowed. There was the vaguest of possibilities that his human had the minisculest of points. Silence reigned for several paces until …

Sandwich, he thought. Did someone say sandwich?

Chapter 21

~

Janet Just Wants

Amanda had started the job early anyway, but it had also gone more quickly than the duration allowed for it. So, with some time to spare before the rendezvous with Trelawney, there was one more cast she could make.

She had sent Joan a text asking for a quiet chat if Janet was out. Janet, apparently, liked going for walks around the village and had declared she wasn't used to sitting about and never had been. The postlady sent a text to say the coast was clear, and she could take her lunch break and chat in comfort while Janet was wherever.

They sat in the sitting room, a tray of cheese-and-ham flan and salad on Joan's lap, with a cup of tea for Amanda on the coffee table. Jim had the kitchen table and was getting on with his baking and serving thin slices of meat to Tempest. They left the door open so he could hear them and comment if he wanted to.

'Well now, dear, I expect what you're after is a bit of profiling,' remarked Joan with a gleam.

Amanda laughed. 'Yes, I suppose so. I'm new to this, remember.'

'We know, we know. All right, so I been thinking, and this is what I think. Only what I *think,* mind you.'

'And that's gold for me,' Amanda assured her trustingly.

'All right. Well, I've listened to Janet a good bit since she got here. She seems like a very hard-working woman who believes in doing the right thing. She does work long hours that a lot would divide a bit more with their family … but you see, that's the nub of it: I think she absolutely loves her job.'

'Fair enough,' responded Amanda. 'I can understand that.'

'So can I, dear. But I'll bet Janet has had plenty of judging over the years for not being there more for her family, even though the children have always been cared for by their dad, and she *has* provided the family with a good life. And I think, love, all Janet wants is to be appreciated. I mean not just the automatic "thank yous" but *really* thanked and told she's done well and a good thing. And that's why she's always saying, and you must have noticed, "it all falls on me, you know".'

'Joan, you're doing very well, love; just keep going,' called out Jim from the kitchen. 'Pearls she's giving you, Amanda, pearls.'

Joan grinned. 'See? That's what I get from my Jim. So, you see, I think over the years, the feeling that she wasn't getting the sort of praise that she craved has given her a … a shell … a skin that's just got thicker and thicker. And not just harder for people to get through to her, but harder for her to get through to people, especially the ones she loves. So "it all falls on me, you know" is like a cry for appreciation, except it sounds more like an accusation, more like –'

'"I have to do it all because you're not doing enough", sort of thing?' suggested Amanda.

'Exactly!'

'I see,' said Amanda slowly. 'But why is she here with you? I mean, I shouldn't think she takes much time off. Why not spend it with her husband? Why is she here with you, strangers, miles from home?'

'Projects,' Joan stated.

'Projects?'

'Yes, you see, I have this theory. And I did mention it just in passing to Sylvia, and she said I was right. See, it's all about what they call frame of reference. You know?'

'Yes,' Amanda responded curiously.

'Well, see, a parent or whoever cares for a child, like your grandpa and granny, they build up those little shared moments. See how they are when they come out of school. But it's often at bathtime if they're little, or bedtime that things come out. What they're worried about or hoping for or whatever.'

Amanda nodded. 'Things often came out when I was with Grandpa in the workshop, during quiet times when we'd both be working on something, or I was sitting up on the workbench while he worked, or when I was studying at the table with Granny.'

'So you know then, dear. Yes, so, having lost the chances for a shared frame of reference with her family, well, you know how sometimes people have a child, 'specially later on, and they say, I'll get it right this time?'

'Do they?'

'Yes, dear. But Janet's a bit long in the tooth for that. So my theory is that all Janet wants is to feel she *can* make a connection with family. So what does she do but go looking for long-*lost* family, and she finds me. And she can start from scratch with me, and Jim too of course, and build up memories and shared things. See?'

'Ah, and how is that going?' Amanda asked.

'Well, that's the thing. Janet's not had much practice, so it doesn't come easy. But she has shared a good bit with me, especially about her childhood and relatives passed on, p'raps looking for connections with me. I do remember my gran saying she came from a big family, but, to be honest, not much beyond that. So, anyway, I think we're making a bit of headway, us and Janet. And opening up to us might even help her back home.'

'Let's hope so. I'm glad you're helping Janet, both of you. It's very kind indeed of you, really. I mean taking a stranger into your home, making her so welcome, being so … when Mrs Oglethorpe doesn't seem a terribly warm person,' Amanda observed.

'Yes, and that's half the problem. She's less likely to get compliments. People probably think she'd easily take offence. But when the approval of other people is the most ….'

There came the muted clang of the oven door closing. Joan looked up as Jim came into the room, apron floury, sat down on the sofa next to his wife and said, 'Tell Amanda, love. Tell her what happened with you.'

'Well, another time, but the long and short of it is that I did have a difficult customer. And I admit it did give me a bit of dip in my confidence, and I did get such a lot of help, and I just wanted to … you know, pass it on, help someone else, and seeing as she's family. And I know she's not the easiest person, but … I am happy to 'elp 'er' We both are, aren't we, Jim?'

'Course we are,' he agreed heartily.

Amanda smiled. 'Well, thank you both.'

'That's all right, dear.'

'Now then,' said Jim, standing up and tying his apron more snuggly. 'Would you like some of these strawberry jam tarts to take home? Course you would,' he answered the rhetorical question without pause.

Amanda beamed. 'Yes, please, Jim.'

'And some for your Inspector.'

Chapter 22

❦

The Big Tease, Beards, and Temptation

'Did he have any distinguishing facial characteristics?' asked Ruth, adjusting her spectacles. Ruth was Amanda's favourite young teen in the village and one whom she had, from time to time, helped with history homework. They had become firm friends, and Ruth's long brown plait was an echo of Amanda's lighter-shade, working coiffure.

Amanda heard Ruth put the question to Dennis as she and Joan entered, having arrived at the café at the same time as Trelawney.

'Oh, Amanda! Inspector!' Ruth called out excitedly. 'Guess what? Mr Hanley-Page has remembered seeing someone about to cross the road on Sunday morning when he was out driving. I'll bet it was someone suspicious, and they were up to No Good!'

Dennis hailed the newcomers with a smile.

'Yes, that's right. It would have been just after 9, when I took the BMW 750iL out for a spin, as I told you. I didn't really look at him. Just registered a pedestrian at the kerb, that's all,' he replied.

'Him?' asked Kieran, Erik's son and best friends with Ruth, thanks to Amanda's kind offices some time ago.

'Well, yes, I say "him", but trousered, at any rate, and short-haired.'

'Tattoos? Scars? Beard?' pursued Ruth.

'Well, he might have done,' pondered Dennis. 'After all, facial hair of some description is à la mode these days, it seems.'

'Oh, don't tell me,' said Joan, to whom Amanda had given a lift. She was just there to drop in and deliver Jim's strawberry tarts and also some butter tarts he'd made from a recipe sent to him by a dear Canadian friend. 'My Jim said he was thinking of growing a bit of a beard, and I said, "Well, your face is your own, and you must please yourself, but don't try and kiss me. In fact, don't come near me with it. If I want to take a cheese grater to my sensitive complexion",' she added, running her fingers along her sun-and-wind-weathered cheek, '"I've got a perfectly good one in the kitchen, thank you very much." And that's what I told him.'

'I take it that he dismissed the notion?' hazarded Dennis.

'He did. His choice, mind,' answered Joan with aplomb.

'Indeed,' Dennis commented with a grin.

'Oh,' Sylvia chimed in comfortably as Amanda and Trelawney sat down at a table by the window, 'it's just a passing fad.'

'Like bellbottoms,' Alexander called from behind the counter.

'Or flapper dresses,' suggested Dennis, happily visualising what was, in his imagination, the highlight of the 1920s.

'It's just a fashion,' Sylvia went on. 'Well, I don't mind a beard. My second husband – or was it my third? … No, I tell a lie. It were an "in-between." 'Ad a beard. Lovely man, 'e was.'

'It didn't end at the altar, though?' asked Dennis.

'No, is 'w-but that's a story as'll keep for another time.'

'Well,' said Ruth reflectively, undistracted by revelations of Sylvia's chequered and extensive romantic past, 'I did read that it's the urban male's response to feeling that his masculinity is challenged by 21st-century life. I do think there's something in that. After all, what can men do now that women can't?'

She put the question to Kieran. She was gazing at him with earnest bespectacled brown eyes, clearly expecting a supporting comment.

'Er ….' Kieran, captain of the second 11 school cricket team, not only had given the matter no thought but was currently feeling challenged by nothing more than an oncoming maths test. 'Sport?'

'In 300 BC in Athens and Sparta, yes, but now is there a sport in which women cannot participate right up to competitive level?'

'Um … not that I know of ….'

'So what else, apart from grow facial hair, can men do that can be on public display that women can't?' she enquired pointedly.

Kieran blushed. 'Um ….'

'Excellent point, young Ruth,' intervened Dennis.

Turning to him, she replied, 'Simple deductive reasoning when you think about it. Oh, of course, Mr Hanley-Page,' she added respectfully, 'I don't include you and your moustache. I expect you've had that since … the 20th century,' Ruth concluded with a touch of awe in her voice at someone of such antiquity.

'That's right, dearie,' said Sylvia. 'I think 'e was born with it!'

Trelawney grinned appreciatively as they picked up their menus. 'You've got to admire Ruth,' he murmured to Amanda.

'I adore her and Kieran too. I thought he weathered the storm courageously.'

He nodded, then turned towards Dennis, 'So, Mr Hanley-Page, someone crossed the road at around 9 a.m. on Sunday morning. Which road was that? And in which direction was the person going?'

'Well, you see, when I go for a drive, I like to choose the prettiest roads, so I drove south-east then up to join Camelot

Way. Then north up Stagg Rise and back along Waggon Lane, then I steered north, then across east towards Cuffley. It was on Waggon Lane. That's when I saw the, er, person crossing from my left to my right, so that would have been going … north east.'

'Coming out of the Wood on the east side of the village?'

'Er, well, could have done, or just walking along the pavement up to the point where he wanted to cross the road. But heading away from the village, if indeed that was where he had come from.'

'Thank you, Mr Hanley-Page.'

'Not at all, dear chap, always happy to be of assistance.'

The excitement over, all returned to their lunches and Joan to her deliveries.

'See?' asked Amanda confidentially, leaning forward.

'Yes, it's still a possibility that Mr Nightingale took a detour from his route East, around to the north.'

'With the Wood for cover.'

'And came out by the priory.'

'Exactly,' Amanda agreed enthusiastically. 'Committed the crime then doubled back on his proposed cross-country route towards Hertfordshire.'

'In time to be seen by Mr Hanley-Page. Rather a lot of "ifs" in there. Assuming it was Mr Nightingale who was the mystery pedestrian.'

'Yes, and if it *was,* it wouldn't have taken him that long to walk from the Sinner's Rue to that spot, so what was he doing in the meantime?' she asked significantly.

'Indeed. Or it could have been, and this is the more likely option, an innocent resident or rambler out for a Sunday morning walk: someone who had not been through the Wood at all but, as Mr Hanley-Page suggested, had been using the pavement all along.'

'Oh. True,' Amanda admitted, deflated. Thomas was moved by her crestfallen expression to add kindly,

'However, the possibility that you suggest must remain on our books until the case is proven either way,'

Amanda was visibly cheered, and she chose a sausage roll, chips for them to share, salad, mustard and chutney to celebrate. Trelawney chose a ham and local Wobble Bottom Farm goat's cheddar toastie, salad, and Branston Pickle.

'So how did it go at work?' he asked Amanda, between mouthfuls.

'Job went well, learned a lot about Mrs Vine but not much else, I'm afraid. I also went to see Joan. She was so kind, confiding in me a little about her past and well, her explanation of why Janet is here seemed absolutely understandable. You and Erik?'

'Well, I learned quite a bit about *Erik,* which I expect you already knew, but mainly, I completely understand why he's taken on Mr Nightingale. Erik certainly knows what it's like to have been through a rough patch and be trying to rebuild or build anew.'

'Indeed.' Comparing Nightingale's past with Erik's time going through the mill could not help but evoke Amanda's compassion. 'Well, perhaps poor Mr Nightingale was just trying to take a walk to clear his mind and, hopefully, think about a bright future.'

'Quite,' agreed Trelawney. 'So, what time is our appointment with the Curate?'

'Not for another half an hour. We have plenty of time.'

Kieran and Ruth came to their table.

'Would you like us to ask around at school,' Ruth offered, eager to help.

'If you would, please,' answered Trelawney. They moved off as,

'My luvvies,' announced Julian coming out of the kitchen, 'our Sandy has completed the baking – nay the creation – of what is voted the most difficult dessert to make: a glorious lemon …. meringue … pie!'

Applause and cheers followed as Sandy emerged bearing the aforesaid confection. It was a favourite among the Big Teasers.

'It looks delicious, but I don't want to be drowsy from too much lunch during our interview with the Curate,' said Thomas conscientiously.

'Then just a very small piece?' Amanda tempted him.

Trelawney looked at her face, alive with delighted anticipation of his enjoyment of the treat, as she turned from the pie in Sandy's oven-gloved hands to him.

He sighed. 'Oh … all right then.' This, thought Thomas, must have been exactly how Adam felt.

Chapter 23

THE CURATE

'Hello, Inspector and Miss Cadabra. What a pleasure! The Reverend Goodword has told me so much about you. Every word glowing with praise, I assure you. Won't you come in? I'm Kay Landen,' she said as they shook hands. 'As you can tell, I've come to my vocation later in life,' she added cheerfully, her white-blond ponytail, lightly silvered, bouncing as they followed her tall slim form into the rectory.

'Hello, Inspector, Amanda,' called Jane, the Rector, from the kitchen. 'Tea's ready.' A dark bobbed-haired woman of middle years and comfortable aspect, who exuded warmth, came out carrying a tray. Trelawney helpfully took it from her and deposited it on the coffee table.

Amanda greeted her affectionately and Trelawney with a friendly air.

'It's all right,' Jane assured them, 'we know you have to ask any newcomers their whereabouts in such an instance as this. Shall I go away?'

'I'm sure there's no need,' replied Trelawney amiably, as they all took their seats on the aged, sturdy, William Morris print, three-piece suite. Tempest perched on the arm of Amanda's chair and stared at Jane in a marked manner until she went to the kitchen and fetched some tuna on a plate, which she placed before him. The assembled company was somewhat distracted by these antics until the scene was concluded successfully.

'So … The Rev–' began Kay.

'No, no, it's Jane,' interrupted the Rector kindly.

Kay smiled.

'Jane explained what you'd need to know: what has brought me to Sunken Madley and where I was when the unfortunate event took place. Is that right?'

'Please,' replied Trelawney.

'What was the time when …?'

'Between 8.15 and 9 p.m.'

'Well, I was at the Daily Office then.'

'In the office?' queried Amanda.

'Oh, I see, yes, daily prayers. I find it such a helpful way to start the day. One reads certain passages from the Bible and so on.'

'Ah, right.'

'Of course, you need to know how long that takes: 20 to 30 minutes. And then, I began preparing for the Sunday service at a half past ten.'

'Shall I be mother?' asked Jane, picking up the teapot.

'Please,' replied Amanda, with a smile.

'And where do you perform the Daily Office, Reverend Landen?' asked Trelawney.

'Kay, please. Usually in my room, but on Sundays, I like to say them in the church to sort of feel the atmosphere into which the parishioners will come later.'

'So did you say them together?' asked Amanda, looking from Jane to Kay.

'I'd said mine earlier,' answered the Rector. 'But I did look in to see if Kay had finished, and when I saw she was still saying them, I withdrew for a few more minutes. Then I went in, and we got the church ready together.'

Cups were distributed, and milk and sugar were added.

'About what time was all of this?' Trelawney enquired.

'Kay was finished by 9, I'm sure,' said Jane. 'We both wanted to have plenty of time.'

'To prepare the church and … for me to prepare myself,' Kay added ruefully.

'Help yourself to shortcake, Inspector, and, of course, the gingernuts are for you, Amanda, dear. Kay was to give the sermon,' Jane explained. 'Well, I knew that the usual slender ranks would be, at least, slightly swelled by those curious to see what the new curate might be like. So I thought, why not capitalise on it and have Kay do the service?' Jane smiled at her curate.

'And they were a most kind audience,' put in Kay cheerfully, helping herself to a jammy dodger. 'No snoring and they sang the hymns with gusto. Both plusses.'

'So you began your Daily Office at …?' asked Trelawney.

'A half past eight, I'd say. Yes, I see what you mean. That doesn't account for the quarter of an hour before.'

'True,' admitted Jane, dunking a chocolate digestive. 'We had breakfast at about half past seven. Kay offered to do the washing up so I could say my own Daily Office.' She withdrew her perfectly tea-infused biscuit and relished it while Kay took up the thread.

'So yes, Inspector, I was alone during the first quarter of an hour of the time you mentioned. And I suppose it would do little good to tell you of my ardent embracing of the fifth and ninth commandments.'

Amanda had got the 'thou shalt not kill reference' but was looking vague about the latter.

Trelawney supplied helpfully, 'Thou shalt not bear false witness.'

'Ah.'

'As I say,' Kay continued, 'I have come to my vocation later in life. I've worked as a portfolio management advisor and have been thinking of this for the last few years. I'm self–funded, so I had to get together what I would need to see me through this time.'

Seeing that Amanda had finished her first gingernut, the Rector offered the plate for a second, which was happily accepted. She took up the thread: 'The Bishop wrote to me and asked how the plans for the new church hall were going and if I would like some help. He told me a little about Kay, and that was more than enough for me to say, "yes, please".'

'Do bishops email these days instead of writing letters?' asked Amanda.

'They do both, my dear,' Jane replied with a smile. 'I can show you the letter, and, yes, I am confident that it did come from the Bishop. I recognised his handwriting. He likes to write the envelopes by hand, with a fountain pen.'

'I don't suppose you'd made any pastoral visits to the Biggerstaffs, had you?' suggested Amanda to Kay. 'Harold does seem to have been a rather troubled young man.'

'I'm afraid not,' responded Kay. 'I had yet to meet the family. I'd rather hoped to become better acquainted with the villagers at the cricket match on Sunday afternoon, but Mr Forbush at Pipkin Acres had requested a visit.'

'Heard there was a pretty, bright young thing newly at the rectory, I have no doubt,' put in Jane with a roguish look.

'Comparatively young!' returned Kay. 'He's 86 next month.'

'Ah, not the last rites then?' enquired Trelawncy, amused.

'I'd guess that's some years off!'

Tea drunk and the biscuits polished off, Trelawney rose, and Amanda followed suit.

'Ladies, thank you for your time and for being so open. You've been most helpful.'

'Not at all, Inspector,' responded Jane.

'I do wish I could have been of more assistance,' said Kay earnestly.

'Well, if you do –'

'If I think of anything at all, then, of course, I shall contact you,' she promised.

They shook hands, all except for Amanda and Jane, who hugged one another goodbye.

Back in the car, Tempest installed, they strapped themselves in, and as Trelawney turned on the ignition, Amanda pre-empted his question.

'I think Kay is telling the truth.'

'Yes, I think she did tell the truth,' he agreed.

'She was completely open,' Amanda pointed out.

'Hm … unusually so,' Trelawney remarked.

'But perhaps that's just the sort of person she is.'

'Perhaps.'

Chapter 24

∽

ORDINARY PEOPLE

They arrived back at The Elms to be intercepted by Irene.

'I hope it's all right. I let Mrs Biggerstaff in. She's waiting in the kitchen. Shall I send her in?'

'Most kind of you, Mrs James. Yes, please.'

Sharon, clearly in a turmoil of anxiety, was visibly relieved to see them. She accepted a seat next to the desk between Trelawney and Amanda, who offered her tea. Tempest took up a supervisory post high up on one of the shelves.

'Oh well, that's very kind of you, dear. Yes, I will have a cup if you're making one.' Amanda got up, switched on the kettle, and put bags in the mugs. 'Only I don't want to leave Gary and Ellie too long. Only I had to come.' She looked down at her green linen shorts and floaty white top, then helplessly up at Amanda. 'I wanted to wear black, but Ellie won't hear of it.'

Amanda at once came and sat down and took her hand. 'Did Harold like you in black?'

'No … no, he didn't. Back when he used to notice.'

'Well then, I expect Ellie is right. Anyway, you look pretty, and that's always good for the spirits, however low, don't you think?'

Sharon smiled wanly. 'Yes, ... I suppose so.'

'Is there something you've remembered, Mrs Biggerstaff?'

'No, no, it's not that. I ... I was just wondering,' she asked Trelawney, 'if you'd found them yet? You know? They say the first 24 hours is the most vital, and it's been more than that now.'

'I understand, Mrs Biggerstaff,' he assured her gently. 'That's what they say regarding the abduction of a child. This is a different sort of case.'

'Oh,' she sighed. 'Oh, I see. Well, you are working on it, aren't you? My mother says when it's a VIP, then it's full steam ahead, but ordinary people just get pushed under the carpet. Time goes by, and the murderer is never found, and they just chalk it up to experience. And Gary said it's better I come and talk to you instead of bottling it all up. I'm not supposed to get agitated, you see. Blood pressure. I know Harold could be a bit wayward, and he was just a teenager, but that doesn't make him less of a person, Inspector.'

'Absolutely, Mrs Biggerstaff. We are doing everything possible to find out what happened to Harold and the person responsible, I promise you.'

'But it does take time.' Amanda explained kindly, responding to the click of the boiling kettle. 'It's a procedure, a process, and we have to work with what we've got. If we had a smoking gun and a set of fingerprints and witnesses, then it would be a lot easier.'

'Not much off a rock, I expect,' Sharon agreed reasonably, somewhat calmer now she had got her worry off her chest.

'I'm afraid not. We're still asking around for witnesses and interviewing anyone at all who might be of help.'

'Oh, all right,' said Sharon, with another sigh. 'Early days then.'

'Early days.'

She looked up straight into Trelawney's eyes,

'But you'll get the person, won't you? The one who did this to my boy?'

He returned her gaze with resolve. 'We shall make every possible effort, Mrs Biggerstaff. Of that much, I can assure you absolutely.'

Sharon nodded and said, on second thoughts, she'd like to skip tea and get back. Amanda showed her to the door and asked her how they'd liked the pie Jim brought over.

'Oh, it was lovely. Wouldn't have thought I was hungry and didn't feel like cooking, but then I thought I should try it since Jim had gone to all that trouble, and once I started, I did feel like eating, and I do feel better for it. We all did. Bless him.'

'That's good.'

They said their farewells, and Amanda returned to the office. Knowing the villagers, the next day, there would be another pie from Jim, or a stew from the Snout and Trough, or kebabs and chips from Iskender, or a chilli from the Sinner's Rue. They looked after their own.

Amanda sat down opposite her partner and waited to see his reaction to the conversation that had just taken place with Mrs Biggerstaff.

'All right,' remarked Trelawney, 'if we needed a spur, we certainly just got one. Let's look at what we have.'

She got up and went to her board while Trelawney finished the tea.

'So ... we have chancer Finley Flemming, taking a break from the daily grind, nitwit Edward Nightingale recuperating and rebuilding his life, obsessive, underappreciated Janet Oglethorpe connecting with family, and the candid Curate, here on an ecclesiastical posting,' Amanda listed. 'All with holes in their alibis for the time of death between 8.15 and 9 a.m. And all with perfectly reasonable explanations for their presence here. What interest could any of them have had in the ruins? None of them is a dog walker. Was one of them exploring the village and just decided to hit Harsh with a rock? Even if he *was* as obnoxious as his sister says.'

'True. Hit with a rock; pretty much anyone could do that. So technically, they all had means. And opportunity, as none of them has complete alibis. Joan and Jim were having their lie-in, so Janet could easily have slipped out without their being any the wiser.'

'Nightingale was lodging at the Sinner's Rue and Finley at The Other Pub, and either of them could have got passed the staff or other guests unnoticed.'

'Yes,' agreed Trelawney, 'with the staff working and guests with their attention on their food and their plans for the day. We have just one witness.'

'The dog.'

Amanda was about to work the conversation around to the location, its history and what leads might be found therein when Trelawney's phone rang.

'Baker … yes … well done …. Any time? …. About an hour from now? … Just a moment.' He looked at Amanda. 'Fancy a trip to the seaside? Now?'

'Oh yes! Lovely!' she replied, clapping her hands quietly.

'Baker? … Can you let her know we're on our way? ….Thank you. Any news? … All right…. Good.' He hung up.

'I do love the seaside,' Amanda said enthusiastically, and then responsibly: 'But shouldn't we be concentrating on the case?'

'We are. Baker called to say that Amber Tang, erstwhile girlfriend to our deceased, has been tracked to Southend-on-Sea, where she's been staying with her friend. She's happy to chat, so let's see if she can shed any light on the life and times of Mr Harold Biggerstaff.'

'Then I'll skip the tea and biscuits,' she said dutifully, with a tinge of regret in her voice.

Thomas grinned. 'I'll buy you an ice cream on the promenade after.'

'Will you?' Amanda brightened up. 'Thank you. But only if you have one too.'

'Oh, I shall. I promise.'

Chapter 25

AMBER

Amber Tang was a sublime heritage fusion of the three generations of genetic contributions, with almond eyes of vivid blue in golden brown skin and dark hair down to her waist. She was more, however, than just a pretty face. Her friend, Lauren, whose mother's house it was, informed Amanda and Trelawney that Amber had received an offer from the prestigious Coxspan College *before* her A-level results had arrived.

No wonder, thought Trelawney, the lofty Harold had considered her a suitable consort.

Miss Tang invited them into the sitting room. A warm beige sofa with cushions of tan, cream and deep blue, and matching armchairs were set around a circular, oak veneer Ikea coffee table and afforded a good view of the plasma screen above the inset gas fire. It was a pleasing arrangement, and the atmosphere was both relaxed and convivial. There was a pile of pain au chocolate on the table and a glass pot of green tea. Two partially filled cups belonging to the girls, and two clean ones, sat beside it.

Amanda and Trelawney accepted tea but passed on the pastries, saving themselves for ice cream.

Trelawney imparted the news about Harold. The girls appeared dumbstruck. Lauren put an arm around her friend.

'Harold *Biggerstaff*?' asked Amber, as though there could have been some mistake.

'Yes.'

'But … how?'

'A blow to the head.'

Amber shook her head. 'I can't believe it. He was …. But … a *blow to the head*? Did he, like, walk into a door or slip in the shower or something?'

'He was struck with an object with sufficient force to induce death.'

'Oh, my g… who on earth would …?'

'We're hoping you might have some idea. As someone who was close to him,' explained the inspector.

'I *was*, but not recently. There were plenty of people he'd pi– irritated, but … *kill* him?' She shook her head again, this time firmly. 'No.'

'May I ask how your relationship with Harold came to an end?' Trelawney asked respectfully.

'Erm.' She was trying to clear her thoughts.

'Have some tea,' recommended Amanda kindly. 'This must be an awful shock.'

Amber reached for her cup and took a couple of sips.

'Yes, erm, ok, so ….'

'You were study partners, weren't you?' her friend prompted.

'That's right. Harold's idea, actually. But …'

'He *was* good-looking,' explained Lauren helpfully, pulling some of her long, mid-brown locks over her left shoulder.

Amber concurred. 'And he seemed ok, and I didn't mind helping him. And at first, it was great. He really did his homework and focused on assignments and revision, and yes, I *liked* him, and one day he said, like, could we be girlfriend and boyfriend, and I said I didn't mind trying.'

'On a probationary basis,' put in Lauren.

'That's right. And it wasn't long before I started to notice that Harold was putting me down in front of his friends and, well, anyone really. At first, I let it go, but then I wasn't prepared to just laugh it off or let him say I couldn't take a joke and just wanted to be the centre of attention all the time. I mean, my dad and my mum agreed with Mr Otieno, who teaches social studies, when he said we should tell ourselves, "I accept only respectful treatment". And this just played in my head, and so in the end, I told him it was over.'

'How did he take it?' asked Trelawney.

'He was rude, but I just ignored him. Ignored him every day until I left after my last exam.'

'Do you know if he was rude or unkind to anyone else?' asked Amanda.

'His friends just left him to it, or ignored him, or gave as good as they got, but he had less and less of a crew around him. I think, in the end, everyone got sick of him, to be honest.'

'May I ask where you were yesterday morning between 8.15 and 9 a.m?' enquired Trelawney.

'Here.'

'Can anyone verify that?'

'Amber shares my room when she stays over,' Lauren replied. 'My mum said she looked in on us just before 8, I think, because she was hungry and thinking of starting breakfast. But she said we were both out cold, so she went back to bed. You can ask her when she gets back from work.'

'If you think,' put in Amber, 'somehow I caught the train all the way to Barnet Hill to thump Harold with a whatever, then that just makes no sense. I didn't have to kill him to get rid of him; I just had to dump his sorry ar–'

'Thank you, Miss Tang. I believe you,' Trelawney assured her.

'Look, I wish I could help. However foul Harold could be, he didn't deserve to die. He didn't need a blow to the head; he just needed … a therapist, if you ask me.'

'Oh yes, clearly self-esteem issues there, or rampant narcissism,' diagnosed Lauren.

'Lauren's mum's a counselling psychologist,' put in Amber by way of explanation. 'But like I say, I wish I could think of someone who would do that, but I just can't.'

Back in the car, Trelawney had a missed call from Ruth. He called her back and put it on speaker.

'Hi, Inspector. We just asked around a bit, and Shuna, who's in our class, well, she said her sister, who was in his year, said that by the end, Harold didn't have any friends that he hadn't upset, but no one hated him, would want to kill him. He didn't have any actual enemies. And anyway, they were all leaving school anyway, so he'd be out of their lives. Want us to dig any more?'

'Thank you, Ruth, and Kieran too. I think we have all we need. If you do hear anything different, though –'

'We'll report in,' offered Kieran. They hung up, and Amanda summarised:

'That does seem to be a bit of a dead end, then.'

'Yes, I fear so. Let's cheer ourselves up, shall we?'

In the golden light of the afternoon sun, they sat on the esplanade on a bench. It was near the kiosk that had provided Amanda with a cone of vegan chocolate ice cream with mixed nut sprinkles and a dark chocolate version of the Cadbury's Flake, in Trelawney's raspberry ripple cone.

The blue sky above, comments from the gulls, a fishing boat or two, and seaweed on the outgoing tide reminded him of home.

'This is a good place for thinking,' Thomas observed.

'Isn't it?'

'And what are *you* thinking, Miss Cadabra?'

'That it doesn't look like it was about *who*. I don't think Harold was killed because he was *Harold*, but because of *where* he was.'

'Where and when, I'd say.'

'Yes, yes. The thing with where and when is ...,' began Amanda.

Trelawney's phone rang. He took it out of his pocket and checked the screen.

'Hello, Vanessa. What can I do for you? ..... Yes .... Aha .... It does? Are you sure? .... Excellent .... I'll send Nikolaides over to collect it .... I will. Goodbye, and thank you, Vanessa.'

Amanda looked at him expectantly.

'Vanessa has found the swab she used to clean up Finley's head. It has tiny pieces of rock on it from the wound. I'll ask Nikolaides to collect it and find out if the residue on this swab matches that of the priory.' Trelawney made the call, and once he had hung up, Amanda began,

'Yes, but ...'

'But?'

'Mrs Vine, who has the cabinet I went off to do?'

'Yes ..?

'She told me that the priory has never had protected status.'

'This village is a law unto itself,' he observed

'Well, I expect it's just passed us by.'

'The Law, you mean?'

'Well ...'

Thomas grinned. 'Sorry, do go on.'

'Well, Mrs Vine told me that the village has been helping itself to the stones, the raw material of the priory, for hundreds of years. As the Sinner's Rue is at least four hundred years old, there may be a good chance that the hearth was made of stone taken from the priory.'

'In which case, the residue could be proof either way.'

'I'm afraid so,' Amanda concurred regretfully.

'Hm. Still, it's worth pursuing. I'll make sure we get a sample from the hearth, too, then.'

'At least it would narrow it down. If it's from the hearth, only then Finley was telling the truth. If it's from the hearth or the priory, then either he was telling the truth about his head or ….'

'It places him at the priory,' concluded Trelawney.

'If the sample matches only the priory or doesn't match either, then ….'

'Mr Flemming is being less than honest with us.'

Chapter 26

∽

AT THE NAUGHTY PRAWN, AND HUMPY

'Hello, you two, do come in. I suppose it's too early for drinking, and you're on duty. I can tell. Tea?'

'Please, Claire.' They followed her into the kitchen, where Amanda, who knew where everything was kept, helped out, and Trelawney, who didn't, leant against one of the counters and tried not to get in the way. Having obtained some background information on Janet and Edward and put the Curate at the bottom of the list, there was now the matter of Finley Flemming.

Claire picked up a Jaffa cake and asked,

'Everything all right? Apart from a murder, of course.'

'We're hoping you can give us some background information on one of the suspects,' explained Trelawney.

'Oh good. A virtuous excuse to dish the dirt. I only wish I could. Don't know either Janet's sister or Erik's new sidekick from Adam, I'm afraid.'

'What about the man staying at the Snout?'

'Haven't seen him. Heard about him, of course, in The Corner Shop.'

Amanda handed her a photo. Claire peered at it studiously, and then light broke over her face.

'Oh *him*.'

'Yes, he said his name is Finlay Flemming,' Amanda said.

'Is it now? Well, I'm absolute rubbish with names but faces ….'

'Good, because according to him, we met, and if it was a date, then it would almost certainly have been a double.'

'That's right, it was, but you wouldn't remember it or him, darling.' Claire looked at Trelawney. 'She wouldn't. Honestly. It was just a one-off.' She struck a dramatic pose with the back of her hand to her forehead and a tragic expression on her face, uttering, 'Like so many heart-broken souls cast by the wayside in her pitiless march toward the One and Only.'

Amanda giggled.

Claire added, 'Oh, Thomas, I'm joking. Most dates are first dates and never go anywhere. Frequently not even beyond a beverage, alcoholic or otherwise.'

'Oh yes, yes, of course.' Except, thought Thomas, I can at least recall all of mine.

She turned to Amanda, 'Darling. It was at The Naughty Prawn in Islington.'

'Oh yes, I really liked the shrimp there!'

'You remember *that* do you?' observed Trelawney with a mixture of amusement and pleasure.

'Yes, and the chef did the sauce for me with coconut cream. He was so kind.'

'You don't remember anything apart from the restaurant?' asked Trelawney.

Amanda stared into space in an effort of concentration until finally:

'Sorry.'

'Oh Inspector,' put in Claire, 'he was nice enough, rather charming actually. I might have dated him myself. Decent looking, easily a 7 or 8, a sort of … I don't know … uplifted vibe, optimistic, you know? And quite entertaining too.'

'Anything else?' he asked.

'Well, I was rather focused on my own date, but …. If you're asking me whether, based on my recollection, I could put Finlay whatever-his-name down as a murderer, I'd say no.'

'Ah.'

'But then what do I know? I've been asked to produce a film where a gangland boss is executed by a pedigree hamster.'

Claire's phone rang.

'Oh, sorry, darlings, I have to get this. Could be a long one too. Can we pick this up another time?'

'Of course,' replied Trelawney readily.

* * *

There was just time for one more interview before dinner. Soon, they were sitting in the comfort of the small salon at The Grange.

When Nikolaides had gone round the village asking if anyone had been about on Sunday morning, Humpy had made no secret of it.

'Yes, I was,' he confirmed to Amanda and Trelawney. 'Out on the toddle. But didn't see anyone at the priory ruins. Footprints: probably mine. I do like the peacefulness of that place. I feel it retains some of the solemnity of its former life and shares the space, if not the time, with those who dwelt there. Oh dear, listen to me, lapsing into the poetic, or more like purple prose, when I should be thinking how I might help. But no, no one was there.'

'There were paw prints on the ground,' Trelawney prompted.

'Paws? Well, dog walkers do pass that way sometimes, I imagine, although usually, they make a beeline for the woods, as far as I've seen. But then, you see, I learned at an early age that you see the most interesting things when you look up, and I always do, you see. Sometimes trip over things, I have to admit. But the downside is more than compensated for by the glories one detects from head-height to the firmament. I do tend,' Humpy concluded, 'to look at the sky a lot.'

'Can you recall the route that you took?'

'Just a morning saunter, work up an appetite for lunch, you know. Let's see, from The Grange up Trotters, round the church, read the epitaphs – some jolly witty ones, you know. My favourite Victorian offering: he lived each day as if it was his last, especially this one. Apparently, that was old Enoch Topernose. Very fond of his home-distilled spirits and partied until the final curtain.'

'And after the church?'

'After the church, crossed the road, sat on the bench in the sun for a bit, then wandered around the priory, in and out the Wood a bit, then back to the pub for a pre-lunch pint of Stinking Rych. The local brew, you know, Inspector.'

'Yes, I am familiar with it,' Trelawney assured him.

'It's good.'

'I agree. And in all of that time, you didn't see anyone?'

'Not that I remember. Hardly anyone about that time of the morning. As you'd expect on a Sunday, I suppose. Hillers was making an early start, before lunch, on cleaning out the mess the pigeons had made when they'd got in through that hole in the roof, and so I thought I might as well make the most of the fine weather. I offered to take Churchill, but he was still asleep. But, no, definitely no one by the priory. Probably a good thing, don't you think? Not in the market for a bang on the bonce, personally. Must have come and gone.'

'Did you see anyone or anything unusual while you were in the Sinner's?' enquired Amanda.

'No … I just did what I usually do: sit in the garden, do the crossword, read the Sundays, that sort of thing. I expect there were people coming and going, but head in the papers. Sorry.'

'So you didn't see anyone, and no one saw you on the way, or in the pub, or when you left?'

'No one that I can recall. Except for the bar staff. I'm not "village", of course, and I don't know that many people here. Most people don't walk their dogs until around 10, and I was probably ensconced in the Sinner's by then. Was back by midday to help with any lunch things, of course.'

Amanda smiled. 'Thank you, Humpy.'

Chapter 27

༄

THE WISDOM OF CLAIRE

Claire detected that her guest was a little less than his usual composed self. She sat him down and made him tea and a plate of shortcake biscuits. He had excused himself from a takeaway with Amanda, saying he had some work to do. Thomas had, in fact, one more conversation he needed to have before he would have an appetite.

'Ok, so how can I help with Suspect Finley?' Claire enquired, curling up on the sofa beside Trelawney.

'You were most helpful earlier. You said you met him on a double date with Miss Cadabra.'

Claire smiled and said, 'Let me be *really* helpful. You're wondering what Amanda was doing on a date with a man like Finley.'

'Well …'

'We looked at each other's possibles on the dating sites we were using at the time,' Claire explained, choosing her words carefully. 'Panning for gold ideally, but ready to take a look at an unpolished diamond or two, if you get my drift.'

'All right.'

'So I've been thinking about that evening and recalling whatever I can. Yes, I did wonder about Finley, but Amanda said she liked his cheerfulness, his positive outlook. He had a profile photo of himself smiling, in focus and the right way up, for a start. He displayed literacy, humour and intelligence. And I think it was also what he *didn't* say: like no list of things he hates, no mention of a recent breakup or a fondness for exertions of a sporting nature, in which we hoped to find a partner to participate. Showed more interest in learning about Amanda than in talking about himself. And he was attractive, of course,' Claire threw in airily.

'Hm. I see. And what did you think Flemming saw in Amanda,' asked Thomas, paying assiduous attention to his mug of tea. Claire saw how he could not resist drifting somewhat away from the professional.

'I didn't meet him for long. Of course, I had an eye on Amanda's dates to make sure she'd enjoy herself, but I was also focussing on my own. If I'd had to sum up Finley: a sweet guy but a chancer. He'd take a spin of the wheel on anything that he thought might reward him in some way. I don't think he was interested in plumbing the depths of Amanda's character. He saw a photo of a pretty girl within striking distance and knew the right things to say. He read her profile, picked out a couple of things to message about, asked her a well-thought-out question and pressed "send".'

'And …?'

'I was with Amanda when she got it. She laughed and said, "Why not?" I was lining up an assignation, so we arranged the double date.'

'And it was drinks and dinner and ….'

'And nothing. Oh, possibly dancing. I think there might have been a DJ, and they cleared some tables. And then we came home.'

'Ah. I see.' Claire observed him visibly relax. He took up a piece of shortcake, dunked it into his tea, and enjoyed the luscious result as she responded,

'Yes. That's the way most of our doubles evenings went. Sometimes, we might go our separate ways after dinner, Amanda would text me where she was ending up, and I'd go and collect her at about 11.30. Home by midnight. I might go back for more, but usually, I succumbed to the lure of a mug of cocoa, comfy jim-jams and an episode of *Midsomer Murders*.'

That broke Thomas's tension, and, having finished his mouthful of tea-infused biscuit, he laughed. 'I'm sure there's a lot to be said for that option.' He sipped his tea.

'Naturally, the trick is to find a man who'll enjoy all of that with you. Someone who is the real deal. And I'm holding out for that. Because I deserve it, and so does Amanda.'

'Of course,' he agreed warmly.

'And so do you, Thomas. So does everyone!'

'I'd like to think so.'

'Well, Amanda has pursued it. I'm sure she must have mentioned a few weekends away and the three that showed promise who turned out to be dead ends. Oh, ask her about it, darling.'

'But we …' Thomas began to object.

'As a friend. Oh, she won't mind at all. You know, Ammee isn't embarrassed about the same things most people are.'

'I had noticed. And her grandparents …?'

'Oh, they actively encouraged Amanda to explore all possibilities,' Claire assured him. 'And to try before you buy, as my grandmother used to say. A tenet by which she still abides, I might add. My grandfather passed on several years ago, by the way, to give you some context.'

'And your grandmother dat…?'

'Sees more action than I do,' Claire answered wryly, taking a consoling biscuit from the plate.

'My word … what a sheltered life I lead.'

'I've often thought so, Thomas. However, Sunken Madley is here to educate you.'

'Believe me, I'm learning all the time. But back to Finley. A chancer?'

'Yes,' Claire confirmed.

'How much would he be willing to risk?'

'As to that, I couldn't say. Risk murder? It's altogether possible. Under that chirpy chappy exterior, who knows what murky hidden depths might lie? So if you're hoping for a testimonial from me on Finley's sterling character, I can't give it, alas, Thomas. He might WYSIWYG – What You See –'

'Is What You Get? Yes.'

'Or he might have the soul of a gambler, an addict to the thrill of the roll of the dice and the dream of the big win.' Claire clearly spoke with the benefit of experience. 'Such men can be expensive and dangerous.'

'And Miss Cadabra did not mention seeing him again?'

'She said she had a nice time, but they were not suited and declined a second encounter of any kind.'

'Ah. Well. Thank you.' He stirred his tea again, unnecessarily.

'Thomas,' Claire said compassionately, 'I can see this is all a bit of culture shock for you. But perhaps, on some unconscious level, you have been confusing the cottage next door with a convent.'

'Er, I ....'

'I know that Amanda has a very young side to her,' Claire acknowledged, 'and in some ways, she can't grow up in the way that ... that we have. But she has lived the years of her chronological age and, during that time, has accumulated certain experiences consonant with that.'

'Yes, yes, naturally.'

'And if you could appreciate just how much pressure she's been under since, well, especially since she graduated, to find a suitable husband, you'd understand why she's tried so hard to find her… her match. And it's for the very reason that, in some ways, Amanda is so young that everyone seems to think she can't take care of herself when ... she can. She really can.'

'Oh yes,' Thomas concurred whole-heartedly. 'Except, well, in circumstances where we all need a hand.'

'Yes, those naturally. Anyway, Amanda being Amanda, took a practical approach and, with a little help from yours truly, checked out dating sites. And you know, most dating sites weren't going to be likely to entertain the sort of person that would go well with her. Pinder and Catch.com or whatadish.com or fixme.com. She did try them but had better luck on Outsidethebox and WandW.'

'WandW?'

'Weird and Wonderful,' elucidated Claire. 'Geeks. I think she met Finlay on Outsidethebox if that's relevant. If he's still got a profile up, it might tell you more about him. In fact, shall I have a gander for you now? Unless, of course, you're already signed up?'

'Thank you. No, no, I'm not …. It's, erm, not something I've ever really ….' Thomas murmured.

'Well, how have you met your past lady friends, then?' asked Claire, reaching for her iPad on the table.

'I … just meet … people … them.'

'I suppose you are out and about in the world more than the rest of us. Amanda's favourite customers are the ones that send their furniture and have it collected by van and whom she never has to talk to. And for me, it's all work and ships in the night.'

'Yes, I suppose you do have a point there, Claire.'

'All right. Here he is. "Bayley". Clever. The name: posh hotel in London, and makes you think of Baileys. Creamy, lush and intoxicating. Right. He says …. "Can you appreciate the finer things as well the simple pleasures?" Good interrogative opener, using "you", notice? "As an East London boy made good, I certainly can. Do you love your life as much as I do? If so, message me because I can't wait to hear all about you."'

'Sounds, erm … fine.'

'Sidebar says: Single, degree, no pets, no children, doesn't smoke.'

'Anything else,' asked Trelawney hopefully.

'Yes, he's filled in the "What your friends say about you" section: "Great guy. Great sense of humour. Easiest to get along with out of everyone I know. Good listener". Of course,' Claire added the rider, 'this could all be made up, but just the same, it does make appealing reading. And you can see from the pics that he's fit and doesn't need to take his shirt off to advertise it. And notice: no pics of him with a beer in his hand. This is extremely well-crafted. What you might expect of an estate agent, did you say he is? But anyway, yes … this is a great hook.'

'Hm, I can imagine.'

'That's not to say,' Claire added dampeningly, 'that he couldn't be a smart serial killer.'

'Ah.' Observing the concerned expression on Thomas's face, she went on reassuringly.

'But it's all normal, this Internet dating thing, for this day and age, and for single people who hope to find their Someone.'

'Yes, well, quite.' Thomas took a breath. It felt like a lot to take in. He had yet to decide how he felt, on balance, about all he had learned. 'Thank you, Claire. You've been very helpful, as always.'

She sensed that he was still a little perturbed on a personal level, and as Thomas stood up and she showed him to the door, took pity and said,

'Thomas. As far as I know, Amanda has not been trawling any dating site for some time now. Any dates … just find her.'

'So when you two go …?' he asked tentatively, wanting very much to know without prying.

Claire grinned. 'Girls' nights out.'

'Ah.' He was visibly relieved, which was what she had set out to achieve. But Claire felt she should add a codicil.

'But I can't promise, however … that that will be the case indefinitely.'

Thomas looked at her, then nodded and said sincerely.

'Thank you, Claire.'

Chapter 28

NICK

The next morning, after magic practice that had once again gone awry and with which Amanda felt no need to distract Thomas, she was back in the office. They reviewed the situation.

'So, who's left?' she pondered. 'Finley's friends?'

'Yes,' concurred Trelawney. 'I think it would work best if you go and have a quiet chat with Mr Nicholas Gosney informally. See if he has an alibi and what insight he can provide into the character of his two cronies.'

'Shouldn't we both go?'

'No, my instinct, from the brief glimpse I got of him, is that he's the sort who sees me as competition.'

'Ah, regards you as another lion. Whereas I'm the antelope?' Amanda suggested ruefully.

'I wouldn't put it quite like that. But, anyway, I'm sure you can outrun him.'

'And Stew?'

'I shall pay a visit to Mr Stewart Croft.'

Naturally, the appointments had to wait until after Nick and Stewart had finished work. Amanda and Trelawney spent the day examining what they had so far.

The late afternoon sun found Amanda in a pleasant café, picturesquely situated on the canal in Hackney. It was close to Stratford, east London. This was a prime location for those who worked at Canary Wharf, that towering business bulwark of the City of London. Many of the workers who toiled on its floors described themselves as those who liked to 'work hard and play hard'.

Nick was dressed in stone French chinos and a white Ralph Lauren shirt. It was turned back at the cuffs to show the tan, courtesy of a booth at the Hot Roast Club, and carefully judged muscular development, thanks to dedication at the gym.

It was a pity, in a way, because turning back the sleeves hid his carefully understated Savile Row Company silver cufflinks, studded with a small single diamond. Still, he could always roll the sleeves down later. Not bad for a boy from the East End, who came off a council estate. Well, his family had moved when he was eight, but that wasn't the point. He hadn't had the most affluent start in life, but he'd made his way and kept his friends back home and here.

He spotted her at a table outdoors and was glad he'd made the effort. It was an official sort of meeting, but these things could sometimes … she wasn't a 10 or even a 9, but at least she wouldn't consider herself out of his league. Anyway, it was shallow to give a person marks out of 10 for physical appearance. And Fin had said she was sweet and a good listener. It would be nice to be listened to for once.

Amanda rose and smiled as he approached.
'Hello, Mr Gosney.'
'Oh, Nick, please.'
'Well, thank you.'
'And may I call you Amanda?' he asked politely.
'Yes, of course.'

He gestured her back to her seat and took one opposite, asking,

'Have you ordered?'

'Not yet, just looking at the menu.'

'It's very good here,' Nick assured her.

'I'm glad you suggested it.'

Flourish was a community café and art space that used only ethically sourced products. Not the most trendy or upmarket, but Nick wanted to keep in touch with his roots and show Amanda that, in spite of his designer cologne, he was still a man of the people.

'Thank you.' They got the business of ordering over with. Nick was careful not to show off his knowledge of coffee and made sure Amanda got dairy-free. 'So, how can I help?'

'I was hoping that you could go over your stay in Sunken Madley, and may I apologise on behalf of the village for the unexpected ….'

'Excitement?' he supplied, with a slight smile. 'Awful though it was that someone lost their life, it certainly is an attention grabber to say that you stayed in a village that had a murder that weekend. No, no need to apologise. It was a great time, and I'd certainly go back.'

'Well, that's good news,' Amanda responded. 'We like to treat our visitors well.'

'Great. I expect you'd like me to see what I can recall, yes?'

'Please. You just never know when an apparently insignificant detail may turn out to be helpful,' she explained.

'I know. So that weekend,' Nick began. It was the same story Finlay had told her and Trelawney in the restaurant of The Snout and Trough. The drive up for the jolly with the mates, the game they'd watched on the screen in the Sinner's Rue and drinks they'd had, the accident with the hearth, the return to the Snout and Trough, about which he recalled very little, and the long sleep until late morning.

'You slept right through the night?' Amanda asked.

'Well … actually, I would have done only Stew bangs on the wall, then stumbles in asking if I'd brought a Paracetemol for his hangover.'

'What time was that?'

'About … just after 8.'

'And you went back to sleep?'

'Yes … no, he came back for another one a bit later, daft muppet, then I can hear him snoring through the wall and banged on it, and he stopped and then I went off to sleep myself.'

'Thank you, Nick. So you and Finley have been friends for …?'

'Not that long, I suppose, in the grand scheme but quite a while. We met when he was working in the city too, and we just hit it off, I suppose.'

'What would you say he's like?'

'Fin's all right. He's got this … I'm not saying you don't need staying power to work in the city or keep up the gym routine and all that stuff, but he's got this tenacity, this dog with a bone thing about him. That's why he left the company, you know.'

'No, I didn't know,' Amanda answered.

'He didn't tell you?'

Chapter 29

The Chancer

'Finley might have mentioned he used to work for a firm in the City, but it was some time ago that we dated, and people are not one of the things that my brain files in the front office, I'm afraid,' Amanda explained apologetically, stirring her oat milk cappuccino, and enjoying the ambience of the Flourish café and the light on the canal nearby, in spite of being 'on duty.'

'Ah yes, I get it, honestly,' Nick Gosney assured her, 'my cousin's the same. Ok, so, Amanda, he was working in property insurance. He was looking at risk assessment, and he kept saying that the seller obviously got this fault or that past the survey or whatever, and that he was in the wrong game.'

'I see.'

'So he set up his own estate agents online, and then it took off. Finley can talk the talk, you see. Oh, he'd never do anything illegal, but he's a chancer, if you know what I mean? I have to say, though, that he sticks with his risks after me or Stew would have given up, and I have to say he's made a go of his little company. Got a little unit and left the company, then moved more upmarket and broadened the scope of the business until he was also finding plots, empty or built on, for self-builders or developers. Even found one for a *Grand Designs* project.'

'Impressive,' marvelled Amanda. 'So you met when you were working for the same company?'

'Well. not exactly. Actually, we met in the Piranha.'

'The Piranha?'

'Casino. I'm not a gambler,' Nick hastened to add. 'It's just a fun evening out now and then. We met there a few times when we were both there with mates. He .... I guess we had different strategies.'

'Strategies?'

'Well, I go with a certain amount of cash that I might have spent on a theatre ticket, say, or I don't know, a white-water-rafting day or whatever. Anyway, I go and play, and if I win by the end of the night, I'm quids in; if not, when the money's gone, it's gone. I'll have had fun, a few drinks, chance to dress up, maybe some great food, and maybe meet someone, you know, attractive.'

'Sensible. But Finley had a different strategy?'

'He'd sometime dip into pots of money that were for other things. Got himself into debt, I think, more than once but always managed to dig himself out. I think he has a problem. Gambling. You know? The risk thing, the big win. But it's hard to say anything to a mate, you know? I have once or twice, but he just laughed it off. And I suppose I'm not one to talk. I can go a bit far with the alcohol. Had a few falls and knocks, horsing about with the boys. Stupid really. I suppose I should be past that by now. Maybe I should … get some help.' He didn't want her to think he wasn't working on himself and his personal development. 'Maybe, I just need a good friend to listen to me,' he offered hesitantly, then, seeing the consternation on her face: 'Sorry, Amanda. You're just so easy to talk to. I didn't mean ….'

'No, no, not at all. And yes, I think you would feel a lot better if you were drinking the drink rather than feeling it's drinking you. Oh, I don't know if that makes sense?'

'Yes, yes, it does. I just don't know who or where I'd go. I wouldn't want to, you know, bump into anyone from work in the waiting-room, if you know what I mean?'

'Well ....' Amanda did have an idea who might fit the bill, but Aunt Amelia, although well qualified, was a bit close to home.

'Yes?' asked Nick gently.

'I could suggest someone.'

He looked at her appealingly. 'Please.'

'I mean, you could talk to her on the phone and see how you feel, but ....'

'Sure.' She texted him Amelia's contact details. 'Thanks, Amanda,' Nick said with a warm smile.

'It's the least I can do,' she acknowledged fairly. 'I really do appreciate your sharing with me all you've told me ... so far.'

Chapter 30

Ask Me Anything

'Look. Let's get some more coffee, and you can ask me anything,' offered Nick. The mood felt much lighter. They ordered more cappuccinos and some olives.

'You know, Nick,' Amanda began, as the waiter moved on to his next table delivery, 'I don't quite understand what brought Finley to my village of all places. I mean, I would have thought Essex or Sussex or much further north into Hertfordshire would be more suitable for a countryside break than us.'

'I suppose there was something particular about Sunken Madley,' Nick admitted.

'Really?' she prompted.

'He was always interested in the property possibilities of anywhere close to London. Commuters, you know, but the real reason was – and perhaps you'll like this – a romantic one.'

Amanda smiled. 'A romantic one?'

He nodded with a grin. 'Oh yes. In search of The One.'

'Oh?'

'One lunchtime date that ran into the evening. Just one date, but Fin never forgot her. She gave Fin a card with her number, and Stew got hold of it later and threw it into the air for Fin to catch. Just … joking around. But it was windy … Fin laughed it off. All you can really do with Stew. He does take things a bit far sometimes, though. Can be a bit much. Sometimes I get out of going for drinks with the boys. Get a break from him, you know?'

Amanda gathered a response was called for. 'Understandable.'

'But anyway,' Nick continued, 'when it's been just us, Fin has mentioned her a couple of times, and I think that was why he was ready to take time off to stay up there. It was the only thing he really knew about her, that she was from that area.'

'Her name?' Amanda suggested.

'Sarah Smith. But that has to have been a profile name. I mean, come on. Anyway, I know he still carries a torch for her.'

'Ah. That's a sweet story, and I hope it has a happy ending,' Amanda wished sincerely.

Nick looked up from his coffee at her and asked casually, 'I take it that the lady in question was not yourself.'

'It was not,' confirmed Amanda.

He nodded, pleased. 'Ok.'

'So in conclusion,' she resumed the thread, 'regarding the incident ….'

Nick knew at once what Amanda was asking.

'No, of course, Finley had nothing to do with it. He'd never seen the victim before – they did show us his photo and, yes, we'd done the tour of the village, including the ruins, but he had no special interest in the priory, as far as I know. I think he was more interested in the Sinner's Rue!'

Amanda grinned. 'Understandably.' Coffee and olives were coming to an end. 'Well, thank you, Nick. You've been tremendously helpful.'

'Not at all.' He needed to make a move now if he was going to at all. 'I've actually enjoyed it. I, er … when this is all over, I wonder if you'd be interested in another round of coffee here, out of your professional capacity.'

'That's very nice of you, Nick. But I'm not really a city girl, you know.'

It seemed like a rebuff, but not all was lost, 'Ah yes, and I'll never make a village boy, I'm afraid. But all the same. Just a coffee …?'

Amanda hesitated. Suddenly Thomas flashed into her mind. Which was absurd, seeing as they were just … Well, she wasn't … there was no … there was no reason why not to. It was just coffee, after all, and it was so pretty here, and he was pleasant company.

She smiled.

'I'm sure that would be lovely.'

'May I text you then when the case is over?'

'Of course.'

They rose and shook hands.

Amanda drove back to Sunken Madley thoughtfully. In more ways than one.

Chapter 31

༄

RECAP, RECALL, AND THE SWORD OF DAMOCLES

Amanda went back to the office to find Thomas already returned.

'I'm sure you'd like a cup of tea after your drive,' he said, getting up and making for the kettle.

'Please. How did your chat with Stew go?' enquired Amanda.

'Straightforward enough. It seems that he and Nick can –'

'I know,' Amanda finished with evident disappointment, 'Alibi each other for Sunday morning.'

'Quite. I can see how let down you feel,' Thomas observed with amusement. 'Have a gingernut,' he suggested consolingly.

'Thank you,' she accepted. 'It always helps, doesn't it? Tea and biscuits.'

'Rarely fails,' agreed Thomas. 'And Shelley the cleaner said their door signs had been left on 'Please service my room'. She looked in on them at about 8.45, and they were both asleep. Flemming's was on 'Do Not Disturb'. So what about Flemming, then? Any nuggets from Gosney there?'

'Well … apparently, he's a chancer, a risk taker, and like a dog with a bone when he's on a project. That's what Nick … Mr Gosney said.'

The quick shift from first name to title and surname did not escape Trelawney's notice. Perhaps, though, Amanda had just been trying to warm up the potential witness by using his first name.

'Anything else?'

'Yes, that he was always interested in properties near London. Is not just an estate agent but also finds plots for self-builders and developers. He better not have his beady eye on the priory, that's all I can say,' Amanda pronounced militantly and then calmly, 'except Mr Gosney said he didn't think Finley displayed any particular interest in the ruins. Although that doesn't mean he didn't have any.'

'And Gosney's character?'

'I don't know. He seemed pretty straight up. I'm not so sure about their friend, Stewart Croft, though. Nick said he sometimes takes things too far.'

'Yes, I gathered that,' agreed Thomas.

'I mean, what if they didn't come straight back from the pub?' she asked. 'What if they went to the priory for a laugh, or whatever they call it? And what if Harold was there and Stewart took a prank too far, but the boy didn't actually die until the following morning?'

'Would they have come back to the Snout and Trough in such spirits if one of them had murdered a teenager?' queried Trelawney

'What if it was an act?'

'I'll ask Baker to check at The Sinner's – see how much they all had to drink. See if he thinks they were all as far gone as they seemed.'

It was Nikolaides who called back later and confirmed the statement of the proprietor: 'Legless. All three. They had all the signs of being highly intoxicated, but, on the other hand, he wouldn't want to have to swear to it in a court of law.'

There was nothing more to be got from the crime scene, which was tying up a uniformed police constable needed elsewhere. The tape was removed, and Trelawney asked Nikolaides and Baker to keep digging into Harold's history.

Thomas had opted for an early night to approach the case fresh in the morning. But his repose was disturbed at midnight by a call from Nancarrow. He sent a text to Amanda for her to open in the morning and soon was throwing his overnight bag into the boot of the Mondeo, and disappearing into the night.

* * *

Amanda saw the text as she switched on her phone when getting up. She skipped magic practice, which was proving too discouraging, and Tempest, in the Royal Box, was clearly finding it exhausting to observe. Instead, they went to the office to which Trelawney had given her a key, not, as her familiar pointed out, that it was necessary for him.

'Yes, but we want to minimise the use of you-know-what,' his witch reminded him firmly.

Once inside, Amanda stared at the whiteboard, went through the files on paper and on her computer that Trelawney had copied her in on, and came up … blank. She sighed. This was clearly not the way forward for her. Amanda went up to the priory with Tempest. She stood, trying to feel the air. There was something … sage … the aroma of … sage, yes. Amanda slowly moved to where she had stood that Sunday when they had seen …

There he was. Was it a "he"? Cowled? Looking out at her, just for a moment, benevolent but anxious; it was much stronger this time, more than anxious … afraid? Then the whoever ducked back behind the pillar.

'Hello?' she whispered. Nothing. Amanda stayed still to see if more would be shown to her … nothing. She slowly approached where she had seen the person … nothing. And the smell … gone on the breeze.

At lunchtime, Sharon dropped in again for any news at all.

'I was thinking of writing to our MP to ask for more resources for the inspector. Move things along.'

'Oh Sharon, I don't think there's any need for that,' Amanda countered calmly, despite her inner alarm. 'We're making all of the progress we can at this stage. Inspector Trelawney is an excellent detective –'

'I know, I know, but ….'

'And DS Baker and DC Nikolaides are both experienced and efficient, I assure you.'

'Hm, all right.'

'Would you like to have some tea?'

'No, dear, no … I'll get back. Thank you, dear.'

Involving the local Member of Parliament? Good grief. Sir Francis Crossly, Trelawney's boss at the MET, would not be a happy bunny at all. Hopefully, Amanda had at least forestalled that. Of course, Sharon wanted to feel she was doing something. It must be awful to just have to sit and wait for … for closure.

'We have to solve this, Tempest. Somehow …'

His citrine eyes glittered at her knowingly.

Chapter 32

MATTY

'It's an opportunity,' said Grandpa, looking at Amanda in the mirror as she combed her unruly hair, 'to keep your ear to the ground.'

'I know,' she sighed. Amanda preferred her ear, both ears in fact, in the seclusion of her workshop, preferably listening to reggae while she set about her restorations.

'It is the least you can do,' added Granny, 'while the inspector is busy with yet another crime on his hands. Put on your cream jacket, dear. You'll be glad of it on the way home.'

Amanda automatically withdrew the garment from her wardrobe and slipped it on over her orange, linen, fit-and-flare dress.

'You look lovely, bian. *Pur deg.*'

That brought a smile to her lips. 'Thank you, Grandpa.'

It was a business networking meeting in the function room above the Sinner's Rue. Amanda used to go to them with Grandpa. They were held periodically, in rotation, in one of the three villages of Sunken Madley, Upper Muttring and Romping-in-the-Heye. Grandpa always admitted that a seller will never get far in a room full of sellers, but it was only right to put their head around the door and say hello.

Granny always declined to come, preferring to spend the evening catching up on sewing or some other 'armchair task'. Except it wasn't, strictly speaking, in an armchair. She and Tempest spent an exhilarating evening at opposite ends of the sofa, periodically taking time out of their task or nap, depending, to glare at one another.

Senara was also fond of the operas of Wagner's *Ring of the Nibelung*, with *Götterdamerung* as a particular favourite. It provided a suitable soundtrack to the hostilities.

Amanda had tried to excuse herself from the event, but ….

'I'll go if you think it might be useful, though,' she had told Trelawney on the phone. He had picked up on the faint note of martyrdom.

'Ear to the ground. People do open up to you.'

'Yes, I do wish they wouldn't, but I suppose on this occasion it ….'

'We need any and every lead we can get,' Thomas appealed to her.

'All right,' Amanda agreed, attempting to infuse a modicum of enthusiasm into the words. Trelawney could not help smiling at her valiant attempt.

'What time does it finish?'

'10.'

'If you do learn anything that you consider to be of value, perhaps you could let me know?'

'Yes, Inspector,' replied Amanda.

And so it came about that, with a sigh, Amanda entered the Sinner's Rue. It was also something of a social event, with the conviviality that inevitably followed the business session, and the locals who drank there, in the Sinner's Rue, were by no means excluded. As if that were possible.

After a laborious 20-minute speech by an accountant from Romping-in-the-Heye and another 40 minutes of having multiple business cards pressed into her hands, Amanda needed some respite and wandered down the stairs into the family-friendly bar. And that was where she met him. Matty.

The connection was instant, even if it was only to be a chance, one-off encounter. The rest of the evening was spent sitting on the wall outside, talking and talking and looking at the stars, about which Matty was surprisingly knowledgeable. One or other of his parents popped out every now and then.

'This is Amanda,' Matty explained with delight, 'She's lovely! We are having int'resting discush'ns on a number of sujjex.'

'Oh good. Hello Amanda,' said his mother, shaking hands. 'I'm Dennis's cousin's daughter. Such a pleasure. Dennis has always spoken so highly of you. Now. I do hope Matty isn't monopolising you.'

'Quite the reverse,' responded Amanda warmly. 'This is by far the best evening I've spent at one of these networking events.'

'I'm so glad.'

'And Matty is … just pure gold,'

'Oh isn't he?' she replied lovingly. 'He's my sunshine. Does more for me every morning than any cup of tea or coffee.'

'Mummy says I'm her orange juice!' smiled Matty, revealing an endearing gap where a new front tooth had yet to appear.

'And so you are, my darling boy,' said his mother affectionately. 'Well, I'll leave you to it.'

Matty gave her a little wave as she returned to the interior of the pub. 'Mummy's lovely, isn't she?'

'She is indeed, Matty,' agreed Amanda.

'And Daddy's lovely too,' he added frankly.

'Well, I haven't met him yet, but I trust your judgement.'

'You will meet him, though. He'll come to check on you in a bit,' Matty predicted.

'Check on me?'

'Yes, to make sure I'm not tiring you out.'

Amanda laughed. 'Well, aren't you tired?'

'Not a bit. I don't sleep early, you know,' Matty explained. 'Well, I go to *bed,* but then I try to read my book.'

'You can read?' asked Amanda, impressed

'Oh yes, but not the big words, so then I get a bit bored by that, so I just lie there and think and then I sort of dream. And I remember when I was here before. Last night, I remembered about being here.'

'In Sunken Madley?

'Well, it might be because you've got one like I was in,' Matty offered by way of explanation.

'"Got one"?' enquired Amanda, all at sea.

'A house like the one I was in,' he explained. 'Only it's mostly fallen down now.'

Amanda cast her mind about for a derelict house in the village and came up blank. 'I don't think we …' There was only one place. 'You mean … the priory?'

'I don't know.'

'Did you live here when you were very little?' Amanda suggested.

'Oh no. I've never been here before. It was when I was here *before.*'

'Here before?'

'Yes, that's right. Mummy said I'm dreaming, but Daddy says I'm remembering a past life.'

Amanda's interest was growing with every word.

Chapter 33

༄

MEMORIES, AND THOMAS'S PERTURBATION

'And which do you think?' Amanda enquired. 'Dreams or past life memories?'

'I'm aclined to go with Daddy, on account of the fac' that I remember when I'm *not* asleep, you see,' said Matty reasonably.

'Ah. That does make sense,' Amanda agreed. 'So … what do you remember about it? About being here?'

'Well, I wore a long black dress with a fat string round my waist, and I might have had pockets, but I'm not sure. And I used to sing and pray a lot, and there were other big boys – grownups – who had dresses too like mine, and we all had dinner together. I think it was quite nice until the leaving time. I don't remember much after that.'

'It sounds like you were ….'

'A monkey, yes,' supplied Matty. 'That's what Daddy said. But I don't think he means a animal, coz I could *talk*.'

'I think your Daddy means a monk. They're people who live together in a community, a group, and they might have a school or a hospital or help out in some way or just do ….'

'Spichal things?'

'Spiritual things, yes.'

'Oh well, I didn't think I was an animal. But just the same word,' Matty concluded wisely.

'They are very similar words,' agreed Amanda.

'I wish I could remember more because I think it was quite nice. Can I see your prayery?'

'The priory?' asked Amanda. Matty nodded. 'How about tomorrow?'

'We're going home first thing.'

'Ah.'

'Wait, please, Amanda. I'll getta parent.' He jumped down and soon returned with Daddy.

'Hello, I'm Ben, Benjamin, parent. Pleased to meet you, Amanda. I gather my son wants to take you on a walk now.'

'How do you do, Ben?' she replied with a smile. 'Yes, I promise we'll take good care of one another. It's just a bit along this road. The old priory.'

He looked at his son keenly but tenderly. Matty was beaming up at him. Ben nodded.

'Yes … yes, by all means. Matty, you may escort Amanda.' Ben turned to her. 'He … remembers things … you never know … it might prompt something that will help him to sleep. Although, I can't say you ever lack energy, do you young man?'

'No Daddy. I'm indefactable.'

'Indefatigable, indeed. Enjoy your walk. Thank you, Amanda.'

Matty and the village witch strolled along the quiet street and crossed the High Road hand-in-hand to the west side. The setting sun was turning the pale stones of the priory to orange.

* * *

Amanda duly called Trelawney.

'How is it going there?' she asked.

'A potting shed, rarely used and unoccupied at the time it was set fire to. Same as last time: no accelerant, no witnesses, the usual suspects all have alibis.' Mr and Mrs Gwynsek, the owners, had neither heard nor seen anything. 'Anyway, how was your evening?' he asked

'Oh, amazing! I met Someone.'

'Oh?' Thomas tried to keep the suspicion out of his tone.

'He was … extraordinary. Wonderful.' It seemed to him that Amanda's voice was positively radiant.

'He?'

'Matty. We spent most of the evening sitting on the wall and looking up at the stars.'

'Really?' This was sounding worse to Thomas's ears by the minute.

'I've never met anyone with such a glow inside them,' Amanda continued enthusiastically. 'When we hugged goodnight, it was like I was being infused with light and warmth.'

Good grief, thought Thomas with alarm. 'Hugged goodnight?

'That's right,' she agreed brightly.

'Are you …. going to meet again?' he asked, wanting to know the worst.

'I don't know.'

'He didn't give you a phone number or ….'

'I don't think he has a phone.'

Clearly, a Luddite judged Thomas, then chided himself and suggested fairly, 'Ah … well, not everyone is into tech.'

'I think he has some sort of iPad, though,' Amanda offered.

'So … you'll keep in touch? I mean, he sounds … you seem … Is he … open to the idea of magic?'

'Absolutely and more,' confirmed Amanda.

'Ah. ….' He couldn't help himself. He had to ask: 'Romantic possibilities then?'

Amanda came to an abrupt halt, then:
'Romantic?'
'Yes.'
'I shouldn't think so. I'd have to wait an awfully long time.'
Oh no, what mess was she getting herself into? 'Really? Don't say he's married, pending divorce?'
'He's only six.'
The relief that swept over him was so dramatic that Thomas felt slightly faint and leaned on the desk for support for a moment.
The line had gone strangely silent, prompting Amanda to enquire,
'Are you quite all right, Thomas?'
'Yes, yes … probably didn't have enough … dinner.'
'Make yourself a cup of tea,' she encouraged him kindly.
'Yes … yes.'
'And then I'll get to the main event of the evening.'
He went to click on the kettle, encouraging her to continue.
'Now,' Amanda began in response, 'I don't know how concrete this is in the way of evidence, but it's a thread, and it's all we have to go on at this moment. So …. when we reached the priory, Matty went very quiet and then sighed and said:
"It was so lovely until the bad men came. The light was a bit like this then. But it was early morning. But I don't like to think about that bit." Then he talked about other things, and I took him back to his parents and came home. The point is, when would bad men have come to the priory and spoiled everything unless during the dissolution of the monasteries? And clearly, the priory resisted the handover to the Crown.'
'Fair enough.'
'And why should I meet Matty now and hear his memories or dreams *now*? It *has* to be significant. The past, I mean. There must be a connection between then and now.'
'I see where you're going with this, and by all means, look into as much history as possible relating to the priory,' said Trelawney diplomatically.

'Will do,' agreed Amanda.

'Thank you for letting me know.'

'Not at all. I'll let you get on.'

'Yes, I'm afraid I must get back to business here, but I'll come back to Sunken Madley at the earliest possible moment.'

That was going to be earlier than either of them could have anticipated.

Chapter 34

୬

Another Body

This time it was found by a dog walker.

Trelawney zoomed back from Cornwall and arrived to find that Baker and Nikolaides had the situation under control. The area was taped off again, and the body was covered and shielded from view by a tent. The inspector peeled back the sheet over the victim. On this occasion, identification was easy and immediate: Janet Oglethorpe.

The medical examiner was having lunch and doing *The Hertfordshire Chronicle* crossword in the Big Tease, so she was still around.

'Blow to the head,' Dr Carter said shortly. 'I'll know more when we get back.' Trelawney knew that by 'we', she meant herself and the deceased. 'I'd put the time of death between 2 and 2.45.'

Amanda and Trelawney searched Janet's belongings and Joan and Jim's spare room where she had slept, but nothing of note was to be found. They began the rounds.

'I was on my way to The Manor, as it happens,' said Finley airily

'By car?' asked Trelawney.

'On foot. Thought I'd take a walk through the village.'

'What time did you arrive?'

'Let me see, it was well after lunch… about 4 o'clock maybe?'

'And you left when?'

'Not sure, really.'

'You left your key at the desk when you went out?' asked Amanda.

'Yes.'

'So that's all right. Don't worry. Sandra will be able to check,' she said reassuringly.

'Ok. Let me think. It must have been about 3 o'clock.'

'Hm …,' Amanda pondered, 'well, it takes only a few minutes to walk from the Snout and Trough to The Manor.'

Finley gave a nervous laugh. 'I'd need a very slow walk, I know, for that. Actually, I took a bit of a detour. I went to look at the school.'

'Why is that, Mr Flemming?' asked Trelawney amiably.

'Well, it's an old – a historic building.'

'Oh, are you interested in history?' enquired Amanda with a smile.

'No – yes, yes, isn't everyone?' Finley finished.

Trelawney leaned back. Let the silence hang heavily. Finally, he said quietly,

'Why don't you share with us what you are really doing in Sunken Madley, Mr Flemming?'

'I told you. A holiday', was the slightly defensive answer.

'You haven't been completely open with us, have you, Mr Flemming?' Trelawney opened the file he'd brought with him. 'You are not, as you represented yourself, an employee in an estate agent's doing the daily grind. You own the business, and you specialise in finding land, with or without structures built upon it, for those interested in development. Is that not correct?'

'Oh, all right, yes, it's true,' Finley admitted. 'But you know what people are like. "Developer" is almost a dirty word. People think concrete over green fields and all of that. I was just being sensitive.'

'And what piece of land interests you in Sunken Madley?'

'Well, a lot of village schools close, and the buildings are under-modernised and often come with playing fields, a car park, or a playground at least. There's a lot can be that done with … a situation like that, to the benefit of all parties.'

'And The Manor? That is occupied by recent buyers set on restoration.'

'Well, a manor will often have land attached to it. You know, historically, that the family may not have sold off.'

'Or the priory?' suggested Amanda casually.

'Oh no,' Finley replied at once. 'That's probably got listed building or monument status. Waste of time, but … like that bit of meadow in the middle of Madley Wood, for example.'

'For example, or in particular?' asked Trelawney.

'I'm just scouting,' Finley insisted. 'No one's ever looked at Sunken Madley properly. The land the estates are built on, was never on the open market. There might be other undeveloped land, still belonging to the original owners. There are all sorts of possibilities.'

'So you took a detour to look at the school?' summarised Amanda, with a friendly air.

'That's right.'

'Did anyone see you? Did you chat with any of the villagers?'

'N-no. No one about, really.'

'And at the Manor? Did you meet the Poveys? They're such lovely people, aren't they?'

'Yes. Mr and Mrs Povey said they didn't own the meadow, and I could try The Elms or The Grange. Both being old houses.'

'Ah, I see. And then?'

'Then I came back here. And got my key from the desk and had a pint.'

On the way out, they checked with Sandra. 'Yes, he went out at 2.57, according to the record,' she said, gazing at the desktop screen at the end of the counter. She looked at Trelawney. 'But you know, Inspector, not all guests leave their key every time they go out. Yes, they are supposed to, but sometimes people forget, or reception is unstaffed, so they just go. It's not something I make a fuss over.'

'Understandably,' responded Trelawney. 'I'm sure it's something we've all done.'

'Oh yes, even I've done it. But what it does mean, for your purposes, is that I can't swear that Mr Flemming didn't go out and come back before he officially checked in his key. Although … I did see him in the restaurant … and yes, he did seem to be taking a long leisurely lunch. Which,' she admitted ruefully, 'we by no means discourage.'

Trelawney smiled. 'Yes, the final coffee of lunch can easily become after-lunch drinks. Thank you, Sandra.'

As they walked to the car, Amanda uttered sincerely:

'I do hope Finley doesn't manage to get hold of our meadow!'

'Don't worry,' Trelawney assured her.

'Why not?

'Because he's lying.'

Chapter 35

❦

A Tentative Suggestion

Erik had been in an afternoon meeting in Cockfosters and sent his assistant back to the office for some papers.

'I'm awfully sorry, Inspector, Miss Cadabra,' apologised Edward, 'I'm not sure what time that was, but I had to go straight back once I'd located the documents.'

'Cockfosters?' queried Trelawney.

'Oh yes, I can show you.' Nightingale took out his phone and brought up Google maps. 'It's here, to our east ... well, east-south-east, perhaps we'd say. So I drove into the village, to the office on the green, from the south and back out again the same way. If only I had come from the north, I might have seen something. And to think we were at Upper Muttring later!'

'North?'

'Exactly, Inspector. Then I would have passed the priory and perhaps seen something.'

'Thank you, Mr Nightingale.'

The Curate had been out on pastoral duties but had got rather lost.

'I'm afraid I'm still familiarising myself with the village and the area. But I didn't visit the priory, I'm sorry to say.'

'Can you recall any times that you saw particular people?'

'Let me see … I collected Mrs Duner's little son from daycare because she wasn't at all well and stayed with her until Dr Patel had been, and then got her prescription from Mr Sharma, but … I'm not sure about times.' Neither, alas, were any of the other parties involved.

Humpy had been reading in the grounds of The Grange.

'All afternoon, yes,' he said. 'Apart from when I fell asleep. *Gin, Sin, Flappers, and Jazz* is an awfully good book. History of the 1920s, you know, but you can't beat a snooze under a tree on a summer's day.'

Nick Gosney and Stewart Croft were both at work. There must have been any number of people who'd seen them.

'Hm. Again,' observed Trelawney, 'too many alibis or people without them and no motive. But the same MO, at least: struck from behind with a piece of stone from the priory,' He looked at his laptop screen, hoping that something would jump out at him, that there would be a link somewhere, a hole somewhere.

'There is, perhaps,' Amanda began circumspectly, 'one thing that I could mention.'

'Oh?'

'Yes, it's –' She was interrupted by Trelawney's phone ringing.

'Sorry, it's Nikolaides.'

Amanda waited. It was a short conversation, and as soon as he hung up, the inspector relayed its purpose. 'Nikolaides took samples from the Sinner's Rue hearth and the priory and got them compared with the flecks on the swab used to clean Flemming's injury. Now, both match because – you were right – the hearth was made from a priory salvage job. But what is most interesting is that it's Cornish granite.'

'Hm, that is interesting,' agreed Amanda. 'I know that it was used for a lot of buildings in Cornwall but … here?'

'Yes, so Nikolaides did some research and found that it's one of the materials that was used for Westminster Abbey, so it's not unheard of for it to have made it to this side of the Tamar.'

'Aha. But I suppose the important thing is that it does support Finley's account of the night before Harold was found.'

'Yes, but ... we're still at a bit of an impasse. You were saying, though, that you did have something you could mention.'

'Yes, well ... it's not perhaps what you'd describe as concrete.'

This flagged up on Thomas's alarm system, rigged expressly for detecting any suggestion of using magic. He raised his eyes from the computer to her face, his features schooled into an expression of amiable interest.

'Well,' continued Amanda, encouraged by the slight smile she observed, 'you remember the monk I mentioned I saw at the priory?'

'Vividly,' he returned lightly.

'Well, I saw him again. The other day.'

Thomas took a deep breath and resolved to attempt to treat this as "normal" data. 'Do you think he was trying to warn you?'

'I don't know. It was more like he was trying to .... It was something that had already happened, I think.'

'Right,' Trelawney responded vaguely.

'Well .... It could just be a recording in the stones, but maybe, if he was occupying the same space, just in a different time, he could have seen something ... you know ... that happened in the present.'

'Hm.'

'If I could make contact....'

'Are you thinking of holding a séance?' he enquired neutrally.

'What? No, I don't know how to do those. Granny and Grandpa always said don't because you can't be sure who or what you'll get unless it's your gift and you're highly something-or-other, and it's not, and I'm not, so I don't. And well, no, I wasn't thinking of holding a séance,' Amanda finished.

'Then …?'

'Instead, I was thinking ….'

'Of taking Mohamed to the Mountain?'

'Yes, you see, if I could cast a … a time spell and go back to when the priory was the monk's space and speak to him ….'

'Back to … when would that be?' Trelawney enquired.

'Well, I'd have to research that,' Amanda admitted.

Relieved that there was a roadblock, however temporary, he responded affably, 'Right, well, I'll leave that with you. And, for the time being, let's follow procedure, shall we?'

'Yes, only …,' Amanda began, then found herself without a destination.

'Only?'

'Yes, of course. Leave it with me.' Amanda was visibly relieved to have got broaching the subject over with and not having the suggestion met with any protest.

'So …,' Trelawney moved on smoothly, 'Mrs Oglethorpe's daughter, Linnie, is coming down to identify the body.'

'Oh good. Do you think she'll talk to us?'

'Yes, but I'd like you to solo this one if you would, Miss Cadabra. I have the feeling, from speaking to her, that she'll open up more to you.'

'Really? Why?'

'My instinct is that she'll feel that you'll understand her as a woman.'

'But I don't know anything about women,' Amanda objected reasonably.

He grinned affectionately.

'I know you don't. But she'll think you do, and that's more than enough. Trust me on this one.'

'I do.' She smiled seraphically, her strange blue eyes flecked with brown, looking up at him. He had the impulse to behave unprofessionally, and quickly added:

'Dunstable, I believe, is where she'll be staying. With a friend from schooldays.'

'Oh, Dunstable!' responded Amanda with delight. 'Then, if she doesn't mind, I know just the place!'

* * *

That evening, as Amanda sat on the chintz sofa of the cottage, stroking Tempest with one hand and holding a cup of Ovaltine in the other, Senara and Perran paid one of their impromptu visits. Granny, in a long blue silk satin gown and collar of sapphires, solidified out of the ether in her place beside Amanda and Grandpa, in evening dress, in his favourite armchair. They were holding what appeared to be cocktails in elegant crystal glasses. Clearly, they were not preparing for bed.

They exchanged warm greetings, and Perran's next words explained the reason for their visit.

'Case getting to the end of its tether, is it, *bian*?'

'I expect young Thomas is desperately labouring his normal methods to their very end,' remarked Granny. She took a sip of her drink.

'Yes,' answered Amanda.

'Well, make sure you both have explored those methods and exhausted them before you do anything risky, love,' Perran urged Amanda.

'Of course, Grandpa.'

'Remember that magic –'

'is a serious business. Yes, Grandpa.'

'And,' stated Granny, 'is not a shortcut.'

Amanda had some idea as to the subtext here. She'd been … 13, perhaps?

* * *

'Now Ammee dear,' Granny opened as they sat at the burgundy, velvet-covered dining table where lessons usually took place, 'we return to the thorny and treacherous matter of time spells.'

Amanda's eyes brightened, and she pushed one of her two long plaits back behind her shoulders with a business-like air.

'Really? You think I'm ready, Granny?'

'Possibly,' Senara answered in measured tones. 'We shall see. Time spells are part of Advanced Magic and are not, I repeat, *not* to be used lightly.'

'No, Granny.'

'Of course, all, I say *all* magic ....'

'is a serious business,' Amanda repeated conscientiously.

'Quite.'

'Yes, but surely ... if one knows what one is doing ....' Amanda offered, in a mixture of confidence and hope.

'And one does, does one?' Senara asked her granddaughter, her violet eyes regarding her with amusement.

Amanda suddenly recalled the unfortunate affair last week. Hungry and somewhat tardy, she had attempted to speed up Sunday lunch using magic. The chicken had exploded, and Grandpa, as ever, had looked for the silver lining.

'Well, it's not in so many bits as last time, and I'm sure chicken pieces taste just as good.'

'At least we hadn't put the vegetables in yet,' added Granny. 'Next time, I'm sure we can wait for the oven to do its own job, without any *assistance*,' she finished pointedly.

Having observed her granddaughter's reverie, Senara recapped.

'Magic *is* a serious business and time-spell-casting even more so. People have got themselves into disastrous situations through lack of knowledge and understanding of how they work.'

'Yes, Granny,' Amanda replied meekly, wondering if her grandmother was about to drop the whole idea of the lesson. However,

'Well, we shall see how far you have progressed and try a small experiment.'

'With a time spell?' Amanda's hope was renewed

'Yes, dear. Now, do you remember how we begin?'

'Wand to heart, and address Lady Time. *Hiaedama Tidterm, Hiaedama Tidterm.*'

'Correct. An abstract concept, of course, but it helps to focus the intent. Next?'

'Request permission to enter the gate.'

'Good. In Wicc'yeth?'

'*Ime besidgi wou. Agertyn thaon portow, hond agiftia gonus fripsfar faeryn ento than aer deygas.*'

'Well done. Now, wand out, focus and cast.'

Amanda placed her wand at her chest, concentrated on going back in time, and chanted. There was a slight shiver in the air around the table.

Something was wrong. Wrong with her body, it was ... her hands were definitely smaller and ... She put a hand to her hair. Just one plait, the way she used to wear it when she was .... younger.

'Remain calm, Ammee dear,' Granny bade her serenely. 'No lasting harm will result. There was a slight issue with your spell. We shall request a reversal.'

Once back in her 13-year-old form, Senara asked her if she had looked out of the window just now.

'No, I was a bit distracted by ....'

'Indeed. The state of the garden would have been able to show you whether you were back in time or not.'

'Oh yes, of course. And, er...?'

'Not on that occasion. We shall proceed with a little more practice.'

Chapter 36

༷

LINNIE

There was a flying school at the bottom of the bluff. From the top, there was a vista of fields. Kite flyers and picnickers coloured the foreground, with the white wings of the gliders in the middle distance against the blue vault. Here, they were above the world.

Amanda, matching the woman coming from the carpark with the image on her phone, waved her arm in greeting. Linnie Tweedy, née Oglethorpe, was a tall woman, big-boned yet graceful, with shoulder-length, dark-brown hair and blue eyes. They held a friendly, down-to-earth expression as she joined Amanda at the picnic blanket on the grass, looking out across the valley below. They shook hands.

'Shall we sit down?' Amanda invited her, 'Thank you for meeting me, M….'

'Linnie, please. Not at all.' Linnie hitched up her khaki capris at the knee, put down her canvas bag and took a seat beside Amanda, remarking appreciatively with a mild Yorkshire accent, 'This is gorgeous. Better than a police station.'

'I thought so,' agreed Amanda, 'and that you'd like being out of doors in beautiful, natural surroundings.'

'Aye, I do.'

'You're a horticulturalist, is that right?'

'Aye. Basically,' explained Linnie, 'I grow plants for sale, an' I do special commissions too for exotic species. But the ones I supply reg'larly, customers who visit my plot or the local outlets, are me bread and butter.'

'You didn't want to follow in your parents' footsteps?'

'Management and accountancy? I think I'd 'ave withered and died! But each to their own; I couldn't see ma'self doin' that?'

'I couldn't agree more,' Amanda smiled. 'Your mother was very successful, though, I gather, and liked what she did.'

Linnie was quiet for a moment, then said frankly,

'Aye, you're wantin' to know what she were like. Well, she were an odd woman. I 'ope it's all right to say that about me own mother.'

'Of course.'

'I don't know. Mothers and daughters, right?'

'Hm,' said Amanda vaguely.

'She were always saying,' Linnie went on, '"It all falls on me". But that were never true. It were Dad as brought us up, looked after the 'ouse, played with us, 'elped us with our 'omework, cared for us when we were poorly. And he worked as well, at 'ome, you know. But we were lucky it were that way round.'

'You were lucky?'

'Oh yes, because our Dad, he were always fun, he still is. But when we were kids, he could be daft with us, muck about, never fussed. And, course, 'e were our Dad, and we did respect that, but 'e could also be one of us, you know?'

That reminded Amanda of Grandpa.

'Yes, yes I do.'

'Yeah.' Linnie stared meditatively out at the fields. ''E deserved a better life. He de*serves* a better life, and now that 'e's free … I hope he teks 'is chance …. Hm …. Anyway, she were always saying as how it all falls on 'er. She did do right by us; I'm not saying nothin' against 'er.'

'Of course not.'

'We 'ad a good standard of livin', better than a lot of our neighbours and friends, you know? Good food, nice clothes, 'olidays abroad. And mam were good at her job, mind, though not liked that much, I 'ave to say. She didn't suffer fools gladly, as she always said. If sumat or someone wasn't up to scratch, she could come 'ome in a right mardy mood. But she expected no less of 'erslf, she used to say. Oh, she worked at 'er job. That's 'ow she was, when she got on a … a project … caught the scent, if you know what I mean? She wouldn't let go. Like ….'

'Yes?' Amanda encouraged gently.

'Well, at the time … it were always all Freddie and then his mate, too, who lodged with us. I don't think she ever wanted a daughter, but I were never jealous of either of them. Me and Freddie were always close. Anyway, one day there was this girl at school: tall, not so well-to-do family, though there's nothin' in that. Plenty of kids not so well off was lovely, but this one …. and she had two 'angers on like Crabbe and Goyle to the blonde one in Harry Potter.'

'Malfoy?'

Linnie nodded. 'Aye, 'im. Anyroad, one day this bully said sumat to me, can't remember what it was, and I answered her back, and she took a pet and slapped me round the 'ead. I were that shook up, and I did report, but nothing came of it. You know what it was like at school.'

Amanda didn't but looked at Linnie in what she hoped was an understanding manner. Linnie went on:

'Only somehow it got back to me mam. Well – and I don't know how she did it – but she talked to the other parents. You know, for all her cold ways, she could get stuff outta folk. Prob'ly too intimidated to say 'er nay! But she got to the bottom of all sorts of bullying by those three and blow me down if she didn't get them all expelled! Aye! I think it came as a relief to a lot of kids to 'ave them gone.'

'Well, that was good,' observed Amanda.

'Aye … a good deed, but I don't know as she did it to be "good" or she did it because she couldn't 'elp herself once she were onto it, you know?'

'Ah, I see. Yes, quite a difference.'

'Aye … you know … that streak in 'er … this is off the record,' Linnie stated firmly.

'All right.'

Linnie lowered her voice.

'Just between you and me, … I'm not really … deep down … surprised …. someone killed 'er.'

Chapter 37

❦

History Lesson

Amanda duly reported her conversation with Linnie to Trelawney, back in the office. Tempest had found a file box at one end of the desk with a shallow padding of important documents. He had nimbly flicked it open, ensconced himself therein, and gone to sleep.

'Interesting,' was Trelawney's first somewhat enigmatic comment when Amanda completed her narrative.

'You mean the fact that Linnie wasn't surprised someone …?' she checked.

'That certainly.'

'Or that it looks like Janet was on a project, and her mother was, in so many words, obsessive.'

'Yes, that. According to Mrs Oglethorpe, that project was seeking out a hitherto unknown family member and, according to Joan, establishing a successful relationship.'

'To prove to herself that she could do that,' said Amanda.

'Yes, but what if she had a hidden agenda that involved herself in something that resulted in her death?'

'That has crossed my mind, Inspector, but she's never been here before, nor has … unless …. Has either the sergeant or the constable unearthed any previous link between Janet and Sunken Madley? Or Harold?'

'Not yet. Baker rang earlier to say that they haven't found anything on either Harold's laptop or phone that suggests his life was threatened in any way. Nikolaides is going over it all again, but she's not hopeful. Janet's home computer and phone are both password protected. Her workplace one has revealed nothing so far.'

'Hm, shame. One thing we can say is that this second death has compounded the urgency to solve this case. If the same killer is responsible for both fatalities, then they are certainly capable of striking again.'

'I agree. Erm, so,' added Amanda, 'we've been going through the same procedure as post-Harold's demise, and, er, do you feel that the picture is clearer in any way?'

'These things take time,' Trelawney reminded her. 'Both occurred at the priory ruins, and I think that's significant.'

Champagne corks all but popped in Amanda's head. This was the opening she had been waiting for. Now to ….

'Maybe,' suggested Amanda gently, 'we're thinking too three-dimensionally.'

'That is usually considered to be a good thing,' Trelawney replied with a glimmer of humour. However, he had a fair idea of what was coming, but every lead had to be explored, and so replied: 'Time.'

'Yes.'

'You're referring to the monk you saw. It could have been just a recording of an emotional event that imprinted on the stones, that played out because you were near it,' he countered. 'You've shown me how that works before.'

'Yes, but Inspector, even if it *is* just a recording, there must be a connection. I've been coming to the priory for picnics on Sundays for years and never seen the monk … until recently. That has to be of some significance. And then Matty ….'

'Yes, I do see. Please don't imagine that this carries no weight with me. There may, however, be normal avenues to pursue. Nevertheless, I am open to your thoughts on how, *hypothetically*, one might proceed with following up this possible lead.'

Relieved to find Thomas so willing to contemplate her proposal, Amanda attempted to reign in her excitement.

'Well, as it so happens, I have been doing a little preparation.'

Preparation, thought Thomas with foreboding.

'Just in case,' Amanda mitigated.

Preparation for what she regarded as the inevitable, he concluded. I might as well go with the flow.

'Yes?' he encouraged. Amanda looked at his face doubtfully. He smiled and nodded. 'Tell me.'

She breathed a sigh of relief. 'I've been doing research about the dissolution of the monasteries.'

'Ah.'

'You see, it didn't all happen overnight.'

'I imagine not.'

'It happened in sort of two stages,' Amanda explained. 'A law was passed in 1535 called the first Act of Suppression. Following this, first Henry VIII's people did an audit. And all of the monastic houses earning less than £200 per year were closed and passed to the crown along with their assets.'

'£200 doesn't sound like a lot, but I imagine it was more substantial then,' he hazarded

'Yes. The rough equivalent, I think, of about £200,000 today.'

Trelawney raised his eyebrows. 'Monasteries could have made that much?'

'It's a lot, but not unachievable. They had land so they could be self- supporting.'

Trelawney nodded. 'Hm, that makes sense if they were orders that didn't interact with the outside world. If they were orders dedicated to prayer, lots of silence involved.'

'But there were others that did go out into the community and further. But the point is that land was a source of income.'

'Yes, crops, animals.'

'And fish ponds.'

'Those too,' he concurred. 'Yes, and the surplus could be sold to the villagers. If the income was calculated to include the value of everything they produced, then over the course of a year ....'

'It could mount up, couldn't it?'

'But smaller houses with only a few brothers, or sisters as the case may be, would have fewer needs, and so the value would have been lower.'

'Right. So they were closed first,' said Amanda.

'Yes. Was our priory among those, do you know?' Trelawney asked.

Amanda smiled. She liked it that he had said 'our' priory.

'It seems not, from what I've been able to find about the Hertfordshire ecclesiastical houses. So ... the larger houses may have concluded, "Phew! Storm over," and gone back to business as usual.'

'But we know from our history that it didn't end there,' remarked the inspector.

'Quite,' she agreed. 'Look, the monk I saw was definitely anxious, possibly alarmed, even fearful, maybe.'

'It was most likely a recording, bound to the stones of the priory, but I'll admit it that only an emotion, a strong one, could have done that.'

'Yes, what was the most anxious time for the monasteries if not the dissolution?' Amanda asked reasonably.

'True. But,' went on Trelawney, finding himself getting caught up despite his reservations, 'that would have been protracted. Surely, this monk must have been anxious about something specific. And you said he seemed to be looking straight at you.'

'Yes, so what if it was *more* than just a recording? What if he was appealing to me for help? And if I go and help him with whatever it was that he was troubled about, maybe he can help us know what happened to Harold and Janet.'

'Agreed, but that's "if", "if", and "maybe". Nevertheless, let's follow this line of reasoning. So, anxiety-causing event?'

'We have to find out what it was.'

'Indeed, but a bit more history, if you please, Professor Cadabra.'

Chapter 38

A Dangerous Habit

Amanda was more than willing to continue their dip into history. Of course, they needed tea and biscuits in order to do the job properly. While Thomas filled the kettle from the office amenities, Amanda took the biscuit barrel over to the desk and dropped teabags into their mugs.

'What happened to the monks who were evicted from the monasteries during the first Act of Suppression of 15 …?' asked Thomas, plugging the kettle back in and pressing down the switch.

'1535. Well, the higher-up monks, at least, were given a state pension or redundancy money, I gather.'

'Provided they cooperated, I expect,' Trelawney remarked, sliding back one of the cupboards to access the little concealed 'mini-bar' fridge, so cleverly fitted by Bryan. He leaned in to take out the milk and left it open for Amanda to extract the smoked salmon, with which she had stocked it for Tempest's delectation.

Amanda agreed. 'Well, yes. And many, I think, found positions as preachers in the community.'

'And those monks who had skills they had learned in the monastery ….'

' … could find work in the secular environment.'

'Larger houses would surely have taken some in,' he speculated, pouring milk into the tea tray jug and returning it to the fridge.

'I would have thought so.'

'So they weren't made destitute? I'd always assumed that that was the case.'

'Me too,' answered Amanda, nodding. 'But.' She paused to allow the kettle to have its vocal moment as the water came to the boil. 'That's a wonderfully fast kettle,' she observed admiringly.

'A present from my mother.' That reminded Thomas of how much Penelope Trelawney would relish the current historical conversation. And how little she would relish its objective. He put that out of his mind and poured the water onto the tea bags, prompting Amanda to continue with:

'But?'

'The brothers and sisters, it seems, were provided for, though only if the Abbot was cooperative and there was a peaceful handover.' She put the salmon-laden plate on a napkin next to Tempest, who stirred at the aroma. 'I gather that either way, the lay workers were not so fortunate.'

'Oh?'

'I read,' said Amanda, rearranging the desk a little to make space for the tea tray in the middle, 'that they could be suddenly and forcibly ejected from their homes if those were on ecclesiastical land, in the clothes they stood up in, not allowed even to bring their goods. Whole families, with children, elderly family members. It must have been devastating.'

'Couldn't the houses warn each other?' Thomas asked, bringing over the tray.

'You'd think so, but communication was so much more limited than today. I'm sure many just didn't see it coming. But …'

'Yes?'

They sat down in their chairs opposite one another, and Amanda picked up a teaspoon. 'I've been thinking, what if an abbot, say, in one house had inside intelligence that the big cull of all of the large monastic houses was coming. Wouldn't he or she, if an abbess, want to warn any houses in the same order or that were nearby? To be prepared?'

'That would make sense. Ah ha … and I *think* I see where you're going with this, but do go on.' He stirred the water in his mug to help the tea from the bag to percolate.

'So,' began Amanda, following suit, 'let's say the abbot or prior of a house in Cornwall, like Tresco Priory in the Scilly Isles, maybe of the same monastic order or who is a friend of our abbot here, gets intel that the end was nigh, so he sends one of his brothers to Sunken Madley Priory. With a letter.'

'Aha.'

'Well, in a *hypothetical* scenario,' continued Amanda carefully, 'that would get me into the priory, in disguise as a monk, of course. And then I could find whoever I saw that day at the ruins and see if he saw anything of our present-day murders.' This was met with silence and, to Amanda, an inscrutable expression. She asked, hopefully, 'What do you think?'

'What I always think,' Trelawney replied baldly. 'It's a hare-brained scheme that will almost certainly end in disaster.'

'Why?' protested Amanda.

He leaned back and crossed his arms. 'I see. So you, a female, are planning to go back to the 16th century and infiltrate a monastery. Right?'

'You don't think I can get away with it?' she enquired tentatively.

Thomas viewed her kitten face.

'Pass for a man?' he asked her with a practical air.

'Boy?' Amanda suggested.

He grinned. Even when he'd seen her begrimed from the workshop and her hair off her face to him, her features were unmistakably feminine.

'All right. To be fair, there would be an outside chance. People do see what they are expecting to see. And if they expect to see a boy, then ... yes.'

Amanda smiled with relief, but Trelawney added a rider:

'Yes, so if, and I say *if* we are thrown upon this last resort, then ... you'd better have some company from the genuine article, don't you think?'

She laughed. 'Yes, very well. Point taken, but we're not planning a lengthy visit!'

'But,' Thomas pointed out seriously, 'we do need to come back alive with whatever it is you think you'll find there.'

'I see what you mean. Yes, *not* die or be arrested. Very well, Brother Thomas. We shall go together.'

'As partners should, Brother Amanda! But only *if* there is no other way to solve this case with proper patience and procedure during the coming days.'

'Yes, Inspector,' she agreed meekly.

Tempest, back in his file box nest, opened his eyes just a little. Through the lids came a livid yellow gleam.

Chapter 39

HILLERS AND HUMPY, AND LOST AND FOUND

Nikolaides reported that Gordon French had told her that Edward Nightingale had told *him* that he'd known Hillers back in the day, and said he would like to talk to her or her husband.

'Maybe he was just interested in what sort of man she married?' suggested Amanda.

'Or … if he had something on her that was disreputable, perhaps he was going to attempt blackmail.'

Amanda gave that a definite no.

'Hillers is unembrarassable.'

'But,' Trelawney countered, 'Humpy was out walking that day that Harold was killed, and surely he could have left The Grange grounds unseen. It's not like they have staff on every lawn.'

She shook her head. 'I don't believe it.'

'Nor do I, but for the sake of due diligence, we cannot rule either of them out until we have spoken to Hillers and Humpy,' Trelawney pointed out. Amanda agreed and phoned The Grange. Moffat answered, informed her that they both were at home, and confirmed that Miss Cadabra and the inspector would be most welcome to visit.

'Knew him?' asked Hillers, spreading butter on a hot toasted crumpet as the four of them sat around the tea tray in the small salon at The Grange. 'Oh yes, we did have a very short fling, if you can call it that,' she continued frankly.

'Did you know this, Humpy?' Trelawney asked her husband.

'No, but dear boy,' he replied with a twinkling smile, 'I knew my girl had had a few tours of duty before she settled on me, y'know. No harm in that.'

'Let me see … what year was that?' Hillers asked herself rhetorically. 'Oh yes, I was up for that committee at the time. I remember him saying that they might not approve of what we were up to.'

That got Trelawney's attention. 'Did he mean that in any threatening way?'

'Good gracious, no,' Hillers replied at once. 'It wouldn't have made a mite of difference. Lady Charnington, the chairwoman, was a lady of the night before she met Charnington. How they met, the word was. No, no, no one was going to be in the least interested.'

'How well did you know Nightingale?'

'Just a few evenings' worth – theatre, dinner, and the rest – and a weekend, I think. He was a no-can-do from the off. A bit intense, don't you know. But thought I might as well take him out for a spin. We must have had some good times. Couldn't have been awful; I'd have remembered. He wanted something more serious, as I recall, so I had to pull the plug. I was never a girl for leading men up the garden path.'

'Can you remember anything about him,' asked Trelawney. 'Did he mention friends, family, problems?'

'Hm … Not that stands out in my memory, I think … he had a rather nice Tiffany lamp … or that might have been someone else. There was … yes, a rather attractive coat of arms on the wall. The Tiffany lamp was in that other chap's penthouse in Mayfair. That's right.'

'Would you object to a visit from him now?'

'What? Course not. Might know something about removing pigeon droppings from roof tiles.'

'The more, the merrier,' agreed Humpy. 'Tell the chap to come for tea.' Then, even more brightly, 'Perhaps he likes 1920s jazz!'

* * *

'A Mr Colin Parker called, sir,' Nikolaides, who had dropped in at the office, told Trelawney, 'and left a message to say he and his partner have found the dog that identifies as that of the Biggerstaffs.' She recited the number. They concluded the call. Trelawney relayed the news to his partner on the other side of the desk, dialled and put the phone on speaker.

'It's ringing. … Hello, Mr Parker? … This is Detective Inspector Trelawney calling regarding the dog you've found.'

'Ah well, it's more that he found us. He was our son's, you see,' Mr Parker explained.

'Bit of a well-meaning, but thoughtless, Christmas present, I'm afraid, from my wife's aunt. More money than sense, though I say it as shouldn't,' agreed Mrs Parker. 'But he's off to uni, and we both work now and can't give Woodie the attention he deserves, so we had him rehomed.'

'But then he came back!' finished her husband.

'Yes, I'm afraid his new owner,' Trelawney said diplomatically, 'was involved in an unfortunate incident. Regarding which, I wonder if we could borrow your dog. Or rather your son's dog.'

'I'm afraid not, Inspector,' replied Mr Parker regretfully.

'We would take good care of him and bring him back safely,' Trelawney assured the couple. 'You could accompany him.'

'Oh no, it's not that. I'm sure you would. But we don't have him anymore.'

'No?'

'I took him to the rescue home,' Mr Parker explained.

'Ah. Would you have an address?'

'Yes, it's the Maysea Centre. Got a pen?'

Trelawney wrote down the details, thanked Mr Parker and finished the call.

'We have a lead,' Trelawney announced with satisfaction to Amanda. 'You never know. If this pans out as I hope, then no extraordinary methods will be required.'

With spirits lifted, they set out in the Mondeo for the Maysea Shelter and Rehoming Centre. Tempest was enthroned on his travel blanket on the back seat.

'I can't imagine why … your … would want to come to a dog home,' Trelawney muttered to Amanda.

She looked over her shoulder to be met with a smug gleam.

'Power trip,' was her answer.

At the entrance to the Maysea, Trelawney showed his warrant card, made the introductions, and they were shown in.

Barking fell silent as Tempest patrolled the space between the kennels. Even Bludger, who had Issues, decided to glare from the safety of his basket rather than the front of his accommodation.

Having reached Howard, the cheerful person in charge, the inspector said,

'I was wondering if we could borrow the dog that was recently rehomed but returned to you yesterday. By a Mr Parker? Woodie?'

'Oh yes, we contacted the rehomers, but apparently, they didn't feel able to take Woodie back. Apparently, they'd had a bereavement, and it seems the dog was there at the time, and the association is just too much for then.'

'So the dog is now here?' Trelawney asked hopefully.

'Oh, no need to worry. A lovely couple visiting the area popped in and fell in love with him at first sight, and Woodie is with them. They live in a beautiful place, and there'll be other animals, and they've invited us to visit. I was so happy for Woodie. He has such a sweet nature.'

'Are they still in the area?'

'I don't think so,' answered Howard. 'They went home the next day.'

'Do you have an address?' asked Amanda.

'Yes, lovely place. Bute.'

'Bute?'

'Yes, it's an island off the west coast of Scotland,' Howard explained.

'Ah.'

Back in the car, Trelawney said energetically,

'It's a long drive, but it may just be the lead we need, no pun intended!'

He dialled the number Howard had given him.

'Hello, this is Detective Inspector Trelawney. I am investigating a case to which your dog may have been a witness, and I was wondering, Mr Han ….'

'Sorry, Inspector, not Mr Han. The name's Joosun; I'm Mrs Han's brother. They're not here, I'm afraid.'

'When will they be back, do you know, Mr Joosun?'

'Not for a while. They're out of the country. I'm here cat-and-house-sitting and doing a refurb on the property.'

'Cat? Not dog?'

'No, they decided to take Woodie with them. Got his chip checked, got the shots, passport and paperwork, and so it's just Maygame the cat, and me, which I must admit makes it easier to get on with the job, even though there are great walks around here.'

'Passport? Where have they gone, may I ask?'

'Bahrain. My brother-in-law is an engineer, and Hannah works remotely, so she can do that from anywhere. They both left for Manama this morning.'

'When will they be back?'

'October 29th. Shall I ask them to call you when they return?'

'That's most kind, but hopefully, the case will be solved by then. If not, I'll ring again.'

'Yes do. I'll tell them you called then.'

'Thank you, Mr Joosun.'

Chapter 40

WOODIE'S PEDIGREE, THE MUSEUM, AND PRESSURE POINT

'Bahrain. Not exactly a drive away,' observed Amanda.

'However,' rallied Trelawney, 'perhaps we can run a sort of thought experiment of a scenario in which he may have been helpful.'

'Yes, what if someone had dropped some valuables at the priory and, when they returned to get them, the dog and, therefore, Harold had already found them and refused to return them?' Amanda suggested. 'Didn't we think of that before?'

'And Janet? *More* valuables? Harold might be the sort to resist handing them over, but Janet?' he asked practically.

'But what if the dog was really sniffing out something someone *didn't* want to be found?'

'If the murderer was watching the priory, he would have seen that dogs investigating wasn't an unusual sight.'

'Hm, I suppose so,' conceded Amanda. 'And when you think of all the dogs that are walked past there, why should *Woodie* have zoned in on the whatever and not the others?' That rang a bell. 'Wait … Cats … white … dogs. Yes, Mrs Vine is a dog specialist of sorts. She used to help out at Crufts, and she said that some dogs are really good at finding things, and some are mad for shiny things. What if …?'

'Well, let's take this one step at a time. Let's find out what breed of dog our Woodie is.'

'Agreed.'

Trelawney called the Centre. The exchange was short. Amanda looked at him expectantly.

'The person who answered the phone doesn't know what breed he was. And Woodie had only just come in when the Biggerstaffs saw him. The staff didn't have time to take a photo to post on the website with particulars, as they normally would have done.'

'All right, but Mr and Mrs Parker would surely have one because I'm sure Mrs Vine would be able to tell us about him.'

The Parkers willingly obliged and sent a few photos to Trelawney's phone. Amanda made a call, and soon they were sitting in Mrs Vine's kitchen as she studied the images.

'Oh yes. Yes, I know what breed your Woodie is. It's rather special, you know: Lagotto Romagnolo. There was a wonderful story on the news about a dog just like Woodie who found buried treasure!'

* * *

'All right, Miss Cadabra,' conceded Trelawney, back in the office. 'So, what if this *is* about location, not Harold. Could something be buried there? Then let's, at least, find out more about what is known about the priory now.'

Consequently, they paid a visit to Barnet Hill Museum. The volunteer there sighed.

'We don't have much on it.' She showed them some black-and-white photos from the 1950s. The priory had more stones then, but that was about all it told them. 'It's not the sort of place that has ever attracted much interest. It's about funding, you see. And there are so many projects on the books with, well, better credentials, if you know what I mean? Besides which, I think the locals are very protective of it.'

'Are they?' enquired Trelawney curiously as they walked back to the car. 'The locals. Protective of the priory?'

'Yes, it's a valuable source of building materials. Has been forever. The door stop for the back doors of the workshop comes from the priory. I only just realised the other day.'

Returned once more to the office, Trelawney sat and stared at his notes on the computer screen. Amanda stood gazing at her whiteboard. Tempest assumed the position in the visitor's chair and snored unhelpfully.

In the silence, Trelawney's phone rang. Amanda started slightly.

'Mike?'

'Thomas. Amanda there?'

'Yes.'

'Put me on speaker, would you?'

'Hello, Uncle Mike,' Amanda called cheerfully.

'Hello, my dear. I'm afraid this is not a social call.' His voice sounded serious.

'Oh.'

'Quite. Just had a call from Crossly.'

'Sir Francis?' she queried.

'The very same. Not a happy bunny. Not a happy bunny at all. An email reached his inbox and flagged up for his attention because it contained the words "Sunken" and "Madley" in the same sentence.'

'From?' asked Trelawney.

'Forwarded by the MP of Chipping North from a Mrs Sharon Biggerstaff.'

'Oh no,' said Amanda with foreboding.

'She expressed her anxiety that her son's case will be shelved in favour of the new victim. Mrs B has urged that extra resources be assigned.'

'Oh dear.'

'Yes, that sort of interference is the very last thing any of us, including Crossly, wants. What he *does* want is this whole business put to bed *tout de suite*. In short, you have to find the killer. As close to now as possible. And, Thomas … by any means necessary.'

They all knew what that meant. Amanda was regarding Trelawney hopefully.

'Understood,' said the inspector calmly. 'Miss Cadabra has suggested … an historical line of enquiry.'

'Is it all you've got? Hogarth asked frankly.

'Yes.'

'Have you consulted Amelia?'

'No.'

'Then do so now, and call me back.'

'Will do,' promised Thomas.

'Yes, Uncle Mike.'

Chapter 41

༄

THE GLASS

'Come in, come in, my sweeties,' Amelia invited them warmly after exchanging hugs with Amanda and Thomas. Her chestnut bob whirled as she turned her head. She led them into the sitting room, her long, embroidered, peach silk coat alternately wafting behind her and brushing her ankles. Tempest was already settling into his favourite chair.

'Tea first! I have scones. We shall do this properly. I popped them into the oven to warm when you called. They should be perfect now.'

'Is there jam?' asked Thomas.

'Strawberry, raspberry and apricot, and anything else you can find in the cupboard.'

'Is there cream?' enquired Amanda.

'Yes, sweetie, non-dairy for you, ordinary for us, Thomas, and Jersey for Tempest.'

Soon they were seated at the round, lace-covered table, stirring tea and spreading helpings of jam and then cream onto their scones.

'Everyone feeling better?' asked Aunt Amelia of her nephew and honorary niece, to whom she had been 'aunt' since Amanda was seven years old.

'Much, thank you,' replied Thomas.

'Definitely,' answered Amanda.

'Then, as this appears to be a matter of some urgency,' observed Amelia, getting down to business, 'perhaps we should begin. Although you didn't say what it was about which Mike has instructed you to consult me, it took only one look at your face, darling Thomas, one look at Amanda's, and one glimpse at old glitter-eyes over there for me to have an inkling.'

Thomas grinned. Amanda chuckled.

'There's no hiding anything from you, Aunt.'

'Well then, I gather that you've hit the buffers with this case of yours, and it would seem that your only option is to seek what leads the past might offer.'

He nodded.

'Thomas, as always, you recognise the risks. Ammee, you, as always, see only the end without comprehending the peril of the means.'

This speech clearly gave the former a degree of satisfaction and a slight frown of confusion to the face of the latter.

'Oh, but I do. As long as I'm careful. I'll have Tempest. Although he always seems to wander off … but anyway, I've always come back alive.'

'Barely,' put in Thomas. 'And some might say, if they were being severe, that it was more by luck than judgement.'

'That would be severe,' agreed Referee Amelia. 'Nevertheless, I gather that this case has become time-sensitive?'

'It has,' confirmed her nephew, and added with a note of frustration, 'If only I had time, I know that I could arrive at the killer's identity through normal procedures.'

'But you no longer have that luxury?'

'Correct. The mother of the first victim has written to the Chief Constable.'

'Oh dear, oh dear. Francis has been on the phone to Mike, then. I quite understand. Very well. You have no other option. Well, tell me about the case, so I have some idea of what to ask the globe.'

Amanda and Thomas took turns relating the case so far, as they made their way through two pots of tea and a mound of scones. Thomas was scraping out the last of the jam pot as Amelia commented,

'Matty. Now that was most interesting, Ammee, and more important than either of you,' she added with an amused glance at her nephew, 'might think. But thank you both. I have what I need. Now, if you two clear the dishes away, I'll fetch the globe.' The younger people accordingly took the empty plates and bowls to the kitchen.

Amelia was an award-winning glass-blower, although she practised her art but rarely these days, diverting her energies into counselling. For some clients, it was just talking; others liked her to use her exquisitely crafted balls of crystal filled with cunningly wrought shapes and colours.

Of all the works up on her shelves, her favourite was the largest, an apparently simple clear globe, in which, on closer inspection, slivers of gold and silver could be observed, floating in an intricate dance around one another. This she now brought to the table on its strangely carved wooden stand of ash and rowan, made by Perran many years ago.

Once they were all seated again, Amelia stilled herself, focused and looked ….

'Matty … there he is … oh, he is a little sweetheart … and now his presence is … yes … monk … where? … Yes, your village … the priory … which one was he? … Not clear … it shows me a group of monks … hm ….' Amelia shook her head gently and moved on. 'When? … A king … Henry … hands … reaching … spires … cloisters … habits and sandaled feet upon the roads … the globe darkens … stars …. The night the bad men came ….'

'Yes,' contributed Amanda softly. 'That's what Matty said.'

'Hm … before dawn …. A new question … the vision at the priory … a man … Yes, murder …' Amelia shook her head a little in confusion. 'Then or now? … It is clouded … I cannot tell …. Will Amanda and Thomas find what they seek there? … The gold within glows … yes. … Yes, but … danger from … from? … Dark … or … something … I cannot tell …. But yes, you find the treasure you seek.'

'Good,' breathed Amanda.

Amelia exhaled and was about to lean away when suddenly her face grew concerned, and she peered into the ball.

'Hm …. Darting … figures … in and away … few …. Very few … but one … perhaps more …. I see only one … the mist … too thick … holding … a staff? … no …. the glass …. Show me … It is clouding … clouding.'

She blew out a breath and sat back. Her face cleared into a smile. 'Well. There. What you seek is there. Amanda, Matty's words provide your fixed point to which to direct your spell: Henry VIII's time. I saw his portrait.'

'The dissolution of the monasteries?'

'Yes. Sunken Madley priory on "the night the bad men came".'

'Got it.'

'Then you must calibrate to a day or so before. That is by no means simple. Time is a slippery customer where magic is concerned. But you can't rely upon turning up at the exact optimum moment. You could turn up during the bad men's advent, which would be disastrous, or just after ….'

'Which would be of no help at all,' observed Amanda. 'What do I do if we get there after the event?'

'Turn round, come back out and recast. That's a lot of magic for one session, though. I'd strongly advise against it. But be positive; visualise the outcome you want, not the ones you don't want, sweetie.'

'Yes, Aunt Amelia.'

They waited for her to say something about the last thing she had seen in the globe, but she was not forthcoming.

'What did you see, Aunt?' Amanda asked. 'At the end?'

'Oh nothing really, not that I could interpret. Perhaps it was something for me or someone else.'

'Ah.'

Chapter 42

The Wisdom of Aunt Amelia

Amelia left the globe on the table while they chatted about Amanda's research into the turbulent times of the 1530s. Finally, Amanda got up to visit the bathroom, and Amelia diverted her to the one upstairs.

Left alone with her nephew, Amelia nodded towards the globe and asked him gently,

'Will you look into the glass, Thomas?'

He started a little.

'What? No. No, thank you … I wouldn't see anything anyway.'

'Are you sure?'

'It would be a waste of time,' he said, falling back on practicality.

'Would it? Of course, if you are sure you will see nothing … then will you not look?' Thomas was silent. He was curious. And yet, the idea of magic still faintly repulsed him. 'You cannot deny you have the gift.'

'The gift of the Flamgoynes,' he objected. 'I refuse to become one of them.'

'The gift of divination is pure,' Amelia answered, 'and cannot be tainted simply because of the nature of those who have possessed it too.'

Thomas could not refute the inescapable logic of this. It calmed him.

'You're right. And I'm sorry. You are nothing like them, of course, Aunt Amelia.'

'Then you have nothing to fear, Thomas.'

He nodded. 'But I *am* afraid. You can resist any …. You have such … goodness … such strength within you.'

She smiled. 'And you have those things in no less measure, my sweetie.'

Thomas nodded again. 'I hope so.'

'You know,' said Amelia, 'I expect to be here for a few decades more. But far in the future, when I am no longer sharing your plane of existence, who will look into the glass for you? Who will look … for Amanda?'

'Can't she …?'

'She is Cardiubarn and Cadabra, my dear, not Flamgoyne. She has not the gift. So who?'

This carried no little sway with him.

'One day. But not yet.'

'I understand. When you are ready, then.' She changed to a lighter note. 'Magic is still far from flavour of the month with Penelope. I did get her to laugh over the predictions for the month on some charlatan astrologer's website, though. I like to think that that's progress.'

'That's further than I've got,' remarked Thomas. 'I can't get anywhere *near* the subject before my mother changes it.'

'She still sees it as what broke up her family.'

'I know. But it was my grandmother's family who did that, not magic,' objected Thomas, then abruptly stopped himself. I can't believe I'm defending it, he thought. Amelia was smiling just a little. He grinned. 'I'm clearly on the slippery slope. Yes, I still "do my thing", as Mike calls it. And I'm pretty comfortable with that.'

'It's a good start.'

'What's a good start?' asked Amanda, returning to the room,

'The work so far,' replied Amelia, as Thomas excused himself to go upstairs.

'I think so. And Aunt, I *do* recognise the risks,' Amanda promised.

'Good. … Good.' A silence fell, until Amelia looked at Amanda and asked,

'You are careful, aren't you, Ammee, when you go into the past?'

'You asked me that before, Aunt. Yes, of course.'

Again a thoughtful pause ensued.

'Have you ever considered …' Amelia began carefully, 'that you are not the only witch in history to have cast the time spell?'

'Erm … well … have there been others?'

'Spell-weavers have largely come from one witch-clan, … by and large,' Amelia observed.

'The Cardiubarns?'

'Yes, and among them, the ones with sufficient power to conjure the charm have been rare. And even those could only manage one large enough for a mouse or perhaps a rabbit ….'

A low purring growl issued from the grey fur mound on the chair by the fireplace. Yellow eyes caught Amelia's brown ones.

'Or a cat,' she added ruefully. 'But one the size of a human … almost unknown.'

That sounded hopeful to Amanda. 'Well then.'

'However, I can think of two others who would have been *capable* of it. One of whom would never harm you.'

'Granny?'

'Of course.'

'Granny once cast the time spell and went back …?' Amanda was astonished.

'No, never that I know of.'

'The other then?'

'One who was perhaps her equal in power … but you are safe from her here … and *now*. And there may have been another. I cannot see …. But you must be careful. I saw but vaguely, not who or when or how. And you must not be alarmed, for these things are open to such wide interpretation, and it is very far from clear to me. I feel in my heart only that I must … not *warn,* but *mention* it to you.'

'Aunt Amelia, what is it? What is it you … saw … you sense?'

'The past is a vast ocean, Ammee, vast. You can travel through it for many, many lifetimes without ever encountering a particular person.'

'All right, but ….'

'Upon or beneath that vast ocean, Ammee, someone … I think ….. oh, I may be wrong. I may have misread entirely …. No, I cannot say.'

'Please, Aunt. All right, I know you may be wrong or have misunderstood. But what is it you *may* have seen?'

'It may be, … and I say only *may* be, that someone, my dear … is hunting you.'

Amanda nodded calmly.

'So I must beware. Be extra careful when I … *if* I visit the past.'

'Yes, sweetie, and you should go for the shortest possible time. Every moment you linger ….'

'I understand.'

'Just be aware. That's all.'

'I promise. I don't take this lightly. I know that magic is a serious business. I'm more and more careful, honestly.'

Amelia smiled. 'Good. That's all right then.' She changed the subject. 'So you've got costumes ready for this venture then, have you?'

'Oh yes,' replied Amanda, her enthusiasm returning.

'Has Thomas seen his yet?'

'No. One thing at a time.'

'Quite right, my dear.'

'What's quite right?' asked Thomas, returning to the room.

'Amanda's preparations. When do you go?'

Thomas looked a question at Amanda.

'I was thinking evening,' she answered. 'If we're supposed to have travelled, then we wouldn't have done so overnight. And the best chance to talk to the monks will be after their working day.'

'Good call,' agreed Amelia. 'What do you say, Thomas?'

He nodded. 'We depart this evening, then.'

Amelia looked at the globe.

'I shall be watching you, my sweeties. Light be with you. And Amanda … when you get there …. do not linger.'

Chapter 43

～

COVERT PREPARATIONS

Amanda and Thomas contacted Hogarth when they got back to the car and related what Amelia had seen and said. Neither mentioned their private conversation with her. Both had independently decided not to.

Thomas will only freak out, Amanda had thought.

Amanda will only start thinking I'm fine with magic, Thomas had thought.

Consequently, Mike got the need-to-know, and was privately well aware of it. He wisely let it go.

'So you're sure this lead is all you've got?' he checked.

'Unfortunately, yes,' admitted Thomas. 'Unless *you* can …?' he asked, clutching at straws.

'Cupboard's empty here, I'm afraid,' confirmed Mike.

His last hope gone, Trelawney said, 'In that case, I can see no other way forward that might get to the truth in the time we have.'

'Then both of you: report on return, good luck, be careful and, for goodness sake, come back alive.'

* * *

At the cottage, where Amanda said she had some things to pick up, Trelawney asked,

'So what's our back story? You're a stripling bringing a message from – Why a *stripling* with a missive of vital importance?'

'The stripling is a nephew,' Amanda replied promptly, stroking Tempest, who was napping across her lap in preparation for the, no doubt, arduous hours to come.

'Oh, *that* sort.'

'Well, could be, or a real nephew or the son of some relative or other, to whom the abbot of the Cornish priory, Tresco, we'll be supposed to be coming from, owes care. Our Tresco abbot thinks that if trouble comes to our abbey, then the young tyro may be safest on the road. And so entrusts him, and a letter, to the care of his faithful Brother Thomas, on account of his excellent English.'

'Bravo. And if anyone happens to drop by from home while we're at Sunken Madley Priory?'

'We have to hope they don't. We shouldn't be there long enough for that,' Amanda added.

'Hopefully. And you're right. Brother Amanda.'

'Austell, I thought,' she suggested.

'Very good. Brother Austell speaks little English.'

'Agreed. But I speak enough should the occasion necessitate it for our advantage. It would make sense that in public, I'll have to speak to you in Cornish, and you'll have to translate or reply as though you've understood me.'

'Hm. Well, if you speak slowly and don't use any long words,' Thomas replied ruefully.

She grinned. 'I can interject some broken English here and there.'

'How kind.'

Amanda laughed.

'Right. We'll most likely meet the guest master first, then, of course, we'll get an audience with the Abbot.'

'Of course?'

'His right-hand man is the prior or sub-prior – I think the two titles are interchangeable – and his Number 2, according to my research, will be the cellarer.'

'Hm, we can expect some opposition from one of those probably,' remarked Trelawney. 'Like a receptionist whose job it is to vet incoming and ensure the boss's time isn't wasted.'

'Probably. Anyway.' Amanda turned her computer screen towards him. He came and sat beside her on the sofa, a safe distance from Tempest, while she explained. 'Here's a plan of a standard abbey of the time, though there were variations and rebuilds. They were set around four sides. See this grass square in the middle? It's called the garth. Now, the church had to be on the north side –'

'Facing east, of course.'

'Yes, I think that much was set in stone, er, so to speak. The accommodations for the monks were down this east side here, along with the Chapter House – a sort of boardroom for daily meetings. The guest quarters were opposite, on the western side, where the gate was set, and along the sound side, the dining room and kitchen.'

'What was the redorter?' he enquired, reading the labels on the plan.

'Dorter was dormitory, and redorter was the lavatory block,' Amanda explained.

'Where's the one for the guests?'

'I can't see one. I'm sure there would have been some sort of arrangement. Now, if we're housed in the guest quarters, the difficulty will be that the monks will be on the other side of the quad, where we can't talk to them.'

'You're sure it was a monk that you saw?'

'Well, I think so. I can't be sure,' Amanda admitted. 'Everyone dressed similarly, I think, in those days. Unless you had stacks of cash.'

'Hm. Ok. Well, we'll have to work with what we've got.'

'Anyway,' Amanda continued, 'if we're lucky and it's one of those monasteries where they have supper, we might get a chance to talk to whoever's next to us then. According to the rule, you didn't get any supper, but, well, it will be after the working day, and even if there's no food, they'll have time to talk to us between services. Besides, as I say, we can't turn up at dawn *before* they start work.'

'Yes, we wouldn't have been travelling overnight. Not with the dire medieval streetlight shortage on country roads,' Trelawney remarked humorously.

'Exactly.'

'Where will you … you know … make that magic gate thing?'

'I'll cast the portal at the edge of the trees,' replied Amanda.

'We'll walk there from The Elms then,' he recommended.

'Yes. What about my car, though? If … by the remotest of possibilities,' Amanda added hastily, 'our stay is protracted, if my car is parked outside your place all night ….'

'Quite, that will undoubtedly give rise to speculation, until the village is used to our occasionally pulling an all-nighter.'

'I'll pretend my asthma or something is playing up,' Amanda offered.

'To give me an excuse to drive from and to the cottage. Good. So, portal in trees. But, surely anyone watching at the priory in the past would be expecting travellers to come from the road,' Trelawney objected.

'We could have cut across the Wood between the Great North Road and Sunken Madley, couldn't we?'

'Yes, I suppose so. Rather daring, considering it's thick in places with wild animals and footpads. Still, I'll say our steps were guided.'

'Ah. *You'll* say?' Amanda queried doubtfully.

'Yes, me.'

'My English would certainly be good enough to speak that line.'

'I thought we agreed. I'll have to take the lead on this one.'

'Hm.'

'It's only practical. If you're posing as a youthful acolyte, it would make sense,' Trelawney said persuasively. 'And … it would probably be to our advantage if you spoke as little as possible.' As soon as he said it, Thomas knew he had phrased it unwisely.

'Oh, it would, would it?'

'Only,' Thomas replied quickly, 'because your voice could easily give you away.'

'I can make it lower if I try,' Amanda insisted.

'I'm sure, but that sort of thing is difficult to maintain.'

'Hm.'

'Look,' Thomas offered appeasingly, 'if ever we are called upon to go back in time and infiltrate a harem, I promise to take the lead from you.'

This conjured up such an entertaining image that Amanda's umbrage evaporated, and she smiled.

'All right. Point taken. Well then, you can say I speak only a little English. I have a little skill with herbs, which will give me a reason to go wandering around the grounds, ostensibly foraging, but mainly I work in the carpentry shop or whatever at our monastery. No ….'

'No?'

'Not "work": "work*ed*". That's our story. We've been sent on the road because our abbot believes the end is nigh for our abbey, and there may well be no carpentry shop for me to go back to.'

'Fair enough. And what do I do?' Trelawney asked.

'Erm … look after the fish in the ponds?' came Amanda's inspiration. 'You know about fish, don't you?'

"Hm. I do, at least, know the theory, but fish in the sea, not in ponds. I expect I can bluff my way, though.'

'So, this evening, having been guided through the dangers of the forest, as you suggest ….'

'Thank you,' he said modestly.

'Oh, stop it,' she chuckled. She regained her countenance. 'At about 6, say, we leave The Elms and make for the trees beyond the priory. I cast the portal far enough into the trees so as to be beyond the border of the priory. I have to shut it once we're through. Can't risk anyone finding it. So once in, we come round to the gate.'

'You'll have your hood up,' recommended Thomas.

'And my hands tucked inside my sleeves,' added Amanda.

'Yes. I'll introduce us and state our errand. We gain admittance, and then what?'

'I suppose we'll be shown to a guest cell.'

'Hm, my first night in a cell,' mused Thomas. 'That should be a memorable experience.'

Amanda laughed

'You know it's not that sort of cell.'

'I do. Go on,' he invited her.

'We'll either be called to see the Abbot before or after dinner, I'm guessing.'

'Probably after. Either way, you will be with me,' Thomas stated firmly. 'You never leave my side. I promised your mother on her deathbed. In the final conversation before she breathed her last.'

'That was very nice of you. Good.'

'So within that loose framework, we're winging it,' he observed drily.

'Well …. yes.'

Chapter 44

∽

THE PROP

'Got costumes then?' asked Thomas, now caught up in the spirit of adventure.

Amanda held up two large carrier bags.

'Robes, rope belts, scrips –'

'Scrips?' Trelawney queried as she handed him his gear.

'Leather pouch. You can attach it to your belt,' Amanda explained. 'We'll each have a larger messenger bag that I've put a few likely things into. We probably would have been expected to carry very little and rely on the charity of wherever we passed through or whomever we encountered. But hopefully, they'll put the luggage down to our strange Cornish ways.'

'Excellent.' He looked inside the carrier bag. 'Beard?'

'Yes. Monks were usually clean-shaven but could grow a beard when travelling. I gather. I couldn't find a wig with a believable tonsure, so we have to explain away your hair. With a beard, it supports your plea that it's grown out on the road, and you only let our brother back in Tresco do your hair. You can say you're going to shave off the beard, and the next time you appear, you're without it.'

'Good thinking.

'And,' – her eyes sparkled – 'I've got something else.'

Between sanding, glueing, and other jobs, Amanda had found a handy block of fine wood and set it to turning and bevelling. Senara had had a necklace of seed pearls that had burst its string. Both she and Amanda, to whom she had given it, had made several attempts at rethreading, but the wilful gems made so many repeated breaks for freedom that they had both agreed to donate the collection to the workshop. It had sat in an old jewellery box for years until ….

'In addition to our costumes. I also made some other little preparation.'

He looked at her in amusement. 'You astonish me.' Then recalling that irony tended to elude Amanda, 'Did you indeed?'

'Yes. I was thinking that a gift from our abbey would go down well, so I made this.' Amanda produced from one of the bags a waxed wooden box, set with a tiny lock and key and offered it to the inspector.

'Hm … what have we here?' Thomas wondered.

'Open it,' Amanda invited him.

He turned the key and lifted the lid. Set within a red felt-lined bed was a cup that appeared to be gold.

'May I?'

'Please.'

He lifted it out carefully.

'I turned a wooden goblet,' Amanda explained. 'Then covered it with Dutch gold foil, you see. Then I set the seed pearls around the base and just below the rim. Oh, and I put a weight in the base to make it feel heavier so that it might, on sight, pass for gold.'

'Clever,' Thomas remarked admiringly. 'It's quite exquisite. Yes, I imagine this would please the recipient greatly. Well done, Amanda. Well done.'

'Thank you, Thomas. You'd better be the one to present it.'

'I suppose I had. It seems a shame that you should not get the credit.'

'Oh,' answered Amanda, gazing heavenward, 'that would be prideful.'

'So it would! Good point.'

Once arrived at The Elms, while Trelawney finished up some admin, Amanda retired to the bathroom to effect her transformation. Presently she emerged, hood up, hands tucked in her sleeves and her eyes downcast.

'Ah, Brother Austell, I presume?' commented Thomas.

She looked up with a mischievous smile. Her face scrubbed free of makeup, looked more youthful than ever.

'What do you think?' Amanda asked hopefully.

'Pretty convincing. If you avoid that expression.'

She grinned and put back her hood. A wig of short brown hair covered her usual untameable locks. A leather pouch hung from her rope belt. Thomas looked over her appearance.

'That will certainly do. No tonsure?'

'I'm just a novice, so I wouldn't have shaved the crown of my head yet. Actually, I wouldn't have been sure about which way to do that because, I think, the Celtic monks didn't do the helmet hair thing but instead did the front half of the head. But I'm not sure which centuries they did that in.'

'Well, we'll leave it at the no-tonsure-for-tyros then. Er …' he glanced at her flattened upper torso. 'Ah. Er, how did you, er …?'

'Sports bra,' Amanda replied succinctly. 'And I've got an old cotton petticoat underneath for a shift, and I don't care what the true-to-history requirements might be; I am *not* sacrificing my 21st-century lingerie.'

'Quite.'

'It's not like either of us is going to be dancing on any tables.'

'I should certainly hope not!' Thomas agreed heartily. 'All right. My turn. I shan't keep you waiting long.'

Amanda stashed her modern clothes in a corner of the sitting room. After a few minutes, he came out of the bedroom, bearded and robed. Amanda gazed in horrified astonishment at his transformed countenance.

'What do you think?' asked Thomas.

'Dreadful,' she replied at once. 'That is … er, you look the part.'

He grinned. 'The beard, eh? Don't worry, I won't try to kiss you …' Thomas had no idea why he'd said that. 'Er, I mean … The Big Tease … Joan … Ruth … you, er ….'

'Oh! Haha, yes indeed,' Amanda responded quickly. 'Of course. Yes, haha, well, thank you for your consideration …. Of course …' Suddenly, she knew and didn't know what she was about to say.

'Of course … if I …?' Thomas began.

It hung in the air for an instant as they looked at one another, somehow rooted to the spot, until they both said at once:

'We should go.'

Chapter 45

୧ଓ

BEYOND THE GATE

Amanda and Trelawney made it out of The Elms, across the Upper Muttring road and into the edge of the Wood unseen. Once screened by sufficient trees and to the south of where the priory wall was going to be, Amanda took out her patent Pocket-wand. This invention of Dr Bertil Bergstrom's hid a slim shaft topped with citrine within an ordinary-looking Ikea pencil, with a cunningly concealed lid at the end. She withdrew the wand from its holder and, holding it to her heart, she addressed Lady Time,

'*Hiaedama Tidterm, Hiaedama Tidterm, Ime besidgi wou. Agertyn thaon portow, hond agiftia gonus fripsfar faeryn ento than aer deygas.*'

There came the expected jolt in her vision as she saw the other side of the portal. Amanda led the way with Tempest, and Thomas followed. They were only just inside the trees. The priory ruins must have been swallowed up by the Wood in the present. Gone was the estate opposite, and the priory wall stretched out in front of them to the left; to the right, they could see the entrance and someone pruning greenery nearby.

Having established that they were, apparently, in the right place and time, Amanda turned back.

'I have to close the portal,' she said quietly. Thomas nodded. She spoke the words of the spell. He saw it collapse and vanish.

'Ready?' Trelawney asked.

Amanda smiled, put up her hood, shouldered her pack more comfortably, and hid her hands in her sleeves.

'Ready, Brother Thomas. Lead on.'

They approached the west gate, which according to Amanda's research, would be where guests would be received and settled in the block on that side of the cloister.

A man of middle years and height, in thigh-length tunic and hose, was tending the grounds before the priory and looked up. As they approached, he put back the hood protecting his head from the last of the sun and hailed them with a smile and a wave.

'Welcome, good brothers. I am Abel, both in name and body, still, for which I am thankful.'

'Greetings, Abel. I am Brother Thomas, and this is Brother Austell. We have journeyed from our house, Tresco Priory in Cornwall, with a letter for the Abbot here.'

'Oh, by all the saints, you have come far! Though not as far as some. Yes, come, come in.'

As they followed their guide, Amanda glanced down at the plants Abel had been tending, for there, in the air, was the unmistakable fragrance of sage. Sure enough, there was a bush of the herb a little to the right of the gate.

The entrance hall was a wide corridor that gave onto a cloister that ran around all four sides of the central garth.

'Well,' said Abel amiably, 'if you'll follow me to the guest quarters.'

'Thank you. Accommodation with our brothers will do very well for us,' Thomas essayed.

'The guest house has the more comfort, and the dorter is only for those of our house,' explained Abel.

'Of course,' Trelawney conceded with a smile.

Abel led the way, observing,

'Your young brother's pack is fragrant.'

'Brother Austell has some knowledge of herbs and found some as we walked through the woods.'

'A healer?'

Amanda kept her head down. She'd crammed an assortment from the garden in there. 'He has some small skill,' replied Trelawney, with an air of modesty on his companion's behalf.

Abel opened a door and gestured for them to enter. They had been expecting a small, bare-walled room, perhaps with pallets stacked in a corner. But it was surprisingly large, panelled, and fitted out with two beds, a table on which candlesticks were set, a chest with a bowl on the top, and a cupboard.

'Aye, t'is better appointed than many you'll find in a holy house,' remarked Abel seeing their surprise. 'And the Abbot keeps a good table thanks to Brother Cellarer, though it gives me little pleasure to own it. But so he does, for all his finical ways and goin' about like the air isn't good enough for his nose. Even the Abbot himself is not so high and mighty, although he has his ways. But like I say, our quarters are better than most, and so it must be, so close to London and many a fine gentlemen and lady passing this way, as well as royalty, if we're out of luck.'

'Out of luck?' enquired Trelawney, keen to keep the man talking.

'They are a costly crew. Still, it is also to the credit of our house and perhaps may mean we are spared if there are more bad times to come. The King claims otherwise, insisting the bigger houses are safe. Though few credit it, if all that comes to my ears is to be believed. Still, I must not be tattling when there's work to be done. Let me show you where you can wash, though I shall bring you water presently too.'

Abel showed them a small room where they might perform their ablutions and an even smaller one that he called an 'easement' room, the progenitor of the lavatory. Amanda had thoughtfully supplied them with linen squares for loo roll.

'I dare say the Abbot will see you after supper, which is not long now. I will take word of your arrival to the Abbot and fetch water.' As Abel departed, Trelawney saw him giving Amanda a shrewd but kindly glance. He mentioned it to her once they were alone.

She looked at Thomas with concern. 'Oh dear. I hadn't calculated for a lay servant who would have more experience with the contrasting forms between the genders. Do you think he's seen through my disguise?'

'Possibly. Hm. Awkward, but he seems a well-meaning soul. I was hoping we might at least be able to visit the redorter as an excuse to go about the priory at night, if necessary.'

'Same here,' Amanda agreed wistfully.

'Never mind. We'll work with what we have. Anyway, it's most likely communal, which could be a bit awkward for you. Now, I'll leave you two together when Abel comes back. See if he says anything to you that suggests he's seen through your monk's habit.'

Abel returned with good news:

'The Abbot will see you at supper after Vespers and afterward in his study. Shall I point out where everything is? So you get your bearings.' Trelawney accepted with thanks. 'I have served here man and boy, and my father before him. My wife and children and I live yonder, close by on priory grounds. I help the guest master, who is getting along in years, but still much respected by the brothers. A good man and master. I am happy to give him ease from whatever duties I can.'

'Most kind,' responded Thomas.

'I do not go much beyond the west side here but am called at times to aid further within the priory. So I can at least point out – wait. The brothers are at prayers. Perhaps I can *show* you where all is situated if you are interested, Brothers?'

'Please,' said Trelawney.

'Wait here, if you will, while I make sure ….'

They watched him cross the quad, looking around the cloisters as he went. Then, having reached the east side, Abel leaned out between the pillars and beckoned.

Amanda had a strange sense of déjà vu.

'All right?' Thomas asked, seeing the slight frown on her face.

'Yes, I just …. We'd better go to Abel.'

Chapter 46

∾

THE CLOISTER

They walked along the south cloister and around to the east to join their guide. Abel pointed behind him and up, and spoke softly.

'That's where the brothers sleep.'

The dorter, Trelawney recalled the label on Amanda's priory plan.

'And here is the Chapter House. As guests, I don't know if you'll be called to meetings about the running of this abbey, but just in case. You'll need to know where the refectory is. Now, if you'd come in my grandfather's time, I'd have sent you there,' he said, gesturing to the south side.'

'Has it moved?' asked Thomas curiously.

'Yes, when the watercourse below shifted. The buckets from the well came up dry, and father said as they hired a *druid,* would you believe? And he divined the new path of the water. I don't know as how much you'd credit such a story, but in any case, the refectory and kitchen beside it were shifted to by the wall of the church there, and a new chimney built between them to heat the stove and, on cold evenings to warm the refectory, where there is a handsome fireplace. Though t'is warm now and so not lit; in winter, it is a fine sight!'

Trelawney smiled. 'I'm sure. You have seen it, then?'

'Oh yes, when there are large parties, I do help to serve the food and clear up after.'

'Are you shorthanded?'

'Have been these past few years. Ever since … the smaller houses … the King … many brothers, and sisters too, have thought better of their calling and found it elsewhere.' He lowered his voice. 'My old aunt. Passed these eight months since, rest her soul, used to say rats leaving a sinking ship. She had no love for the church, you know, but she did have the right of it. They say, behind their hands mind, that t'is only a matter of time until all the houses are gone. But for such words, I could be put in the stocks, so I beg you, Brothers, you will not repeat it.'

'It is no less than we have heard whispered elsewhere, I promise you, good Abel,' Trelawney assured him.

'Ah well, Brothers, you had best make ready for supper. And I will bring you water.'

'Thank you. I must shave,' said Thomas.

When Abel returned, he found Amanda alone. He was bearing a large earthenware jug, a piece of cloth, and a chamber pot to which he drew Amanda's attention as he slipped it beneath the bed. She looked at him with a smile from the shadow of her hood.

Amanda attempted some broken English: 'You do say … be your family here in abbey grounds?'

'Yes, Brother,' he confirmed, pouring water from the jug into the bowl on the top of the chest. He seemed unsurprised that she could speak in his tongue.

'Abel … you seem a good man.'

'So I should hope … Brother.'

She decided to abandon her ruse of the English language beginner but kept her Cornish accent and uttered in lowered tones, 'We are here on the business about which we spoke. We come with a warning for this house. The thing about which there is talk? It is imminent.'

Abel showed no surprise at Amanda's suddenly acquired grasp of his mother tongue but looked at her, holding the jug close to him. 'Henry is coming for our house?'

'It is certain sure.'

'But all are pensioned off, are they not?' he asked hopefully.

'Not the servants. There have been stories of lay servant families thrown in the streets. Deprived of lodging and even their goods without recompense or warning. You must make provision for you and family, good Abel, and be ready to get them away at a moment's notice.'

He came to her side and asked earnestly, 'Are you sure, Brother?'

Amanda nodded. 'I am certain of it. You must not expose your family to mistreatment by Henry's men.'

'Is the King truly set upon this course?'

'He is.'

Abel stood and stared at the floor in thought. Finally, 'Thank you then for this warning. I shall make preparation. My wife's brother is the baker in the village. He and his wife will take us in.' He looked around. 'This has been my home … all I have known … and my children too …' He turned back to Amanda. 'But all will be well. Thank you, Brother… or should I say … Sister?'

Amanda's eye's widened.

'Nay, mistress, I have a wife and three sisters. Shame on me if I did not know a woman when I see one. And what better excuse to hide your sweet voice than to say you have not the English tongue? But take no thought to it. The brothers will not see through your disguise, I promise you. They have few dealings with those of your gentle kind. Your secret is safe with me, though. What of Brother Thomas?'

'He, too, is privy to my concealment,' she assured him, relieved by his kind response.

'And so I thought. Well, he seems a good man and true. You have done me and my family a great service this day. If there is any way in which I might repay it, you have only to say.'

'Thank you, Abel.'

Trelawney returned.

'All well?' he asked.

'Truly, Brother. I have something to attend to. I'll be back when the bell sounds for supper. After you have spoken with the Abbot, you can find me hereabouts if you have need of anything for the night.' With those words, he departed.

Thomas removed his beard and hid it in his pack. Amanda pushed back her hood, washed her hands, and dried them on the length of linen Abel had left by the bowl.

'I hope you don't mind,' she whispered. 'I told Abel. To get his family out.'

'Won't this change history?' asked Thomas uncertainly.

'Well, I'm hoping they'd have got out anyway,' was Amanda's tenuous reply.

'Hm. Well. Fair enough.'

'Oh, don't forget your dinner knife. I put one in your pack. Everyone had one.'

'Bring-your-own-cutlery, eh?' Thomas remarked.

'Yes, but we're in the pre-fork age,' Amanda explained. 'so it's knife, spoon and fingers.'

'Got it.'

'So let's get supper over with, and then you can talk to the Abbot and find out what's going on here,' she urged.

'Oh, I can, can I? Just like that?'

'Yes,' came the confident response, 'you've won, erm, commendations for your interview technique. If anyone can get any info out of the Abbot, you can.'

'Those legendary interviews took place over weeks, months even,' Thomas informed her.

'Well, but can't you sort of do a condensed version of your technique?' Amanda suggested optimistically.

'No,' answered Thomas shortly. 'Then again … if the Abbot is only slightly less arrogant than the Cellarer, as described by our new friend, then I suspect the man at the top is an inveterate snob. I could do little name-dropping, I suppose, to soften him up.'

Amanda's face brightened. 'There! I knew you'd come up with an idea,'

'No, you didn't; you hoped I wouldn't come along at all,' he pointed out.

'Yes,' she freely admitted, 'but that was *before*.'

'Before what?'

'Before I could see how useful you'd be,' Amanda said frankly.

'Oh, "useful"? Delighted to be of service, ma'am,' Thomas responded with the slightest hint of acerbity. Amanda beamed at him. 'All right. Well, you'll have to give me some names to drop.'

'Erm … the Arudells were a distinguished Cornish family. And mention the Treffy family. They helped keep the French at bay during the last century before this one. Oh and … ' But the bell rang, and Abel could be heard returning to escort them.

Chapter 47

༼

The Refectory

Amanda pulled her hood further down over her face as a monk who was Amanda's image of Friar Tuck – elderly, portly, with a slightly rolling gait and friendly aspect – approached. He was still blinking and a little bleary-eyed from his nap.

'Ah, welcome, Brothers! I am Bernard, the guest master, and I see our Abel has made you at home. Brother Thomas, is it?' he addressed Trelawney.

'Good evening, Brother Bernard. This is my companion and charge, Brother Austell.'

Amanda respectfully bowed her head.

'From Cornwall, are you?' Brother Bernard enquired as they set out with him around the covered walk of the cloister.

'We are, Brother. Brother Austell has but the Cornish tongue and a few words of English.'

There was no chance to say more, for a tall monk with close-cropped blonde hair and pale eyes was coming to meet them. His head was held high on his craned neck. No doubt, surmised Trelawney, he topped most of his brethren, and was accustomed to looking down his nose at the slightest infraction. The monk progressed towards them with an officious walk.

'Ah,' said Bernard with mixed emotions. 'Here is Brother Pius; come to greet you.' And so he was, by name and nature. He gazed down his nose at Amanda. 'Here is Brother Thomas and Brother Austell, Brother.'

Pius nodded at them graciously.

'Welcome, Brother Thomas and Brother Austell. I am Brother Pius, the Cellarer.'

Figures, thought Amanda.

'Forgive my not greeting you earlier,' he went on, 'I have many things to attend to. I trust Brother Bernard has settled you in your quarters?'

'Indeed. Thank you, Brother,' Thomas answered.

'It is unfortunate that you did not arrive in time for *Vespers*.' There was a critical note in Pius's voice.

'But we look forward to Compline,' replied Thomas calmly.

'Hm. I see you do not take the tonsure, Brother Thomas. Is it not the rule in your Cornish house?' The word 'Cornish' was spoken with a note of disdain.

But Amanda had prepared Trelawney for this one. 'Indeed, Brother Pius, it is, but our journey has been lengthy, and it has grown out upon the road, as has my beard.'

'Well, our brother Theodoric can attend to it for you before Compline if Father Gideon concludes his meeting with you in time,' stated the Cellarer.

'You are kindness itself, Brother Pius,' Trelawney replied smoothly, 'but I would not rob our Brother Caradoc back home of his privilege. It means a great deal to him to express his devotion by this office to all in our house, and our abbot is most insistent that we allow no other to see to this matter. The beard I shall attend to before service.'

'Hm. As you wish. And this is your novice, I see?'

Amanda bowed her head.

The Refectory

'Yes, Brother,' confirmed Trelawney. 'He does not have much English as yet.'

This did not seem to please the Cellarer. 'But he must learn,' insisted Pius. 'Our services are being conducted in English and with the King's Bible.'

'And so I have been instructing him upon the journey.'

Pius regarded Amanda's covered head doubtfully. He ushered them into the rectangular refectory. From the shadow of her hood, Amanda observed the long table flanked by benches. The wall opposite the door bordered that of the church; to the left, in a short wall, was a fireplace, unlit, as Abel had predicted. In colder months, however, it would provide comfort, especially for the occupant of the carved chair that was clearly reserved for the Abbot.

Brother Pius looked at the visitors and gestured towards the middle of the bench by the church wall side and near the Abbot's end of the table.

'Brother Cury, you shall sit beside Brother Austell today.' he stated, signing for the man to move down the table to allow places for Amanda and Trelawney. Then addressing Thomas: 'Brother Cury is a fellow countryman of yours. Perhaps he may be of assistance in improving your companion's English.'

'It would be my privilege,' responded a stocky, dark-brown, curly-topped and tonsured monk of middle years, with a smile at Amanda. She bobbed her head respectfully.

'Brother Barnabas.' A young light-brown-haired monk with violet eyes and a gentle demeanour that held an otherworldly gaze seemed to return to earth at hearing his name. The Cellarer motioned Barnabas, whose seat Amanda was taking, to go to the opposite side.

'Yes, Brother Pius?' he asked.

'Today, you shall sit between our pilgrim, Brother Venables and Prior Stephen.' Amanda gathered Prior Stephen had yet to make his entrance. Venables had little that was memorable about him, apart from a pair of soft, deep brown, what Amanda immediately labelled to herself as 'puppy eyes'. Next, Pius introduced some of the other brothers as they came in and took their places,

Now, a somewhat portly man with a worried expression came into the refectory. From the lines on his face, it would seem that this had been a permanent fixture for some time.

'Brother Stephen, we have guests. Brother Thomas from Tresco Priory in Cornwall and his companion Brother Austell. This is Prior Stephen.'

All three bowed their heads in greeting.

'Welcome, both of you,' said Stephen. 'Brother Bernard has, er …?'

'Most kindly,' Thomas answered warmly.

'Well, good, good,' replied Stephen, as though relieved at having one thing fewer to worry about. 'Cornwall? Ah yes. All is … well there, I trust?'

Amanda knew that this was a reference to the uprising of the Cornish against the Crown only some 40 years ago. Suddenly she recalled that an Arundell had been involved and executed. I must head Thomas off if he tries to name-drop that one, she reminded herself.

'All well, I thank you, Brother,' Trelawney was answering, concealing his bemusement at the emotion behind the man's question. One of the dates that Thomas did know was that of the Prayer Book Rebellion, but that was not going to take place for another ten years.

But now, here entering was one on whom Brother Pius could not look down. Equalling Trelawney's six foot, he had a slightly heavier build though he carried it lightly, and it seemed only to add to his physical presence. This was enhanced by the plentiful silver-grey hair on either side of the bald crown that extended forward from his now natural tonsure. The light-brown eyes appeared kindly, and the man exuded a slightly vacant, distracted air.

Pius gestured as one pulling a rabbit from a hat.

'Father Giles, Abbot of our priory. Here we have Brother Thomas and his novice Brother Austell come from Tresco Priory, our order's house in Cornwall.'

'Ah,' the Abbot uttered benevolently, 'our visitors. We shall be relaxing our rule of dining in silence this evening, that we might exchange news of such matters of the outside world that may have a bearing on our life here at the priory.'

'Of course,' agreed Brother Stephen anxiously. He turned an ear to Pius, who imparted something in a low voice.

'And here,' went on the Abbot, 'is one of your fellow countryman whom, no doubt, you have already met. Brother Cury, come take your place by our guest, Brother Thomas.'

'Or perhaps, by Brother Austell,' suggested Prior Stephen, going to his place at the Abbot's right hand, 'as he speaks little English, I gather, from Brother Pius.'

Pius inclined his head in a gesture that combined both pride in his organisational skill and a proper degree of modesty.

'Indeed,' concurred Father Giles.

Pius took up his station at the left hand of the Abbot with Thomas on his left.

With all in position, the Abbot intoned the words of grace, and the monks got into their seats on the benches.

Food was brought in by one of the brothers and a lay monk. There was bread and roasted fish – 'From our own ponds,' Brother Pius informed Trelawney with pride – and vegetables, early apples and blackberries.

Cury turned blue-green eyes to Amanda with the same warm smile as before. '*Gorthugher da, Broder.*'

Amanda, still with her hood forward, returned his smile and greeting, hoping her Cornish was up to a medieval test of it.

His first question, she gathered, was asking where she was from.

'*Dhyworth bargen tir war Goon Brenn, Broder.*' Amanda was glad she'd prepared her backstory of being from a farm on Bodmin Moor.

'*Ah. Ty a wor Melor Minear?*'

She had anticipated someone at the priory knowing someone there and asking if she was acquainted with them.

'*Ni wruussyn ni diberth an bargen tir yn fenowgh,*' Amanda replied, claiming a secluded life. '*Kyns my dhe glewes an galow.*' "Until I heard the call." Cury was listening carefully as though struggling with her dialect but, hopefully, was putting it down to an isolated family existence.

'Ah.'

She had to get him talking and trust she'd be able to follow him. '*Ha ty?*'

Cury replied that he was from St Neot.

Good grief, thought Amanda, just my luck to meet someone from the edge of The Moor!

But Cury was going on to say that they would have more opportunity to speak after Compline, as he had been given leave by Father Giles.

Trelawney, meanwhile, was being asked about 'his' abbey and was being general. The subject of the closure of the monasteries was only lightly touched upon. Of course, any rumours that the larger houses might be likewise seized by the Crown were forbidden by law.

During the conversation, Amanda had leisure to observe, from beneath her hood, those at table. She could not help but allow her gaze to alight on Brother Barnabas; he was, in a word, beautiful. She noticed how his eyes watched the Abbot and turned often and long toward those he addressed, but especially Trelawney. Puppy Eyes paid proper attention to the Abbot but otherwise maintained a respectful silence, when not requesting someone to pass the bread. They probably usually signed that, thought Amanda. Must make a nice change to say it out loud.

Thomas asked about the Priory. Amanda followed the conversation closely, alert for any clues that might explain the deaths of Harold and Janet in her own time. Or the identity of the monk whom she had seen.

Her facial recognition was minimal. She recalled nothing of the features of the person whose image had appeared to her so briefly. But surely there was one here who might give her information about her own time. So far, her fellow countryman seemed the most promising candidate, and yet Abel was the more likely. Of course … although he wore, not the habit, but tunic over hose, he also sported a cowl to shade his head from the sun. Amanda had assumed the figure was that of a monk simply because it was at the priory, but … the man had leaned out from behind one of the great stones, only showing his upper half. Was it possible that the person she had seen was …. Abel?

* * *

They had been gone some two hours. In the darkness of the office at The Elms, a phone in the desk drawer lit up, but its ring was silenced.

Chapter 48

∽

The Study

With the meal concluded, the Abbot requested the guests' attendance in his study. The Prior and Pius seemed to take their own invitation for granted. Cury was asked to come along but to wait outside the door in case there was need of him. Barnabas was dispatched to bring a little mead.

Once within and invited to be seated on the other side of the table, Trelawney turned to Amanda, who brought forth their gift from her scrip and handed it to him. He, in turn, rose and, standing, presented it to the Abbot. Pius scuttled over to intercept it and took it to pass it on himself.

'A gift, Father,' Thomas explained, 'from our Tresco Priory: a gesture of our Abbot Petroc's good will toward a sister house.'

The Abbot expressed surprise. 'Petroc? Is Father Sulien no longer with us?'

Amanda coughed.

'A sickness took him,' replied Thomas solemnly.

'Ah. Well, this is most kind.' Giles inspected the wooden box, turned the little key and opened it. The raised eyebrows and smile indicated his approval. He looked up from under bushy eyebrows. 'Pearls ... most generous, most generous.'

There was a knock at the door, and Barnabas, on being invited to enter, brought in cups and a bottle, placed them on the table and retreated to a word of thanks from the Abbot. 'And now,' he said, as Pius dispensed the wine, 'to the letter.'

Trelawney rose again and pre-empted Pius by saying. 'I have vowed to place it in your own hands,' and suited the action to the word.

The Abbot opened the seal. Amanda had watched a video on creating medieval letters. She had followed the instructions on how to fold a sheet of paper and apply wax to form an envelope.

Giles read it with every appearance of polite interest. Then he put it aside and steepled his fingers while he contemplated. The company maintained silence. Finally, the Abbot cocked his head, looked first at his prior, then the Cellarer, and came to a decision.

He turned his gaze on Trelawney. 'It would seem that you are privy to the contents of this missive, Brother Thomas.' Brother Thomas realised he had omitted to enquire of Brother Austell exactly what the contents of the letter he was carrying might be. All he could do was go with the flow.

'I am, Father,' he answered confidently.

'Very well. Brother Stephen and Brother Pius, tomorrow at Chapter, I shall be informing our brothers that the King is to pass an edict granting him appropriation of the larger monastic houses. Our own, no doubt, to be among them. I have been approached in the past, urged to offer cooperation in return for a pension or compensation of some sort. This temporal reward has been accepted by many smaller houses and even those of greater size. But know this: ours shall not be among them. This priory shall make a stand. Thus far and no further shall the King's hand go in seizing what is spiritual.'

'But, Father,' protested Stephen, 'surely the King's men will be armed and shall overpower us if we resist. What of our brothers turned out destitute upon the road?'

'Henry's men shall not dare trespass,' stated Giles. 'Was not he who touched the Ark of the Covenant struck down?'

'But did not Jerusalem fall, Fa–?'

'Father Giles has spoken, Brother Stephen,' intervened Pius. 'His faith does us credit. We all do well to emulate it. Our father does, after all, speak for our House, and I, for one, shall follow his example in faith.'

Stephen looked from one to the other. Then turned to Trelawney as if for support.

'Your own abbey, Brother Thomas …?'

'When we return,' answered Trelawney, 'we have no expectation of being able to go back there, Brother Stephen. We intend, once we have seen what can be done to aid our brethren, to go to my family on the coast.'

'Father,' Stephen entreated Giles, 'surely you will not say that the Abbot of Tresco lacks faith? Surely he has only a care for those under his ….'

'It is not for me to pass judgement on another. I have long expected this and come to this decision. It is done,' ruled the Abbot.

'Amen,' intoned Pius.

The Abbot rose and addressed Trelawney and Amanda.

'Thank you for your delivery of this letter and your gift. You are welcome to spend however many days you wish with us, Brothers, before you make your return to your own land. And now let us prepare for Compline.'

They found Cury and Barnabas outside the door in conversation. They were dismissed to get ready for the last service of the day. Trelawney and Amanda returned to the guest house to wash.

'What did you make of all of that?' he asked her.

'He seems determined.'

'Did you get anything from our Cornish brother? What were you saying, by the way?'

'Just dodging questions about my place of origin,' answered Amanda. 'Nothing more, but we have permission to speak after Compline – briefly, I expect. And you?'

'Table chitchat for general consumption, but ... I did notice one thing: Giles's eyes. I was never quite sure if he was looking at me or beyond me or ....'

'Perhaps he sees, well ... like I do Granny and Grandpa?' suggested Amanda.

'Possibly. Did *you* see anyone from their ... plane of existence?'

'No,' she admitted. 'I noticed Barnabas seemed fixated on Giles.'

'Hm, yes, but perhaps it's not often he hears the Abbot speak so much outside office hours,' Thomas replied reasonably.

'Could be. Oh, by the way, if do need to name-drop, don't mention Arundell after all. He was involved in a revolt and came to a sticky end.'

'Noted.'

Soon, responding to the Compline bell, they headed to the church. Amanda had wondered what it would be like, going into the whole structure, a part of which was so much a part of her life in the present. There, to her right, as they entered through the west side, were the nightstairs, the flight that led from the dorter above down into the church for services held in the hours of sleep. For a moment, she had a flash of the ruins with her makeshift platform above those very stairs. Then it was gone.

The church lacked the homely feel of the parish's St Ursula-without-Barnet, but then this place was mainly for the monks.

They followed the service as best they could. Amanda could not help her attention drifting again and again to the nightstairs in the corner of the church. *Her* nightstairs, at the top of which was *her* 21st-century eyrie. And then her gaze would sweep to the wall, amidst whose broken stones she had seen the figure that had beckoned to her that Sunday far, far in the future.

Chapter 49

༷

THE GUEST CHAMBER

Compline concluded, Thomas returned to the guest house and removed his beard to his pack, and Amanda waited to have a few words with Cury.

'So … the last Cornish houses are to go,' he said regretfully in Cornish as they sat on a bench in the east cloister.

'And this one … what will you do?' Amanda asked.

'I think we have no choice. If it is the Abbot's will … and yet he seems certain that Henry's men will yield to the voice of the church at the front gate. What can any of us do … but have faith?'

'Could you not approach the Abbot?'

'No, no, Brother. He says he has everyone's best interests at heart, but,' Cury said, then lowered his voice, 'I am not sure that he included me.'

Amanda was surprised. 'Why ever not? What makes you think that?'

'Father Abbot keeps looking at me. At every meal, except last night, probably because he was paying attention to Brother Thomas. But usually, whenever I look up, I find him … studying me as though he suspects something. But I have done nothing, nothing,' Cury insisted.

'Perhaps he thinks you look like someone he knows?' hazarded Amanda.

'Then why not ask me?'

'Well … perhaps it is someone he doesn't get on well with,' she suggested lamely.

He shrugged helplessly.

'I suppose so.'

'You could mention it to the Prior, perhaps? Brother Stephen?'

'No. No, I don't want to make a fuss or seem too much concerned with something that is personal.'

'I understand.' That subject having run its course, Amanda had to take what might be her sole opportunity to follow the line of enquiry she had come to the monastery to pursue. 'May I ask, Brother, on another subject, have you ever seen anyone in strange garb? A young man, here? With a dog? Perhaps here in the refectory or … upon the garth?'

'In strange garb? Why no, Brother.'

'Or a woman?'

'A servant?' Cury suggested.

'In strange attire?'

He shook his head.

Amanda phrased her next enquiry carefully, 'Perhaps one who appeared as a spirit?'

'A vision? Of our blessed St Ursula? No, Brother, that has not been granted to me.'

Pius then called Cury to go to his rest, and Amanda went to join Trelawney.

'Well?' he asked as she entered their quarters, where Abel had lit the candles.

'Nothing much,' she replied regretfully. 'Just it seems that if Giles says "we shall not be moved", then the rest of the house must follow suit and damn the consequences.'

Abel knocked on the door.

'All well?' he asked.

'Yes and no, in truth,' replied Amanda, 'The Abbot intends to make an announcement tomorrow that he will oppose the handing over of the house to the King.'

The man's face grew grave.

'I don't suppose Father Giles is amenable to reason?' asked Thomas.

'No.' Abel shook his head. 'Of that, I am certain. For all his mild manners, there is a core of iron there and no mistake. But I have said more than I should. What will be, will be. Have you all you need for the night, Brothers?'

'Yes, Abel, thank you. But will you not sit a while?' Amanda invited him, hopefully.

He hesitated for a moment, then, 'Well … I shall. Let me bring us a little wine.' He disappeared for a few moments and returned with a skin bottle and three goblets. Seated at the table, he poured it, saying, with pride, 'T'is of my own making, Brothers. Elderberry. An old family recipe.'

Amanda had been caught out before with homemade elderberry wine and knew from experience how potent it could be. But this seemed mild.

'Most pleasant, Abel,' she remarked with a smile.

'Well, and so my wife says too.'

It was clear to Trelawney that Abel had warmed to Amanda, so he left the enquiries to her while he sat back and listened and watched.

'What can you tell of those whom we met this evening?' she was asking.

'Well, now.' Abel leaned back comfortably. 'You should know that Father Giles is of an aristocratic family. So no surprise Brother Pius fawns over him, for he is also of minor gentry and sets great store by such things, in spite of disdain for earthly matters. He harbours a secret jealousy, I have no doubt, of Brother Barnabas, who is distant kinsman to Father Giles.

And even of the Prior, even though he himself had some station in the world too before he took the cowl. T'is all writ in a book – but only the Abbot's eyes light upon it – because all renounce their worldly titles on entering the priory and speak of them to no man. But there will always be talk amongst the lay monks and we servants.'

'You are not bound by the rule of silence?'

'By no means. But even the monks will talk, given opportunity. To be silent goes against the rule of man's nature, after all, if you ask me. Or woman's, though my daughter is the more the thoughtful of our children and t'is our son has plenty to say!'

'Let's say the nature of humans, then,' Amanda suggested with a smile.

'Aye, I'll raise my cup to that.' They all took a sip, and then, casually, she enquired,

'And Brother Stephen, the Prior, what is his position? The measure of his influence.'

'He supports the Abbot, of course,' Abel replied at once, 'but would steer this house to a different tack in many things, I think, if he were in Father Giles's shoes.'

'And our Cornish brother?'

'A kind and devout soul, I would say. I know more of Brother Bernard, the guest master. Now he is a kind soul. I try to give him as much ease as I can. You'll have seen him at table, no doubt. Been here, man and boy, and his brother too. Brother Peter. Passed away long since. He was a stone mason, you know, and so made all the repairs for us.'

'Really?'

'Yes. The fireplace in the refectory, now, that was done specially. The Abbot designed it, you know. Oh, he spent long hours between the services in with Brother Peter, wanted it to be perfect, and so it is. You have a proper look next time and see all the little bits and pictures in there. He's a good man, Father Giles. Can get a bit set in his notions, but still, he's a good man.'

Amanda nodded as though in accord, but wondering if you could have a good 'core of iron'.

'What of Brother Barnabas and Brother Venables, who sat opposite us at supper.'

'Ah, Brother Barnabas,' Abel sighed. 'Now, there's one as is too good for this world. I think he is already half in heaven.'

'He certainly does have an other-worldly look about him,' Amanda concurred. 'But I couldn't detect any family likeness to Father Giles. Though, of course, I was not looking for any.'

'No, perhaps there is no likeness, except, in their different ways, both are good men, I like to think. For I would rather think well than ill of any man until I have just cause.'

'I think that's a good rule to live by,' Thomas put in and sipped his wine, suggesting he was a little tipsy and too tired to contribute much to the conversation.

'And Brother Venables,' asked Amanda, thinking, 'Puppy Eyes'. 'The Abbot called him a pilgrim.'

'Aye, for he has visited many a shrine and brings the blessings of those saints to our priory. He has leave to travel to one and the other and now comes to stay with us and make his devotions to St Ursula.'

Amanda was at once diverted.

'There is a relic of St Ursula here?'

'The rope she loosed with her own blessed hands that bound the bear,' declared Abel on a note of pride. 'In our very priory. Though t'is kept safe tucked away, except on holy days.'

A holy rope? thought Amanda. No such thing in our day. I wonder what happened to it?

But Abel was continuing,

'Not had much speech with him or heard anything. Seems a hard worker and always ready to give a hand to any task, and always gives me a friendly look with those great brown eyes of his and a nod and smile in passing, not like I'm invisible, like for Brother Pius. But for the most part, I have not so much to do with most of the brothers and can speak only from those times when

I have been called to help somewhere and receive orders. Their rule of silence does not encourage chatter,' he added humorously.

They laughed, and he took a breath.

'Well, and so I must –'

'Abel, what of others you may have seen here? A young man, perhaps, in strange garb?'

But Abel's replies were much the same as Cury's. Finally, Abel declared,

'And now I must be home to the wife and my night's rest. Until tomorrow … Brothers.'

They bade him goodnight, and off he went.

'That was helpful, wasn't it? Lots of background there,' observed Amanda brightly.

Trelawney came straight to the point. 'We have been here four hours, and are we any closer to gaining any insight into our own times' murders? Abel hasn't witnessed any ghostly future events, and I gather, neither has Cury.'

'Well … no,' Amanda conceded. 'But I saw the monk for a reason. I'm *sure* this is where I'm supposed to find answers, and Aunt Amelia saw that we'd find what we were seeking.'

'"Find the treasure you seek" were her words, which are highly ambiguous. It could simply be that you discover more of the history of this place that is such an important part of your life.'

'I suppose so.'

'I can only be away so long, Amanda. I am on call.'

'Yes … but … now we're here …,' she entreated.

'All right. We shall see what the night brings, and if nothing, we must go back in the morning. Agreed?'

'Agreed,' she concurred reluctantly. Thomas put one candle on the hearth where it would cast little or no light and blew out the rest, so it would appear they were asleep. Amanda and Thomas each lay upon their bed … and waited.

* * *

In the darkness of the office at The Elms, the phone in the desk drawer lit up, its ring still silenced and went to voicemail. Multiple messages were listed in the text on the screen.

'Any luck?' Detective Sergeant Harris asked Detective Constable Nancarrow, seated at her desk in Parhayle police station.

'No sir. I'm going to try Sergeant Baker if that's ok with you?'

'Yes, go ahead.'

'He won't mind, I'm sure,' Nancarrow said confidently. 'It's ringing …. Not going to voi– Ah … Sergeant Baker, DC Nancarrow here from Parhayle. I've been trying to reach Inspector Trelawney. Would you have any idea of his whereabouts, sir? …. Oh yes, I've emailed and called and texted. … Yes, sir, of the utmost urgency. There's been another fire. … Yes, arson …. Hm. Thank you, sir …. Yes, I'm sure he does have a good reason. … No … yes … Former Chief Inspector Hogarth?.... Yes …. Yes, I shall … Thank you, sergeant.'

Harris looked at Nancarrow expectantly as she hung up. 'Any ideas where the inspector is?'

'No. But he recommends we call the former chief.'

'Want me to do that?' Harris offered, not wanting her to feel in the least like his secretary.

'No, no, that's all right, sir; I know he won't mind. He's … he's rather nice ….'

'He's old enough to be your grandfather,' came the disapproving tones of Harris, who had hopes of a romantic nature in a certain direction himself.

'I didn't mean that,' Nancarrow uttered defensively and dialled Hogarth's number. Then added, 'Anyway, my grandfather has a girlfriend!'

Chapter 50

಄

THE NIGHT

Trelawney was accustomed to all-night vigils. Amanda, less so. The bed was not as comfortable as her own, and she rarely slept in her clothes. Those, together with Tempest draped over her waist, and the presence of Thomas a short distance away were sufficient distractions. All the same, her eyelids began to droop.

However, before the last light had faded from the sky, they heard hooves galloping up to the gate and a voice urgently calling forth for attendance. Amanda sat up, disturbing Tempest. The visitor managed at last to rouse the guest master. Trelawney watched through a crack in the door for Bernard to pass toward the gate, then gestured to her to follow with him to within earshot of the visitor. It was a man's voice.

'A letter for the Abbot. I am come from Bentley Priory.'

'Come, come in, Brother,' Bernard answered, his voice a little gruff from sleep.

'Make haste, I beg you,' the newcomer urged.

Amanda and Thomas waited until the two had passed, then followed circumspectly in the shadows, Tempest at their ankles.

Bernard knocked on the door of Giles, whose sleeping quarters were next to his study.

'Forgive me, Father Abbot, but a brother comes with urgent news that cannot stay until Matins.'

The door opened shortly, and Bernard repeated his words. Giles nodded. 'Of course.' He disappeared for a few moments, then came out again, carrying some keys and greeted the agitated visitor. 'Come, Brother.' He unlocked the study door, and Bernard, carrying a rush light, went in and saw to the illuminations. 'Thank you, Brother Bernard. Some of the brothers may have roused, hearing of the arrival of our brother here. Give them assurances, and send them back to bed.'

'Yes, Father.'

But it was too late to forestall the arrival of Pius and then Stephen.

Amanda and Trelawney retreated deeper into the shadows as Bernard passed toward the dorter, and the Cellarer and Prior came from that direction. The Abbot's study door remained ajar.

'Now, Brother,' came Giles's voice, 'unfold to me your errand.'

'I am come, Father, from Bentley, which was once my home, but no longer. Our Father Prior is signing over all to the King this night but dispatched me as the fastest rider to bid you prepare. For the King's men lodge tonight there not 10 miles from your gate, and were heard to say they would surely be here the day after tomorrow. Some are to lodge at the Green Man in Whetstone and may come as the vanguard at dawn, not two days from now.'

'Thank you, good brother. Take refreshment and return to your prior with my thanks.'

'Thank you, Father.'

'Brothers, leave this with me. I shall seek guidance in a night of prayer. No, thank you, Brother Pius. I shall do so alone. Now, back to bed before service, and bid Brother Bernard see to refreshments for our guest.'

Quickly, Amanda and Trelawney returned to their quarters. Bernard commended the messenger to Abel's care and retired. Soon all was quiet once more.

Trelawney went to watch the quad. His intuition told him someone was still up … in the shadows, perhaps. Within the hour, his vigil was rewarded. There was a light in the refectory …

'Amanda!' Thomas whispered. 'Wake up. Something's going on in the refectory. I'm going to take a look.'

'I'm coming with you,' she insisted.

'All right. But we must be careful. Give me one minute to check the cloister is clear.'

'Ok.'

Trelawney stealthed from shadow to shadow around the cloister, drawing close to the refectory deep in the shadow of the church beside it. He listened, and, hearing nothing within, he turned toward Amanda.

She saw him beckon, and again there was that strange flash of memory. But she lost no time in joining him at the refectory door.

Suddenly there came the sound from within of something falling with a clatter. Thomas carefully opened the door. They entered, and Amanda ducked down to search for the light source between the table and the far wall. A candle dying on the flagstones illuminated a human form lying beside it.

She hastened across to it, and, seeing the door to the kitchen was ajar, Trelawney went to check there as a figure exited to the courtyard and flitted past the refectory windows. Trelawney gave chase as the fugitive disappeared into the church. He followed, but within, there was no one in sight. No sound. Only that of his own breath. Then the furtive slap of feet upon the nightstairs. Now the man would be swallowed in the mass of his brothers, while there might be help for his victim.

Amanda was bent over the man on the floor, Tempest observing from the tabletop. She looked up at Thomas, 'It's Giles!' she whispered as Trelawney came over.

'Is he still …?'

She shook her head. He was, indeed, lifeless, the cord mark upon his throat telling its heinous tale.

'We should tell Abel,' urged Amanda.

'Yes,' Thomas agreed, 'then make ourselves scarce. We must distance ourselves from this.'

They hurried back to the guest wing, and while Trelawney went to ensure that the visitor was out of the way, Amanda had time to ponder and Tempest to observe her shrewdly.

Thomas returned, saying, 'He's seeing to it. I just said I saw a light and went to investigate.'

'Which is true. But, Thomas, did you see where the body was? Close to the wall? That's right near the place where the monk or whoever beckoned to me. What if it was Giles whose apparition I saw, and he was calling me across time to solve his murder? Or –'

'Either way, this must have something to do with his decision regarding the priory.'

'Could it have been the Prior, Stephen? He was clearly of a very different mind. What if he killed Giles, so he could gain control over the fate of the house and save everyone in it?'

'That would follow,' agreed Trelawney, 'but he wasn't the only one who knew about Giles's decision. Don't forget Pius.'

Amanda nodded. 'And Cury and Barnabas were right outside the door. They could have overheard.'

'But why in the refecto–'

'Brothers!' Abel was at the door, holding a candle and in much distress. 'All of value is missing from the Abbot's study and the sacristy. Our chalice is gone, and the cross, plate, candlestick and censor used on holy days, as well. Even some sacred relics! Oh, brothers, I hope they don't think you –'

'They are welcome to search our bags, Abel,' returned Amanda.

'Well …, there is such turmoil … perhaps …. I must go back and see what aid I can render.'

With Abel gone, Trelawney turned to Amanda and said urgently,

'He's right. As strangers, suspicion must fall upon us. We must go.'

'But –,' Amanda began.

'No. *Now*. It's not safe, and no one is going to tell us anything after this.'

'Oh … I suppose. But,' Amanda began to object.

'Now! We are strangers here. We cannot afford to be exposed.'

'All right,' she agreed, shouldering her pack, as Tempest jumped wearily down from her bed. They hurried to the gate and slipped out into the wood.

She looked back.

'Please, Amanda,' Thomas urged her.

'Of course.' She cast the portal spell, the three of them stepped through, and she shut it behind them.

Chapter 51

∽

Retreat

No sooner had Amanda closed the portal than she turned to Trelawney.

'We must go back, Inspector! Before Henry's men come. You heard Abel. All the valuables missing: treasure! What if that's what this is all about? Not just Giles but Harold and Janet. We have to go back. There has to have been a record of where the treasure was stashed. How else could anyone now know about it?'

'Yes, the Abbot or Prior, perhaps, must have written about it in a will or a letter,' Thomas conceded.

'Yes! So we have to go back and look through his papers,' Amanda urged him. 'That book Abel mentioned will tell us who everyone was, and there might be a family link between the priory then and someone in the village now.'

'It's too risky. Far too risky. Look, we know about some treasure, and it may have been hidden somewhere here, and there's no record of it ever having been found. Treasure as a motive for murder is a lead of some sort, and we just have to follow it in case it does lead to the killer of Janet and Harold.'

'But how?'

'We have four newcomers to the village,' he pointed out. 'Plenty to investigate.' Amanda was doubtful. Thomas reminded her strategically, 'And Humpy to clear.'

'Oh yes,' she agreed at once.

'Come on, back to The Elms.'

'Yes, I must collect my clothes.'

'Then I'll drive you home.'

Back around through the trees and across the road, he led them to the new porch of the side door of his flat. Amanda and Tempest followed Thomas in and across the sitting room to the door of his office.

He crossed at once to his desk and opened the top drawer. By the light of the desk lamp, his consternation was visible even to Amanda.

'As I feared,' Thomas said. 'In my absence, I have missed calls. I must leave at once.'

'Cornwall?'

'Yes, another arson attack. I'm sorry, Amanda. I'll drop you home. I'll be back as soon as I can. Tomorrow evening, if possible.'

As he gathered his things, she spoke quickly. 'Missing treasure. Henry's men about to arrive. The Abbot must have hidden it. And in the refectory somewhere.'

'It's possible.'

'If I could go back …,' Amanda began persistently.

'No. I'll return as soon as I can.'

Once in the car, Tempest, on his blanket on the back seat, curled up and tucked his tail over his ears. He already knew what the outcome of the conversation was going to be. Amanda, however, did not, and had another go. 'The treasure might still have been there after all the monks left.'

'Of course, Henry's men most likely would have found it when it was demolished,' Trelawney pointed out, buckling up and turning on the engine.

'But what if they *didn't*, and someone – *our* murderer – found out about it and came to hunt it out?'

'And killed anyone who they thought was snooping near where they think the treasure is. Yes, it's possible,' Trelawney agreed again, pulling out and driving swiftly but legally along the empty High Road.

'Exactly. They found Harold and then Janet Oglethorpe on what they thought was the same mission.' Amanda offered with enthusiasm.

'Well, that follows. Especially if they were partners in crime. As I say, it's a lead, and I'll set Baker on looking for ties between Janet and the other newbies and anyone else in the village. It could be a good lead.' He turned into Orchard Way.

'But how could someone 500 years later have found out? There *must* be a link between someone at the priory back then and now. I just have to find it. Abel had been there all his life, and he knew about the background of everyone there. If I could just –,' she tried persuasively.

'Wait. Please.' He pulled up outside the cottage. 'Just wait until I'm back. Sorry, Amanda.' He popped the boot lid. 'I have to go. Hold the fort till I'm back, won't you?

'Of course.' she assured him. 'Good luck in Cornwall.'

'Thank you. See you soon.'

Amanda got out, opened the back passenger door, gathered up Tempest, closed it, grabbed her bag and shut the boot lid. Thomas turned around efficiently, waved and sped off up Orchard Way.

Chapter 52

༄

A CHANGE OF HABIT

Back inside, Amanda still in her costume, she and Tempest were soon in the kitchen to supply her familiar with a midnight snack and herself with cocoa. The washing-up had accumulated, and, the sink being full, a dish was standing soaking on the counter beside it. Tempest got up on the windowsill to oversee her efforts regarding his food.

Amanda was not sure how or why it happened, but when she bent to get a tin of Ortiz tuna out of the cupboard beneath the counter, suddenly she felt the splash of cold water on her back. She stood up at once with a gasp. It was one of Tempest's bowls that had been soaking. After a day, the contents had become a noxious fish-infused liquid, which was now permeating and befouling Amanda's habit.

'What the ….!?' The bowl was now empty, and the direction of the slop was clear to see. Tempest was still seated on the windowsill, an impish look in his livid yellow eyes. 'Tempest! Did you do that?' Amanda tried to look over her shoulder as she reached a hand back to feel the saturated cloth that she could smell all too keenly. 'Honestly!'

She pulled off the habit. The foul water had also gone through to her shift, so that had to be removed too. Amanda went up to the bathroom, carrying the garments, some stain remover and detergent. By the time they had been restored to an acceptable level of cleanliness, both layers of clothing were wet through. But they'd soon dry on a radiator. She slipped on her dressing gown and came downstairs.

With the warm weather, it had been three weeks since the central heating had been on. Amanda switched up the thermostat, waiting for the telltale click and muted whoosh of the boiler lighting. Silence. She turned the temperature up higher. Silence.

'I don't believe this! I'll have to get Bryan in, in the morning.' Still, there was another way to do the drying. The fire in the hearth was soon kindled, a clothes horse fetched, and her habit and petticoat draped over it. Amanda tended the coke and wood into a promising blaze and returned to the kitchen to resume her cocoa-making. It would surely soothe and calm her.

Tempest had picked at his snack and gone off.

'Typical,' Amanda remarked, observing this as she poured some milk into a pan and set it to heat on the hob. She added a splash of it to the cocoa powder she had spooned into a mug and stirred them both into a smooth paste. It was an almost therapeutic procedure. Her breathing slowed, and the late hour and fatigue of the day and evening were making themselves felt. 'I must get to bed,' she yawned. Nevertheless, it might be worth tackling some of the washing up while she waited for the milk to come to the boil.

It was when Amanda was stirring sugar into her now-ready drink that she smelt it. She sniffed suspiciously.

'Is that … smoke!' It was coming from the sitting room. Running in, Amanda saw her habit on fire with the wet patches steaming. Swiftly, she smothered the flames with another part of the cloth, coughing from the smoke. Once all was made safe, Amanda had pause in which to look around suspiciously.

Tempest sat on the sofa nearby, smirking.

'Not funny, Tempest! Oh, how could you!?' Her costume was ruined: charred and holey. What on earth am I ….? No, this is serious. I have to go back. What am I … Oh, let me think,' She fetched her mug and sat down beside her clearly unrepentant, mischievous familiar.

Tempest dropped gracefully to the carpet and went to resume his snack with the air of a job well done, which won him no favour with his witch.

Amanda sipped her cocoa and decided, 'There must be something among Granny and Grandpa's things I can use. Hm …. There's that long black coat Granny got for a funeral. I think she only wore it once and said she'd make something out of the fabric but never got around to it. Hm … tomorrow. I've had more than enough day for one day.'

The ensuing morning found Amanda, refreshed by a decent amount of sleep, masked and in the attic, rooting through one of her grandmother's trunks. Finally, she drew out the coat and took it downstairs to the sitting room, and Tempest continued his night's rest on the sofa.

'Well, the length is right,' Amanda announced, inspecting the garment, 'and the colour, and it's wool, but … buttons down the front will never do. What about …. back to front. Hm. The hood ….'

She quickly unpicked and removed the hood and its fur trimming. 'It's generously sized. Let's see … I could just close it with ties and leave it loose on the shoulders, and remove the buttons, then find something to tie around the waist. There's bound to be an old curtain cord or some rope in the workshop, maybe, that I can use. Yes … it'll be fine. No thanks to you, you naughty kitty,' Amanda added, rubbing his tummy.

Presently, the emerging habit was ready to try on. Amanda regarded herself in the hall mirror.

'It's ok. The back does look odd …. I wonder …' She hurried off to the workshop to find a roll of black felt that Grandpa had bought for a customer who wanted a card table recovered in that colour.

There was just enough to make a short scapular. Sleeveless and sideless, it would hang fore and aft and hide, at least, some of the back. If anyone in the priory commented, she could say it was in her pack because she felt the cold. It was done. The back-to-front coat, some dun-coloured upholstery cord around her waist to tie it shut, the hood loose on her shoulders, and the scapular over the top did just about look the part.

Amanda needed to call Bryan, but first, she gave the thermostat one last try. There was a click and a whoosh, and the boiler came on. She sighed with a mixture of relief and exasperation and looked at Tempest suspiciously. He was, predictably, napping.

Now all she could do, as far as a return to the monastery was concerned, was wait. She received a text from Trelawney. He said he'd called the Biggerstaffs to let them know he and Miss Cadabra had a new lead. The message, however, said nothing about his return.

* * *

Trelawney arrived in Parhayle after dawn. He drove straight to the location given by DS Harris and approached the smouldering caravan at the end of Mrs Boscawen's garden.

'It belonged to my old uncle,' the lady told him. 'Bit of a state, I know, but this is how it came to me, and I've been meaning to do something with it, make it fit for tourists and so on, but I just never got round to it,' she explained apologetically. 'All the same, as I tell the insurance, it was an asset and did have sentimental value too, Inspector. But the main thing is, these…

these fires. They've got to stop. We're not that sort of place where such things go on.'

'You're right,' Trelawney concurred.

The fire had been set alight at night. There was no trace of an accelerant; it was dark, no witnesses, and no one so far had seen or heard anything unusual. Again.

Chapter 53

JANE IS ALARMED

Amanda breathed a sigh of relief when her phone rang. But it was not Thomas's name on the screen.

'Amanda, sorry to disturb your work,' came the unusually shaky voice of Jane.

'Hello Rector, are you all right?'

'Could you please come over when you have a spare moment?'

'Now,' Amanda assured her friend at once. 'I'll come now. Be right there.'

A few minutes later, a pale-faced Jane was answering the door of the rectory to her.

'Dear Rector, whatever has happened?'

'Oh. Amanda … I am a little, well, concerned. Do come in.'

'Let me make us some tea.'

'Oh dear … I am the one here to assist others and ….'

'It's quite all right.' By the time Amanda returned with the tray, Jane was more herself, and Tempest, who liked the church, had located what he considered to be the most comfortable chair.

Once seated with Amanda on the sofa, the Rector, holding a folded A4 sheet of paper in her hand, explained,

'I've had a letter. I've been so busy I hadn't had time for the post until just now. I saw the official-looking envelope and thought it must be something about the church hall. ... I never ... Here. Best you read it – aloud, if you would, dear – so I can believe my own ears, if not my eyes.'

'Of course.

Dear Rector –'

'Never mind the opening paragraph, dear: just standard.'

'All right.

It has reached my ears of late, that Sunken Madley has attracted a series of unfortunate events. It would seem that certain of your sheep, in particular, a Mr and Mrs Biggerstaff, are feeling untended in their hour of extremity. I am sure that this is a situation you will be quick to remedy.

Nevertheless, it would seem that there is something rotten in the state of Sunken Madley. No doubt, you are doing your best to hold back the tide of misdemeanours. However, I feel that you may welcome some assistance. I am prepared to send Father Werthiman unless you are confident and able to reassure me that all is in hand. It may be that you and your new curate are on top of the situation. In which case, I would not wish to interfere.

On the other hand, if you feel that the situation is beyond your capabilities, perhaps a less demanding post may be more suited to you. However, you have rendered sterling service in your little community for many years, and I am confident that I may leave this in your capable hands. I look forward to hearing from you regarding your successful progress with these matters by the end of the week.

'Closing salutation ... from the Bishop?' Amanda marvelled.

'Yes, the Bishop! You see?'

'But I don't, Rector. These "unfortunate events" have all been to do with outsiders, I'm sure, not the villagers whom you shepherd so ably.'

'But I don't,' protested Jane. 'Only three people in the congregation on Sunday.'

'But the Apple Festival service was packed out,' countered Amanda gently. 'And on special days ….'

'Oh, I know.'

'And people know that you're here, and they talk to you.'

'Yes, yes, I've always thought I was …. And now … if I was sent away ….' Jane looked at her in distress. 'I've been here for years and years. This is my home … my people.'

'Well,' Amanda replied with calm practicality. 'I think there's a long way to go before your being replaced is any real possibility. Who is this Father Werthiman, anyway?'

'He's rather young, and, oh, I don't want to say "ambitious", I'm sure he's …. oh, but he would *never* understand Sunken Madley,' Jane insisted anxiously.

'Well, it's only a possibility. The Bishop does say it's in your capable hands.'

Jane exhaled. 'You're quite right, Amanda. I am overreacting entirely. It's just that I've never had … But this is most likely all just a result of Chinese whispers and the ….'

'And the ambition of one who probably saw an opportunity to make his mark?'

'Well, let us say aspirations to be a force for the light, dear.'

'Yes, Rector. And I'm sure that somehow we'll have an opportunity to present a clearer picture of the spiritual health of the parish.'

'That's right. But… by the end of the week? There's a murderer abroad and two people in my parish dead. How will I have news for the Bishop in such a short time, unless …?'

Amanda took a breath and a commitment. 'I am hopeful of a resolution any day now.'

Relief visibly washed over Jane. 'Oh my dear, that is wonderful. I shall have good news to send him, then, and all will be well.'

'But who could have been talking to the Bishop about Sunken Madley? You don't think it could have been the Curate?' suggested Amanda.

'Kay? Oh dear me, no, surely not. I can't bel … Oh, I don't know ….'

'Well, if we discount Kay for now …. Rector … you are sure this really did come from the Bishop?'

'Oh, well … I …. Wait just a moment.'

Jane went to the desk and looked through a file. 'Here. This is the letter from the Bishop about the new church hall.' Amanda came to her side, and they compared the signatures, the handwritten address on the envelope, and the greeting, then checked the postmark on the newly arrived letter. The opening salutation, paragraphs and language were the same.

'I wonder,' said Amanda, 'if someone is leaning on the Bishop.'

'Oh no, surely not Kay. She said she doesn't know anything about it.'

'If not the Curate, then … who?'

'Dear Amanda, if you can get to the bottom of these murders, I'm sure you can find the person behind *this*.'

With Jane reassured, Amanda returned to the cottage to find a stranger on the mat.

Chapter 54

༄

Pressure Points

'Hello,' Amanda ventured in friendly terms to the man at her front door.

'Hello there, Miss Cadabra.'

He knew her name. That, at least, was a clue. Yet she was sure she'd never encountered him before. He was light-grey-haired, tall and large-framed. Despite his rounded middle, in films, they would have regarded him as a useful man in a fight, even though she would, if pressed for a guess, have put him in his sixties, perhaps more.

'Have we met?' Amanda enquired politely.

'Terry Biggerstaff. Your granddad did our G-plan chairs, and I served you some of my cider at The Feast of St Ursula of the Apples last November.'

'Oh yes, of course!' she exclaimed, none the wiser, except that here was a relative of Harold's.

'You must be Harold's …,' she fished.

'Grandfather.'

'Ah, yes. Won't you come in?'

'Oh, that's all right, dear, I'm just looking for the inspector,' Terry explained.

'He's not here, I'm afraid.'

Mr Biggerstaff looked disappointed. 'Oh ... nor at The Elms.'

Amanda shook her head regretfully, 'No, he was called back to Cornwall, unfortunately.'

'Well, really!' responded Terry in some dudgeon.

'They've had a series of fires. Arson attacks,' Amanda added quickly.

His mood at once changed to sympathetic. 'Oh dear. Anyone hurt?'

'Not so far,' replied Amanda, to stress the gravity of the situation

'So not as serious as murder then?' countered Terry.

'True, but it could escalate and harm a great many people,' Amanda offered, hoping to conjure an image of a rapidly spreading inferno.

'Yes, but that's "maybe". Two killings right here in Sunken Madley, and one of them my grandson, and what's being done about it, I ask you?' Terry enquired with growing indignation.

'I promise you, Mr Biggerstaff, we are doing everything we can. The Inspector called your son and daughter this morning to tell them we have a new lead.'

'But the Inspect–'

'I am on the case,' Amanda responded rashly.

He objected at once: 'But you're not trained.'

'But I am helping, and the inspector will be back very soon,' she retrenched.

'But in the meantime? I'm sorry, dear; I don't want to make any trouble for you, but this is just going on and on, and it's as much as my family's nerves can stand, and I've always been a man as gets things done. If the inspector is busy in Cornwall, we should have someone take his place.'

'But....'

'No, dear, I'm sorry. I'm going to contact the Commissioner of Police and –'

'All right, Mr Biggerstaff. All right.' There was nothing for it. She would have to act, with or without Trelawney. 'You've every right to do that, but please, give me until tomorrow night. If we don't turn up something by then ….'

He stood and considered. Finally, he gave a nod.

'Ok. We have an agreement, then?'

'Yes, Mr Biggerstaff,' Amanda said solemnly.

'I'll be back.'

Amanda let herself and Tempest in and entered the sitting room to find an only slightly ethereal, laden tea tray on the coffee table. Perran and Senara were seated on either side of the fire, leaning forward and toasting crumpets on long forks. She could not help noticing that Grandpa was dressed in white shirt and trousers, and Granny is a similarly snowy, calf-length, dropped-waist, sleeveless dress.

'Wonderful!' exclaimed their granddaughter with delight. 'You can help me. I have a dilemma.'

'Course, *bian*,' responded Grandpa warmly.

'Yes, you need to get this matter sorted out, Ammee, dear,' enjoined Granny. 'You missed magic practice.'

It hardly seemed important by comparison with a murder, but Amanda desisted from pointing this out and, instead, asked, 'but what do you think I should do? The inspector is away, I've got the Biggerstaffs on my case, and the Rector has the Bishop on hers, and actually, at this moment, we're no closer to working out who the killer is. Or are. We need to know what the link is between then and now, and quickly! I need to go back, don't I?'

'The path will become clear to you,' assured Grandpa cryptically.

'Erm, … do you think you could be a little … more helpful than that?'

'We would, naturally,' said Granny, 'if we did not consider you sufficiently trained to handle the matter yourself.'

'Myself?' asked Amanda doubtfully, 'As in, independently? So I should just go back to the monastery?'

'You can do this, *bian*.'

'Is that all you're giving me? And,' Amanda's curiosity overcoming her, 'why are you dressed in whites?'

'We have a tennis engagement,' Senara explained.

'Which is why we can't stay long,' added Perran. 'Just dropped in to give you some moral support.'

'Well, thank you, Grandpa. Aren't you hot by the fire?' she could not help asking, observing their summer-wear.

'Can't beat a crumpet, and tea cools you down, you know, *bian*.'

Granny withdrew her crumpet from the blaze, applied a generous helping of butter, wrapped it in a white damask napkin, took a sip of tea, and said to her husband,

'I think we'll have to take these with us, or we shall be late.'

Amanda, alarmed at their imminent departure, protested, 'For *tennis* when I …?'

'Doubles, *bian*,' responded Grandpa informatively, packing up his own snack.

'This is a crisis and … doubles?' their bemused granddaughter enquired.

'With Katherine and someone she's bringing along. Judy, I think,' answered Granny.

'Katherine?' Amanda could not help herself.

'Hepburn, dear. Very keen tennis player. Going to help us improve our game. Must go. You'll be fine. Just don't … well, you'll know.'

'Bye for now, *bian*.'

And with that, they faded and vanished.

'Well, that was no help at all!' Amanda checked her phone in the hope of inspiration there. She found the volume had been low, and she had a missed call from Hogarth.

'Uncle Mike?'

'Amanda. Any developments?'

'We, er, paid a visit in ana historical context, and I think I know what this is all about, but I need to find the link between the people then and the suspects now.'

'You need to go back.'

'Yes! But. ...'

'Ok, the "but" says it all. Well, you may have to go ahead. I've had a call from Crossly.'

'Oh no.'

'Oh yes. He had a call from your MP's office, wanting to be seen to do the right thing, and another from the Bishop, who just said he wanted to get "a picture of the situation." Crossly wants an arrest.'

'But who?'

'The chap staying at The Grange.'

'*Humpy*? He can't be serious! Humpy wouldn't hurt a fly! It's absurd,' Amanda protested.

'Yes, he'd be released very shortly, but it would buy some time and look like "something is being done".'

'No! No, please, Uncle Mike. Look, I just had Harold's grandfather here, and I managed to cut a deal with him.'

'How cloak-and-dagger! Do tell.'

Mike's lighter note both calmed and slowed Amanda down.

'I have asked him to give me until tomorrow night to show progress. If I come up empty-handed, he's going to go to the Commissioner and ask for a replacement for the inspector to deal with the case.'

'Yes, that would be disastrous,' agreed Hogarth, 'especially as you, my dear, are now in deep.'

The path, as Grandpa had predicted, had become clear. There was no crossroads, no fork in the road, not so much as a track leading off into the trees. There was only one way ahead.

'Yes, Uncle Mike. It's come to this: I have to go back. The Rector is in danger of losing her parish, and now Humpy has an arrest hanging over him, even if he doesn't know it. I have a deadline for tomorrow evening. There is no way that the inspector's normal methods are going to solve the case by then. I've *got* to go back. The only leads are there.'

'I spoke to Thomas earlier, and his presence here is essential. It's becoming a serious case. It could be seen as a dereliction of duty for him to absent himself now.'

'Yes, well, I am resolved: I'm going by myself.'

'When?' asked Mike.

'Tonight.'

'Does it have to be? Thomas would say if it's the past, can't you go back at any time.'

'These things are hit and miss as it is, Aunt Amelia says. We were lucky to get there when we did,' insisted Amanda. 'Timing is everything. If I go back now, I have the best, maybe the only chance to get the information we need. If I leave it …. If it's to do with the same time of year as now, same time, in the same season, – oh, I don't know how it works, but if I have to wait until next year – if this *is* my only chance I can't afford to miss it. It would be disastrous for Humpy and Hillers and the Rector and all of the village if she's replaced with someone who –'

'All right, all right, Amanda. But no … *extraordinary measures* while your there,' Hogarth counselled her.

'No … I know …. I know the rules. I think I can do this with minimal … extraordinary measures. There's someone there that I know will help me to … do what I need to do. And then, I'll be right back,' Amanda promised.

'When tonight?' asked Mike

'After 3 a.m., after the last service of the night but before dawn.'

'You think Henry's men will arrive that early?'

'The vanguard could do so easily. Uncle Mike,' Amanda pleaded, 'I have just this one window in which to get back to the monastery and find out what happened. I know it's all connected. I'm *sure* of it. The monastery will almost certainly be taken at dawn tomorrow; everyone and everything that might give us clues to our murderer then will be out of reach.'

'Thomas will not be happy,' Hogarth pointed out.

'He doesn't understand.'

'He does. But he trusts the methods he knows,' he reminded Amanda.

'But it's only a few hours away, the moment when the evidence could all be destroyed or taken who knows where? Please, Uncle Mike, ask Sir Francis Crossly to give us – give me – just 24 hours.'

'I'll try. It will be more like 12 or 18 at the most, Amanda. And, as I say, Thomas is not going to be pleased.'

'I know. But I was hoping …,' she began tentatively, but Hogarth saw her plea coming and forestalled her kindly:

'No, no, you have to tell him yourself. That will mitigate his wrath far more effectively than any soothing words from me.'

'Really? You think he'll be *angry?*'

Mike thought. Irritated, yes. Frustrated, yes. Bemused yes. Angry …?

'Angry, no,' Mike responded carefully. 'But he'll be ... not overjoyed.'

Amanda was subdued by the thought of the impending Conversation. 'Hm … I expect not.'

'Might as well get it over with, young Amanda,' Hogarth recommended.

'Yes, Uncle Mike. But do I have your …?'

'Sanction? And if I didn't give it?' he asked knowingly.

'Well,' Amanda prevaricated.

'Quite. Very well, my daughter. *Te absolvo. Vade.*'

'*Gratias, pater,* or should I say "*avunclus*"?'

After the call was concluded, Amanda paced and practised her speech, regarded with amusement by Tempest, who was enjoying the drama.

Hogarth, moved, if amused, by his honorary niece's plight, sent a ground-laying text to Thomas.

Amanda is about to call you and tell you something. Be nice. H.

The response was almost instant but unpromising:

I'm always nice. T

Chapter 55

∽

WAIT UNTIL DAWN

Nevertheless, forewarned by Hogarth, Trelawney was forearmed. He had a fair idea of what was coming. Mike's message indicated some sort of approval, and so all he could do was try to get his head around what the situation might be.

However, before he could do so, Amanda's name flashed up on his phone screen to the accompaniment of the ringtone.

'Inspector, hello, how are things in Cornwall?' she opened, hoping to soften what was coming with a little diversion.

'Hello, Miss Cadabra. Somewhat confounding at the moment. I gather this is not a social call.'

There was no point in prevarication. Amanda launched boldly into her narrative exposition:

'I have to go back. You know it's reached Sir Francis Crossly's desk and the MP ... and now Uncle Mike says they want you to arrest Humpy! And Jane is about to lose her parish, and it would pass into the hands of someone who could never... and Mr Biggerstaff senior is threatening to go to the Commissioner, and I have until dawn when Henry's men will take or destroy anything that might help us, and I'm absolutely positive then and now are connected.'

Trelawney responded levelly, 'I understand, but I simply can't leave here. This is a situation that is threatening to escalate. The next fire could kill. I'm sorry.'

Amanda stated quietly, 'Then I must go alone.'

Exactly what he'd feared. 'Oh, good grief. Let me think. Just…. give me an hour. I'll call you back. I promise.'

'All right,' she agreed.

Thomas thought. Flash 'n' dabs had done their job. There was still the meagre CCTV footage and whatever snaps or videos had been taken in the area during that evening; locals, shop owners to be interviewed, and tourist accommodation canvassed for any input from visitors. Above all, he needed personally to revisit the girls, Ty, Hardy and his probation officer, and the apparently reformed fireworks enthusiast. The perpetrator had got away with it twice and might return to the scene of the crime to witness their triumph. The Losows' stall was a danger to livelihood, but unlikely as it was, someone could have been in the Gwynsek's shed and been harmed or even killed. Had the arsonist checked whether it was empty? Had they cared?

Thomas tried to imagine one of the girls, Ty, Hardy, or the young pyrotechnics fan. Did anyone of them fit? What would Mike say? Of course: 'Do your thing.' Why, oh, why was he constantly tripping over magic?

Nevertheless, Thomas drove a little way out of town to a quiet lane, parked and turned off the engine. He looked out over the landscape, then took some deep breaths, focused and closed his eyes. He waited. The lights came: lines of light tinted in orange, green, blue, racing parallel to the gold one and then a maverick … outlier … purple … purple … In an explosion of illumination, the vision was over. He opened his eyes. What had he seen lately that was purple?

It wasn't much help at all. Anyway, he couldn't leave, unless … during the night possibly. He would have to come straight back: Sunken Madley, in and out of the monastery and straight back on the road. He could be back in Parhayle by tomorrow morning. Just about, with the aid of the siren. Flashing lights, at least.

Trelawney rang Amanda.

'Miss Cadabra. Give me till dawn to get to you.'

'But they'll be here before then,' she objected. 'I mean there … then.'

'4.30?'

'All right,' she agreed doubtfully.

Amanda tried to get some sleep after setting her alarm for half past three. She ended up watching the clock for the last hour and then pushed Tempest off her stomach, got up and dressed. After putting the kettle on for a cup of tea, she appeased her disgruntled familiar with a very early breakfast. At 10 past 4, she looked out. Her eyes widened in alarm.

'The sky! Tempest! The sky is starting to get light! We can't wait.' She rang Thomas.

'Inspector.'

'I'm on the road,' came his voice on the speaker.

'It's starting to get light. I can't wait.'

'Are you sure?'

'I can't risk it. Look. I'll cast the portal deep in the trees, but I don't know how to keep them open for long. It's a risk, but hopefully, no one will see it at that time of night, and it will stay open long enough …. It's the best I can do.'

He could have tried vetoing it, but ….

'All right. Please take care, and get out at the first sign of trouble!'

'I promise.'

'I'll be there as soon as I can. Do your best and, for goodness sake, be careful.'

Amanda said reassuringly. 'Tempest will be with me,'

'That's what worries me.'

'I'll be fine,' she promised him rashly.

'We have different definitions of that word,' Trelawney replied drily. 'All right. I suppose this has Mike's blessing, does it?'

'It has his consent,' she replied diplomatically.

'All right. Text me just before you leave and as soon as you're back.'

'Yes, Inspector.'

If you come back, he thought. One thing was for sure: tonight was going to be eventful.

Chapter 56

༄

CONFESSION

A tap on the gate was all that was needed. Abel did not seem to notice Amanda's change of raiment. He said he was making preparations for his and his family's departure, and going up at intervals to the church tower to scan the horizon for the approach of Henry's men.

'But, mistress, where have you been?'

'Brother Thomas was called away on an errand. I came back because there is something more I must do before I leave. And I pray you, Abel, will you help me?'

'Anything, mistress,' he assured Amanda, glancing down at the strange cat that seemed to accompany her everywhere.

'You spoke of a book where it is written who each monk was before they took the cowl?'

'In truth,' agreed Abel.

'Where might it be?'

'In the Abbot's study in a locked drawer or chest, for sure, I'd say,' Abel replied confidently. 'T'is the safest place in the priory.'

'Can you get me there? To the Abbot's study. Without being seen?'

He shook his head. 'I could bring you there, but t'is locked at night.'

'I ... I have a way with locks,' Amanda responded vaguely, 'if you can only get me there and help me to search and keep watch ....'

'Well, the brothers are now to their beds unless any keep vigil in the church.'

'And the Prior?'

'Asleep too, I should think.'

'So we shouldn't be disturbed,' Amanda checked hopefully.

'No, but Brother Stephen and Brother Pius have wondered at your absence, mistress, and especially that of Brother Thomas.'

'You could say we have been unwell. Some minor indisposition from the long journey, but hopefully, it won't come to that. For I must leave as soon as I have seen the book.'

The Abbot's study was on the south side of the Chapter House. On the north and adjacent to the church was the sacristy, where all that was required for mass was stored. The study was sufficiently spacious and furnished to please noble guests, elevated clerics and envoys from other houses: only the Abbot and the Prior held keys.

They moved out into the shadow of the south cloister.

'Wait here, mistress and I will check all is safe.' Abel crept around the central garth. Suddenly, Amanda observed him stop in the moonlight as though listening, then hurry to the door of the refectory and go in. Moments later, a candle was lit, and she saw him leaning out of the door beckoning to her, and suddenly there it was:

Hooded – cowled – leaning out, benign but anxious yet, hopeful she could help. Surely this was the vision at the priory ruins.

Amanda hurried across to him.

'Quick!' Abel urged her. At once, she saw a body … No, two – no, three – on the floor of the refectory floor. She went to the one lying by the hearth.

'Brother Pup– Venables?' she asked Abel in a whisper.

'Yes, but that one is dead, mistress. And Brother Pius alive but unconscious. Do you make haste here to Brother Barnabas.?'

True enough, he was opening his eyes, but his breathing was shallow, and he was as pale as death. He tried to raise himself. Amanda knelt, supporting Barnabas's head.

'Brother, are you unwell?'

He glanced down at his hand. It was over a wound below his ribs.

'Abel, get the infirmerer!' Amanda said urgently, but Barnabas raised his other hand and shook his head.

'No. No, Brother. No infirmerer. I must pay with my life for my transgression. This wound from Brother Venables' knife is his gift to me.'

'What?' Amanda looked at him in confusion. 'What transgression?' She saw the blade gleaming wet on the floor beside him. It looked far more like Barnabas was the one transgressed against.

'I must confess,' he insisted weakly.

'I cannot take conf–'

'I must. I killed Venables …. Spy for the King …. struck down Brother Pius.'

Amanda was incredulous. '*You* are a spy?'

He shook his head. 'No … Venables.'

Puppy Eyes? thought Amanda, almost equally surprised by this revelation.

Barnabas went on:

'House to house … pretended … shrines. But any treasures … hidden money …anything … … every house he went to … now … gone … or doomed. And he had to encourage … Abbot … give away priory.'

'But the Abbot is dead now and … It was you?' He nodded slowly. 'You killed the Abbot?'

Barnabas's distress was evident. 'To my shame. But it was for my brothers. They do not deserve to be destitute and homeless.'

'Of course, they don't, Brother. What were you both doing in here in the middle of the night when you …. When the Abbot died?'

'I watch … Father Giles. Followed him … here and … I saw … hit him with … candlestick.'

'Why was the Abbot in here?' Amanda asked curiously.

'Putting away a box in the secret place.'

Of course, she thought. It all fits. It has to be in here. But Barnabas was still speaking:

'It had a cup with pearls. Of great value.'

No need to say that she knew it personally. More importantly: 'What did you do with it?'

'In the place with the other treasure he had buried – to be safe from the King's men.'

'Are you sure they won't find it?'

'I have sent a letter for my father … Only one I trust… he will tell ….. so that they might return when all is safe and … make use of what lies within to aid themselves and … to begin the priory anew when … the storm is … passed.' After this slight burst of life, he was growing visibly weaker.

'Oh, Brother Barnabas, was there no other way than killing Father Giles?'

'No sure way, my Cornish brother. And now … you must get away from here.'

'Yes, I shall. But I must help you first,' Amanda insisted.

'No … my life is done. My work is done. I believe … that Father Stephen will be one with me now … in the cause of our brethren.'

'Your life is ….'

'It drains away. Do not mourn for me …. I go with joy. I did it for … no man hath greater love ….'

His eyes now stared as though unseeing of Amanda but something beyond.

'Brother! Please … where is the treasure? In case your letter is intercepted or destroyed!'

His gaze was distant. She wasn't sure if he had even heard or understood her.

At first, there came only, 'Kee …' then, 'Keep safe … whhh ….' He raised a finger.

Amanda knelt by his side as he slowly reached a hand out to her, weakly beckoning her to listen to him. She took it and put her ear close to his lips to hear the last thread of his words. It was soft, but she was sure she'd heard it:

'The night… stairs.' They came out with his final breath. His hand lay limp in hers. She closed his eyes.

Chapter 57

༄

DEFILER

There was nothing more to be done for Barnabas but considerably more elsewhere. Amanda rose and entreated Abel,

'Can you give me a few minutes before you raise the alarm? I must see the book you told me of.'

'Yes, but quickly then.'

With Abel shading a candle from the refectory, they hurried to the late Father Giles's study.

'Keep watch, if you will, toward the church door,' she requested to distract him.

As Abel trod a few silent paces in that direction, Amanda slipped her Pocket-wand out from the rubber bands securing it to her forearm, and whispered to the study lock:

'*Agertyn.*'

Once sprung, the heavy door pushed open with a sigh, and Amanda silently called down blessings on whoever kept the hinges well-oiled.

Hearing the slight whoosh, Abel turned, rejoined her and led the way in. He pointed to the chest and desk, then hurried to the window and peered out.

'Dawn is near, mistress. Will you make your search, and I will look from the tower for Henry's men.'

'Yes,' Amanda said, accepting the candle from him. He left, and she swiftly began checking the writing desk. Her profession stood her in good stead. She knew her way around this piece of furniture and every nook and cranny. Coming up empty, she took the candle and moved across to the chest, kneeling beside it. Out came the wand again.

'*Agertyn.*'

The lock gave, and Amanda raised the lid. She searched the contents. Mostly it was scrolls or expensive-looking editions of what appeared to be sacred texts and commentaries in various shapes and sizes. All hand-inscribed, some illuminated and neatly stacked.

It was clearly not much used or important: just a small, brown- leather-covered book near the bottom of the chest. It seemed to date from long ago. Amanda hastily but carefully, mindful of its historical value to come – if it survived - turned to the more recent entries. There was the name of Brother Barnabas! A good start. On a folded A4 sheet with which Amanda had supplied herself, she began to copy down the monastic and corresponding secular names of all at the priory whom she remembered. Just one more left to find …

Abel dashed in.

'Henry's men! Upon the road. They will be here in minutes. Mistress!'

Amanda glanced up briefly. 'You must go, Abel. To your family. Now.'

'But you –'

'Go!'

He hurtled out of the door as she found and scribbled the last name.

'Hold!' came a shout from the cloister. 'Who is in the Abbot's study!?' It was Pius. Oh no, thought Amanda, he must have revived.

Amanda grabbed her pencil and paper and thrust them back under the bands on her arm, retreating to the cover of the desk. Pius entered, rubbing his head, and, seeing her, stood and pointed an accusing finger.

'You! You have slain Brother Barnabas. I saw him lying dead. You have poisoned him.'

'No, ... I ....'

'You,' he spat out, moving towards her, 'with your Celtic ways. It is some potion. Some witchcraft.'

Amanda suddenly dodged around the desk and broke for the door, pushing a chair over to impede his progress as he came after her, crying out,

'Brothers! Stop Brother Austell! Seize him!'

Adrenaline gave wings to her feet. Tempest stopped and turned toward Pius, hopping on all fours, back arched. All at once growing in size and baring his teeth, he let out a hiss that momentarily halted the pursuit.

'An evil spirit!' shouted Pius to the monks coming to join him. 'Do not let it deter you.'

Tempest turned to follow Amanda. He had bought her a precious few yards. She fled towards the gatehouse, pulling out her wand.

Rapidly, Amanda judged roughly where beyond the gate she might have reached by the time the spell was uttered and was about to begin her chant.

At that moment came a violent thud upon the gate and a cry of: 'Open in the name of the King!'

There was no help for it; she would have to cast the portal this side of the gate in full view of her pursuers. Amanda was no runner and had only the shortest of sprints in her. Muttering the spell between gasps that were ever more asthmatic, her head fizzed.

Despite his condition, zeal spurred Pius on. He closed on Amanda, and his hand grabbed her hood and, with it, her wig. Her hair flew out as she dipped her head out of the hood and scapular with it.

'A woman!' The shock of discovering slowed him. 'A woman! Defiler!'

He reached out once more and took hold of her sleeve.

Quick as a flash, Amanda ripped off the cord at her waist, ducked and spun around. As the garment came loose in Pius's hand, the portal opened. With one arm still in the coat, she flung herself through it, her legs collapsing beneath her and Tempest leaping at her side. Her arm came free, and she began the closing spell as she arched towards the ground on the other side. And surely would have hit it. Trelawney, too late for the portal in the trees, was alert for the eerie fluctuation in the air that proceeded its opening. His waiting arms caught her.

He heard her chant and then, breath barely squeezing out of her lungs, 'I got it ….'

The last words she heard were, 'Amanda … it's all right …. You're safe.'

Chapter 58

༄

THE LETTER

Amanda became aware of the softness of the sofa, the blanket over here, the cushions beneath her head and a warm furry mass up against her side and under her left hand. At the same time, she recognised the voice of Dr Neeta Patel.

'She will be fine, Inspector … with rest. But running around a lot of dusty old stones at night is far from my recommendation for one with asthma of Amanda's severity. Perhaps you can convince her of this. And make her some tea when she wakes up properly.'

Amanda was woozy for some time, drifting in and out of consciousness or sleep. In one of her lucid moments, Dr Patel asked,

'How do you feel, dear?'

'Oh fine … yes. Bit weak.'

'Breath slowly in and out.' Amanda complied. 'Can you take a deep breath? Yes … good. All right. Just rest. The inspector will stay with you.'

'Thank you, Doctor.'

'No more running around tonight, hm?'

Amanda smiled. 'No, Doctor,' and returned to the arms of Morpheus.

Assured of her future recovery, Thomas's annoyance bubbled up to the surface. He had been waiting outside the priory with a mixture of anxiety and frustration, lightly seasoned with irritation kindled by fear for Amanda's life.

She opened her eyes and looked for Thomas. He was sitting opposite with his laptop and, at once, put it aside and came to her. Amanda smiled blearily.

'I did it. I got the list, and I know what happened.'

'I congratulate you,' he said sincerely. 'On the other hand, I cannot help but ask myself what part of the word "team" seems to be causing you the most difficulty.'

'Oh, I am so sorry, Thomas,' Amanda said contritely. 'But you were still on the road, and it was … timing. And I was only *just* in time, without a moment to spare.'

He was disarmed. 'Ah. Well, in that case … all right.'

Amanda looked down and pulled Tempest close.

'Let me tell you what happened,' she said, moving deeper into the sofa to make room for him to sit beside her.

'Yes, but I'll get some tea first. Doctor's orders.'

By the time he returned to her side, Amanda was sitting up. While the tea in the mugs brewed and cooled, she began to unfold all that had transpired.

'It seems that Barnabas came upon the "Puppy Eyes" Venables, the spy who he'd been keeping an eye on, in the refectory. Puppy Eyes had struck down Pius, who was probably nosing about, and then Barnabas and the spy fought and got out their dinner knives. Barnabas killed Venables, but Venables mortally wounded Barnabas, so he was on his way out when I got to him. In his final minutes, he wanted to "confess" that he'd killed Abbot Giles when he came to open the hidey-hole and stash the extra treasure, in order to save the priory.'

Amanda told him how Pius had grabbed her habit and how, if it hadn't been for Tempest spoiling her real set of monk's garb, she would never have cobbled together the replacement that she was able to get out of in time. It was like he'd known, Amanda said fondly as she cuddled her familiar.

Even with the successful outcome, the tale was no easy listening for Thomas. Especially as he had been doing some research and read what befell the abbots of Glastonbury, Colchester and Reading, who had stood out against Henry's takeover. But he waited until she had concluded her narrative before responding:

'You took an enormous risk. What if Pius had caught you? What if the Prior had handed you over to Henry's men under a charge of murder? Pius, at least, would almost certainly have tried to pin the death of the Abbot on you rather than on one of their own. Then accuse you of having poisoned, at least, the mind of brother Barnabas with your evil foreign Celtic ways.'

'I know … I know … but … now we know. You found the list?' Amanda asked, who had felt the elastic bands, Pocket-wand and paper gone from her arm.

'Yes, while I waited for Dr Patel. Easy to interpret, knowing everyone's monastic name.'

'And now we know Harold and Janet's murders were about *place*. The letter Barnabas sent to his father, telling him the location of the hiding place, must have come to light. But for whom?'

'Quite. And how?' Thomas added.

'Papers can be stored, left unsorted, passed from generation to generation. Bearing in mind, too, that not everyone was literate. Less than twenty per cent then, and only half the population could read as late as the 1800s.'

'But Barnabas was an educated man, was he not? And of a noble family, according to Abel.'

'But not all of the nobility could read,' Amanda informed him. 'Fewer women than men for a start, and if the man's main thing was soldiering, then he'd be less likely to be literate because he wouldn't need to be. But let's say Barnabas's father could read. The monasteries weren't restored during his lifetime, and Barnabas wrote that the treasure was to remain where it was until such time as the priory was re-established.'

'And, all too clearly, it never was,' Trelawney remarked.

'So the letter would have passed from generation to generation, or at least ….'

'… from one homeowner to the next. Until it was found by someone in the village.'

'Most likely one of our newcomers,' Amanda put in.

'Indeed.'

Chapter 59

༄

THE NIGHTSTAIRS

'So Barnabas told you where the treasure was?' asked Trelawney.

'No, that's just it! It was the last question I was able to ask him before his final breath. He made this sort of "whhh" sound, which I expect was just breath, and then he just said what I'm sure was, "the nightstairs".'

'Well, you've spent quite a bit of time, over your Sundays in the present, going up and down them. Do you know of anywhere on them, or under them, that a box or bag of treasure could be hidden?'

'No,' Amanda admitted flatly, but then her mood changed. She sat up and gazed into the empty hearth. 'Unless … what if it wasn't "stairs" as in "flight of" but "stares" as in looks at?'

'The night stares?' Trelawney queried.

'It was dark. Maybe, he might have seen eyes in the dark. The Night stares?'

'He wasn't stabbed by an animal,' pointed out Trelawney.

'Someone, a human, with light eyes?'

'Humans don't have eyeshine,' he countered.

'Unless,' replied Amanda, 'they have cataracts or some other eye condition more serious. But Barnabas may not have been entirely sentient at the end. Maybe he thought I didn't know he'd killed the – Wait. Please, pass me the list, Inspector!'

Trelawney went over and got it for her.

'Thank you.' She looked closely at her scribbled notes. Then, 'Ha! As I thought. Look,' invited Amanda turning the paper for him to see, and pointing.

'Brother Stephen, Sir Piers Blatchford?' he asked.

'And the last one.'

'Brother Giles, Sir Erkred Hukkelham. Erm…?'

'See? What if Barnabas wasn't saying "night", as in opposite of "day" but ….'

'Knight with a "K". And we have two of those here,' Trelawney observed.

'Yes, what if he was trying to say, 'Keep safe where the knight stares!?'

'Why would Barnabas call one of them "the knight"?'

'Well, look, he's listed here: Brother Barnabas, Basil Hukkelham. If he was a poor relation,' reasoned Amanda, 'and his parents wanted to stress their noble family connection, or out of respect, they might have referred to second-cousin-once-removed or whatever as "sir knight or "the knight".'

'Bit formal,' objected Trelawney.

'But people were. You know, in Jane Austen, *Sense and Sensibility*, Mrs Jennings always refers to her son-in-law as "Sir John", doesn't she?'

'Does she?' responded Trelawney vaguely. His knowledge of Austen was less thorough than Amanda's. 'Right. Ok, so your theory is possible. But if true, then it must have been Giles to whom Barnabas was referring. But where did the knight stare?'

'At supper. Barnabas was watching the Abbot like a hawk and following his gaze.'

'Yes, I did think at times it seemed Giles was looking through me, but he could have been looking ... at the wall behind me. Where ... he hid the treasure.'

'Yes!' Amanda's enthusiasm was mounting. 'Because Cury, who usually sits where you did, said the same, that the Abbot kept looking at him funny, or words to that effect.'

'So, in the wall. Yes .... and that would be where both Harold and Janet's bodies were found too, and that of the Abbot. It fits. Well done, Miss Cadabra,' Trelawney congratulated her with a smile. 'And so, recently, one of our suspects found the long-stored letter and came to seek their fortune, and not above board.'

'No,' concurred Amanda, 'because surely someone legit, prepared to hand over treasure trove to the Crown ....'

'... And just picking up a comparatively meagre finder's fee would never have been violent. On the other hand,' Thomas added the rider, 'if the treasure belonged to a predecessor, then it would go to the present-day heir.'

'But what if the finder was *not* the direct heir? The trail leads us through Barnabas's father, and that, I'm sure, is where the connection is to today! One of these surnames has to mean something; it has to take us down through 500 years to one of our suspects, who has some kind of family link.'

'Let's assume you're right,' responded Trelawney cautiously.

'Well, it *couldn't* be Humpy. He's an historian. He would have gone through his attics and cellars and every corner of their property over the years and catalogued every scrap of a document there.

'Yes, true. He was never a contender,' Trelawney assured her.

Amanda smiled gratefully, 'Thank you for that. But the others ...?'

'Follow the money,' Trelawney advised, 'or, rather, the need or lust for it. Flemming: in property, "one of the boys" likes the good times, holidays, alcohol. Probably collects something expensive, as well. All of that is high maintenance. And above all, he's always after the big win.'

'Janet always going on about how she has to do everything now that her husband is ill. Likes cleaning and creating order, during which she could have found the letter. Oglethorpes could have been there for generations. She was righteous like the monk, Pius, but he wasn't a murderer – still, that doesn't mean she wasn't. She could have been Harold's killer. Many's the murder committed in the so-called cause of Right, in the eyes of the perpetrator.'

'Only, if she did find the letter, she didn't have it on her when she visited the priory for the last time, nor is it in her luggage,' Trelawney pointed out. 'Ok, next: Nightingale. Probably here to learn about property law in relation to the local land. Aspires to the good life. Coat of arms on the wall, but he doesn't have a title or land or fortune. We need to dig into the ancestry of all of them.' A thought came to him. 'Just a minute.' He got out his PCN and leafed through the pages. 'Yes, here it is. Hillers referred to Nightingale as "Forty".'

'A nickname?' Amanda suggested. 'He couldn't have been forty years old at the time. It was too long ago when they were dating.'

'Or it could be his real name,' offered Trelawney. 'I've always thought that "Edward Nightingale" sounded like a stage name, and he has worked in the theatre for many years, even if not as an actor.'

'True. Forty? Fortiscue? Does sound grand. Like he comes from a posh family.'

'Agreed.' Thomas was reading his notes from the interview that day. 'Here, Hillers mentioned she saw a drawing on his wall with a coat of arms. Maybe she can describe it.'

'Let's call and ask her,' suggested Amanda eagerly.

Thomas got out his phone, put it on speaker, and soon reached Hillers.

'Can you recall the coat of arms on Edward's wall?' Trelawney enquired hopefully.

'Yes: had an eagle and a motto. Given the occasion, I found it memorable: *Resurgemus*: We Shall Rise. Motto of the Fourtisque family. With a "U" and a "Q", by the way.'

'But he gave his name as Nightingale?'

'Yes, said he found it smoothed his path more effectively. Fourtisque was his mother's family name. Bunch of cashless snobs, he claimed, as far as I remember. Blanch said he was only permitted to dwell upon the perimeter of their reflected but dim former glory. However, he was determined to make his own way.'

'Blanch?' queried Amanda.

'Blanchard. Blanchard Fourtisque. That's his real name. Or it was.'

'Thank you, Hillers.' They said their goodbyes, and Trelawney hung up.

While listening to the call, Amanda had also been re-examining the list.

'What if Blanchard was a descendant of the prior? Stephen Blaxford. Blaxford, Blanchard. Sometimes people gave their children family surnames as first names.'

'But the Prior didn't know about the treasure. Or did he?' asked Trelawney. 'But, we're straying from the point. It was not the Prior who Barnabas was watching, was it? Or who I thought was looking through me. We come back to Giles, who probably couldn't resist to keep on checking that the wall had no tell-tale signs of a hidey-hole. But when and how would he have created such a hiding place, anyway, without anyone else in the monastery knowing about it? Because if others did know about it, that widens the field considerably of those to whom that information could have come over the centuries.'

They sat and pondered, Amanda staring again into the fireplace, the silence broken only by the occasional snore from the furry heap on her lap.

Chapter 60

☙

The Cloister and The Hearth

Tempest stirred himself, having observed the humans' abject failure to ignite what few brain cells they possessed. He sighed, hopped off Amanda's lap and went to sit by the empty fireplace.

As though Perran and That Woman hadn't given her enough of a clue, he thought.

Amanda looked up.

'I suppose … is it a little bit chilly in here?'

'It seems warm to me, but I'll light the fire if you're feeling cold,' said Thomas, getting up. Amanda watched him set a match to the kindling and encourage the flames to spread to the coke and wood.

Amanda was more than warm enough, but it was typical of Tempest, she thought, who would be happiest sitting in his fur coat, in the tropics, in a greenhouse built over a thermal vent. Still … he was looking pointedly from her to the fire and back again.

'What?' Amanda asked him. He regarded her with laboured and weary patience. Suddenly she said: 'Oh.'

'Oh?' responded Trelawney.

'Are we slow, or what?'

He smiled. 'Are we?'

'Hearth. In the refectory.'

Thomas thought. The penny dropped. 'Hearth …stone … *mason*.'

Amanda nodded. 'The guest master's brother who did the hearth, designed and supervised by Giles.'

'Being closeted with the mason daily. Anyone would take the hammering and chiselling for work on the hearth. It was the perfect cover.' Trelawney had to admire the ingenuity of the plan.

'Giles must have had the cubbyhole hollowed out then,' deduced Amanda, 'blocked up carefully and the mortar matched to the existing stuff in the wall. And that wall is double thickness.'

'The refectory is built against the church wall: take a bit out of the outer skin of the church and the refectory wall adjoining and, hey presto, you … have … your … cavity.' They smiled at one another. 'Henry's men would have had to tear down every wall to find it,' Thomas remarked.

'But,' Amanda assessed, 'I don't think the Abbot was a devious man by nature. I think the fact that he was concealing something from the authorities would have weighed on him, given the divine right of kings and all that.'

'So he couldn't help looking at the wall, checking it was flat enough to deceive the eye. But that must have been done some time ago. Abel said the guest master's brother was dead. So why worry about the wall now? Unless he wanted to add whatever valuables he had in his office and those that were stored in the sacristy for regular use.'

'Yes,' agreed Amanda, 'because he must have guessed that the letter from our Tresco Abbot contained a warning about a royal takeover being imminent.'

Trelawney nodded. 'So had to stash everything precious he had, pronto. Even hastily, and may have feared he wouldn't be able to do a good enough job of putting the stones back just the way they were before.'

'But,' continued Amanda, 'even though not a devious man himself, he was being watched by someone who *did* have a devious mind. Puppy Eyes the Spy was watching the Abbot, but he wasn't watching Barnabas and didn't see Barnabas was watching the Abbot *and* him.'

'So that was it.'

'And then Giles had to add our new cup to it, so that's why he was in there when Barnabas caught him.'

'That does all fit.' Trelawney returned to the crux of the matter. 'But how does it help us now? If Blanchard, Finley or the Curate found Barnabas's letter, how does that explain the death of Janet or any possible involvement she might have had? Harold, I think, was just unlucky. His dog was probably onto something and observed by Fourtisque, let's say, had to be stopped along with its owner, who might have been about to find whatever the dog had sniffed out.'

'I agree, Inspector, that doesn't explain Janet. Surely lots of people must have wandered across the priory ruins. If they were walking from the estate, say, up towards the asthma centre, it would be a bit of a shortcut. Why single out Janet?'

'It is hard to see her involvement. Let's look at the list again.'

'Pius. He was such an officious busybody. Wouldn't surprise me if somehow he'd found out about the treasure,' Amanda commented frankly. 'Tobias Velander, he was before he joined the monks. Hm, sensible, Pius; Tobias.'

Trelawney retrieved his laptop and came back to the sofa. He Googled. 'Velander … Belgian origin … Flemish ….'

'What if? Velander, Vlander, Flander, … Flanders, Flemmish … Flemming! Now,' Amanda added, getting into the swing, 'we just have to see if we can link up Janet and the Curate to Barnabas or one of the other monks! Although the Rector seems pretty adamant about ruling Kay out.'

'Too many possibilities,' Trelawney stated flatly. 'And to be honest, I don't think this game is all that profitable. I'll bet you could find any name from the past that you could *somehow* link to someone in Sunken Madley.'

'Hm, probably.'

'And time is running out,' he observed seriously.

'In that case, now we know where the treasure is, there's only one thing for it: we must set a trap!' she urged, eyes shining with anticipation.

'Not "we",' Trelawney responded crisply. 'I.'

'Of course, Inspector,' Amanda replied compliantly. 'But I can just come along, can't I?'

'To observe only,' came the concession.

'Of course,' she repeated, apparently biddably.

Thomas was not in the least taken in by that tone. 'May I remind you that you have very recently been through a life-threatening experience?'

'Yes, and in books and films, when the hero gets shot or beaten up, he gets up and goes out and gets the baddie,' Amanda pointed out energetically.

'Fiction,' remarked Trelawney acerbically. 'Such a splendid guide to real life.' Amanda's literal mind interpreted this favourably. She smiled.

'Isn't it just? So that's agreed then.'

'What is?' Trelawney asked suspiciously.

'I'm coming with you.'

'Oh, that. Yes, fine,' he allowed. 'We'll find a safe place from which you can watch. *Watch*.'

'Hm. So how do we go about setting the trap?'

Chapter 61

❧

THE BAIT

'I expect,' hazarded Amanda, 'we circulate the news that we intend to go and find the treasure tomorrow?'

'Yes,' Trelawney confirmed, 'that will draw out the rat or rats. They'll have to get it out tonight. Actually, it would have to be dusk, while they can still see without a torch, which would draw attention from the nearby houses.'

'In case they don't take that bait, we should say that *I'm* going to check it out,' she recommended. 'If they don't know the exact location, they'll be waiting until I get to it, then make their move.'

'Say you're going to check it out so that you can risk your life again? Oh, what a splendid idea.'

'Of course, I won't be at risk,' Amanda insisted. 'You'll be there, concealed. Ready to intervene as they raise their blunt instrument of choice.'

'And if it's a bullet?' he asked pointedly. 'Fired from the shadows?'

'I'll be fine,' came the rash promise.

Thomas was irritated by her apparently cavalier attitude to her own danger. 'Oh so, you've been shot before, have you?'

'No,' she admitted. 'Hm, I'd really rather not. I expect it's awfully painful. But I doubt any of them will do anything so noisy.'

'You do know that silencers have been around since 1869?'

Amanda regarded him with surprise. 'Have they? What a fascinating detail. Who came up with the notion?'

Thomas, however, was not to be deflected.

'It is a *real risk*.'

'I'll wear a flak jacket or whatever,' Amanda offered.

'Yes, you will. If there is no other way.'

'Well,' she began reasonably, 'no one is going to tackle a policeman, are they? I don't think Finley, for all his gym sessions, would get the better of you, nor would Edward. The Curate most certainly not. And we don't know which one of them it is. If you show up, it will scare them off.'

'Well ….'

'If we can't think of any other way. As a last resort?' she appealed.

Thomas sighed. Amanda and her last resorts, he thought.

'Agreed.'

She looked at the clock. 'The Biggerstaffs. I told Terry, until tonight. I wonder how long into the night they'll wait.'

'We'll forestall them,' Trelawney said decisively. 'Let's pay them a visit and let them in on the plan. I believe we can trust them to keep it to themselves.'

'An edited version of the plan,' recommended Amanda.

'That will be calling on your particular skill,' he observed with a lifted eyebrow. But this ironic reference to her selectiveness with information was overlooked by Amanda, who urged,

'Yes, so let's go now before one of them turns up on the doorstep again!'

They were soon informing the Biggerstaffs that a document pertaining to the priory had been found, and it seemed that treasure was rumoured to be hidden there. The dog, Woodie, being a skilled natural hunter, had likely located it, and Harold, as he investigated, was struck down by the treasure hunter. The same with Janet. They now had a strategy to catch the killer that night and asked that the Biggerstaffs keep safe indoors.

Gary and Sharon thanked them and were even excited at being made privy to the plan. Gary duly promised to prevent his father from taking any action, and Sharon said they'd keep their daughter at home and wait to hear from them. Sharon apologised to Amanda and hoped her father-in-law hadn't sounded threatening or anything. Amanda assured them both that their concern was quite understandable and thanked them for agreeing to keep quiet about the evening's agenda.

Next, they went to drop in on Erik and his assistant for a casual chat about the law governing buried treasure. They called at the rectory to ask the Rector and the Curate about church valuables. They went for a snack in the Big Tease and discussed the subject when members of the owners' teatime crowd were within earshot. Consequently, the rumour quickly circulated that there was treasure at the priory, which the inspector and Amanda were planning to investigate the next day.

Back at the office, there were phone calls to make. Trelawney asked Vanessa to keep an eye on Finley, and Amanda persuaded Jane to be aware of Kay's movements, just in case. They had no time alone with Erik to ask him to watch Nightingale, as the assistant was both helpfully and unhelpfully present during their conversation. They requested Humpy to stay indoors and with a member of the household at all times in case anything was going to happen, for which he'd need an alibi.

Now, all they had to do was wait until dusk. Tempest curled up on a cushion and got some ever-much-needed naptime in. Trelawney, every now and then, covertly looked out from the office window from which it was possible to see the edge of the priory.

He was accustomed to the tedium of the stakeout. Amanda was not, and soon her mind turned back to what Trelawney had earlier referred to as a game.

She looked at the list from the Abbot's study. Giles … Hukkelham …. Erkred Hukkelham … Erkred? Saxon? She got out her laptop. Googled …

'Inspector?'

Thomas turned from the window.

'Found something?'

'A link!'

Chapter 62

∽

THE PIECES

'Yes. Giles, Sir Erkred Hukkelham, and Barnabus Hukkelham – Hukkel – Hoggel – Ogle!' exclaimed Amanda.

'Hmm, and both "thorpe" and "ham" refer to habitational names.'

'Yes!'

'Ok … but if it was Janet who found the letter,' Trelawney reasoned.

'Makes sense, though, doesn't it? According to Linnie, her daughter,' Amanda recalled, 'Janet was a born organiser. But she was up in Yorkshire. How would she have met either Finley or Edward down in London … unless ….'

'You've thought of a link?'

'Possibly. Linnie said they had a lodger, a friend of her brother's, who was a bit older than Freddie. What if …?'

'Male, yes? Flemming would be too young, perhaps? But let's try.'

Trelawney made a call.

'Hello, Mr Oglethorpe?'

'That's me.'

'This is Detective Inspector Trelawney.'

'Oh aye, you're working on my Janet's case.'

'That's right. Your lodger when your son was at university. Could you tell me if it was one of the two men in the photos I'm sending to you, please?'

'Course. Go ahead, Inspector.'

He waited while Thomas dispatched the images and then looked carefully at them. Then,

'Aye, that's 'im. Older, of course, but yes, that's Forty. Blanchard Fourtisque.'

'Do you know if your wife had been in contact with him recently?'

'I don't, sorry. But she might 'ave. 'E was like family, and she liked to keep in touch, I expect.'

'Thank you very much, Mr Oglethorpe. You've been a great help. Er, do you have any old papers in the house, old family documents, records, anything like that?'

'Oh aye, up in t' attic. In a trunk. Always passed on. Never been bothered about 'istory. I'm more of a numbers man. And besides, I don't need a lot of papers or to know what's in my genes to know who I am. I know who I am. I'm Keith Oglethorpe. I'm me.'

'Quite right, sir. But do you know if your wife might have taken an interest in them?'

'Well, no, she always said she didn't like the attic, dusty place. But she did respect it was the family's old 'ouse and never said to throw anything out up there that wasn't 'ers. Mind you, since I 'ad my heart trouble, she'd been cleaning from top to bottom.'

'Did that include the attic?' Trelawney enquired.

'Well, I wouldn't be surprised.'

'Would you be able to check, sir? It would be tidy, yes? Hoovered or swept?'

'Aye, and I can check, but you'll have to give me some time,' Keith warned him. 'I 'aven't 'ad much truck wi' stairs since I come out o' 'ospital. Only a few at a time, you understand.'

'Of course.'

'I'll call you back if that's all right, Inspector?'

'That's fine, Mr Oglethorpe. Please take your time.'

'Right you are. Call you in a bit.'

Trelawney hung up and turned to Amanda.

'Ok, let's say Janet found the letter Barnabas wrote to his father with the location of the treasure. Father gets it and puts it somewhere safe. His heir clears out his desk and dumps all of the paperwork in a chest in the attic.'

'Or keeps it safe for when the monastery would be re-established.'

'Either way, it ends up in a trunk where no one ever bothers to look for, or at it, stored over the years as the house is passed from generation to generation.'

'Until it's discovered by Janet,' put in Amanda.

'Yes, so, Janet the organiser, the project manager, contacts a solicitor she believes she can trust: her one-time lodger and possibly surrogate son, Edward the solicitor.'

'She must have intended to do this legally, then?'

'Let's give her the benefit of the doubt for now,' Trelawney recommended. 'Edward gets himself here to spy out the land and looks into the legal side of property here. Perhaps, if they can own the land where the treasure is found, it gives them a much better chance of profiting from it. But they need someone in the property market.'

'Finley. But there are dozens of estate agents. Why him?' Amanda asked.

Suddenly the image of Flemming with a piece of sticking plaster on his forehead, imperfectly hidden by his hair, came to Thomas's mind. 'Finley has a lot of accidents from horsing about.'

'Yes. I think his friend Nick Gosney said something about that too.'

'All right, Edward claimed he suffered some sort of a nervous collapse and was taken to Accident and Emergency in a private hospital where his condition turned out to be a panic attack.'

Amanda nodded. 'And Finley said he was in and out of A and E all the time and all the staff know his name.'

Trelawney got out his phone again and dialled.

'Nikolaides, check private hospital Accident and Emergency patients … Ah ok, Urgent Care Centres … Yes, the ones that have them. Over the past six months, see if these two men were seen on the same day at around the same time: Finley Flemming and Edward Nightingale. He may have registered as Blanchard Fourtisque …. Yes, I'll spell that.' Trelawney did so, thanked her and hung up.

'So, if the three of them were in it together … where does the Curate come in?' asked Amanda. 'Or doesn't she?'

'Let's assume not, for the time being. Unless it was that the Gang of Three thought it might be on church property, and Kay could find out for them and so drew her into the circle.'

Amanda shook her head. 'No. Jane is very thorough. I'm sure she's examined and filed every single document within the church and the rectory. There would have been nothing for Kay to find. And anyway, she just doesn't seem the type to do anything bad.'

'All right. So …' Trelawney's phone rang, and he answered it. 'Mr Oglethorpe. Are you all right? … Good. Well done…. Yes …. Yes … You're sure? … Ah, well, we can thank Mrs Oglethorpe for that. … Indeed … Of course … Thank you, sir. Goodbye.'

'He found it?'

'No, but Janet had organised all of the papers in the attic into document wallets, which made it easy for him to check. Mr Oglethorpe got up there more quickly than he expected. Clearly, he's on the mend and promised to have a look around the house, after a rest, in case his wife put the letter somewhere else.'

'So, if the letter was in the Oglethorpe family, and Janet did find it, and it wasn't on her or in her luggage, and if it isn't at the family house, where is it now?' asked Amanda rhetorically.

'Indeed. So, putting the Curate aside, either or both Finley and Nightingale must have seen Janet at the site of the treasure, assumed she was jumping the gun and killed her.'

'Like out of vengeance for betrayal?' suggested Amanda.

'Well, if she wasn't to be trusted. And one person fewer to divide the proceeds of the sale of the treasure with,' Trelawney observed. 'This was a house of cards from the beginning.'

'Hm. Well, I expect we'll find out more soon enough.'

They waited, watching the sky and the priory.

Chapter 63

Armed

Just before dusk, the call came. Vanessa said she hadn't seen Finley. He wasn't in his room or anywhere in the pub. But she'd found something in his room that she thought might be suspicious. 'I've found a gun case. I think. I'm not sure.'

'I'll be right there.'

Trelawney hung up. 'Flemming's gone from the hotel. Seems he might be armed. I need to see the case, which Vanessa thinks might be for a gun, for myself. Please, stay here until I get back.'

Vanessa was waiting calmly, but somewhat anxiously, for the inspector in reception and quickly led him up to Finley's room, saying quietly,

'He hasn't checked in his key. But I can't see him around. It's perfectly legal for me to enter guest rooms, by the way,' she added.

'I know,' Trelawney assured her.

She opened the door and pointed to under the bed.

Trelawney pulled out the hard plastic case. It was not locked. There was the sculpted foam to receive a rifle, sights and ammunition. It was no easy task telling the difference between an air rifle and a rifle that fired bullets. Police were not routinely trained in their use; that was the province of the Authorised Firearms Officers. Trelawney took some photos on his phone and sent them to Baker, who called back.

'Hello sir, got your pics. Sent them on to Mary, sir. She'll know. I'm checking it myself online in the meantime.'

'All right. Thank you, sergeant. I'm going to look for Flemming. Looks like he's armed. I may need backup.'

'Standing by, sir.'

As Trelawney finished the call, Vanessa offered, 'I'll recheck the garden.'

He followed her back downstairs, but as she entered the reception area, she looked out through the front door.

'Inspector! There's his car just pulling out of the car park.'

Trelawney ran to the Mondeo and followed at a discreet distance.

Flemming drove up the High Road toward the ruins. But before reaching them, he turned off to the right, along Vicarage Lane and parked at the end of it, where it turned at right angles into Manor Lane.

Where on earth … ? wondered Thomas.

Flemming got out and headed north-west into the trees between the two estates, one to the west and one to the east. He was carrying a weapon.

Trelawney pursued as quietly as possible. Presently, Finley stopped and looked up into the trees and around him. Thomas stood still.

The man shouldered his rifle.

* * *

The sky had grown dim. Tempest woke up, livid yellow eyes bright in the subdued light.

Amanda looked at her watch, and then her phone, then back at the sky.

'Whoever it is probably won't turn up until darker dusk,' she reasoned spuriously. 'I can't see enough from here. It won't do any harm to get just a bit closer. We can stay in the shadow of the house at the edge of the estate.'

Her familiar began to purr. He stood up, ready to leave. Amanda put her hair into a business-like plait.

'Yes, Tempest, we'll just look.'

Amanda locked the office door behind them, and they slipped into the porch, then across the quiet road. No one was in sight. There were her nightstairs and the platform where they picnicked. So that had been the church beyond … there was what remained of the wall, doubled up where the refectory had been up against it. Yes … must have been …

Drawn by the fascination of history and the strange sensation of shared space over the centuries, stranger than ever in the unworldly twilight, Amanda found herself approaching closer than she had intended. This was the place … yes, the place in front of which she and Thomas had sat at supper, only last night … except it wasn't, was it? It was almost five hundred years ago … She put up a hand almost reverently to touch the wall where, surely … here ….

'That's enough, Miss Cadabra,' came a quiet, chiding voice from the shadows. 'No touching.'

* * *

Finley tilted up the rifle, looking through the sights into the branches. He fired. A flutter went up from the canopy, but nothing dropped.

'Oh well, Fin,' he said aloud to himself. 'If, at first, you don't succeed ....'

'Mr Flemming.'

He turned with a slight start. 'Yes? Ah, hello, Inspector. Oh, it's all right,' Flemming added hastily, 'I do have a permit.'

'Good to know,' Trelawney replied amicably. 'May I see it?'

'Yes, I made sure to have it on me. It's just an air rifle, of course, but … all the same. I know the law.' His jacket appeared to be equipped with myriad pockets. They came up devoid of paperwork, and he made the tour again. 'Sorry about this, Inspector. I know I have it ….' Finally, the errant document was tracked down in Finley's wallet. 'Ah, I can see it.' But the wallet was crammed and took some un-wedging. 'Here.' He handed it to Trelawney, who inspected it by the torchlight from his phone app.

'Hm … yes, that all seems to be in order. But do you have permission to hunt here?' Trelawney asked doubtfully.

'Oh, that's not an easy one, is it? Oh, I don't mean the question; I mean finding out who owns a bit of wood and getting in touch and getting an answer. I expect you have to ask that sort of question all the time, coming from the country.'

'I come from the town, but, yes, I have had to investigate such things. So …'

'Well, when I saw I was coming here, I did see the woods on the map and thought I might have a bit of spare time, and why not? I wasn't having much luck, to be honest, but thought I'd bring my gear anyway. In a case, all secure and locked up and legal, of course. Oh.' A thought occurred to him. 'Perhaps I should have asked the proprietor if it was all right for me to … but anyway I do ….'

'Mr Flemming, what is your purpose in coming to Sunken Madley?'

'Well, in the line of business. Property and development. I've told you that, Inspector. All aboveboard, isn't it?'

'I hope so, Mr Flemming.'

'Yes, so I approached The Grange as one of the oldest establishments in the village, thinking they might own the p– piece of land I was interested in. Well, they were very nice and said, no, they didn't, and then I asked, on the off chance, if they knew who owned the Wood because I thought I might do a bit of shooting while I was here. Just pigeons and squirrels, as no one would mind about them, being classed as vermin and pests. And they said they owned a part of the Wood, and I was welcome to shoot there, as long as I had a licence and so on.'

'Most kind of them, and fortunate for you. Do you have this in writing, Mr Flemming?'

'Oh yes, all good, all sorted. The butler, Moffat, he put it into an email. I'll just check my phone. Hold on, …. I know it's here somewhere … I'll find it … but I get so many … like you do ….'

Chapter 64

~

The Road to Ruin

Amanda stood very still. It was all right. The inspector would be here at any moment. The speaker was hidden, but the voice was one she knew.

'It was you,' said Amanda calmly.

'That's right.'

'You killed Harold and Janet.'

'In an honourable cause,' he countered.

'Which honourable cause?' she asked curiously.

'I am raising the estate of the Family,' he declared, emerging into the fading light. It was enough for Amanda to see that he was holding a large stone in his right hand.

'The Nightingales?'

He looked down his nose at her. 'Don't be absurd. I am Blanchard Fourtisque.'

'Oh,' replied Amanda, simulating what she hoped sounded like admiration, 'I see.'

'I doubt it. Plebeians,' Blanchard remarked, flicking a speck from the shoulder of his jacket, 'I should never have worked with plebs. I should have insisted on handling the entire matter myself as the *only* competent person.'

'Which plebs?' asked Amanda, trying to use his momentary sartorial distraction to manoeuvre herself more into the open. He was too quick for Amanda and took a step towards her.

'That Oglethorpe woman ….'

'What did she have to do with it?' Amanda had to ask.

'A certain piece of information came into her grubby little hands.'

'A letter?'

'You see? You know too much. Too much knowledge is a dangerous thing for the likes of you and the Oglethorpe and that useless estate agent,' Fourtisque spat out in disdain.

'Finley?'

'We had an agreement. She and I would stay *away* from the site while Flemming tracked the owner or created a legitimate reason for being here, conducting a close inspection.'

'And he failed or took too long?' she asked quickly, pulling out all the stops to keep him engaged.

'Lax. What else could one expect of persons of that class?' He tweaked his cravat. 'And then that boy … that dog started nosing around like it knew. I had to take care of the situation, which, I need hardly say, I performed expertly.'

'Of course,' Amanda humoured him.

No more magic on humans. She had had to so resolve so. It had had appalling consequences. Where was Tempest? Why was he always disappearing at crucial moments? Where was the inspector? All she could do was buy him time, time to arrive …

'Then the woman,' he was continuing, 'clearly couldn't contain herself, overwhelmed by greed, no doubt. No self-control, those people. What did I expect?'

'But perhaps she was seeking whatever it is on behalf of you all?' suggested Amanda pacifically.

Fourtisque regarded her with scorn.

'Oh, don't play the innocent with me, girl. You know what's hidden, don't you? Or why are you here? You're working with the police, or,' – he narrowed his eyes – 'you want some share of it, more likely.'

'Just for the local museum,' replied Amanda carefully.

He replied with a jeering laugh, imitating her voice. '"The local museum",' he scoffed. 'Private buyers. That's the market. Oh yes, I know of at least three people who will pay handsomely for what's here. Not that *you* could possibly appreciate the finer things of life.'

Amanda retrenched and pitched the only diversion she could currently think of. 'I'm not a pleb,' she stated, raising her chin, straightening her back and generally assuming a fair imitation of Senara.

'Farmers your lot, *I* heard,' Fourtisque returned haughtily.

'On my grandfather's side,' she agreed, although it went to her heart not to rebut Fourtisque's disdain for them. 'On my grandmother's: Cornish aristocracy.' Amanda felt dreadful even playing along with such arrogance. But it seemed to work. He paused and looked at her measuringly.

Where was the inspector? Surely he should have tracked Finley down by now, and either apprehended him or discovered whether whatever he was about was innocent.

'Really?' Fourtisque was enquiring. 'What is your *real* interest?' Clearly, he was quite unable to imagine anyone, unlike himself, who might have an altruistic agenda.

'The estate. The Hall is hopelessly dilapidated.' Amanda, constitutionally incapable of lying, chose her facts carefully. She knew full well that there was insurance and money bequeathed for the upkeep of the unpleasant pile that reeked of malevolent sorcery.

'You understand,' remarked Fourtisque. That appeared to give them a moment of connection. 'The fate of so many noble families and their estates. Good. You want a cut, then, but ....'

'Wouldn't you say that even plebeians can have their uses, serving the cause of the nobility as they were always intended?' I have to build on what he imagines is common ground, thought Amanda.

'True. That woman, a scion of the House of Oglethorpe.'

'Hukkelham?'

'Precisely. She found the document that expressed where the treasure was to be found. As one versed in the law, she turned to me. Fortune favoured the project and brought Flemming into my path, during an unfortunate strain on my health.'

'Hospital?' she asked, trying to inject a note of concern into her voice.

'A private hospital, naturally,' Fourtisque drawled.

'He had had an accident?'

'Hopelessly clumsy, I gather – no gracefulness of movement, those people. I shall have to attend to him next, no doubt. But first things first,' he said in a business-like manner. He moved towards her slowly but purposefully.

'Tell me, how did you know Harold and Janet were at the ruins.'

He paused, willing to share his accomplishments. 'Mini surveillance camera. I could check on my phone. First thing I did when I arrived. Lots of handy little nooks and crannies to hide it in. I was on my little Sunday walk, making my way around there anyway when I saw him and his dog being a little *too* interested.'

'And Janet?'

'Simple. I checked the camera app when I was out with Erik, saw where Janet was, pretended some papers were missing and volunteered to go back for them. I took the route that brought me to the village from the north and parked in the trees, just here. It took only a couple of minutes to deal with her and get back on the road to Cockfosters.'

'And—'

'No, enough bedtime stories. Time for you to sleep now.'

'Wait. I ….'

'No. I shan't be sharing. You have to go. I have to do this. This is my chance, my chance to shine, and you're not going to stop me.'

His eyes glinted with obsession in the last of the day's light. 'Your chance to shine?' Amanda attempted to distract him once more.

'Yes, my mother always said one day I'd get my chance. My chance to shine.'

'Edw– Blanchard, I'm sure that's not what she meant.'

'Yes, yes, it is. I'm going to restore the family fortunes, whatever the obstacle. Get mother out of that squalid salon, her hands in the hair of peasants, when she should be the one waited upon. And so she shall be. I shall get the House back for the Family. There'll be a portrait of me holding the treasures. It will be hung over the fireplace in the Great Hall. I'll …'

'But you're going to sell them illegally, aren't you? So how could you openly –?'

'You don't understand, Amanda. Of course, the subtle logic of the situation eludes you. I have to do this.'

'No, you don't. We can –' she began.

'You'll just tell. I know I can't trust you.'

He was mad, quite mad; it was clear for Amanda to see. But even so, perhaps he could be shocked into realisation of what he had done. 'You've killed someone, Blanchard: a boy with his whole life before him, and a woman with a sick husband.'

'And they would never understand. I could never serve a prison sentence. The Family name. The disgrace. It is not to be borne. I could never live with that, and so … come here,' he told her in a sing-song voice. 'It will be quick,' Fourtisque assured Amanda with demented kindness.

Amanda knew she could not outrun him. She darted and dodged behind one pillar, then another. But still, he advanced, both of them kicking up the dust of the ages. It crept into her lungs.

I must not use magic, she told herself. Cough. Wheeze. She knew she could not keep this up for long. Even now, she was slowing down. Wherever was Tempest? I must not use magic, Amanda repeated inwardly. All the same, her hand had crept to her pocket and closed on her wand.

She backed up to a low wall overhung by a higher pillar. Amanda sensed a presence above, then as Fourtisque closed the distance between them, a shower of loose rocks and dust showered down from overhead. She turned away, covering her nose and mouth, as Fourtisque flailed his hands at the debris. She moved off quickly, but his recovery was swift, and on he came.

All she had to do was buy some time, time for the inspector to get here. Just a little more. But too late. As she whisked herself behind a pillar, her plait flew out, and so did his hand. Grabbing her hair, he pulled her towards him relentlessly. He held up the rock in his right hand. Deranged, he smiled and nodded.

'It will be quick.'

No choice. She flicked her wand.

'*Tŏglisyn.*' Amanda tugged, and instantly his hand slid rapidly down her hair. The counterforce sent him tottering. Instinctively, she reached out to save him but not fast enough. Tempest, hidden in the rubble, now shot out a paw, strategically scooting a small boulder into place. The murderer reeled and fell backwards, his head making contact with the carefully positioned rock. Thud. He lay, still with signs of life, the telltale pool spreading like a halo beneath him.

Amanda gasped and was torn between concern that he might be feigning and the desire to keep him alive, at least to face justice. She became aware of flashing blue lights and the sound of sirens. Three vehicles skidded to a halt, and three figures emerged.

Nikolaides, former under-18s sprint champion for North London, outstripped the men and arrived in time to hear the words the murderer delivered to Amanda as she stood by him.

'What did you say?' He rasped out between breaths, looking up at her, his eyes wide with horror. 'What … are … y …?'

Chapter 65

∽

Baker Steps In, and Amanda Owns Up

Trelawney, who had arrived with Baker seconds behind Nikolaides, quickly knelt by Fourtisque and felt for a pulse. But the staring eyes told their terminal tale.

The detective constable looked at Amanda, coughing between drawing on her inhaler.

'Miss Cadabra, are you all right?' she asked,

'Yes, thank you, Constable …. Hello, Inspector, hello, … Sergeant Baker.'

'Miss Cadabra. What did he mean?' pursued Nikolaides.

'Mean?' Amanda asked innocently.

'He said, "What did you say? What are you?"'

'No, no, Constable,' Baker intervened smoothly. 'Hard to tell when they're at their extremity, so to speak, but it was far more like "Mott Cardew".'

'Mott Cardew, sir?'

'Probably a partner or friend, maybe even a relative.'

Nikolaides looked doubtful for a moment until distracted by a new thought.

'Maybe he was implicating this Cardew?'

'Yes, well caught, Nikolaides, Baker,' Trelawney joined in. 'Please follow that up, Constable. Although, it might have been "Scott", though, do you think, Baker?

'Yes, sir, quite possibly.'

'Maybe that's why he looked so horrified at the end. Maybe this Cardew put him up to it in some way,' Nikolaides postulated.

Baker nodded. 'Hm. Well, you never know with criminals. Sir, we'll see to this if you want to take Miss Cadabra home and call the doctor, as she's not looking too clever.'

Trelawney turned to Amanda. 'Yes. Miss Cadabra, if that's all right with you?'

'Oh yes, if you would, please.'

'And I'll take Miss Cadabra's statement when she is sufficiently recovered,' he assured his sergeant.

'Thank you, sir.' Trelawney shot Baker a glance of gratitude.

At the cottage, Dr Patel finished examining Amanda while Thomas made tea.

'Yes, well,' remarked Neeta, packing up her doctor's bag. 'You've come through another asthma attack. Not as bad as the last one. But much too close for comfort.'

'Yes, Doctor. Will I be able to …?'

Neeta smiled, 'Yes, you shall go to the ball, my dear. I've always said this about you, Ammee: you're fragile but resilient. If you rest from now until the big day and introduce activity slowly and carefully, then you'll be fine. Perhaps, plan to save your dances for the … the special few, though.' She closed the catch of her bag with a click, then looked up.

'Amanda.'

'Yes, Doctor?'

'You have to stop having these near misses, you know,' Neeta said seriously.

'Oh ….'

'One day, it might not be a miss.'

Neeta patted her hand, smiled kindly, asked Thomas to stay with the patient until she retired to bed, declined tea and left. When Thomas returned from showing her out, Amanda asked,

'Sergeant Baker didn't really hear "Mott Cardew",' did he?

'I strongly doubt it,' Trelawney replied on his way to the kitchen to fetch the tea tray.

'Fourtisque almost gave me away.' Amanda helped herself to her mug of tea. 'Thank you. – Oo, where did you find Battenberg cake? – Why did Baker save me? Does he know …?'

'I don't know. We've been very careful not to discuss it,' replied Thomas, picking up his own mug and taking a seat in the armchair opposite. 'But yes, he knows something …. somethings …. that I know he will never tell, never voice. So *what* he knows or, at least, suspects, *we* shall perhaps never know. He respects beat boundaries. That, I suppose, if asked, is what he would say,' he concluded with a smile. 'So.' Trelawney stirred the sugar into his tea, then asked casually, 'How did you and your murderous cat carry out the deed this time?'

Amanda looked up and protested, 'Me? I didn't kill him!'

'Of course not, Miss Cadabra,' the inspector replied smoothly.

'*He* was trying to kill *me*!' Amanda went on.' He was backing me around the ruins, but the dust … I was slowing down, and he caught my plait and … his hand slipped …. And he fell … onto a rock.'

Trelawney regarded her measuringly, then crossed to the sofa and sat beside her. He reached to her shoulder and took her plait in his hand.

'Please, try to pull that out of my grasp, Miss Cadabra.'

She sat still, looking at him ruefully. He let go of her hair and commented,

'Yes, I thought so.'

'All right, all right,' Amanda conceded. 'I used a slipping spell. But on my *hair,* not on him.'

'And he fell backwards,' Thomas concluded.

'Yes.'

He looked at her shrewdly. 'And there just happened to be a rock on the ground at the strategic coordinates?'

Knowing his dislike for Tempest, Amanda replied airily,

'Ruins. Lots of rocks, pebbles, boulders of all shapes and sizes lying around.'

But Trelawney was not to be deceived. He leaned forward and looked at the deadly grey furry ball of familiar on the sofa beside Amanda.

Two eyes in the depths opened and glittered. Tempest smirked.

Chapter 66

༄

THE BURNING QUESTION

They ordered kebabs, which Iskender delivered personally, and Thomas suggested they watch *Skyfall*. It was long, absorbing and entertaining. Amanda's head had drooped and come to rest on Thomas's shoulder and his cheek against her hair. His eyes had likewise been closed for some time when the call came.

They woke up at the sound of the ringtone. Thomas smiled down at her as he reached into his pocket, and she straightened up. Amanda saw his expression change.

'Harris? … I see. Where this time?... Anyone injured? … Good. All right. Well, you know the drill. I'll be there as soon as I can.'

He hung up.

'Another fire?' Amanda asked with concern.

'Unfortunately, yes. I must go.' He got up and put on his suit jacket. 'And I think this time, I must stay until the arsonist is found.'

'Of course.'

'Don't get up. I'll try to get back for the party, but ….'

'I understand. This is more important. There'll be other parties.'

'Definitely. I'll keep you posted.'

'Please.'

'See you soon, Amanda, and … and well done.'

They smiled at one another, and then he was off down the hall, out of the front door. She heard it close, and in the silence of the night, the sound of his car door shutting and the engine turning on and fading away as he drove up the street and away to the west.

The end credits of the film were rolling. Tempest looked pointedly towards the stairs. His human had kept him up long enough. Her pet had brought him a snack halfway through what they regarded as the entertainment. At least that showed he had potential. His training was underway. Yes, this was going to work out satisfactorily.

Amanda switched off the television with the remote control, heaved Tempest off her lap, pushed her blanket aside, and got up. 'You can walk yourself up the stairs to bed tonight,' she told him, switching off the lights as she crossed the room.

On second thoughts, reflected Tempest, it looks like you can't get the staff these days.

* * *

Siren on, Trelawney sped through the darkest hours of the night to the address sent to him by Nancarrow. The householders were eager to speak to him.

'Inspector, like I told your sergeant and your constable, no one was in it,' Mr Tylda assured them, looking at the remains of the yurt in the garden. 'To be honest, no one's really *ever* been in it, zackly. Come to us from my cousin, you see. Died and left it to us, thinking, well, tourists and such. Bring in a bit of extra, you know. But it's a lot of trouble, and we never really made a go of it.'

'So much mildew, you'd never 'ave thought it would catch fire,' remarked his wife.

'Hot spell we been having would 'ave dried it out, though. And it's from my cousin who died. Lot of sentimental value.'

'I'm sure,' replied Trelawney respectfully.

They'd been in bed asleep with the window open and had smelt smoke when Mr Tylda had got up to use the bathroom. By the time the fire brigade arrived, it was too late.

'But we are insured. Fully,' said Mrs Tylda. 'I 'ave to say I'd rather 'ave the money than the mildew. Besides which, Jori left my 'usband a nice pair of cufflinks, for to remember 'im by. All the same, we can't 'ave these fires, Inspector, not 'ere in Par'ayle. It's gone on too long and too much. They got to be stopped before someone gets hurt.'

'I agree entirely,' Trelawney assured her sincerely. 'We shall do all we can to discover and apprehend the person or persons responsible.'

But it was the same story: no witnesses, no unusual sights or sounds. The usual suspects all appeared to have watertight alibis.

As Trelawney left the house, the owner of the website parhaylepeople.co.uk ran up.

'Any progress on the arsons? Are we safe, Inspector? Could any of us be toast by morning? Is it safe to go to our beds at night? These are the questions the people are asking.'

Trelawney thought it more like the fear-mongering questions the local paper wanted to ask.

'No one has been harmed,' the inspector commented.

'So far. But what, if anything, are our police doing?'

'We are pursuing enquiries,' Trelawney replied politely.

'Do you have any leads?'

'You know that I am not at liberty to discuss the details of an ongoing investigation.'

Trelawney got into his car and drove to the station.

The headlines that morning were variously,various in *The Parhayle News*. 'The Burning Question: 'Where will the Arsonist Strike Next?', *The Parhalye Post*: 'Police Outwitted' and *The Locksmiths Newsletter* 'Be alert! Police Stumped. Attacks Likely To Continue. Is Your House Secure?'

The station received a visit from the Parhayle Holiday Park and one of the estate agents, concerned respectively about it affecting tourists and would-be residents.

At last, the wave of calls abated, and Trelawney went to his flat to grab a few hours' sleep.

Chapter 67

☙

Family Time

It was now the day before the party, with no progress, and Inspector Trelawney, for the umpteenth time, was studying the map of the incidents. Again: what was at the epicentre? Just some houses and possibly a few small shops, including a takeaway. Thomas had an idea. Houses … hm …. Was it possible? But what could possibly be the motive?

'I'm going back over to the area around the fires,' he said to Nancarrow.

'Do you need, er, … backup, sir?' she asked hopefully.

'No, thank you, Constable. I think I can handle this one. Just a bit of reconnaissance.'

'Yes, sir.'

Trelawney parked in the slip road by the shops and took a wander.

Hm. There was the house. It bordered a little alley between the fences. Only a short cut-through that ran the depth of the front gardens, sides of the dwellings and back gardens of the residences that flanked it. Not dark or dodgy. Just a way through to the next street.

He ambled down the grass-and-gravel way. The family to the right had planted some geraniums on their side of it. In one place, they seemed a little worse for wear. Trelawney stopped at this point and looked up at the house. Flat roof, drainpipe, water butt and a small but sturdy willow on that side of the fence, just to the right of the spot with the crushed flowers. Hm …

One had to be very careful in such circumstances. First, Trelawney visited the corner shop and asked a question about the sale of matches.

'Yes, of course, to anyone. It's not like alcohol or tobacco. So, yes, to anyone at all. But that's legal, right?' asked the proprietor cautiously.

'Oh yes, yes. I just wondered.'

'You don't think someone … the fires…? Well, I wouldn't put it past one or two round here.'

'No one is being accused of anything. Just looking at any possibilities,' the inspector explained amicably. 'Thank you for your help.'

Trelawney decided next to pay a visit to an acquaintance of his father. He walked up to the Karrji Jenkin garage and found the owner just handing over a repaired vehicle to a customer.

'Good morning, Mr Jenkin,' the inspector greeted him.

'Your Kyt's lad, aren't you?'

Thomas smiled, 'I am.'

'I remember you when you were a schoolboy. Hm. You've grown a bit since then,' observed Mr Jenkin jovially.

'A bit,' he agreed.

'About the fires, are you?' the man asked shrewdly.

'Yes. I wonder if we could have a chat?'

'Well, I never done it, officer,' he replied with a grin.

'About that, I have no doubt, but perhaps ….'

'Come in the office. Roger …. Yes, start on the Volkswagen. Yes, the Golf. …. Come on, lad. We'll have a cuppa, dreckly …. Charlene, you can 'ave a break, me luvver. I'll man the phone.'

'All right, me 'ansome, but don't touch the printer,' instructed the lady. 'It's very temperamental.'

'Cross me 'eart!'

'So 'e sez!' She turned to Roger. 'I dunno, wozelike?'

'Promise.' He returned his attention to Trelawney. 'Now then.'

'Mr –'

'Dave'll do fine.'

'Thank you, Dave. You know everyone in this street?'

'I'd say so. I do all the cars. Handy, you see, in very easy walking distance!'

'And everyone in the street knows everyone else? Same local, same school, same corner shop, same garage?'

'Oh yes. Bit like a village, you might say.'

'So rumours spread … very easily?'

By the time tea had been drunk, a fair understanding had been established between the two men. Thomas had a willing accomplice for his plan.

'Right, you are, Inspector,' summarised Dave. 'So the Higgins's shed is so old it would go up like firewood, is that right? Especially with this dry spell. And there might be a couple of old fireworks in there, is that so?'

'You never know, Dave.'

'That's right. You can't be too careful, can you, Inspector. Matches … in the wrong hands ….'

Trelawney then returned to the station and shared his plan. Harris enthusiastically volunteered at once, and Nancarrow dutifully agreed to the undercover assignment. They would be posing as a courting couple by the back fence of a certain house with a certain shed.

* * *

Late that night, in the dark, Trelawney sat on a bed next to a couple who were looking anxiously toward the bedroom window.

'Fortunately, they were insured,' the inspector was explaining soothingly. 'The yurt and shed fully, the caravan less so, but it was empty, and the owner had almost got an order from the council to move it. The stall, too, had business insurance, but it will hike their premiums.'

'I'll replace the stall,' the man promised. 'My brother will help me. He's a builder: decent enough carpenter. I'll see the Losows, right. We won't have them suffering because of one of us.'

'I'll make a new awning,' added his wife. 'My neighbour's got a sewing machine. I'm sure she'll help me.'

Trelawney nodded, then put a finger to his lips. Someone was progressing up the back of the building onto the flat roof.

Izzy James's 8-year-old fingers appeared over the window ledge. Quick as a flash, Trelawney crossed the space, took her arms and hoisted her into the room. He placed her, protesting, on the carpet opposite her astonished parents.

'The game's up, Izzy,' he informed her as her father switched on the light.

'Izzy!' exclaimed her mother, going to her daughter, who was dressed in black leggings, a navy top, and matching bobble hat to hide her blonde hair. Her face was smeared with some dark slate eyeshadow borrowed from her mother's makeup collection. Of course, no one would have seen or heard the small figure creeping through the shadows armed with a box of matches.

Lips pursed, with narrowed eyes, Izzy regarded Trelawney speculatively. Then her face relaxed as she uttered judiciously, 'All right. It's a fair cop.'

'Why d'you do it?' he asked her.

'They wouldn't take me to the Jubilee Beacon Party,' Izzy explained frankly, as though this was clear justification.

'But darling, you were sick!' protested her mother.

'You had a temperature,' added her father kneeling beside her and gently taking off her hat. 'You could have given something to someone or caught something in that state.'

'I woulda bin fine,' Izzy insisted. 'I *told* you I was fine. Anyway, doesn't matter; I done my own beacons and better ones too and up close, and I lighted them myself. 'Cept tonight; a stupid couple were in the way.'

This ignited further protests and concerns from her parents. Trelawney, meanwhile, looked around and saw the bear on the bed. Purple. Of course. The colour of the maverick line he'd seen when he'd done "his thing". Izzy was carrying it on the morning after the stall fire when she came along the street with her mother.

'Who's this teddy?' he asked. The change of subject caught Izzy's attention,

'Not a teddy,' she replied with scorn. 'A bear: shape-shifting druid.' She gave him his name.

'Rogue?' queried Trelawney, thinking how appropriate that was if he'd been colluding with his owner.

'R. O. Q. Short for Roquen, of course.'

Izzy was looking at him with a don't-you-know-anything? expression as perfected by 8-year-olds.

'Tolkien,' offered Mr James helpfully.

'Ah, well, yes. Unusual. Roq.'

'Yes, and he's mine.'

'So he is,' agreed Trelawney. 'What if someone climbed in here and set fire to Roq?'

The look that appeared on Izzy's face was a mixture of alarm, protectiveness and belligerence as she declared: 'They'd never find the body!'

'Hm. How do you think the stall holder feels about his stall or Mrs Boscawen about her caravan, or the Tyldas about their yurt, then? That stall was his father's, and the caravan belonged to her uncle, and the Tyldas don't have a lot of money, but they had that yurt that might have helped them.'

Izzy looked troubled. 'Do I have to give them Roq?'

'You have to give them something that will mean more.'

'Wassat?' she asked with an eye to a bargain.

'An apology,' replied Trelawney.

'Say sorry? S'pose. Will I get sent down?'

'You will not go to prison, but you may have to go to court.'

'Before the beak?'

'Yes, and the beak will most likely impose a child curfew order, which means you must not be away from home in a public place without an adult between 9 o'clock at night and 6 o'clock in the morning.'

'And you can be very sure that's kept to,' put in her mother.

There were going to be consequences that Izzy had not considered.

Chapter 68

༄

Potential, and Aunt Amelia's Warning

The arson case was solved, and to Thomas's satisfaction, it had been achieved by using good, solid, normal, police methods, instead of a lot of …. Of course, his 'thing' had given him a hint that must have acted on his subconscious, but *other* than that …. And it seemed to have ended equably. Although, Trelawney wouldn't put it past Izzy to get into trouble in the future. Still, one could only hope for the best. Many a respectable adult had had a misstep or two in their childhood. Yes, one could only hope for the best.

Izzy certainly seemed to have given in a little too quickly. Nevertheless, his discussion with her had revealed pivot points. Hers was a mind that craved purpose and challenge, preferably for the public good. Thomas had an idea.

He had to admire Izzy's motivation and execution, if not the results. If she had only pulled off the stunt once, she would have got away with it. There was an agile mind there. One that might, one day, be of value to society. He wanted to do what he could to protect that potential. It might be that Izzy was an ideal candidate for The Detectives Project, with which she could join classes and workshops to learn to be alert for and solve crimes. There would be consultations to be had, and it all added to the inevitable paperwork. It was going to be a long day.

Thomas called Amanda and expressed his regrets. It was difficult to see how he could get back for the party.

She was understanding. She was always understanding, he thought. That somehow made it even worse.

*　*　*

'How long do you think you can get away with this, Amanda?' asked Amelia, who had invited her over for tea and slices of freshly baked Victoria Sandwich.

'With what, Aunt?'

'Visiting the past. That's deep magic, sweetie,' Amelia pointed out gently. 'Magic is not our toy.'

Amanda looked up from the delicious cream, jam and sponge cake on her plate at her aunt's serious tone. 'Of course not. But if it's the only way to get to the truth in the present, to stop killers ….'

'Oh, Ammee, no one could possibly fault your motives or your actions, but … these tiny changes you are effecting ….'

'But when it's a matter of life and death ….'

'Saving a life that may give birth to other lives, and down the years …what if that descendent, who otherwise would not have existed, is the one …?'

'What? The one what, Aunt?'

'The one who ends up here. The one who takes a life, the one you will hunt and the one who may bring the stab in the back that you don't see coming?'

'Oh, that's very extreme, Aunt Amelia …. I mean … but …. Perhaps … you're saying that I need to be more careful?'

'Yes, dear. *More careful.*' Amanda was grave. 'Then again,' Amelia added on a lighter note, 'you do have Tempest. And I pity the fool who tries to creep up on you when you have him lurking in the shadows.'

Amelia looked over at him, deep within the cushions on the sofa. His citrine eyes glittered back at her, his expression unmistakeably ... smug.

Chapter 69

༄

THE PARTY

While Amanda cooked a batch of that staple of the British menu, chilli con carne, for the freezer, Granny kept her company, sitting at the kitchen table experimenting with nail art. The pins had already been tapped into the canvas, and Senara was now winding silk thread around them.

'What's got you into that?' asked Amanda.

'Pablo's idea.'

'Pablo?'

'Picasso, dear. Do try to keep up. Make sure you have a rest before the party, won't you, Ammee?'

Tempest, perched on the small wine rack, had turned up his nose at Senara's mention of the evening's gathering.

'Still being spurned by Lady Natasha of The Grange, I see,' she remarked with a certain amount of *schadenfreude*.

'It's a new experience for Tempest,' explained Amanda with sympathy.

Indeed, there had never been anything or anyone upon which he laid his eyes and wanted that he could not have because of his appearance or charisma or simply Who He Was. Tempest did not believe in coercion of any kind. Where was the achievement where there was no free will? Force was the act of a lower form of life.

'In anyone else, I'd say it was a salutary experience. I hope Natasha has the wit and will to stand her ground,' Granny remarked drily.

'Well, perhaps it's an opportunity for character development for Tempest,' suggested Amanda.

Senara eyed the cat askance and then looked at her granddaughter.

'Really, dear?'

'Oh, all right. Probably not, but there's always hope.'

* * *

It was a quarter to eight, but the Cornish summer sky was still light. Trelawney was at his desktop computer, periodically scrolling and typing when a knock came at the door. The invitation to enter brought Detective Constable Nancarrow into the room.

She had struggled over this. It went to her heart to encourage him into the arms of Another. Even though the Another was really nice and cared about him, and his biscuits and everything. Maybe, he would one day remember … Anyway…. Oh. He was looking up at her with that ….

'Nancarrow? How can I help you?'

'Well, sir, I was thinking. It's well after hours, considering what time you started, sir.'

'True, Constable, but there's work to be done. Please don't feel you must stay. Get along home, now.'

'That's all right, sir. But I was thinking … if you clocked off now, say, and were back by tomorrow lunchtime … I'm sure you could catch up, and you wouldn't be missed, especially if someone covered for you. And you do need to interview that estate agent man, and these things are an opportunity for you to observe any strangers to the village ….'

'Erm …? Do you mean ….'

'Yes, sir. I think you should go to your party, sir. If you leave now, you could ….'

Thomas was sorely tempted.

'Well, that's very kind of you, Constable … but … I really should …. But anyway, you've certainly done enough for today. Please, go home and get some rest.'

'Yes, sir. Thank you. But you'll think about it, won't you?' She glanced up at the wall clock. 'And not for too long. Good night, sir.'

'I will. Goodnight, Constable.' Nancarrow felt more than repaid by the smile he gave her as she departed.

His phone rang. It was DC Nikolaides.

'Sir, I regret to say that I've made no progress on locating Mr, Mrs, Ms or Miss Mott or Scott Cardew. No person of either of those names seems to exist. It must have been an alias.'

'Perhaps some long-lost sweetheart. I wouldn't devote any more resources to it, Constable. You can just leave a note in the file.'

'Yes, sir. I called on Ms Fourtisque, by the way: Mr Fourtisque's mother. She said she had no idea he'd become so obsessed with the family. He was always fascinated as a child by stories about them, and they used to go there on Open Days and Family Days. She said it was a picnic for relatives on the lawn. A bring-your-own-food-and-drink affair because, in her own words, they never had two farthings to rub together. The house has been handed to the National Trust. The owners just live in a part of it, and Miss – well, Ms Fourtisque said they all have jobs, and there's really nothing romantic about any of it anymore.'

'*Miss* Fourtisque?'

'Yes, she never married his father. They went their separate ways, amicably, early on in Blanchard's childhood. The father contributed and even helped her get going with the salon she owns. They never experienced hardship. She said he was always a rather odd, dreamy boy, but she had no idea that this was festering. I thought she was a nice lady. Offered me a free nail-art session.'

'That's kind,' remarked Trelawney.

'I said I couldn't take it, of course, sir. It might have looked like a bribe. So she added her business to the Blue Light Card – first session free! Oh, it'll be neutral on nude, to fit in with regulations, of course.'

'Very thoughtful. Please thank Ms Fourtisque on my behalf. If I ever need nail art, I'll know where to go.'

Nikolaides laughed and bade him goodnight.

* * *

Claire insisted on driving Amanda, who was still recovering slightly from her 'running around the dusty ruins' again. Claire was in a little black dress with sections cut out in strategic places and covered with fine net. Amanda was in a favourite frock that had been a present from her best friend: a fit-and-flair scoop-neck of transparent silk that was self-patterned in a light matt gold over cream satin.

Miss de Havillande had been correct in her assessment of Sunken Madley being thin of company. Ryan was away, so was John and the new teacher, Jonathan too, and Jessica, Irene's supermodel daughter. The Poveys were in India, and the younger Patels in Portugal. The core of the village was present, however. Nevertheless, there was still plenty of space in the large salon.

Amanda enjoyed the evening, the delicacies, the carefully chosen partners who would give her a gentle tour of the floor, and the music. And yet … the thing she most looked forward to, as she was becoming increasingly aware, at the end of each ball … was not to be. Still, she determined to make the best of things and relish this time with her friends and neighbours. And very well indeed she did. But as it grew closer to midnight, her heart could not help but sink a little.

Over the music and the voices, she failed to hear it. The crunch of tyres slightly skidding to a halt on the drive. The solemn chime of the front doorbell. Moffat's footsteps going to answer it. Nor did she see the butler speaking to Bill MacNair on the sound system. One minute she was looking across at the fireplace, and the next … there he was, standing before her, and the opening bars of *Roses of Picardy* were playing.

'I'm not too late, I hope?'

'Insp–Thomas! You made it! What happen–? Oh, never mind.' She took his proffered hand. 'No, of course, you're not too late. How on earth did you manage it?' Amanda wanted to know as he led her into the dance.

'I stretched the regulations slightly.'

'Oh,' she asked, smiling with curiosity. 'That doesn't sound like you. Whatever did you do?'

'I do need to interview Mr Flemming, and so I escalated my need to be back here to an emergency.'

'Oh, you didn't …?'

'Yes, I was obliged to deploy the siren.'

She laughed in astonishment. 'No!'

'I couldn't possibly miss this, nor, after all, you have done to help solve this case, disappoint you.'

'You did this … for me?' she asked hesitantly.

'Of course.' He smiled at her warmly. 'Never doubt it.'

'Look at those two,' remarked Joan, comfortably circling in Jim's arms, 'glowing at one another.'

'Oh yes, just a matter of time. Like you always say to me, love,' he replied, 'there's no rush.'

'Aww,' said Sylvia, tripping the light fantastic with Dennis, 'think 'es finally tellin' 'er?'

'Probably not,' replied her partner. 'Remember, they still have to work together. Putting romance and business together;

that's the sort of dovetailing that makes the box. I'm just an amateur compared to Amanda with carpentry, but I do know that it takes careful … adjustments.'

'S'pose you're right, dearie. Still, they're young. No hurry, I'm sure. I'll wait to buy a new hat.'

'Oh no, don't wait to do that. But buy one for the autumn, and we shall go to the races! I'm sure your husband would like that too.'

'Oo, yes, I'm up for that. P'raps there's another couple as would like to come?' Sylvia nodded suggestively in the direction of Amanda and Thomas.

'We'll ask them, shall we? But we shan't call them a couple, I think,' Dennis recommended.

'No. Well, they're not there just yet.' Sylvia looked at them again. 'Aww.'

Tempest had declined a lift with Amanda in Claire's car. He had his own arrangements. Shortly thereafter, he was to be observed by Natasha, watching from the sill of an upstairs room, promenading nonchalantly through The Grange grounds with Bella of The Elms Annexe at his side. Unfortunately, the youthful lady caught sight of the cool, amused, blue gaze of the Nevskaya Maskaradnaya above and thought that it was time she was getting home, deciding that the candle, however sumptuous the beeswax, was not worth the farthing.

Thereafter, Tempest had remained resolutely in the small salon throughout the evening, employing his strategy of giving Natasha the cold shoulder to indicate that she was no longer a lady of interest. She responded by sashaying in and out of the room at intervals to the adoration of her many human admirers. During these performances, Tempest settled himself more deeply into the folds of a £2000 cashmere wrap and gave every appearance of being asleep. Natasha, undeceived, enjoyed the evening immensely. Amanda's familiar less so.

Having observed something of the display during the evening, his witch wisely forbore to ask him how it had gone with the object of his desire. He had, however, been served throughout the proceedings with lavish offerings of salmon and caviar from Claire, Joan and Mrs Pagely, the librarian, and a treat from Mrs Sharma. He also consoled himself with the knowledge that he had one more card up his sleeve: Bella was four months old and booked for an appointment at the vet's in Romping, who had been doing rather well out of Tempest's preoccupation, as Lord of the Manor, with preying on the village maidens. There was that sweet but brief window of opportunity to furnish the environs with a new litter of either grey-furred or, especially, yellow-eyed kittens.

Trelawney had noted their number and muttered that that infernal animal was turning Sunken Madley into the feline equivalent of Village of the Damned.

Chapter 70

∽

THE BRAINS BEHIND THE OPERATION

The next morning found Amanda and Trelawney in the office with Finley. Janet had known what she was about, and her hardware was well protected. The techies were still trying to access the data on her laptop and phone.

Nikolaides hadn't yet got back about any shared time at an A and E for Flemming and Fourtisque. However, tucked out of sight was Fourtisque's phone. At first, it appeared that Flemming had no connection with either Janet or Blanchard. Amanda, however, made a suggestion.

'Claire says that she puts all of her exes and frenemies under Z in her phone contacts list, so if they call her she can ignore them.'

'Hm, there's an idea.' Trelawney turned the phone towards Amanda so she could observe as he scrolled down. There it was:

ZFF. Had to be Finley Flemming.

And a little further: ZJO. Not Jo, but Janet Oglethorpe. It did indeed tally with her mobile number.

Trelawney looked at Finley, seated at the end of the desk between him and Amanda,

'Would you like to tell me about your connections with Nightingale now?'

'But I don't have –'

'Or shall I just ring this contact number on his phone,' suggested the inspector, placing it on the desk, 'and we'll see if yours rings?'

Flemming sighed. 'Ok, fine. We met in A&E – well, Urgent Care, they call it, being private. We got chatting. He said his nerves were all shot to pieces, and I'd had one of my stupid clowning-about things. We swapped details, and he got in touch. Said there was this prospect that might interest me. Look, it was just a possible big property deal. I've got companies on my books that would kill … I mean, look, I never thought I'd be mixed up in anything like ….'

'Please go on, Mr Flemming.'

'It was his old landlady that organised it. She seemed to check out all above board and everything. Nightingale said she had a family interest in the site. Might even have the rights to it or the right to buy, said he was on the case, and then one of my clients could purchase it from her. There might be something valuable there too, he said, a family legacy of his old landlady's, and I'd get a cut from the sale of the proceeds, and so would he, and he would investigate the legal side. That was two shots at the jackpot for me. But we had to be discreet. He was very insistent.'

'Did he say why?'

'Just that there were bound to be other parties interested. So I was being circumspect: just making enquiries, looking for any parish or other records in the library. And then, the boy and then Mrs Oglethorpe turned up dead. Nightingale said it must be one of our rivals. I admit I got pretty jittery, but he said, no wonder because it was a once-in-a-lifetime opportunity, and we should just keep our heads down until it blew over. Look, Inspector, I had no idea he would ….'

Finley leaned back and shook his head.

'My sister always said I'd take a risk too far.' He looked anxiously at Trelawney. 'I'm not in trouble, am I?'

'You have not broken any law, Mr Flemming. Once you have made your written statement, you will be free to go.'

Relief flooded over Finley's face. 'Thank you. I … I wouldn't have got involved, really. I mean, I wasn't decided, because it all seemed pretty vague, but it was the area you see. Yes, I've been hoping to bump into someone – Oh, not in a stalkery way or anything. It was just I lost her number, and she's probably been thinking all this time that I wasn't interested, you see.'

'Yes, well, my admirable Detective Sergeant Baker has informed me that in the course of seeking anyone who might have inside information on the suspects, which included yourself, he found a certain young woman that it appears was an acquaintance of yours and had been expecting a call fro–'

'What? You found her?'

'He could possibly send her your email address on the off-chance that she may be interested in re-establishing contact with you.'

'You would? That's ….' He suddenly stopped and sat, thoughtful. 'I would be very grateful, Inspector. But not just yet. I think my sister's right. I need to get some help. Getting mixed up with a murderer. That's not me; that's *just* not me. When I'm ready, can I call you then?'

'Of course.'

'We just seemed to me like the perfect match.'

'Then, Finley,' put in Amanda. 'Has it occurred to you that if you get help and you change, that she and you won't be a match anymore?'

'Hm … I guess. But I'll just have to take that chance, won't I?' Suddenly, he grinned. 'I guess … that's what I do.'

He stayed to type out his statement on Trelawney's laptop, then, with thanks, departed. Amanda returned from the door, sat down and gazed impishly at her partner.

He looked a question.

'Why Inspector Trelawney, I do believe that under that practical exterior, you are an incurable romantic.'

Thomas grinned. 'Guilty as charged. No bad thing, I hope?'

'Not at all, Inspector,' Amanda responded with a smile. 'Not in the least.'

Chapter 71

WHO TOLD THE BISHOP?

With Flemming out of the way, Thomas set out for Parhayle, paperwork and persuasion.

Amanda went home and was engaged in checking the clamps on a table she'd glued when the doorbell chimed. She stopped and went to answer it.

'Rector! How nice to see you. Do come in. Tea?'

'Oh Amanda, dear, thank you, no, I must get back. You'll never believe it, but I had another letter from the Bishop's office. It seems he got a very nice letter from Sir Francis Crossly, saying the case was solved and what a great help I'd been to the investigation. And he had gathered from the reports of his officers that I had been essential in supporting the villagers through the traumatic experience of losing one of their own, in a way that only I, with such a long-standing relationship with them, could possibly do. And that I clearly was an indispensable pillar of the community!'

'That's wonderful, Rector!'

'But I don't feel I did anything. Of course, I did look in on the Biggerstaffs, but … well! Anyway, it was all dear Kay.'

'What? Who complained to the Bishop?'

'No dear, who told him what an asset I am to the village. Well, not herself. But she asked Sir Francis Crossly to write. Her aunt is a friend of his wife, and Kay looked after their cat in the summer, and they said they owed her a favour and, well, she called it in!'

'I'm so pleased. And I'm sure Kay will be an asset to the village too, just like you, Rector.'

'So am I, but still, it's a mystery, isn't it? Who told the Bishop there was trouble in Sunken Madley in the first place? But the point is that all is well. Now Kay and I can concentrate on the plans and arrangements for the new church hall. We hope to begin in the spring. Well, I say "begin", but those lovely boys from Germany will no doubt have it all up and done within a week. Oh, won't it be nice to see them all again, Amanda? I'm sure you'd like to see Hugh again. You too got on so very well.'

'Oh, course, Rector. I'm so relieved it's all ended happily, and perhaps one day, we'll find out what happened behind the scenes.'

'Yes, indeed. Well, I'll leave you to your Sunday, and I must get back and help Kay prepare to give the sermon. She's doing so very well, you know. Goodbye for now, dear.'

'Goodbye Rector.'

Amanda returned to the workshop and Tempest, prodding a detached upholstery cushion to test its nap-worthiness.

'I suppose *you* know who was behind the whole Bishop business,' she speculated accurately.

Naturally, came his voice in her head.

'Oh well, I suppose one day ….'

"One day", however, was much closer than Amanda imagined. For no sooner had she resumed her inspection of the complicated clamping on an antique card table than the doorbell chimed again. Amanda sighed and answered it to find a lady whose distress was evident even to her.

'Oh, Miss Cadabra, I'm so sorry.'

'Mrs Biggerstaff – Sharon, whatever is the matter. Please come in.' Amanda urged the agitated lady.

'Thank you, that's very kind, but I must get back. Oh, look, I only just found out, and oh, I never meant … I haven't had my head straight since that dreadful day. I couldn't help it. I just told my nan. You know, about it all and how nothing's got solved yet and ….'

'Well, that's all right, surely, that you told your grandmother?'

'Yes, but she told her *neighbour*,' answered Sharon, as though that explained everything.

'Erm …?'

'Well, my nan lives in quite a posh area, you know, and her neighbour is friends with the PA to the Bishop.'

The penny dropped. 'Ah,' replied Amanda, 'and so ….'

'Yes, my nan rang me the next morning and said the Bishop is onto it, and I heard the Rector had had a letter and, oh, I never meant it to get … I'm so sorry, Miss Cadabra. I don't know what to do. I can't undo it, and my nan's neighbour can't get hold of her friend and … and, now the Rector has had another letter and, oh, I'm so sorry.'

Relieved to know the source of the do-to, Amanda replied soothingly, 'I'm sure the Rector will understand. I know it would do her so much good if you popped around to let her know, and she may have some good news for you.'

'Really? Oh, I don't know …. I feel so …. but I must make amends, I'm sure. I'll go straight there.'

Amanda returned once more to check her glueing and make a start on removing any excess that had seeped out. She might even have time to give it a wax; then, that would be another job done. She was leaning over the clamps when the phone rang.

'Oh, good grief!' Amanda exclaimed in exasperation.

Chapter 72

❦

TREASURE

It was Claire on the phone, and in a froth of excitement.

'Darling, you just *have* to come to the library. Now!'

'Oh. Do I? All right.'

'Quickly!'

Amanda shed her boiler suit to reveal a t-shirt and orange linen shorts underneath, exchanged her work boots for sandals and drove library-ward. Inside, she observed a knot of villagers around one of the larger tables.

'Amanda!' called Mrs Pagely, the librarian.

She went over but was forestalled by Jonathan, the assistant, who said to her quietly,

'You know our very odd stacks?'

'I certainly do,' she answered with feeling.

'Well, you know we keep a copy of *Fordyce's Sermons to Young Women* down there?'

'Oh yes, for Mrs Dowerly.'

'She only asks for it when her daughter's upset her, but it isn't often, so we can't afford to give it shelf space up here.'

'All right,' replied Amanda patiently, wondering where this was all going.

'When I went down to get it, I accidentally selected a different volume of his: *Addresses to Young Men* 1777. Well, it's not the sort of thing anyone ever asks for, but it's rather old and could be valuable too. When I took it down, a bookmark fell out, or rather a document someone had folded up and used as a bookmark. Come and see, Amanda.'

Jonathan led her to the table, where a carefully creased yellowing piece of parchment lay open. It appeared to be close written with ornamented capitals and an official-looking seal. It was being studied by Erik while the assembled throng waited with bated breath. Finally, he raised his head.

'Yes, oh, hello there, Amanda. Yes, this does appear to be a legal document. It does seem that in 1832, the priory was assigned to the parish church of St-Ursula-without-Barnet in the stewardship of the Rector thereof and his successors to the post, in perpetuity.'

'Really?' asked Jane, who had received the call and been sent forth by her Curate, who promised to take care of the sermon

'Hm, it seems it's belonged to our church for the last 200 years,' observed Erik.

Jane stood amazed for a moment, then, 'Well, it won't be built around or demolished or whatever. Not as long as I'm rector of this parish!' she declared stalwartly.

A chorus of cheers went up.

'That's good to know, Rector,' said Amanda, 'but would you be willing to allow a little excavation? You see, I think there is something of value hidden there. It may be of interest to Barnet Hill Museum, and even the British Museum could be interested in purchasing some of it. That would certainly help the church funds.'

'Permission granted!' cried Jane jubilantly. 'Do you know exactly where it is?'

'I think so,' replied Amanda.

'Then let's go there at once.'

'I'll need some tools.'

'I've got tools,' called out Bryan.

And so it was that the troupe headed off. After some cautious scraping and chiselling and some more cautious scraping and chiselling a little to the right, the blocks slid out into the strong arms of Bryan and Iskender, who'd come over to help. Within, the wood of a plain wooden box could be seen that was more of a lining for the cavity than a chest. The front acted as a door that hinged down. After some more application of tools, the men carefully manoeuvred the receptacle, placed it on a rug on the patchy grass and stood back.

There was no lock, for the person for whose use it was intended believed no one would ever find it.

'Rector,' said Bryan. 'You should be the one to open it. It's the church's, after all.'

'Oh … Amanda, you do it,' requested Jane.

'Of course,' she answered.

Amanda knelt on the rug and carefully opened the box. Inside were brass altar candlesticks, a silver censor, a small box containing what appeared to be a bone and another with dark hair. There were also purses with coins and some other sets of candlesticks and ecclesiastical paraphernalia, including a large ornate cross that might have been of gold and seemed to be set with precious stones.

But none of these drew Amanda's attention. For there, nestled in a corner, was a carved wooden box. As in a trance, she drew it out and twisted the little key in the lock. Within was a turned wooden cup covered with gold leaf and decorated around the base and the rim with seed pearls. She knelt, frozen to the spot. Aunt Amelia's words came back to her—she had changed history. Effected a small change that …. She had also saved Abel and his children ….

'Are you all right, dear?' asked Jane with concern.

'Oh, I'm fine, just amazed by this find!'

'As are we all. We must call the museum at once and inform, er, whoever we must inform that we have treasure trove. Oh, what a day this is!'

'Yes,' murmured Amanda, 'what a day.'

It was hard to wait, but, at last, the confirmation came back that the old document was legal and the priory would now be safe. As for the treasure trove, once Jane knew the whole story, she insisted the finders fee should be split between Mr Oglethorpe and the church fund. That would supply the new hall with some equipment for the crèche and the classes that would be held there, and all of the other hidden costs that would present themselves once the building was completed.

'The roof,' Jane told Amanda, 'will last us quite a few years, but the village could do with the church hall facilities as soon as possible. Some of the treasures will be taken to the British Museum, but Barnet Hill will be permitted to retain and display some items of lesser value. Except for that cup. That's being very closely examined. It does indeed seem to be hundreds of years old, but experts say that it was turned on a device that is identical to a modern one. Still, I expect a lot of these things have changed very little over the centuries.'

Amanda agreed. She looked down at Tempest at her feet who raised an eyebrow. She left in a state of some perturbation. This was observed by Miss Hempling, former owner of Ye Olde Tea Shoppe.

'All right, dear? Hello, dear little kitty.'

'Yes, thank you. How are you, Miss Hempling?'

'Wonderfully well, my dear.'

A sudden thought came to Amanda.

'Miss Hempling, may I ask you … the teashop. You said it was your aunt's? Has it always been in your family?'

'Not as a tea shop. But it was a baker's. Oh yes, going back generations. Now I know you like history, my dear, so I will try to remember the story …. Oh dear, my mother used to say that I had a head like a sieve when I was growing up, and, strangely, my memory is actually better than it's ever been. But this is an old, old family story …. Now … let me get this right. Yes, now, the first baker in the village – well, he might not have been the first, but it sounds so much more important, doesn't it? – His nephew married a monk's daughter.'

'A monk?' Amanda asked with intense curiosity.

'Well, he wasn't a monk anymore by the time he married and had a daughter. He was a Cornish monk, you know, but he must have fallen in love with a village maiden, and that's why he didn't go home when he finished being a monk, I suppose. And this is the bit my great-aunt always told me that inspired her. The couple – that's the monk's daughter, except he wasn't … er, yes and the baker's nephew, that couple. Well, after the husband died, the wife kept on with the bakery. So she was the first businesswoman in the history of the family. Isn't that jolly?'

'Yes,' agreed Amanda. 'It certainly is.'

'But then, coming into my aunt's time, the supermarkets happened, and people came to bakers less, and so it became a place to sell all sorts baked goods for customers to eat on the spot, and then eventually progressed to a tea shop. And now the dear boys have it. The Big Tease; oh, I do so love that name.'

Relief was spreading over Amanda's countenance.

'Of course,' continued Miss Hempling, 'Sandy and Julian are only distantly related to me, my dear. But that is one of the reasons I sold it to them. Keep it in the family. Well, I must let you get on. Come and visit us at Pipkin soon.'

'I will,' Amanda promised merrily as Miss Hempling went off along the street. 'So,' she addressed her familiar, 'no harm done, after all. Hmm. Just when I think I know everything about this village ….'

Tempest's words came clearly to her mind: *That's one of the multitude of differences between us. I* do *know everything about this village.*

Amanda smiled and bundled him up in her arms.

'All right, Mr Smuggly-wuggly, I *know* oo do!'

Chapter 73

༄

The Judgement of Wallace

Janet had always said it all fell on her, so the extent of her life insurance should not have surprised her husband, but it did. And with the finder's fee, thought Keith, looking at the figures before him, it was enough to … hm … make a new start?

* * *

'I'm not going to dress it up, Mr Oglethorpe. This place is frankly rather dilapidated, but the structure is sound, and the garden's a decent size. You wouldn't be able to change the façade. It is 400 years old. I don't think Mrs Plum had any work done on it since the War, to be honest.'

'Hm,' remarked Keith. 'Can we see upstairs and outside?' Finally, coming in from the garden with his grave four-year-old grandson, he looked down and asked,

'What do you think, Wallace?'

Wallace pursed his lips and looked thoughtful for a moment, before finally delivering his judgement:

'It's got p'tenshal.'

Keith nodded slowly. 'Aye, lad. It's got potential. You going to help me smarten it up, then, are you?'

'Yes, Granddad!'

'Of course, we will,' said his son, Freddie, eagerly. 'What about the family house, though?'

'It'll stay in the family. I'm leaving it so Linnie will have that, and you'll have this place when I go.'

'Oh, Dad, we've both got a house.'

'Now, now. Well, then ... Wallace 'ere has given 'is opinion, and it'd be a nice project, so ... in that case ....'

'I could try and get the asking price down,' offered the estate agent.

'Hm ... no .. it's a fair price. Just one thing, though. This seems like a nice village, but ... is it safe? People do seem to keep dyin' 'ere?'

'Well.' The estate agent shifted uneasily from one foot to the other. 'I'd quite understand if you ... what with your wife passing away here.'

'She didn't die in this cottage, though, did she?' countered Keith.

'Oh no. No, no. Of course, people die all the time, all over the place. But the village does have their own police detective in residence now, and, I hear, a very able assistant, from all accounts.'

'Ah ... well then ... hm.' Keith looked around the room again. 'In that case, I think ....'

'Cooee!' called Joan from the door.

Keith went to answer her call.

'You all right?'

'Doing very nicely, sir,' she replied cheerfully. 'And yourself?'

'Nicely, thank you.'

'You thinking of buying this sweet cottage?' Joan asked hopefully.

'Actually, I was just about to say I think I could be … I could be reet snug 'ere.'

'You've decided?' enquired the estate agent.

Wallace looked up. 'I think we have, haven't we, Granddad?'

'We've decided,' affirmed Keith.

'I'm Joan, the postlady, your wife's distant relative.'

'I'm Keith, the accountant.'

Joan held out her hand, and he gladly shook it.

'Keith the Accountant,' she said grandly, 'welcome to Sunken Madley!'

Chapter 74

The Wisdom of Humpy, and a Present for Amanda

Thomas was back. With all the upset and kerfuffle of the fires and Izzy on informal probation, he thought it best to show a presence in Parhayle for now. However, he had found time to receive a text from his landlady and send back a request. Now, just for the weekend, he had driven up to Sunken Madley that Saturday morning. However, he did not go straight to The Elms but to The Grange.

It was, of course, because Amanda had sent Thomas photos of his desk, refurbished and in place in the office. He wanted to show them in person to Miss Armstrong-Witworth since she had so kindly gifted it to him. Yes, that was the reason he was there.

However, his hidden agenda was first served by the presence on the drive of Humpy, coming in from a walk.

'Hello, Inspector,' cried Humpy jovially. 'Back from the far reaches of the south-west and another triumph of detection, I hear.'

Amanda must have mentioned it in The Corner Shop, the inspector rightly concluded.

'Too kind,' responded Thomas with a smile as they shook hands. 'Strange, I should bump into you like this. I wanted to thank you for your help with the case here. For being so frank and open. Both of you.'

'Not at all, dear chap.'

'It couldn't have been easy … bringing up your wife's past.'

'Couldn't it?' asked Humpy, apparently mystified.

'You – when they crop up … men from her past … you don't feel …?'

Comprehension dawned, and an understanding smile lit Humpy's face. He patted Thomas's shoulder.'

'My dear boy. Hilly loves me. I love her. Want her to be happy. If some chap made her happy before me, then, well … shake his hand. Me, she married. Me, she's stayed with all these years. D'you see?' He shook his head in wonderment. 'After all her chances, she chose an ordinary chap like me.'

'No,' said Thomas decidedly. 'I don't think she did choose an ordinary chap. Not ordinary at all. In fact, quite extraordinary.'

Humpy was quite overcome. 'Oh, my dear boy. Do you really think so? It's what Hilly says. Hm. Thank you.'

Thomas waited. There was something more to come, perhaps.

'Sometimes,' Humpy said slowly, looking earnestly at Thomas, 'the only thing standing between us and our heart's desire is in our own heads. And if we can just get past that, we can have anything … we really want.' Humpy briefly put a kindly hand on Thomas's arm. He gave a nod and a smile. 'Think I'll go and find my girl now. Cheerio, Inspector.' With that, he turned and, with a spring in his step, headed inside the house, leaving Thomas standing thoughtfully on the gravel.

Miss Armstrong-Witworth was delighted to see the photographs and congratulated Thomas on his success in Parhayle and his joint efforts with Amanda in solving the Sunken Madley case. She had some words of wisdom for him too, which he stored up to ponder.

Trelawney drove next to The Elms, went into his flat through the side door, checked the office, unpacked, and let Amanda know that he had returned. Notified that he was on his way back to the village, she was prepared for the message and left within a few minutes.

Thomas was at the door to greet Amanda and, in high spirits, ushered her into the office.

'I have a surprise for you, Miss Cadabra.' From the formal address, she gathered it was work-related. 'Come in. Notice anything?'

Amanda looked around. Then gasped.

'Oh! Oh, Inspector.' She turned pink with pleasure and clasped her hands under her chin as though to try and contain her intense glee.

For there, upon the wall installed by Bryan, hung a large corkboard. On a small ledge was a clear Perspex box of map pins.

'For me?' breathed Amanda.

'For us.'

'Oh, I love it! Thank you, thank you so much.'

'And …' announced Thomas, with the air of a magician producing flowers from the end of a cane. He took a long tube from around his side of the desk, opened one end, took out a sizeable poster, unrolled it and went over to the board.

Amanda hurried to help him pin it into place. 'Whatever? Ah, a map of the village!'

'Hopefully, this will inspire us.'

'It's perfect! *Thank* you, Thomas.' Unexpectedly, Thomas found himself enfolded in an enthusiastic hug, in which he willingly participated for its all too short duration. Finally, Amanda's hold slackened, and he released her as she turned to the board.

Some men, thought Thomas, buy flowers; I buy stationery. Still, it seemed to be having the desired effect. Amanda appeared to be more delighted with it than any number of roses. Clearly, the way to her heart was through office equipment. But there was more.

'Let's inaugurate our pins,' he suggested. They put them in place in The Grange, The Manor, The Elms, next to the church, The Library, Little Madley, and now, of course, the priory.'

'It's wonderful!' exclaimed Amanda joyfully.

But there was one more surprise to come.

'And now,' said Thomas, 'if you go over to your top drawer ….'

Amanda hurried to the desk, smiling with anticipation and opened it. There it reposed: neatly, pristinely wound. She picked it up and gazed at it, then at him, her eyes shining.

'Oh, Thomas, … *red string!*'

Chapter 75

Amanda's List, and Tempest Solves Two Mysteries

They decided on a ploughman's lunch in the Big Tease. Amanda declared it her treat to celebrate the corkboard. Alex and Julian had in some sheep's cheddar and goat's butter that Amanda's system could tolerate occasionally. Consequently, now there reposed upon the table, two plates of deep gold cheese, Branston pickle, crusty loaf out of the oven, butter melting on its soft white inner surface, a pork pie, boiled egg and representatives of the salad family on the side, flanked by two cups of tea.

After a sip, Thomas enquired,

'Do you think Flemming will get help?'

'I don't know. He may have just been saying that to impress you. Like Nick Gosney. He said the same thing, probably just to ….'

Thomas smiled. 'Impress you? But who could blame him?' he asked gallantly. 'So, perhaps you might even remember who Gosney is if you should meet again.'

'Possibly. Although … I don't think I will meet him again.'

Reassured on that particular point, which he had to admit had been slightly bothering him, Thomas asked, 'Tell me, Amanda, how does this lack of facial recognition thing work?'

'Well, this is one theory: most people register a triangle that goes from eye to eye and down to the mouth, but people like me register a bigger triangle, like across the eyebrows to the ears and down to the chin. I remember things like headgear and earrings, and if people change their hat or glasses or something like that, then … that's it. Oh, it's only partial. I do remember some faces. It's … sort of like my brain *does* have a filing cabinet for faces, but it's just a very small one,' she explained.

'I see. How many drawers does it have?' He knew how literal her mind was.

Amanda pondered.

'Three. The top one has people who I'd know anywhere. The second one down, the middle one, has people I'd know if there were where I expected them to be but wouldn't recognise elsewhere, and the third is for faces of some people I'd recall if I was reminded who they were. As I say, the cabinet is very small.'

'Ah. And, er, … who is in the top drawer?'

'Oh, let me see… well,' Amanda counted them off on her fingers, 'the obvious ones like Grandpa and Granny, Aunt Amelia, Joan, Dennis, Sylvia, everyone at The Grange, the library, The Corner Shop, the doctor's, The Big Tease, The Snout and Trough, and proprietor of the Sinner's, Mr Sharma's and the Patels of course, Erik and Esta, Kieran and Ruth.'

'Anyone else?'

'Erm … Uncle Mike!' Amanda exclaimed. 'Of course, Uncle Mike,'

'And …?' Thomas prompted hopefully.

'Oh well, Tempest,' she laughed.

'Right,' he said flatly.

'And you,' Amanda added matter-of-factly.

Thomas smiled. 'Really?'

'Of course. That goes without saying.'

'Does it? Ah well, that's good.'
Amanda giggled.
'I'd say so. You're definitely top drawer.'

* * *

Jim came into the kitchen to find a pot of jam and half a dozen eggs smashed on the floor. The back door was open, but he was too late to see a grey, thick-furred tail disappearing around it.

Hearing his uncharacteristic expletive, Joan hurried in.

'Oh, my life! Whatever happened here, love?'

'The back door was open. Wind musta blown these off the counter.'

'Never mind,' Joan responded comfortingly, opening a bottom drawer. 'We'll have it sorted out in no time. We'll use a couple of the old tea towels, then rinse them out and put them straight in the wash.' Suiting the word to the deed, she pulled from the drawer two aged but clean and pressed cloths. As she shook them out, a manila envelope fell to the floor and had to be rescued from the jam.

'This yours, Joanie? Secret love letters, are they?' he joked.

'Not mine, love. You better write me some!' she replied, wiping off the stickiness and tearing open the envelope. Inside was a small, light brown paper folded into an envelope. Carefully, they opened it up.

'It looks very old,' remarked Jim.

They studied it together, then looked at one another.

'Do you think …?' asked Jim.

'Yes, I do!'

'We'd better call the inspector. And Janet's husband. This belongs to Keith.'

But they stood for a while longer, doing their best to make out more of the words. At last, Joan said,

'I'm glad this man got this letter from his son. Musta loved his dad.'

Jim nodded. 'Says "no one else I can trust".'

'Well, he trusted the right person, looks like. And Janet trusted our old tea towel drawer.'

'Yes, she had this all along to help her know where to look for the treasure. And got herself mixed up with a proper dodgy pair,' remarked Jim.

'Aww, that young chap's not so bad,' replied Joan indulgently.

'Oh, got a soft spot for 'im, 'ave you, then, Joanie?' he teased, putting his arms around her.

'Now then, you! We've got important calls to make … first.'

* * *

Back in the workshop, kneeling on the door, green boiler-suit clad, Amanda prepared for magic practice. She looked up as her grandmother said,

'Yes, Ammee, dear, I am well aware of what day of the week it is, and yes, this would normally, possibly, be a day off. However, in view of the number of days you have missed, this is an admirable opportunity to catch up.'

'Now, *bian*,' advised Grandpa, 'put all of those other attempts out of your mind. You're beginning afresh. Try thinking of the door like a magnet being repelled by another magnet on the floor.'

'Yes, Grandpa,' Amanda responded conscientiously.

Breathe, focus, relax, rise …. And …tip!

Restored to the stability of the floor by Perran, Amanda looked at him helplessly.

'Can I be saying the spell wrong?' she asked.

'No,' replied Granny. 'There is nothing amiss with your casting.'

'Then what?'

The three gazed at the door thoughtfully. The pile of old curtains on the shelf shifted. A grey head emerged. The rest of Tempest followed in a leisurely fashion. He stretched, yawned and finally jumped down nimbly onto the bench and thence to the floor. Tempest stared at the humans one at a time, searching for any sign whatsoever of intelligence.

He sighed. Do I have to do everything myself? As though there weren't *sufficient images that made the answer plain enough*. At last, he crossed to the door on which his witch was still kneeling, stepped delicately onto the wooden surface and took up a position behind Amanda.

'Of course!' she exclaimed. 'A cat sitting behind the witch. It's not just for taking a ride: it's for balance!'

Tempest looked at the ceiling. Finally, he thought. Finally.

Amanda set to once more, closing her eyes, breathing,

'*Aereval.*'

The door rose and rose, remaining perfectly level.

Amanda tried thinking of surfing. The door remained flat.

'Very good, *bian*,' murmured Perran. 'Now try moving forward.'

She softly spoke the spell: '*A-rith.*'

But movement hovering and moving forwards was a bridge too far for the time being. The door shook, and Amanda brought it back down, then, at once, turned to scoop up her familiar in her arms.

'Oh clever, clever Mr Fuffykins!' He submitted to her adoration as his due. 'Don't you think so, Granny?' she asked, with sparkling eyes.

'Hmph,' uttered Senara.

'Nice one, Tempest,' Perran acknowledged. 'Well, *bian*, I think we've accomplished enough for one day.'

We've accomplished? thought Tempest. *We?*

Chapter 76

༄

AMANDA'S THEORY, AND QUESTIONS OLD AND NEW

'Aunt Amelia, you know the Wicc'lord?' Amanda often pondered the identity of the present incumbent of that title. 'The mysterious person who has always moved behind the scenes in the cause of good?'

'And handed down that title from mistress or master to apprentice for millennia. I do.'

'Well, I don't know if I told you, but I did think it was Grandpa – who is definitely good. Or very possibly Granny.' Who was maybe a bit less good, Amanda thought but forbore to say.

'Really? And who do you think it is now?' enquired Amelia with interest.

'Aunty!'

'Mrs Sharma? Nalini?'

'Yes,' replied Amanda enthusiastically. 'She also has this mysterious connection with Tempest, like they each know who the other really is. And if Sunken Madley really is significant in the grand scheme of things, and the heart of the village is The Corner Shop, then Aunty is the *heart* of the Corner Shop, isn't she?'

'Indeed.'

'Well, then!'

'Hm,' responded Amelia, 'Why have you moved your chips off your grandparents?'

'Well! All they ever do is go to grand lunches and cocktail parties and play tennis or whatever with famous people and drink champagne and … and eat toasted crumpets!'

Amelia regarded her niece with amusement. 'Oh, especially eating toasted crumpets?'

'Yes, at my fireplace!' Amanda replied with a measure of indignation, then, 'All right, I suppose it's theirs too.'

'Hm, on the other hand,' Amelia replied judiciously, 'they did give you a clue, sweetie.'

'A clue?' asked Amanda with surprise. 'What clue? When?'

'Toasted crumpets …' hinted her aunt.

Amanda visualised the scene, frowned, and then her brow cleared.

'Oh! Oh, I am such a muppet! The hearth! In the priory, how Giles was able to get the hiding place made. They were trying to get me to think of *fireplaces*. Oh dear,' she laughed. 'And I wasn't at all appreciative of their efforts.'

'I'm sure they saw the funny side of that,' Amelia assured her.

'And then Tempest …. Well, I got there in the end.'

'You always do, sweetie. Still prefer your Aunty Nalini for the role of Wicc'Lord?'

'Hm.'

'Well, what about the monk you saw at the priory ruins? Who do you think that was?'

'Well,' responded Amanda thoughtfully, 'I did think it might be Cury, and then I thought it must be Abel. But I got that feeling of déjà vu three times. Twice with Abel, but once with … Thomas.'

'Thomas?'

'Yes. You see, neither Cury nor Abel saw the future me in their space. So what if the monk I saw was Thomas, in the past, beckoning to me in the future, in the shared space where somehow he knew I would one day be?'

'If so, would that be a good thing or a bad one? Either way, I wouldn't mention it to him quite yet,' advised Amelia.

'I think, perhaps not,' agreed Amanda. 'Not quite yet. That would be a bit too much magic.'

* * *

It was Sunday, and as the villagers could have predicted, Amanda and her somewhat unnerving four-legged companion were on their way to the priory ruins for a picnic lunch. Amanda had parked near the library and was hopeful that none of her neighbours would waylay her, as so often happened on this stretch of road.

'Amanda!' But the call came from one whom she was always happy to encounter. Jonathan, the assistant librarian, was hurrying after her, waving a slender volume.

'Hello, Jonathan. The very odd stacks?'

'Yes, I was taking down volume 8 of the spare set of the *Encyclopaedia Britannica* to repair it, as the tidy one has gone missing again. And what do you think happened? This book fell out. I thought you might be interested, seeing how hard you worked on the priory case. Must get back now. It always gets a bit busy before people's lunches and the cricket.'

'Well, thank you, Jonathan. I'll be sure to bring it –'

'No rush. When you're ready. I issued it for you on your ticket.' He hurried off.

Picnic basket and book in hand, she paused a moment before where she had seen … Abel? She gave a little gasp. There it was: the scent of sage. And with it, a sense of peace. No figure appeared. All was quiet.

They climbed the nightstairs up onto her platform, her eyrie. It would never be quite the same. No. It would be better. Now, she had a sense of the church beyond and the cloister below, the brothers and Abel moving about the buildings and grounds.

She sat down on her platform, served Tempest with some ham and looked at the book Jonathan had found, or perhaps more correctly, that had found Jonathan:

'*Hertfordshire Habits: The Monastic Houses of the County* by Andrea Besse,' she read aloud the title. 'Written 1889. Hm ….' She looked at the contents, and there was the chapter: The Priory of Sunken Madley.' Carefully she turned the pages. There was a lot of information about its founding and a forest of medieval history and names. It was all rather dense, but here was something of interest:

'*The prior, Father Stephen, was commemorated as one of the few who stood out against the edict of the King, honouring the wishes of his recent predecessor, Father Giles. It is thought that he did not survive the transfer of the priory and the estate.*

The brothers were ejected without compensation, and either returned to their homes or, together with the lay servants, were taken in by the kindly villagers, where some remained, their families still bearing their memory by their Christian names if not their surnames: Cury, Abel, and others.

Henry ordered the destruction of the buildings themselves, and the land was awarded to the Dunkleys of Sunken Madley Manor. Later, in our century, the family requested that it be restored to the church, and into the caretakership of the incumbent of the parish and his successor in perpetuity.

'*The ruins are little visited, being of minor interest now.*'

Amanda looked up. So … they were all still here in some way or another; in this space, shared over time. Those brothers with whom she had sat at table, had shared a meal, walked and talked in the cloister ... they were still here… and in the village too … in and out of the same buildings, treading the same streets and lanes. It brought her immense comfort somehow, and even joy.

She believed the deaths at the hand of Barnabas would leave no taint upon its stones, for terrible as the deeds had been, he had acted out of love, and that had to count for something. Even the passing here of Harold and Janet seemed not to have left its mark. Perhaps because this was a place, above all, of devotion and hope and faith. One day, the last stone would be taken for a path or garden wall, and the grass would grow over the last of the foundations. And yet, whoever passed over it, would surely feel their spirits lifted, their faith in themselves and their hope for the future renewed.

It was no wonder that here she had always been able to think the most clearly in this place of contemplation. Here it was that questions new and old floated to the surface of her mind.

Was Aunty the Wicc'Lord? Had she got that right? What was the answer to the riddle of Sunken Madley? What was its significance, this little village, obscure, tucked away in the trees of the orchards and the Wood? At least, she had discovered two more links with Cornwall: the granite of the priory and the monk who had come here from the land of her birth.

Somewhere there was the grimoire, the grimoire of the Cardiubarns with the antidote to the asthma spell that still hung over her.

What if I was well? she asked herself, yet again. If I could run and jump and climb and … chase criminals and ...? Then again … it was magic that saved her ... magic that enabled her to help solve case after case. Would that be any stronger if her body was? She shook her head, knowing the answer. All the same, it would be nice to be able to run further than 20 yards without the doctor having to be called.

Oh well, maybe one day. The spellbook had to be out there somewhere. But other things were out there somewhere, too, of course: perhaps the remnants of the Cardiubarns and Flamgoynes. Were they all still neutralised, or were they gathering in the shadows? Not a nice thought, Amanda stated to Tempest. She looked at him. She strongly doubted all of his thoughts were nice. Possibly they were to him, though. Who was he? Was her guess about him right? Hm.

Amanda's gaze turned upon her village, the village in her care, whether or not anyone knew it. Thomas, of course; he knew. Did he understand? She hoped so. Suddenly his words at the party came back to her, when he'd said he'd used the siren to get back so as not to disappoint her, and she'd said you'd do that for me? And he said … "Never doubt it". The memory gave her a warm glow. Of course, they were colleagues, and there were all sorts of reasons why it would be better not to be … and he'd never actually said anything outright about there being anything else …. except friends. Well, being friends and colleagues was important. And if they could make those work together, then … who knew? Of course, he had bought her a corkboard. And even red string ….

All at once, a feeling came on the wind, and Amanda looked to the West. She heard the call of the land of her birth. Something … something was … She stood up, her familiar in her arms.

'Something is coming, Tempest. Something. I wonder …. but whenever it comes, and whatever it is,… I'll be ready,' said Amanda Cadabra.

The End

Author's Note

Thank you for reading *Amanda Cadabra and The Nightstairs*. I hope you enjoyed your time in Sunken Madley and Cornwall.

I would love you to tell me your thoughts about the book and would be overjoyed if you wrote a review. You can post in on the e-store where you bought the book, on Facebook, Twitter or your social platform of choice, or recommend it on Bookbub. It would mean a great deal to me.

Thank you

Best of all would be if you dropped me a line at HollyBell@amandacadabra.com so we can connect in person. If there is a character you especially liked or anything you would like more of, please let me know. Amanda Cadabra Book 9 is in the making and I am writing it for you, dear reader.

For tidbits on the world of Sunken Madley and to keep up with news of the continuing adventures of our heroes Amanda, Tempest, Thomas, Granny and Grandpa visit www.amandacadabra.com, where you can also request to enter the VIP Readers Group or sign up for the newsletter to stay in touch and find out about the next sequel. The VIP Readers is a limited numbers group. Members receive the manuscript of the next book in order to email me feedback, within 7 – 10 days, that can be incorporated into the book before it is published.

If Tempest has endeared himself to you, and you'd like to read more about him, you can get the FREE short story prequel to Amanda Cadabra and The Hidey-Hole Truth at https://amandacadabra.com/free-story-tempest/

You can also find me on Facebook at https://www.facebook.com/Holly-Bell-923956481108549/

Bookbub at https://www.bookbub.com/profile/holly-bell

Goodreads at https://www.goodreads.com/author/show/18387493.Holly_Bell

Twitter at https://twitter.com/holly_b_author

Pinterest at https://www.pinterest.co.uk/hollybell2760/

and Instagram at https://www.instagram.com/hollybellac

See you soon.

About the Author

Cat adorer and chocolate lover, Holly Bell is a photographer and video maker when not writing. Whilst being an enthusiastic novel reader, Holly has had lifetime's experience in writing non-fiction.

Holly devoured all of the Agatha Christie books long before she knew that Miss Marple was the godmother of the Cosy Mystery. Her love of JRR Tolkien's *Lord of the Rings* meant that her first literary creation in this area would have to be a cosy paranormal.

Holly lives in the UK and is a mixture of English, Cornish, Welsh and other ingredients. Her favourite cat is called Bobby. He is a black, like her hat. Purely coincidental. Of course.

Acknowledgements

Thanks to Kim Brockway of Brockway Gatehouse Literary Services, for enthusiastic support, eagle-eyed, intuitive and sympathetic editing and to Flora for her ongoing encouragement and publicity,

Thank you to my friends Steve Docherty, who inspired 'Roq', and Leanne Perrett for their constant encouragement, and to Emily Jade Dalton, David Bibb and Katherine deMoure-Aldrich for always checking in on me and keeping up with my progress. Emily also deserves a special mention for acting as consultant on the Yorkshire dialect.

This is also an opportunity to express my appreciation to the VIP beta readers, especially my Horsemen of the Apocalapse: Katherine Otis, Jude Gerstein, Colin Ridley, Katherine DeMoure-Aldrich and David Bibb. (They used to be four but five is even better). Thank you to Colin also for offering invaluable advice on firearms licensing.

The Cornish language in this book would not have been possible without the assistance of my superb former teacher, Kensa Broadhurst, and the abundant support of my friend Linda Beskeen and other members of the Cornish language community.

Acknowledgements

Thanks are also due to the rector of St Mary the Virgin, Monken Hadley whose fund of information helped me to shape the village of 'Sunken Madley', and to Stephen Tatlow, the former Director of Music there and the churchwardens for their kind welcome and delight at being fictionalised.

Praise and thanks go out to my outstandingly talented illustrator Daniel Becerril Ureña (Instagram: danbeu) for his beautiful book cover art.

Also due, are thanks to Bruna Marchetti of Facebook and Laurence O'Bryan Tanja Slijepčević of Books Go Social for their expert advice and assistance with spreading the word about both this book and the Amanda Cadabra series. Thanks to TJ Brown, who, in the beginning, gave me the flint and the kindling for my creative spark and who continues to impart gems of wisdom. And thank you to Sîan and Liam for being such delightful neighbours near whom to write.

Thank you, in fact, to all those without whose support this book would not have been possible.

Finally, in whatever dimension they are currently inhabiting, thanks go out to my cat who inspired Tempest, and to my grandfather and brother for Perran and Trelawney. Your magic endures.

About the Language Used in the Story

Please note that to enhance the reader's experience of Amanda's world, this British-set story, by a British author, uses British English spelling, vocabulary, grammar and usage, and includes local and foreign accents, dialects and a magical language that vary from different versions of English as it is written and spoken in other parts of our wonderful, diverse world.

The Cornish Language

If reading this book has sparked you interest in Kernowek – Cornish – here are some useful places to find out more:

gocornish.org

kesva.org

The Cornish Language Office (offering a translation service or everything from house names up. Free up to 40 words.)

I have had tremendous fun over the past three years learning the language, meeting other enthusiastic students and wonderful teachers, all through Zoom, I might add. You can now learn anywhere in the world and join the Cadabras and Trelawneys in experiencing this extraordinary Celtic tongue with ancient roots, now blossoming in the 21st century.

If you'd like to join me in exploring Cornish, you can go to the links above and, or, write to me.

Questions for Reading Clubs

1. What did you like best about the book?
2. Which character did you like best? Is there one with whom you especially identified?
3. If you made a movie of the book, whom would you cast and in what parts?
4. Did the book remind you of any others you have read, either in the same or another genre?
5. Did you think the cover fitted the story? If not, how would you redesign it?
6. How unique is this story?
7. Which characters grew and changed over the course of the story, and which remained the same?
8. What feelings did the book evoke?
9. Who were your favourite characters, and why?
10. What place in the book would you most like to visit, and why?
11. Was the setting one that felt familiar or relatable to you? Why or why not?
12. Is there a character you would like to know more about? If so, who and why?

13. Was the book the right length? If too long, what would you leave out? If too short, what would you add?
14. How well do you think the title conveyed what the book is about?
15. If you could ask Holly Bell just one question, what would it be?
16. How well do you think the author created the world of the story?
17. Which quotes or scenes did you like the best, and why?
18. Was the author just telling an entertaining story or trying as well to communicate any other ideas? If so, what do think they were?
19. Did the book change how you think or feel about any thing, person or place? Did it help you to understand someone or yourself better?
20. What do you think the characters will do after the end of the book? Would you want to read the sequel?
21. If there were a spin-off series, which character would you like to see explored?

Glossary

As the story is set in an English village, and written by a British author, some spellings or words may be unfamiliar to some readers living in other parts of the English-speaking world. Please find here a list of terms used in the book. If you notice any that are missing, please let me know on hollybell@amandacadabra.com so the can be included in a future edition.

British English	AmErikan English
Spelling conventions	
—ise for words like surprise, realise	—ize for words like surprize, realize
—or for words like colour, honour	—our for words like color, honor
—tre for words like centre, theatre	—ter for words like center, theatre
Mr Mrs Dr	Mr. Mrs. Dr.
A1	A road – a main road that is not a highway. This one links London with Edinburgh

Glossary

A3	11.7 x 16.5 inches, similar to Tabloid
A4	8.26" by 11.69"
A-level	Advanced Level course with exam taken at age 18. Similar to an American Advanced Placement course.
Battenberg	Cake made of pink and yellow diagonal squares, wrapped in marzipan
Binbag	Garbage bag, trash bag
Biscuit	Cookie
Boiler suit	Coveralls
Bonce	Slang for 'head'
Boot	Trunk
Brickie	Bricklayer
Cadbury's Flake	Long thick stick of thin folded milk chocolate, especially used for putting into the top of an ice cream cone to make the iconic '99' made by British confectioners Cadbury's found in 1847
Car Park	Parking lot
Chicken Tikka Masala	Chicken cooked in yoghurt and spices, erved with rice. Britain's unofficial national dish.
Chips (food)	Thick French fries
Chocolate Digestive Biscuits	Baked crunch cookie topped with chocolate.

Coupla	Couple of
Corner shop	Small grocery store
Council estate	Public housing or section 8 housing
Crumpet	Romantically desirable person
Crumpet	Cake with holes in, served toasted with butter
Cuppa	Cup of tea
Curtains	Drapes
Different from	Different than
Eyrie	Eerie
Fairy cake	Small round light sponge cake topped with light icing, with a butterfly lid, formed by slicing off the top, dividing it and replacing at angles, like wings
Figgy 'obbin	Traditional Cornish pudding consisting of a layer of pastry covered with raisins and lemon peel or zest then rolled and baked.
Fridge	Refrigerator
Front of house	On reception, where guests are received. In a restaurant: where diners are greeted and served. In a theatre: where audience members are.
Garden	Yard
Gingernut	Hard (like a nut but not containing any) ginger biscuit

Glossary

Grey	Gray
Injera Bread Pudding	Pudding made with Ethiopian bread and eggs, vanilla, butter, and milk
Jam roly-poly	A flat layer of suet pudding, spread with jam and rolled up
Jammy Dodger	Round shortbread biscuit, double layer sandwiching raspberry jam. Top layer has a heart cut out to reveal with jam centre. Similar to a Linzer biscuit.
Jersey Cream	Thick cream from the milk of Cows from the Channel Islands
Jewellery	Jewelry
Jim-jams	Pajamas
Kebab	Kabob
Rogan Josh	Rich, spicy curry with Kashmiri chillis
Licence, on licence	On probation
Lime Pickle	Accompaniment to Indian food
Lili Marlene	A song that became popular in WW2 with both sides about a girl standing underneath a lantern waiting for her sweetheart.
Loo	Restroom, toilet
Loo roll	Toilet paper, bath paper

Mango Chutney	Accompaniment to Indian food
MET, the	The Metropolitan Police Service, policing London
Minibus	Van, minicoach seating 8 - 30 people
Mobile phone	Cell phone
Muck about	Mess around, play with
Momentarily	For a moment
Nitwit	Foolish, scatterbrained person
Naan	Flat bread baked or fried and usually eaten with Indian food.
Off-cut	Remnant
Off the bottle	Not drinking alcohol, not an alcoholic
Pain au chocolat	Chocolate croissant
Paracetemol	Acetaminophen, Tylenol
Pavement	Sidewalk
Petrol	Gasoline
PO	Probation officer
Pub	Quiet, family friendly, coffee-shop style bar
Quid	One pound sterling
Quids in	Having made a profit
Removal company	Moving company
Rupert Brook Poem	Reference to The Soldier
Scone	Smaller, lighter and fluffier than the US scone, served with cream and jam

Shortcake	Crunchy sweet cookie
Solicitor	Lawyer
Takeaway	Takeout
Te absolvo	I absolve you
Tea towel	Dish towel
Tin	Can
Turf out	Encourage to leave
Tyre	Tire
Vade	Go
Van	Delivery truck
Verge	Strip of grass between the road and the pavement or field
Victoria Sandwich	Sponge cake with jam and cream filling
Walnut Whip	Small cone-shaped whirl of milk chocolate filled

Cornish Accent and Dialect

Awright?	Hello
Dreckly	At some point
I'llItellywot	I will tell you what
Me 'andsome	Unisex term of endearment
Me luvver	Unisex term of endearment
Werratting	Worrying
Wozelike (wozz-ee-laeek)	Always up to something, little rascal
Zackly	Exactly

Cornish

Bian	Baby, small
Pur deg	Very pretty

Yorkshire Accent and Dialect

Chuffin' ekk	Expression denoting surprise
Aye	Yes
Yer	Your
T'	The
Ar	Our

A Note About Accents and Wicc'yeth

One or two of the villagers have a Cockney accent indicated by the missing 'h' at the beginning of words such as 'hello' becoming ''ello'. Others have a London accent in which 'th' becomes 'f' and 'ing' become 'in'. Some use a mixture. Still others have a Yorkshire accent in which 'the' is often shortened to 't'' and h is dropped.

Wicc'yeth, is a magical language peculiar to the world of Amanda Cadabra. If you are curious about the meaning of individual spell words, you will find a glossary at http://amandacadabra.com/wiccyeth/ and Amelia's Glossary with Pronunciation.

The Last Word ... For Now

Thank you once again, dear reader, for allowing me to share Amanda's story with you.

Best wishes,

Holly Bell

https://amandacadabra.com/contact
https://amandacadabra.com/come-on-in

Printed in Great Britain
by Amazon